The
GOD
Project

The GOD Project

STAN LEE

GROVE WEIDENFELD
New York

Published by Grove Weidenfeld
A division of Wheatland Corporation
841 Broadway
New York, NY 10003-4793

Published in Canada by General Publishing Company, Ltd.

Excerpt from *The Complete Poems of Carl Sandburg* by Carl Sandburg, copyright 1918 by Harcourt Brace Jovanovich, Inc. and renewed 1946 by Carl Sandburg, reprinted by permission of the publisher.

Library of Congress Cataloging-in-Publication Data

Lee, Stan.
The GOD Project / Stan Lee.—1st ed.
p.   cm.
ISBN 0-8021-1128-9 (alk. paper)
I. Title.
PS3562.E3648G6   1990
813′.54—dc20   89-38362
CIP

Manufactured in the United States of America

Printed on acid-free paper

Designed by Irving Perkins Associates

First Edition 1990

1 2 3 4 5 6 7 8 9 10

To Sandra Lucas

PART I

The Trouble with November

1

NOMINATION

THERE WAS A burned-out quality to summertime Washington that Elmer Jessup reveled in; it was the only time he actually felt at home in the place. For one thing, it was empty. Congress wasn't in session, which was always a plus for the commonweal. For another, the Democrats were all down in New Orleans at their presidential convention busily knocking each other off. The Republicans were on the way to the coronation of President McKay in San Diego. The President himself was still on his ranch in Arizona, pulling strings and twisting arms and patting backs to be sure he was renominated by popular acclamation. Best of all, it was even too hot and muggy for the tourists. In August, Washington was for connoisseurs of the bleak and the blasted. Which was why Elmer Jessup, Director of Central Intelligence, did something entirely out of character for him. He had his driver stop at the Mayflower Hotel so he and his aide, Nye, could watch the roll call of the states in the cocktail lounge.

They didn't go in through the main hotel entrance; it was subtler to enter by the cocktail lounge's own door, which was the kind of calculation that Jessup did on automatic pilot. They entered the darkened room of brown wood and dark red leather chairs and couches and headed straight for inconspicuousness, a darkened nook with a good sight line to the television set.

Washington, D.C., capital of the world, blocks away from the White House, and they had the baseball game on. Jessup waited while Nye bribed the manager. After the roll call, they could switch it back to that opiate of the people, Boston vs. the New York Yankees.

There was a nice muted feel to the place. There were fluorescents, but they were blunted; they were installed behind thick stained-glass panels. The only other light was from dim spots recessed in the ceiling which seemed to disperse before it reached the dark rug. Best of all, the air was good; almost as good as the limousine's.

The room was two-thirds empty, and no one seemed to notice the difference between baseball and politics.

He took out his tally sheets. It was almost as though everything would go wrong if he personally didn't watch it, supervise it, stay with it every step of the way; this thing was too important to leave to chance. Nye came back and took his own tallies out, and they sat there contentedly sipping white wine spritzers as the roll call of the states got under way.

Jessup didn't like conventions, but then he didn't like elections. What? You went around asking Joe Doakes what to do about NATO? The Philippines? The bomb? But he was managing to enjoy this one anyway; it was the quadrennial meeting of the Democrat Suicide Club.

He looked at the names supered on the screen—Halliday, Lindstrom, Rottenburg, and Stonewell—and watched California go ecstatically for the governor of New York, Richard Halliday. He winked at Nye; they'd been worried about California.

Stonewell could conceivably make trouble in November. He had survived twelve years of the shoot-on-sight politics of North Carolina and, unlike most of the Democrats, had a following throughout the South and Southwest. He also had the best campaign organization of any of them. The last candidate Jessup wanted to see running against President McKay was Stonewell.

Rottenburg, a Texan, a solid budget-balancing conservative governor who was willing to spend like a drunken sailor on farm programs, might be a threat. Rottenburg had the second-best political organization among the Democrats as well as eight children, which took care of abortion and prayer in the schoolroom; it was entirely possible that he could pick up the fundamentalists, which McKay would badly need.

The problem was that McKay had too many problems. An even worse

4

corruption record than Reagan, and he had managed to do it in only four years; a noticeable fraction of McKay's political cohort was sitting out the election year in various federal correctional facilities around the country. *Plus* his former Secretary of State had turned out to be gay. *Plus* the worst unemployment since the thirties depression. *Plus* an inflation rate that was running at 9.5 percent annually. Going up against a morally impeccable Rottenburg would be chancy.

Then there was Lindstrom. An imponderable. Lindstrom was a pussycat from Ohio who in eighteen years in the Senate hadn't made a single enemy; in a low-turnout election, he conceivably could squeak past McKay and win it. Only Halliday would be a sure loser in November, and according to Jessup's intelligence, it was going to go all the way to Wyoming before Halliday won the nomination by an eyelash. He sat there happily checking off states, his numbers, so far, correct to the last half-delegate. Jessup's sixty-five-year-old pulse was beginning to make itself felt. Twenty years of mayhem in the CIA had not blunted his ability to get excited, to be on tippy-toes when great affairs were hanging in the balance. In fact, getting excited was his genius. He thought of it as his ability to be revirgined, to be able to go into anything as though it had never happened before, quivering with anticipation spiced with a little dread.

"He'll be the biggest beauty since Adlai Stevenson," Jessup said to Nye. "He'll talk over everyone's head and he'll win three states."

Illinois went for Halliday.

"If I were religious," Nye replied, "I'd say, 'Thank the Lord.' Maybe I should anyway; it couldn't hurt."

"The Lord had nothing to do with it," Jessup said, having managed to bribe the key members of the Illinois delegation into supporting Halliday. At least they'd come cheap; he had gotten nine of them for under a hundred thousand dollars. It always astonished Jessup how cheaply the typical politician sold himself.

"I hate to admit it, but it's looking good," Jessup said, showing a narrow slit of teeth that wasn't so much a smile as a simulation of a smile, or maybe a rough draft of a smile, a tentative, exploratory stab at some kind of nonhostile muscular alignment in the general area of the mouth. Everything was going as predicted. He ordered a rare second drink, but as he looked toward the waiter he spotted Anatoly Malenki half a dozen tables away. Malenki was officially the Second Secretary at the Soviet Embassy but was undoubtedly KGB. Jessup considered him to be the slimiest man in America. Malenki and another Russian had tally sheets out too. Malenki looked over and smiled weakly. Jessup nodded a tenth of an inch.

Malenki had only just finished bribing the manager to switch the TV to the Democratic Convention when he'd spotted the most evil man in Washington strolling into the lounge. One of his eyebrows had gone up, an uncharacteristic display of emotion for him. The one time in months when he'd decided to go out—because there was no one left in either Moscow or Washington who could make trouble for him—and the Director of Central Intelligence strolls in. Out on the town? Drinking? Elmer Jessup?

Malenki was an unusual Russian. He had been born in Kiev, but his parents had immigrated to Brooklyn when he was six months old. He was eighteen years old when they had emigrated back to the Soviet Union. It meant that Malenki could not only talk like an American, he could think like one.

Malenki tore his eyes away from the Director of Central Intelligence and went back to his tallies. There hadn't been any surprises, except maybe Illinois which, some thought, might have gone to Lindstrom but had, unexpectedly, voted solidly for Halliday. Halliday was behind at the moment, but New York had passed, and he was going to get all 212 of their votes. It was depressing. If Halliday got the Democratic nomination, he would assuredly lose in November and they'd have four more years of the conservative fanatic McKay.

The problem traced all the way back to Harry Truman. Truman and Eisenhower, actually. Their idea was to make arms offers that seemed the height of sweet reasonableness to the American public but which invariably contained a joker clause so disadvantageous to the Russians that a "Nyet" was guaranteed. The U.S. establishment had become infatuated with nuclear weapons from the moment of the trinity explosion and didn't want to give them up.

Gorbachev foiled this strategy. Gorbachev simply grabbed at just about anything that was offered—no matter how unfair to Russia—in order to dispel the Cold War mood. Gorbachev had possessed what previous Soviet leaders lacked: a sense of humor.

But George Bush had defeated him. The old Busher, the wimp himself, had done Gorbachev in. It had been easy. He had used the interchangeability of weapons systems to do it. The American public thought in terms of *types* of weapons, which was actually an irrelevant category. If both sides gave up, say, mobile land-based missiles in Europe, that would seem fair and peaceful and equitable to the public. Bush cheerfully went along with such deals while at the same time pushing alternative weapons systems that accomplished the same mission, such as land- and sea-based cruise missiles and attack planes, categories in which the Russians were way behind.

Eventually the Soviet military had clamped down on Gorbachev because he was endangering Soviet military security with his penchant for giving away the store in order to play to Western public opinion. President McKay had continued the Bush game plan. And now there was yet another new American weapons system coming on line.

Malenki's biggest failure in America so far was that he had not yet discovered the nature of the newest Pentagon project. A satellite had picked it up first: a large compound in Colorado. The dominant structure was peculiar. There was a circular installation, mostly underground, that had a diameter of three hundred feet. A second structure was a diameter of that circle, three hundred feet long, seventy feet high, eighty-six feet wide. There was no structure like it in the Soviet Union or anywhere else on earth. You couldn't get near it on the ground. And, for once, American security had held, had been absolutely airtight. There was so much in the American arsenal already that was hellish— Malenki couldn't even imagine what it might be. He'd requested that a seminar be held in Moscow, where leading Soviet experts in all disciplines could cross-pollinate in an attempt to divine—the word came from his American background—what the next ultimate weapon might be. The seminar had produced twenty-five technically ingenious crackpot ideas which Malenki—and everyone else at KGB and the Kremlin—had refused to take seriously. If it should turn out to be a breakthrough system—and in the hands of President William C. McKay, a fanatic and a risk-taker—it could mean mortal trouble for the Soviet Union, where there still wasn't enough money to keep up with the Joneses. Now, Malenki was sitting there appalled.

Wyoming had yielded to New York.

"Watch all the morons go crazy," Jessup said.

The head of the delegation was stretching out his moment of glory, but sooner or later he was going to have to say it: 212 votes for the great governor of the great state of New York and the next President of the great United States, Richard Meriwether Halliday!

7

The convention hall went only moderately crazy; Halliday had done it with 50.05 percent of the votes, a sobering example of democratic, not to mention Democratic, politics.

"He's a liberal," Elmer Jessup said quietly. "An Easterner. He's soft on defense. He's on his second wife. He's an intellectual. And he's talking about a female Vice-President. Six strikes. Out before he picks up the bat."

Jessup ordered an unprecedented third wine spritzer and sneaked a glance at Malenki, who was like all the Russians: stone-faced. They had all taken lessons from Gromyko, who'd learned it on Easter Island. Malenki had to be thinking about four more years of pressure from President McKay. And Elmer Jessup.

But Jessup's victory reaction was beginning to set in. Victory invariably alarmed him. Victory produced the opposite of complacency in Elmer Jessup. Victory made him perspire. All victories had to be protected. He looked over at Nye, who was balling up his tally sheets.

"We've got to worry about overconfidence in the White House," he said.

"McKay will have the longest coattails in history," Nye replied. "Hell, that man will have shirttails."

"Campaign intensively but never take Halliday seriously. Treat him like a leper. That's the way I'd play it," Jessup said.

Jessup's nightmarish thoughts kept returning. Fine, they'd "won" the nomination, but now there was an election that had to be won. It was an election that was fundamental to the political life of the United States. And what was more important, to the economic life. Possibly even the survival of the capitalist system was at stake.

The U.S. had two major problems. For one thing, they had to keep the Soviet Union from conning the rest of the world into disarming. Jessup was immune to the wiles of the Russians. He didn't trust them. If you were a commie you were a commie. There was no such thing as half a commie. *And* they had to solve the Vietnam Syndrome. The Vietnam Syndrome was probably an even worse menace than the commies themselves. And the U.S. was close—within inches. Before long, it would be possible to intervene in Third World countries where and when it was necessary, without having college students marching on the Pentagon or Democratic wimps holding hearings in Congress.

"What do we do if Halliday wins?" Jessup said abruptly.

Nye looked at him as though he were mad.

"Suppose the President sticks his foot in it in one of the debates?"

Jessup persisted. "Suppose he gets caught screwing his horse? Who the hell knows what could happen between now and November 6?"

"You're looking for trouble," Nye said reasonably.

"Damn right." Richard Meriwether Halliday was quite capable of blowing the GOD Project out of the water if he knew about it. "I want a contingency plan covering the possibility that the Democrats win the election, and I want it yesterday."

Nye wrinkled his nose at the commanding tone of voice.

"Yes, *sir*," he said.

2

ELECTION

MALCOLM KEYES WAS working his way cautiously across the swarming hotel lobby—cautiously because the Secret Service made him nervous and guilty and he was trying to look innocuous. There were familiar television talking heads streaming in and out of the New York Hilton, and there were obvious tourists, and there were New York City cops, but the Secret Service were uncountable.

It was after 9:00 P.M. in the East, and power was starting to flow now from all the little levers in the voting machines. You had to be an American to push down one of those levers, but everyone on the planet was affected. The British Green Party was spending the day picketing the American Embassy in London. Their signs said: "No Radiation Without Representation." They had also staged a London tea party, tossing Great Atlantic and Pacific Orange Pekoe tea bags into the Thames.

The Secret Service guy running the elevator looked at Keyes with dead fish eyes. Keyes self-consciously pointed to the laminated credentials hanging around his neck, and the agent nodded and let him into the only elevator car in the hotel that would stop at the twenty-first floor.

When he got out at twenty-one, he was promptly confronted by another one sitting behind a reception desk, who looked for him on a list. The place was the usual political jumble. People scurrying. Stealthy conversations everywhere. A trail of yellow tape running down the long corridor to the horizon, covering bunched up telephone cables.

Keyes spotted Akers strolling down the corridor, proceeding at his usual stately pace. Akers was the eye in the storm; he did not do anything hurriedly. He wasn't tall and he wasn't thin. His intelligent fat face was friendly but inscrutable. He had been in Albany with Governor Richard Halliday for eight years, and was the candidate's chief of staff and campaign manager.

"He's with me," Akers said to the Secret Service agent, without breaking stride. The agent nodded, and Keyes followed Akers down the corridor.

They went into the Presidential Suite, which was a long living room with an adjoining bedroom at either end. There were eleven television sets turned on and he found his boss, Roger Doolittle, sitting in front of one of them while talking into a phone. Situation normal. Doolittle was always on the phone. Doolittle used the phone the way other people used pancreases and gall bladders: It was a vital organ of internal functioning; he couldn't even go for a walk without stopping at a pay phone for a transfusion. Without the telephone, Doolittle would have strangled.

Now he was complaining to the governor of Connecticut.

"We had good crowds in Connecticut," he was saying. "We had the best goddam advance work of the campaign in Connecticut. We had good TV. We had the *Hartford Courant*. We had the *New Haven Register*. What the hell's happening?"

Keyes quickly scanned the TV sets and found one talking about Connecticut. Connecticut was looking bad for Halliday, the anchor was saying, which was the worst possible news; they'd had hopes for Connecticut. The governor there had gotten on Halliday's team early, and a healthy win might influence some of the Western states by demonstrating that Halliday's candidacy wasn't totally hopeless. But Connecticut happened to be one of the most politically volatile states in the country.

Keyes had left his apartment at 9:00 P.M. It was now 9:30. Could the election have been lost as he walked to the Hilton? Most of Halliday's inner circle were in the room now, and they were looking cadaverous. He drifted toward a small group around Norman Pope, who was Halliday's pollster. Pope would know what the situation was. In his long career, Pope had earned a reputation for infallibility and was inevitably referred to as *the* Pope. Pope was now being calm. He spoke in his fake pilot's voice, calmly announcing that there was a little chop up ahead but everything was fine.

"It's early," he said to the group around him.

Pollsters were like weathermen. They could take the readings and study the satellite photos, but there were always unexpected fronts coming in from the West or sucking up from the South, the occasional twister laying waste an entire election district, and always always cold winds from the North for a Democrat: Maine and Vermont.

Keyes wandered around, staying at the fringes, not saying a word; he was low man on the totem pole. He had done Halliday's TV spots, working for Roger Doolittle. He'd been invited up for the election-night vigil as a reward for working twenty-hour days.

On one of the TV sets Halliday was being interviewed live, probably in one of the adjoining bedrooms. Halliday looked his usual confident self, and Keyes was hoping. It had been a tough campaign, with dirty tricks on both sides. War and peace were the issues, with prosperity as a subplot. Which was more or less standard for an American presidential election, but this one had been different. Halliday had changed the rules of the game and had given President McKay a run for his money.

One of the best things Governor Halliday had going for him was his nickname, which the press had given him many years before when he was running for mayor of New York City.

It was late in October, and Halliday had been walking along a Brooklyn street with his entourage, introducing himself to people, shaking hands, doing the standard political mortification before the common man *and* getting some pretty good press coverage; there were five cameras on him. He hadn't expected that much coverage. The five of them moving backward down the sidewalk and out in the street were bumping into each other, they were so eager to get the shot; one of them was almost run over by a semi. Then Halliday understood the situation.

It was a trap.

Out of nowhere he'd suddenly found himself confronted by Morton Fuchs, the incumbent mayor. Halliday had been leading Fuchs in the polls for months. Now Fuchs had decided to humiliate Halliday on camera, take him by surprise, wreck him, win the election with one blow on a Brooklyn street corner.

It was a mortal mistake. It was the last time Fuchs ran for anything.

12

Halliday calmly tore him to pieces. It was hard to take Halliday by surprise. At a very basic level he wasn't hiding anything; his public personality was the same as his private one. He was at ease in his own skin, and his mind was able to focus fast, unencumbered with nameless dreads and fears.

The bonus was that the exchange had taken place at Third Avenue and 33rd Street in Brooklyn, in front of the OK Garage. The garage sign was in the shot for the entire encounter. From then on, Halliday was "Doc" Halliday, which was the perfect image for an American politician: a gunslinger. Halliday himself was appalled by the effect of paltry happenstance on a political career. It had happened in front of a damn garage. It had no intellectual or spiritual content. It was pure, dumb luck. And it made him.

Keyes and Doolittle had come up with a thirty-second TV spot that had been used a lot in the campaign, primarily in Texas and the Midwest. It started off with the line "They call him *Doc* Halliday. Why?" The rest of the spot listed the various "fights" Halliday had "led." This was standard rhetoric—leading the fight—because everyone in politics believed that the public ate it up. The idea was that it portrayed Halliday—who was the peace candidate and advocate of a nuclear freeze—as a fighter; it would have been fatal for him to look otherwise. *All* American politicians portrayed themselves as fighters.

Doolittle had even managed to get a blatantly illegal five-minute spot on all three networks simultaneously. It was illegal because it used footage of President McKay without getting his permission. McKay making promises at the Republican Convention the first time he was nominated. McKay on the stump, making more promises. McKay making fiery speeches, repeating his promises. The spot started off with the line "This is what he promised last time. Remember?"

If elected, McKay was going to balance the budget; he made it worse. He was going to lower unemployment; it went up. He was going to lower taxes; he raised taxes. He was going to make progress in arms control; he didn't. The leader of the opposition in Holland was publicly calling him a nuclear maniac. There were five minutes of it, on all networks, and it ran just once. Behind the scenes, the Republicans went bananas, raging at the networks for allowing it to happen. TV stations always screened tapes of advertising messages for acceptability. How then could blatantly illegal tapes be aired without network knowledge? It had to be a liberal conspiracy among the networks, and the FCC was going to get them for it. But the networks were mystified. They couldn't understand how it had happened. Doolittle wouldn't even tell Keyes how he had managed to switch illegal tapes for the legal ones at all three networks at the last minute without anyone knowing. But he knew it had cost twenty-five thousand dollars.

Then there was the first debate, when Halliday began the process of changing American politics and got away with it. Keyes had written a slogan designed to appeal to both liberals and conservatives: *Halliday: He'll mind our own business.* To liberals, it meant Halliday wouldn't get the country involved in murderous overseas wars. To conservatives, it sounded seductively Calvinistic—the business of America was business, and Halliday would tend to it, would get American business competitive again with the rest of the world. Even labor and the farmers could respond to that. During the debate, President McKay had taken the expected conservative tack:

"Do you mean, Mr. Halliday, that if the communist guerrillas threaten the Philippine government, you will 'mind our own business' and let the Philippines go communist?"

"If I deem the Philippines to *be* our business, I will certainly mind it," Halliday replied. "But I would not mindlessly go to their aid and get us bogged down in another high-casualty Asian land war."

President McKay, unaware that Halliday was about to change the rules of the game, plunged ahead with the cliché.

"Then you might decide to *lose* the Philippines?"

"It is not in my power—nor yours, if I may say so, sir—to *lose* the Philippines. Only the Filipinos can lose the Philippines. That happens to be a distinction that a number of American Presidents have been unable to make. Fifteen years from now, Mr. McKay, I would not want to see a Philippines War Memorial here in Washington, D.C. Would you?"

Halliday's reply was a first in American politics, a total departure from conventional Democratic tactics. The conventional approach would have been to outshout the Republicans, accuse them of a Philippines Gap, of not doing enough to fight the communist insurgency.

Halliday had his reasons. He had started out a virtual sure loser, 45 percentage points behind McKay; he had nothing to lose by gambling and revealing a profound difference between the President and himself. And Norman Pope had been seeing growing evidence of discontent in the country about Pentagon spending. Pentagon spending seemed to have a life of its own, with no apparent connection to external events. No matter how many military concessions the Russians made, U.S. forces were still always stretched to the limit, the breaking point, and this in connection with a putative enemy, the U.S.S.R., which had a GNP only one-third the size of the U.S. GNP. The Pentagon was still throwing billions to the four winds while the country's bridges were falling down.

The problem had started in West Germany, where the people would suffer the most from a nuclear battlefield.

President Bush had found himself in the odd position of trying to woo Otto Muster—the John Doe of Germany—so that he could continue modernizing even as the Soviets were pulling out tanks, divisions, mobile missiles, tactical warheads. Bush had done everything short of going on a whistle-stop tour of the Federal Republic.

President McKay had been even more hawkish than Bush. He'd been a throwback to Reagan, of sorts. But *he* didn't even see the world in Technicolor; it was all black and white. Some said McKay had even reverted to pre-talkies, the silents, because he'd never once sat down to parley with the Soviets.

But the American public was beginning to awaken from a fifty-year hibernation during which, as Dean Acheson had concluded during the Truman administration, they typically spent all of seven minutes per day thinking about foreign policy. During their long sleep they had basically trusted their national leaders when it came to foreign policy. Vietnam had been an interruption to that torpor, or perhaps a nightmare. But now the hibernation seemed to be coming to an end, with the very beginnings of a cocked collective eyebrow. Halliday was trying to tap into that feeling, and he had been willing to go in harm's way to do it.

In the beginning, Halliday's chances were considered so far out that he'd managed to raise only $32 million, as compared with President McKay's $142 million. But Roger Doolittle had been inventive. The first thing he did was enlist the services of a volunteer group that normally worked only for progressive congressional candidates. They had something that was priceless, something that Doolittle would kill to get his hands on. He persuaded them, for the first time in their history, to make a major commitment to a presidential candidate.

The group was called the National Committee for an Effective Congress, NCEF. What they had that Doolittle wanted was data, tons of it. Data on past federal and state elections that had been correlated with census data. NCEF's basic idea was that impoverished progressives couldn't afford to spend money convincing people who would never be

15

on your side, as well as those who were already on your side. The trick was to spend your money in search of the "persuadable voter" only.

NCEF did what they called voter profile analyses for Doolittle, based on age, sex, occupation, education, ethnicity, income: *Who* was persuadable? Then they did precinct targeting studies in order to answer the question: *Where* is he/she? Which precincts? Once the persuadable voters were located, the task was to target the media buying. Doolittle used almost no network TV; he spent most of the money on local radio and television stations, those that covered the precincts that contained those amazing people who *might* vote for a harsh right-wing hawk, McKay, or who *might* vote for a liberal dove, Halliday.

The entire campaign had been a masterpiece of making Democratic penury work in the same league with overflowing Republican coffers— of getting more bang for the buck—and the running joke during the campaign was that Doolittle was going to become Secretary of Defense.

But there was also the basic confrontation between McKay and Halliday, which worked entirely to Halliday's advantage. McKay, with his tremendous initial lead, had simply tried to avoid making mistakes, believing that it wasn't necessary to say anything substantive. As a consequence, he was boring.

Halliday, the long shot, for whom the term "underdog" was a euphemism, was willing to take chances. He had to take chances. He had to get attention. He had to become credible. His comments to TV newsmen were invariably witty and provocative, so that he began showing up on the evening news with increasing frequency. The TV people realized he brightened up the program, and so they covered him more and more, never believing that it would help him get elected; Halliday got the best advertising of all for free.

Halliday, the crapshooter, had also done well with his choice of running mate: Senator Madeleine Smith of California, one of the few major politicians on the scene who was willing to risk her Senate seat to run with him. He'd picked her primarily because he badly needed the West Coast states; he was basically writing off most of the Midwest, the South, and the mountain states.

Smith had turned out to be a superb campaigner. She had vitality and spontaneity, which came across both on the stump and on the tube. She had a habit of departing from her previously distributed speeches in spontaneous outbursts of emotion and humor. These outbursts were so clearly spontaneous that she gave the strong impression of being in command of the issues, of being a political leader who had not been manufactured by a political consultant or a talented staff. The TV journalists soon realized they were missing out on good television by not covering her closely. And there was always the tantalizing possibility that in one of her outbursts she would fall on her nose, which would make even better television. She never did. She held up her end of the ticket, a radiant campaigner in comparison with the rather oafish Vice-President Dunbar.

When the campaign was over, McKay's 45-percentage-point lead had been eroded to 12 points, with a 4-point error.

But the Pope thought it was better than that. Norman Pope was nervously attuned to the traps in polling. The country seemed to be going through a period of change, which was the trickiest moment of all for a pollster. Attitudes were becoming uncongealed, the ice was breaking up, new freshets of opinion were flowing. But if voting patterns were changing, you could only *guess* at what they were changing to. A further complication was the unusual number of undecideds, which was characteristic of a major change coming, complicated even further by the fact that the country had become a nation of ticket splitters. These were what Pope called unquantifiable quantities. You had to *guess*.

Pope had gotten high blood pressure since becoming a pollster. It was a profession built on quicksand, especially when it came to presidential polls. There were two fundamental flaws. You could measure men, for example, or women, ethnic groups, whatever, without having any idea of how many of them were going to show up at the polls on election day.

Then there was the infernal electoral college. A presidential election was not a national election: it was fifty-one separate elections, counting the District of Columbia. But nobody took fifty-one separate polls; they took one national poll.

The Pope did what he could do to minimize the unquantifiable. He used his computer to select those telephone exchanges that gave an appropriate sampling of the entire country. The computer created individual telephone numbers randomly; even people with unlisted numbers—to their surprise—were reached in this way. Then the results were weighted to take all kinds of politically relevant factors into account—household size, age, sex, race, education, ethnic character.

And Pope's last poll showed that the situation had come unglued; the electorate was rethinking, reconsidering, maybe shifting. Long-held

17

popular stereotypes about foreign countries and policing the planet and the limits of American power were beginning to change, set in motion by tough economic conditions everywhere in the country, with the sole exception of the Pentagon, which continued to feast and waste. The number of undecideds had climbed dramatically, and Mr. Infallible's final word was: "Too close to call."

Malcolm Keyes was studying Halliday's face on CBS from the point of view of a media man. The face was a definite plus. Halliday had *the* most fundamental requirement for a presidential candidate—he looked like a President. He was somewhere between JFK and Warren Harding. He had an intelligent forehead, high cheekbones, good skin, faint beard. His lip/teeth relationship was perfect. Keyes believed that if only your lower teeth showed when you spoke, you tended to look untrustworthy and underhanded. Showing only your upper teeth was better, although it looked a trifle dumb. The absolute best was when at least part of both uppers and lowers were revealed in the act of speaking, and Halliday had it.

It was supposed to be a friendly little interview, strictly background fluff, how were the wife and kids holding up. But the aging anchor emeritus slipped in a nasty one.

"Sir, inasmuch as the early returns from the East aren't looking very good for you, have you prepared a concession statement yet?"

Halliday's face slowly metamorphosed. One eyebrow went up. The nostrils quivered. A very amiable smile appeared on the lips. He raised his chin and swung his head to the left and then back, clearing a crick. It was the gunslinger's look; someone had drawn on Doc Halliday.

"Didn't you ask Harry Truman the same question in 1948, Dan?"

The network cut to a commercial and the bedroom door was opening, Halliday striding out. If he had moved a little faster, he might have caught himself on the tube.

"Where's my concession speech?" he asked.

"In the works," Akers replied. Mullins was in the other bedroom trying to come up with something statesmanlike.

Halliday had a habit of reading the room, looking for friends, enemies, spotting weakness, strength, independence, slaves, masters, crooks, whiners, mendicants. He eyeballed Malcolm Keyes. He wasn't sure who Keyes was. Keyes held it for about three seconds and then looked away to a television set. Halliday sat down on a couch next to Doolittle, who was staring grimly at a twenty-eight-inch screen. '

"What do you think?" Halliday said to the room.

"It stinks," Doolittle said.

"Is Connecticut a write-off?"

Doolittle was shaking his head slowly from side to side. He looked ready to kill Connecticut.

"I spent a lot of money in Connecticut," he said.

Halliday was thinking out loud.

"A liberal needs the Northeast. Connecticut, Massachusetts, New York. Maybe even New Jersey. Certainly Pennsylvania. If I got New Jersey maybe I could lose Connecticut. Is that possible?"

No one answered. In the background they could hear yet another anchorman wondering about a concession speech from Governor Halliday.

"Hell, I guess I was a freak to begin with. You all did a good job for me; I couldn't have asked for more." He looked over at an anguished Norman Pope, whose "too close to call" was turning into a wipeout. "Oops," Halliday said to him. "Sic Transit Gloria Tuesday, huh? Get Mullins in here. I want a good-natured farewell to politics."

Malcolm Keyes drifted over to a computer terminal set up on a coffee table; it was connected to Pope's mainframe back in Washington. Keyes hadn't been infected by the mood of the room yet. He was too excited at being admitted to what was, after all, the back room. He did input standing over the terminal and watched columns of numbers flood onto the screen. They were the latest Connecticut vote totals by election district. He looked at the numbers for a moment and then quickly brought up Massachusetts, New York, New Jersey, Pennsylvania.

Keyes drifted back to the group around the governor in time for the most funereal moment in politics: the reading of the first draft of the concession statement, which was like a will in which everyone gets cut out. The people around Halliday had been a shadow government, potentially the most powerful people on earth, but now it was all slipping away and becoming résumé time. And Halliday's people were good people. He had enough ego to tolerate good people, which was rare, rare. He totally lacked the awful need to feel superior, and he never felt threatened by an intelligence, an astuteness, an intuition that might be superior to his own. It was what had made him such an unusually successful executive.

"In conclusion," Mullins was droning, "I urge all my supporters to stand behind President McKay for the next four years. They will be difficult and he will need all of us."

Halliday, sounding like the captain of a sinking ship who is still worried about the brasswork, said, "Give me a funny thing happened on the way to the White House, will you?"

Everyone in the room was now clustered around Halliday, with Keyes bringing up the rear, holding up the totem pole. But it was 10:00 P.M. and the numbers were getting significant. Outlines were emerging, forming, clarifying. The gross totals meant nothing; the networks were so sure Halliday was a loser they weren't checking the data carefully. Keyes went back over it again. McKay, Bush, Reagan, Reagan, Carter, Nixon, Nixon, Johnson, Kennedy. There was total silence in the room while Mullins tried to be creative.

Keyes was still dazzled at even being in the same room with these people. He was rubbing elbows with some pretty famous talking heads. It wasn't too long ago that he'd been selling dog food for a living; now he was standing in one of the most important back rooms in politics: Doc Halliday's inner circle.

Keyes hadn't had any formal preparation or training for what he was doing. He hadn't studied political science at college. He'd gotten a Bachelor of Nothing from Columbia University, with a minor in music; he was a liberal artist. By the time he graduated he still hadn't known what he wanted to do with his life, except that he wanted to be able to earn enough money to afford an apartment in Manhattan. There were only two places you could work that: Wall Street and Madison Avenue. He figured he wouldn't be able to fake enthusiasm on Wall Street but he probably could on Madison Avenue, at least until he figured out what he really wanted to do.

He managed to get himself hired as a junior account executive at a large advertising agency not noted for its brilliance. He quickly found out that he was totally inept at it. He was never able to persuade his client of anything. Ads, commercials, strategy plans, media plans; everything got shot down when Keyes took it to the client. In six months he had the reputation of having the black touch. At the same time, the letters and reports he was doing were turning out to be very well written. Well enough so that it gave his boss a polite way of getting rid of him: He was switched to the creative department and made a junior

20

copywriter. He was given a dog-food account to write on because nobody else wanted it; the account was a dog.

Keyes prospered; he couldn't see anything wrong with exaggerating about dog food. There didn't seem to be an ethical question. Whenever he wrote advertising copy, he pretended he was selling a charming French restaurant on Ninth Avenue that he'd come to like.

He did it so well that his supervisor began to get worried; insecurity was endemic in advertising. So when the agency got the account of a liberal Democrat running for Congress in a conservative upstate district—one of the major stockholders of the agency was an in-law—Keyes was recommended for the assignment, the assumption being that Keyes could only look bad, there was no way a liberal could win that seat.

But the candidate turned out to have a good personality and good looks and was a good speaker. Best of all, he allowed Keyes to get to know him. Keyes tramped through the district with him until he got to know the issues as well as the man. It was his first exposure to politics as it is actually practiced. Keyes soon realized that it was necessary for the TV spots to mirror the candidate's personality, as opposed to the common strategy of polling and telling: Find out what they want you to tell them and tell them. His candidate squeezed in, and Roger Doolittle was on the phone the day after the election.

But the transition from selling dog food to selling politicians was a shock. With dog food there were limitations. The Federal Trade Commission was watching. You could exaggerate only so much. The FTC kept trying to force the advertising agencies to tell the truth about the products they were trying to sell. But there were *no* legal limits to what you could say about the virtues of a politician you were trying to sell.

When Keyes went to work for Roger Doolittle's political consulting firm, he realized that in selling dog food he had stretched the truth, but he saw now that he'd never been in the same league with politicians. If President McKay's Secretary of Defense had been a slab of beef, to take one example, the U.S. Department of Agriculture would have had to condemn him as unfit for human consumption.

Before long he began to realize that deviousness was built into the politics of a democracy, because politicians had to face election day. Anytime a politician took a stand on anything, he or she was bound to offend *some* voters. But politicians *hated* to offend voters. And if the politician advanced, as Halliday had—mayor to governor to presidential candidate—his constituency grew less and less homogeneous, and

21

the problem of offending by taking specific stands on specific issues grew worse and worse, and the politician grew vaguer and vaguer, cagier and cagier. And the job of writing the advertising grew wispier and wispier. Keyes came to the conclusion that political advertising—not to mention politicians themselves—made dog food smell like a rose.

But now, Keyes was watching his political idol, Richard Meriwether Halliday, preparing a gracious exit from politics. It was like interrupting a canticle for the dead.

"Uh," Keyes said.

Halliday's campaign team all turned and looked at him as though one of the chairs had spoken. Keyes was the type who tended to disappear into the wallpaper; he instinctively avoided drawing attention to himself. Now his throat was dry and his hands were moist and he suddenly had to go to the bathroom. But the only politician in America worth a damn was on the point of making a fool of himself, and he had to speak up.

"The networks are getting it all wrong, sir. They've so convinced themselves that you're going to lose, they aren't looking at the nuts and bolts. As of ten P.M. you are not losing Connecticut; you are not losing Massachusetts even better, and Pennsylvania is starting to look funny. New Jersey, I don't know."

It was almost like a shoot-out shaping up, the others backing away slowly to give Doc Halliday a clear shot at him.

"This the guy who wrote my ads?" Halliday said.

Doolittle nodded. Doolittle was speechless. He had gotten Keyes invited to the party primarily as a payoff, so he could avoid giving him a raise.

"Okay, Malcolm," Halliday said. "What do you know that we don't?"

Doolittle stood up and sidled over. He assumed the position he took whenever he thought someone was nuts. His hands were in his back pockets and he was bent over at the waist, with his right ear pointed at Keyes. It was his position of incredulity; he wanted to be sure that he was hearing right, that the other guy really was saying those things.

"The gross totals are misleading," Keyes said. "The key precincts tell a completely different story."

"The governor is doing badly in the key precincts," Doolittle said.

"Compared with what?" Keyes replied. "I mean with whom? Actually, I mean with *when*."

22

Keyes's mouth was suffering from a terminal shortage of saliva, but he was feeling a little braver. He had the numbers on his side. There was a structure of numbers in his head that stretched across the entire country; it gave him an almost physical feel for the situation. He knew what he knew.

"I'm going on past performance of key districts based on time of evening," Keyes told them.

Pause. Looks of disbelief. Shaking of heads.

"That's gibberish," Doolittle said; that stuff coming at his right ear was pure craziness.

"Have you looked at Second Connecticut?" Keyes said.

"We're losing Second Connecticut," Pope put in.

"At ten P.M., Carter was losing worse. The governor is also doing better than Carter and Dukakis, although not as good as Kennedy or Johnson. In *that* district, *that* is significant."

"Somebody get me a drink," Halliday said.

"You're calling Connecticut on the Second?" Doolittle said, still trying to disassociate himself from his employee. He looked as if he wanted to rush to a phone and call someone, anyone.

"I'm not calling Connecticut yet. But look at Third Connecticut. That one's even touchier than the Second. The governor is doing noticeably better than Mondale or Second Carter, *almost* as good as Kennedy. Then there's the Fourth. Fairfield County. A Republican country club. *They* even liked Goldwater. The governor is only losing as badly as Truman. As of ten P.M., I mean."

Now they were all drifting off to couches and chairs, plopping down, thinking, abstracted looks on their faces. He had gotten their attention. Maybe there was even some hoping going on. Maybe even Doolittle was doing some hoping, since he personally regarded any campaign as his own ass on the line, not the candidate's.

"It's not impressive," Moody said finally.

Moody had been Halliday's press spokesman in Albany for eight years. Moody was about thirty-five. He had a face that could go from menacing to hail fellow in a second, and back again. It was his lips that did it. They were thick and long. And his teeth. He had big white teeth. When he smiled there was a sudden tremendous flash of white; when the smile went away it was like turning off all the lights. Moody had undergone a personality change during eight years of jousting with reporters in Albany. He thought of them as animals. He was always on red alert in the presence of reporters, adrenaline flowing, heart

23

pumping. Lately, this tendency had been spreading to more and more of his nonreportorial encounters.

"It's inventive," he said now to Malcolm Keyes. "It's inventive but it's not impressive. It's statistical fantasizing."

Akers was alone in a chair with a scotch. When he spoke it was typical Akers: judicious, objective tone of voice, no curves on the ball, no contempt, a straight question.

"Are you telling us that you know how the vote went by the hour going back to Kennedy?"

"Uh, by the half hour."

"How the hell can you do that?"

"I have a good memory."

"*I* didn't know that," Doolittle said, annoyed.

"Where did you get the data?" Akers asked.

Keyes nodded at Pope. "It's in his computer."

"It is?" Pope said.

Pope turned to his keyboard and did input furiously, his head bobbing back and forth between screen and keyboard for two minutes. Then he sat back in his straight chair and spoke to the wall.

"I forget—did you say the governor is doing almost as good in Third Connecticut as Kennedy? Or Carter?

"Kennedy."

Pope slowly shook his head up and down.

"He does have a good memory."

Halliday was quietly sipping his scotch and staring at the drapes.

"Tell about Massachusetts, Malcolm," he said.

Norman Pope was tall and nervous. He didn't have a whole lot of hair, and his mouth tended to go incessantly; fortunately, he had good teeth. He also had the gift of intensity and gave the impression of knowing what he was about at all times. He had access to energy, sparked by his interest in the world, which was what made him such a good and relentless pollster. Pope really wanted to know what everyone was thinking. But at this moment, *he* didn't know what to think. It sounded too good. In real life the cavalry never showed up when you needed them; when you lost, you lost. He was sitting there now listening to Malcolm Keyes tell about Massachusetts.

"The Fourth tells the whole story," Keyes was saying. "They've got everything there. Yuppies. Yumpies. Wasps. Hard hats. Save-the-

24

whales. You're getting them all. You're ahead of *McGovern* as of this moment."

Halliday and Akers turned to Pope.

"I have to admit that Massachusetts is beginning to look moderately okay," he said.

"Moderately okay," Halliday said flatly.

"Beginning to, I said," Pope replied.

"Well, that's something," Halliday said.

Pope felt Malcolm's arms encircling him. The networks were starting to put up gross totals for Pennsylvania, and Keyes was reaching around him to do input at the terminal, to get the latest vote tallies by district. The vote was still sparse, but it could be compared with other sparse moments. The gross totals themselves were a dirge, a death sentence, but they came from twenty-two election districts, each with its own personality. Keyes was standing there looking at the new numbers and going over modern American political history: first Kennedy, then Johnson, Nixon, Nixon, Carter, Reagan, Reagan, the Busher, McKay.

"Uh," Keyes said, clearing his throat, knowing that in the fairly near future he was going to have to go to the bathroom, "about Pennsylvania."

"What about Pennsylvania?" Akers and Mullins and Moody and Pope and Halliday said. Doolittle was even standing up straight.

"You've got the Fourteenth, of course. Pittsburgh. And the Twenty-second. You've got First Philly, expected. You've got Second Philly, expected. You're holding even in Third Philly, *not* expected. Not as good as Mondale, not as good as Humphrey, better than first Carter, better than Kennedy, much better than Dukakis. The Twenty-third. Always iffy for a Democrat. You're not losing badly at all. The Nineteenth. Death and taxes for a Democrat. You're only losing fifty-five to forty-five. I find that remarkable. I'm having a funny feeling about this whole thing."

Halliday held his glass up and poured what was left of his scotch straight into his bloodstream. He went over to Pope, who was pounding away at his keyboard. He pointed the empty glass at Keyes.

"Is this possible?" he said to the infallible one. "Or is this guy out of his fucking mind?"

Pope was abstracted, lost in numbers, conflicted, hemming, hawing, not wishing to look wimpy and indecisive in front of Doc Halliday. He straightened up in his chair and girded up his loins, but when he spoke it sounded oddly prissy. "I'm sticking to my guns," he said firmly. "It's too close to call."

By 11:00 P.M. the vote was working its way west and the Pope was still infallible. They were having the cliff-hanger of the century and maybe more, maybe going back to Hayes/Tilden.

The complex attitudes of Americans about the issue of war and peace had reached the point of almost total ambivalence. The numbers seemed to be reflecting the conflict in the American psyche, the conflict between wanting to be tough and wanting to be done with hate and hostility—the endless conflict. People wanted to tend to their own problems. Americans were easily aroused; it was easy to rattle their cages. Every military action of a President would raise his poll rating, as long as it didn't last too long. Anything looking like Vietnam had become anathema. There was the slowly dawning realization that the arms race had gone on for fifty years, was continuing with no end in sight, and where was it all going to end? With nuclear winter?

The situation was further complicated by the number of nonvoting voters. Far less than 50 percent of the eligible voters were still taking the trouble to go to the polls in presidential elections. Fewer and fewer Americans were seeing a noticeable difference between Democrats and Republicans. *The* fundamental issue of politics was the distribution of wealth—who gets how much.

And while both sides would—with considerable intensity—shout the same things at each other, no matter who won, the rich still ended up with the lion's share of the nation's wealth; there was no possible alternative to this result. The Democrats and Republicans were actually two wings of the same party, the Democrat-Republican Party, or the Republican-Democrat Party, or, better yet, the Capitalist Party. In that regard, the U.S. and the U.S.S.R. were identical: They were both one-party states. But, on this night, the absence of huge numbers of voters was wrecking conventional projections.

Malcolm Keyes and Norman Pope got into a dialogue that lasted all night and into late afternoon of the following day. There were two computers in the room: Pope's mainframe and Keyes's memory. As they tossed numbers back and forth, slowly moving west in their examination of key districts, Malcolm's boss, Doolittle, the five-foot-five-inch media colossus who believed that he personally had elected fourteen senators, fifty-eight representatives, and a couple dozen governors and mayors,

26

was forgotten and ended up asleep on a couch in front of a twenty-eight-inch color television that had lost vertical sync. Keyes was the one they were turning to. Keyes had all the numbers, all the comparisons, past performances, winners, losers, by how much, who, where, when.

By 4:00 A.M., the electoral vote was shifting back and forth. Ohio, which hadn't gone to Truman until well after sunup in '48, had already swung into Halliday's column twice, each time moving out again, but slower. This was saying something. Politicians tended to regard Ohio as the typical state. It was not Eastern, it was not Western. It was industrial, it was agricultural. Sometimes it went Republican, sometimes it went Democratic. Ohio's ambivalence was fascinating to national politicians. Now it was a signal that something major was happening. Or rather, not happening; the entire nation was sitting on the fence. Farther west, the mountain states, Republican to the core, began to fall like dominoes to President McKay.

That was when Pope started worrying about his blood pressure. Pope was so concerned about his blood pressure—he claimed it was freakishly volatile—that he carried his own cuff, the old-fashioned kind, with him. But he had another problem: He was hard of hearing. He couldn't hear that dark pulse running along his veins, and so he was always asking others to take his pressure. Keyes became the latest victim. As Idaho was falling—he was keeping an eye on ABC—Keyes put on a stethoscope for the first time in his life while Pope pumped up the cuff, and then listened intently for the start of that deadly beat—which marked the systolic pressure—and waited for it to end, which was the diastolic reading.

It was 212 over 130, deep in stroke country, which Pope referred to as "the zone," where you could get clubbed in the back of the head at any moment. He called stroke "the mugger." "The mugger is approaching," he said. Since his blood-pressure medicine didn't work, he used a technique he called belly breathing, which he'd learned from a gestalt psychotherapist.

Keyes waited impatiently. He wanted to get back to the computer terminal. He stood there while Pope used his stomach like a bellows, inhaling it outward to the maximum, then exhaling it all the way inward. He did it twenty times, and then they retook the pressure. It had gone down to 180 over 120, which was still rotten, but better. Pope wrote it down in a little notebook, and then they looked at Montana.

Montana fell.

But Keyes had written off the entire mountain belt hours before. He

27

knew there was Democratic gold to be mined west of the Rockies. That had been Madeleine Smith's assignment, and she'd worked relentlessly at it. Halliday had to have the West Coast to win, and he got it all: Washington, Oregon, and California. The electoral vote now tallied as follows:

Halliday		McKay	
New Hampshire	4	Maine	4
Connecticut	8	Vermont	3
Massachusetts	13	Rhode Island	4
New York	36	New Jersey	16
Pennsylvania	25	Delaware	3
District of Columbia	3	Maryland	10
Ohio	23	Virginia	12
Illinois	24	West Virginia	6
Michigan	20	North Carolina	13
Texas	29	South Carolina	8
Colorado	8	Georgia	12
Minnesota	10	Florida	21
Washington	10	Alabama	9
Oregon	7	Mississippi	7
California	47	Louisiana	10
	267	Tennessee	11
		Kentucky	9
		Indiana	12
		Wisconsin	11
		Iowa	8
		Nebraska	5
		Missouri	11
		Arkansas	6
		Oklahoma	8
		Kansas	7
		North Dakota	3
		South Dakota	3
		Montana	4
		Wyoming	3
		Utah	5
		Idaho	4
		Nevada	4
		Arizona	7
		New Mexico	5
		Alaska	3
			267

as time slowly swept westward out over the Pacific toward Hawaii and its four electoral votes.

President McKay had taken almost all of the South, all of the mountain states, and a big part of the Midwest. Halliday had most of the Northeast, all of the Far West, and the four big states in the center of the country, Ohio, Illinois, Michigan, and Texas, which sometimes had voted conservative, but they were having tough economic times and when the going gets tough, the tough get liberal.

Keyes had predicted it while they were in Texas.

"Hawaii is going to decide this thing," he had said.

Doolittle, bent over at the waist, had said, "Hawaii has four electoral votes."

"I don't think I can last that long," Pope had said, reaching for his cuff.

"Hawaii," Keyes had repeated. By Texas, the entire structure had become clear to him. It amounted to nothing less than a political portrait of a nation. Anyway, for this day, this moment. The organism might shift tomorrow, but for now the structure was firmly in place.

Keyes called it eleven hours before CBS, which waited until 2:00 P.M. on the day after election. ABC waited until 3:30 P.M. NBC and CNN conceded at 4:00 P.M. At 4:15 P.M., Akers handed a phone to the governor, who held a short quiet conversation ending with, "Thank you, Mr. President."

Power had changed hands. Halliday was already showered and shaved and didn't look at all as if he'd been up all night. He was leaving for the hotel ballroom to make a statement, but he paused to shake hands with Keyes.

"Tell me something, Malcolm. Can you do that in real time?"

"Do what?"

"Memorize stuff."

"In real time?"

"Yeah. Like, say, a conversation between two people."

"Sure, if I want to."

"That's very interesting."

Halliday smiled at him and then winked. And then walked out. Keyes was standing there wondering what that portended when a stethoscope was thrust into his hand. He put it on and waited while Pope pumped up his sphygmomanometer and then listened for the dark, dangerous beat that drummed along Pope's veins, doing the mortality rag.

29

It had gone back to normal, 150 over 90.

"What causes high blood pressure?" Keyes said.

"Doctors blame it on salt. They're really out of it. It's got to do with being infallible. Quite frankly, I don't understand how the Pope lives with it," Norman Pope said.

3

TRANSITION

DOOLITTLE WAS ON the phone. He was sitting on the edge of his seat listening impatiently, talking intently, getting physical restoration from telephonic communication, from conquering time and space. Keyes was watching him. Keyes never tired of watching Doolittle; it was necessary for survival. Doolittle's limo—owned, not rented—was parked on a hilltop alongside the New York State Thruway. And a Republican throughway at that: the Thomas E. Dewey, he who'd lost a pretty close election to Harry Truman.

They were heading north toward New Paltz, New York, where Richard Halliday was organizing his new administration. But Doolittle had a problem with the hills. They were getting high; they were starting to turn into mountains, the Shawangunks, which had begun to make telephonic communication with the outside world difficult; so every now and then Doolittle had his chauffeur pull over at the top of a hill. Doolittle without a telephone was pitiful.

On the other hand, it wasn't entirely abnormal. Doolittle had just elected his first President. The presidency had eluded him for years; his candidates had always been too liberal or too flaky or too bruised from previous political office. Now that he was on intimate terms with the

31

White House, the calls were pouring in—Senate races, House races, governorships, mayoralties. Doolittle, in effect, had become the unofficial chairman of the Democratic Party and would go on making money hand over fist from poor liberal candidates. Had he been a conservative, Doolittle would be an easy decamillionaire.

Not that money meant all that much to Doolittle. He was anhedonic, incapable of having fun. It was as though he shot up every morning on something that blocked the flow of the endogenous pleasure chemicals in the brain. Life was work and success—plotting, planning, scheming, kicking ass, staying ahead of the pack. What were you supposed to do when you made it—move to Disneyland? Doolittle hung up the phone and signaled his chauffeur to proceed.

"Hackenlauter," he said.

Keyes nodded. Forbes Hackenlauter. A liberal senator from Nebraska. Up for reelection in two years. Coming to the miracle worker for a miracle. Why did liberals stay in Nebraska?

"I want to ask you something," Doolittle said, as the scenery began to move. "How come you never said anything about that memory of yours?"

"I don't like to talk about it."

"Why not?"

"It makes me look like a freak."

"You know something? I think you're right. I've got funny feelings about you myself now. It's like you're not normal."

Roger Doolittle was ugly. Short and ugly. He'd practically had to pay his mother to love him. You had to take that into account when dealing with him.

"I want to give you a little advance warning," Doolittle said. "This is more than a social occasion today."

"Oh?"

"You're not just going up there to have a hamburger with the next President of the United States."

Keyes looked over at him, sitting on the edge of his seat, ignoring the scenery, busy manipulating. Doolittle was an inveterate manipulator. His politics were liberal, but his personal relationships were fascist. Keyes made it a practice never to let him get away with anything.

"What else would I be going up there for?"

"He's got something he wants you to do for him. He wouldn't talk about it over the phone. I think it's a little out of the ordinary. I told him he could rely on your discretion."

"What's it got to do with?"

"I have no idea."

"He wouldn't talk about it over the telephone?"

"That is correct."

"I don't think I like the sound of that," Keyes said.

"Come on, Malcolm, the telephone's been disinvented."

Keyes looked at that big nose and wide lips and small eyes.

"If you're worried," Doolittle said, "I can tell you this. He specifically said there was nothing to worry about; there was no danger of any kind."

Now Keyes moved up to the edge of the seat.

"Danger?"

"*No* danger."

"What do you mean there's no danger? What are you talking about?"

"You don't seem to understand. I said there is—no—danger."

"Why would the subject even come up?"

Doolittle threw his arms up.

"It was an unfortunate choice of words. All right? It's something a little unorthodox. Don't get paranoid. You don't think Halliday would expose you to any kind of risk, do you?"

"I'm glad we all understand that."

"Stop at the top of the next hill," Doolittle said to his chauffeur.

The limousine wound slowly through the main street of New Paltz for all of five minutes, then sped out across the valley toward the Shawangunks. The Democratic National Committee had rented the entire Mohonk Mountain House for two weeks; it was the lull after the leaf season and before Thanksgiving.

There were four thousand positions to be filled in a new administration, and if they considered only three candidates for each job, that meant processing twelve thousand applications and holding twelve thousand interviews. In the two weeks at Mohonk, they would be able to fill only the very highest ranking of the positions; the process would go on well past inauguration day.

The gatehouse at the entrance had been taken over by the Secret Service, and they had to go through the usual scrutinizing of credentials. Doolittle's chauffeur was a problem. It took two phone calls to the lodge to settle it. The place was crawling with press; they were

33

waiting for a bus to take them to the lodge for the latest announcements; there were columns to fill, minutes to fill. Moody was out there, organizing. Moody's life was built around the 7 o'clock news production deadline. When Moody saw Doolittle's car, he hurried over and got in.

"These guys are hungry," Moody said. "God, are they hungry. I'm going to have a vicious four years. It's kill or be killed. Albany was never like this."

The lodge was about three miles from the gate, at the end of a narrow, twisting road. The whole thing was a Secret Service nightmare. They even had two-man patrols out wandering the roads and countless paths that had been cut through the woods for hikers.

"The Secret Service is going to have a collective nervous breakdown," Moody said. "Halliday has already pushed them beyond their limits by coming up here."

"What else is new?" Doolittle said. "He pushes everyone beyond their limit. That's his executive style."

The entrance to the lodge was another madhouse. Cars unloading baggage and people, the new arrivals; cars loading baggage and people, the already interviewed.

"There's only one thing I want to say to you before you see the man," Doolittle said, as they were going into the lodge. "You've got to start being realistic about politics."

"Every time someone tells me to be realistic, I get fatalistic. Doomsday is coming."

"All I'm saying is that you've still got elementary-school history in your brain. They get to you real young, and you never lose it unless you work at it. Real history is X-rated as far as elementary schools go. Colleges, too."

They were following Moody past the reception desk.

"You're scaring me," Keyes said.

"I am not trying to scare you, there is no danger," Doolittle said in rote tones.

Keyes took a long look at his boss.

"Do you believe in Halliday?"

"Yes, I believe in Halliday. But not the way you believe in Halliday."

"I observe that you didn't tell me that before I did his advertising."

"That's *my* executive style."

*   *   *

34

They found Halliday in the Lake Lounge, crouched before a fireplace making hamburgers and managing to look dapper and presidential in khakis, a heavy gray sweater and jogging shoes. They held back for a while because in addition to cooking Halliday was also hatching a deal with Art Feeny, mayor of Chicago. Moody handed each of them a mug of beer, and they stood there awkwardly, waiting.

"Observe," Doolittle said. "You're seeing politics in action. Art Feeny. Cook County was the only wrong call you made all night. Get me?"

"Got you."

Keyes looked around. Mohonk was all rug and fireplaces and brown wood; there were countless soft chairs and couches for tired climbers and hikers. Through the window he could see out over Lake Mohonk to the rising cliff on the far side; there were little birch huts perched on the rocks here and there and throughout the surrounding woods. Interviews were taking place in them now; the fall weather was mild enough, and even the huge lodge wasn't big enough to hold all of them.

Halliday had laid down the law about interviews: They were to be vigorous. The Reagan administration had been sloppy about it and as a result had nearly one hundred embarrassments, cases of insensitivity to appearances, of conflicts of interest, plus outright indictments and convictions. President McKay had not profited from Reagan's mistakes; he'd had over a hundred scandals in only four years.

So Halliday wanted deep background checking. Every senior appointee would have to go through checking by the White House, the FBI, and the IRS. Halliday had even insisted that the FBI's Standard Form 86, which all appointees were required to fill out, wasn't probing enough; a team of lawyers had drawn up a supplementary list of ten additional questions. Halliday's victory margin had been so thin that he lacked political capital. He considered himself a pauper, and until he earned more across-the-board popularity from the American people, was taking no chances. Keyes regarded it as just another example of Halliday's administrative astuteness.

Then the President-elect was holding out a hamburger on a paper plate.

"It's rare," he said. "In honor of the man who beat all three networks by a country mile. Thanks for coming up."

Doolittle gestured with his mug and then swallowed some beer, looking out of place with a drink in his hand. He wasn't a drinker, but he

35

managed to get some of it down now and then just to be sociable. How could you not toast a President's victory with real alcohol?

"Tell me something, Malcolm," Halliday said. "That memory of yours. It's extraordinary. Is that something you inherited, or did you learn it?"

"It seems to come naturally. But I polished it up a bit."

"Are there any more at home like you?"

"No. It seems to have come out of nowhere." Keyes hated to admit it; he was both proud and ashamed of it.

Halliday was back with his head in the fireplace tending to his hamburgers—rare, medium, and well done, all political bases touched, chef of all the people. Keyes found himself feeling totally at ease, which was one of Halliday's charms.

"Here's what I'm wondering about, Malcolm. You said you can listen to a conversation and memorize it in real time." Halliday said it casually, while flipping burgers.

"Yes, sir," Keyes said.

"I didn't know that," Doolittle said, faintly annoyed.

"As soon as I finish these hamburgers, we'll go over to that group around Moody," Halliday said. "I'm curious to see how this thing works."

Keyes thought for a moment and decided to take a chance.

"To be completely honest with you, sir, I couldn't help overhearing the conversation you were having just now with Mayor Feeny."

A presidential eyebrow went up.

"How much do you remember?"

Keyes looked out over Lake Mohonk to the woods on the far side, where the trees were mostly poles now; autumn clarity had returned to the forest. He thought back a few minutes, and it was all there because he'd wanted to remember it; it was a tiny bit of political history, a collector's item: The mayor of Chicago and the President-elect of the United States decide to level with each other.

"When I got in range," Keyes said, "he was saying, 'That's the way it is.' You said, 'All right, I suppose I'll have to live with it.' He said, 'I didn't say you had to live with it.' You said, 'Huh?' And he said, 'Yeah.' You said, 'No.' It was a happy kind of no. It wasn't a no at all, really. It meant 'Is that a fact?' 'Yeah,' he said."

Halliday flashed a glance at Doolittle and then switched his eyes back to Keyes.

"You were obviously having second thoughts of one kind or another,

36

because you then said, 'It's impossible.' He said, 'Nothing's impossible.' You said, 'What about Hiram?' He said, 'Fuck Hiram.' You commented that you'd wanted to do that for a long time."

"Holy Mother of God," Halliday said quietly.

"At that point," Keyes continued, "you flipped over my hamburger and watched it sizzling on the griddle. The juices were dripping down to the fire and flaring up with little bursts. You smiled into the fire and said it again: 'I've always wanted to fuck Hiram.' "

Halliday was looking wounded. "Is this what politics sounds like?" he said in a small voice. He had forgotten all about his hamburgers. Doolittle, Mr. Sourpuss, the anhedonic, was starting to giggle.

"Then he said, 'Done,' and you said, 'How much?' and he said, 'A hundred,' and you said, 'Balls,' and he said, 'Make me an offer,' and you said, 'Thirty-five,' and he winked."

"I can't take any more of this," Halliday said. He looked at Doolittle. "Do I really sound like that?"

"Yes, you sound like that. That's exactly how you sound. Haven't you been listening to yourself all these years? Sometimes I think I'll have to give the *two* of you a political education."

Halliday was looking down at his shoes. Hamburgers were beginning to burn. He looked at Keyes. "What do you think of me after hearing a conversation like that, which sounds much worse than it was, by the way?"

In a sense, Keyes had grown up with Halliday. Halliday had been mayor of New York City three times and governor of New York State twice. He had heard the name Halliday since he was a kid. His family were all Halliday rooters; he had never heard a harsh word about Richard Halliday in his home. Everyone in his family had felt that Halliday was about as close as American politicians come to having integrity while functioning in the real world. Halliday was about the only mainstream politician who said that people didn't have to be protected from government. The Constitution did that. The Bill of Rights did that. What the people had to be protected from was those sources of power *not* mentioned in the Constitution or the Bill of Rights: the big corporations and the big banks. Although this was not something he shouted from the rooftops.

"I'm only sorry," Keyes said, "that a man of your stature has to deal with the likes of Art Feeny, but it seems to come with the territory."

Doolittle giggled a second time; he was having a real party.

"You're not such a bad politician yourself," Halliday said, putting an

37

arm around Malcolm's shoulder. "Come with me. I've got something to show you."

❧

Keyes's seemingly limitless memory had grown out of two unrelated abilities that he had been born with. One was an extraordinary eidetic memory. Keyes could call up images of things previously seen that were far sharper, more detailed, more intense, more vibrant than other people's. He could recall with total clarity almost any image that had drawn his attention and concentration.

He had also inherited a striking sensitivity to music. He could remember hearing talk as music long before he realized that words had meaning. He had an aunt who spoke in a highly musical way. "Hel-lo," she would say to Keyes when he was still in his crib. "How is my little boy today?" The changing inflections in her voice were entrancing. Questions were especially delicious, because they ended unresolved; there was more coming; the suspense was exquisite. It took him a long time to comprehend that a question was supposed to be responded to.

When he discovered music—which was music that was all music— he lost interest in words. Music was far preferable to talking. He ended up looking oddly retarded and talked late.

As the years went by and Keyes became acquainted with the various musical instruments, he realized that the human voice contained all of them, but that most people used only a few when they spoke and very often only one. He got into the habit of characterizing people as horns or strings or woodwinds or drums; it was the beginning of his memory system.

To which he added harmony.

As his musical sophistication grew, Keyes saw that he was leaving out the most important element: harmony. To Keyes, harmony was so basic that many years later he decided that music was what people were made to do. It came right after eating and before sex, because it had some kind of profound evolutionary advantage; among individuals of a group or tribe it improved all their chances if they engaged in teamwork and cooperation. Darwin had been misconstrued. In prehistoric times the reigning principle was clearly and obviously Survival of the Harmonious. A taste for Mozart had been bred in the tooth-and-claw jungle.

Once he understood the importance of harmony, the concept of characterizing people's voices in musical terms opened out to the entire world of music. For one thing, there were different musics. Classical.

38

Jazz. Blues. Rock and roll. Modern. Romantic. Baroque. Even different composers within each grouping had their own styles, which added further refinements and subtleties for coming up with the most vivid association for any individual's voice.

It was apparent to him that every person—every document, for that matter—had his her its own particular harmony or disharmony. He became acquainted with the typical chords used by the great classical and popular composers, so he could more accurately characterize the speech of anyone he heard. He could not only associate particular individuals with particular instruments, he could further identify the individual as, say, Chopinesque, Tchaikovskian, or even the *Roman Carnival Overture.*

And there was rhythm. In some ways rhythm was the most important aspect of all. Rhythm was a breathtaking quality. It had the wild potential for simultaneously bringing both order and abandon to music. Keyes listened closely for human rhythms. Some people had singsong deliveries, which Keyes heard as *dah* dah dah, *dah* dah dah, *dah* dah dah. Or the reverse: dah dah *dah,* dah dah *dah,* dah dah *dah.* In Keyes's brain even the simple phrase "Good morning" could characterize a person forever. There was the common "Good *morn*ing." Dah *dah* dah. Along with the often phony "*Good* morning." *Dah* dah dah. Or the more deadly—even hostile—"Good morning." Dah dah dah. Big nothing. No inflection. Someone a million miles away. Keyes did not like dah dah dah; he couldn't help it, it was a turnoff.

It was an easy step from "Good morning" to far more complex matters. For example, Keyes had had an algebra teacher in high school who'd had an ominous, tragic intonation in his voice and delivery which was nothing less than Wagnerian. It was like going to the opera three times a week and hearing different versions of Siegfried's Rhine journey, but a Rhine journey that went on for two semesters: chalking up truth and beauty on the blackboard as though leading up to a polynomial which would demonstrate beyond any doubt that doomsday was coming.

There was a disadvantage. While Keyes always got straight As because he remembered everything, he never had a feeling of security about his schoolwork. Although he knew everything, he always had the queasy feeling that he understood nothing. It had turned out to be a lifelong disadvantage: Remembering was easier than thinking. It had resulted in his going through life with a well-informed naiveté, since he'd rarely bothered to make connections and establish relationships

39

among the vast array of facts at his fingertips. The facts alone had seemed adequate.

The most peculiar thing about it all was that when he was a kid, Keyes didn't think of it as *his* memory system. It was too obvious. It virtually built itself, although it was based on his own unique assets. He didn't realize how obsessed he was about memory. He thought everyone had a good memory. But long afterward he realized that he had to be careful with his memory. It was too easy to turn other people's inconsistencies into plots; he remembered, they didn't.

When Keyes was eleven, one of his schoolteachers discovered that he had memorized the Declaration of Independence in one reading. To Keyes, it had been pure Copland. "When in the course of human events" was *Fanfare for the Common Man,* simplicity and grandeur intertwined and simultaneous, ending with its intense and inevitable climax—drums and horns—"we mutually pledge to each other our lives, our fortunes and our sacred honor." There were tears running down his face when he finished reading it and his teacher, also moved, was also somehow appalled. He was a freak, and she never looked at him in quite the same way again.

Years later Keyes read a book by the Soviet scientist A. R. Luria that was virtually a description of himself. It was called *The Mind of a Mnemonist.* It was about a man who had an extraordinary eidetic memory and had built a memory system based on the streets of Moscow. When he wanted to memorize something he would take a mental walk along a street in Moscow and put all the words or numbers in doorways, leaning against lampposts, in store windows. When he wished to recall the material he would take that same mental stroll again, and it would all be there waiting for him to walk past. Luria's conclusion was that the man's memory was infinite; Keyes believed the same of his own memory.

When Keyes got to college, he was still bothered by his oddness; like any other teenager, he wanted to be the same as everyone else. One of the first things he did was seek out a professor of psychobiology to learn the "cause" of photographic memory. The professor got interested in him and gave him the ultimate memory test: lists of nonsense syllables. Fa, la, da, la, ga, fa, and the like. It wasn't even a strain. The professor had stayed in touch with him over the years, to see if he could still remember the original lists of nonsense syllables. His score was always perfect.

The professor's "diagnosis" for photographic memory was pure guesswork, but Keyes found it reassuring. The professor told him that his brain was probably secreting unusual amounts of the chemicals that aided memory, the chemicals that helped rats learn mazes quickly.

"You're probably getting an extra-high dose of the neuropeptide vasopressin. An extra little scootch of norepinephrine. A bit more enkephalin, I'd guess. In fact, you could be ODing on ACTH or the neurotransmitter acetylcholine."

It made Keyes feel better. It demystified the phenomenon to some degree. There was nothing *really* peculiar, it was merely a little more of this in the mix, a little more of that. He was basically sound.

Now, as they wound their way across the big Lake Lounge—dozens of interviews going on around them—Doc Halliday was talking about politics and truth, which were mutually exclusive categories.

"You see, Mr. Lincoln didn't get it quite right. You can fool *almost* all of the people *almost* all of the time. American Presidents have been doing it for the last fifty years at least. But if I'm going to be able to get us a nuclear test ban, and if I'm going to be able to keep the establishment from forcing me into countering other people's revolutions all over the globe, I have to begin the process of *un*fooling the American people. This is dangerous work."

One of Halliday's charms was that he never condescended. He treated you as an equal. Keyes didn't stand a chance; he already knew that he would do anything Halliday asked. They'd left the lounge and were going down a long corridor past the coffee shop to one of the lodge's administrative offices.

"Now, I want to get the truth out, but I have to do it slowly or they'll kill the messenger. They won't want to hear the bad news. And what have I got for a mandate? The jokes have already started. I'm the Pineapple President. Four lousy electoral votes from across the Pacific. My wife and daughters will do the hula at the Inaugural Ball. Visitors to the Oval Office will get leis. Visitors to the Oval Office will get leid. A major part of the establishment is opposed to me. For all I know, the bureaucracy too. My administration is going to leak like a sieve."

They went into an office, and Halliday went up to the double doors of a large closet.

"I want to show you the infernal machine," he said, throwing open the doors.

It was a copier.

"It's the leakers' hydrogen bomb. The Russians keep the damn things locked up. I'm not allowed to do that."

Keyes was hearing Halliday as a piper. Not a pied piper, a benevolent

41

piper. A virtuoso flutist leading people away from war toward peace, conning them every step of the way. As compared with, say, Art Feeny, who was a Mississippi riverboat banjo player with six aces up his sleeve. Now, Halliday was working terrific solo riffs and Keyes was dancing along behind him.

"Did you know," Halliday was saying, "that certain agencies of government are no longer committing certain matters to paper? Contingency plans were the first to go. Think of a Federal Deposit Insurance Corporation contingency plan for a series of catastrophic bank failures. It would look lovely in a headline. If such a plan were leaked it could conceivably *cause* a catastrophic series of bank failures. So they don't have a contingency plan. On paper. Somebody at FDIC has to remember it. That goes for the Federal Reserve Bank, the SEC, and a number of other agencies. Even the Pentagon is doing it. *That* started when a contingency plan for adding hospital beds in the event of a nuclear accident got out. Now *I* have a contingency, and *you* are my contingency plan."

"Really."

"It's probably pure poison. It's probably a ploy, a play to get me some bad headlines." Halliday seemed almost to be talking to himself. "I'd be better off ignoring it completely."

He paced back and forth across the room several times, as though rethinking his decision—in the presence of the God of whistle blowers, Xerox—and managing to come to the same conclusion all over again.

"But on the other hand it could be juicy as hell. Ideally, I'd like to know about it and not know about it—know what I mean? So I want you to handle it for me. In your fashion. Nothing on paper. Get my drift?"

"Yes, sir."

"It occurred to me on election night—when you were flinging numbers around like confetti—that you are the perfect solution."

"What do I do?"

"I want you to talk to someone. Then come back and tell me the he saids and the you saids. That's all."

"What do I talk about?"

"I don't know. He'll do most of the talking. But don't let him be cagey. You'll be in a strong position in this situation. Pick his brain. Pump him. You've got *carte blanche.*"

"Who is he?"

"President William McKay's favorite tennis partner."

"Where do I find him?"

"In Danbury Prison."

4

SUMMIT MEETING

From the road that ran past it, Danbury Prison at first looked like a golf course; there was nothing but grass as far as the eye could see. Then, as Doolittle's chauffeur took the car up a hill, it began to look like an army base where they had the manpower to keep the grass looking crew-cut. Then, at the top of the hill, they saw low, two-story buildings with walls that weren't all that impressive. There were two small parking lots near the entrance, and the place now looked like an industrial park; there was a Chalmer's Cookies van pulled up near the entrance as Keyes went in.

Inside, it was a prison. Twenty feet from the front door there was a heavy sliding glass gate. In between there was a metal detector. To the right there was a men's and a women's, both with the doors open wide. Everything was spotlessly clean; there was manpower available here. Keyes failed the metal detector three times. The thing could almost pick up tooth fillings. He had to take off his watch, his belt, and his shoes before it would certify him as weapon-free. Keyes was feeling intimidated, cowed, afraid to make a false step. This was a place of regulations and procedures; things were spelled out here; there wasn't a whole lot of room for improvising. Then the heavy door was humming open and Keyes was in jail and being treated like visiting brass by the warden's chief assistant. Which he was, Keyes thought. Brass for a day. The appointment had been set up by the Attorney General–designate.

Danbury was a Category 2 prison, one step up or maybe down from a country club. It wasn't oppressive walking through the successive courtyards—there were flowers and shrubs growing everywhere—although none of the inmates looked particularly happy. The aide took Keyes around the long way—showing the place off to the visiting big shot from the new administration—and they went past the athletic field. There was a baseball game going on, and Keyes recognized former Senator Timothy McKnight doing the pitching. And still tossing curve balls, Keyes noticed, and at the former chairman of the board of Federal Steel, no less, who was at the plate trying to look menacing. It looked like there was an ancient Berrigan playing deep in left.

When they got to Lockhart's cell, the warden's aide engaged in some friendly banter with Lockhart and then discreetly disappeared. It wasn't exactly an oppressive, sadistic relationship; it wasn't exactly a cell, either. The normal Danbury cell was about seven by eleven feet, with a cot, sink, toilet, and cabinet. Lockhart's was about three times that size. It was a former "quiet room" where inmates could watch television or write letters. Lockhart seemed to flourish under all conditions.

He was a former arbitrager on Wall Street, one of the most dangerous and potentially profitable fields there was. He had gone from that to being President McKay's director of the Office of Management and Budget, where he had been a middle-aged *terrible* for three years.

Lockhart had been dictating his memoirs to Henry Toomey, a former executive stenographer for the Securities and Exchange Commission. Toomey had used some inside information about Federal Reserve Board policy to pick up a quick twenty-five thousand dollars. He had been forced to "disgorge" it, as the SEC so neatly put it, to get off with a mere ten months in a Category 2 hotel. Seeing the two of them together made Keyes feel as though he had blundered onto the evening news.

Lockhart was about forty. He had a whizbang, outgoing personality and gave the impression of being the man who has everything, even in the slammer. Another inmate came in with coffee and danish for two on a tray. There were only two cups, and Toomey got the hint, closing his steno book and the door behind him.

The main item of furniture in the room was a picnic table. Keyes climbed over the bench on one side and sat down. He was queasy about

44

dealing with the likes of Dewitt Lockhart, partly because he had been such a major figure in the McKay administration but mainly because he was an arch right-winger. He had all the conservative contradictions. He was opposed to abortion, but once the sacred fetus came to life, it was a good-for-nothing loafer feeding at the public trough. He would have been quite capable of labeling catsup a vegetable for free lunch programs if it hadn't already been done back in the Reagan days; he had the conservative's passionate lack of compassion. Keyes had always had trouble even making small talk with people like Lockhart.

Now Lockhart was standing across the room lighting a cigar and looking almost wistfully at Keyes.

"The beginning of an administration is the most tense, exciting moment I know of. By the way, who are you? I never heard of you."

"I'm nobody," Keyes said. "I'm running an errand."

Lockhart nodded. "There's something to be said for that, too," he said, gesturing around at the room as though it were a potential destination for anyone in politics. He had misbehaved with the Office of Stockpile Disposal, making a fast three hundred grand on titanium at fire-sale prices.

"I guess you're wondering why I sent for you," he said, still smiling, circling around the picnic table talking to his cigar, a knife-edge crease in his gray prison trousers.

"You have Halliday's attention."

"Fine. I'll try to make this sound plausible."

Lockhart was ordinary looking; medium height and slightly stocky. But he had a cherubic face and a manic personality. He had a reputation for being effervescent no matter how bad things got. He seemed to have the ability to step out of his skin and look at himself from a disinterested observer's point of view. To Keyes, he was beginning to sound like a drummer—bass, snare, cymbals.

"It occurred to me six months after I got here," Lockhart said, "that I was railroaded."

Keyes put his coffee cup down.

"You mean you didn't do it?"

"Oh, no. I did it. Oh, yes. Oh boy, did I do it. They had me cold." He stopped pacing suddenly and smiled, his arms out in a gesture of total openness. "See? How about that? I'm changing. Prison is rehabilitating me. It works!"

"Maybe we should send our politicians to Danbury *before* we send them to Washington," Keyes said.

45

"There's an idea in there. I might have thought twice. It's just that it was so easy. Oh God, was that easy. The opportunity was handed to me on a silver—no, a titanium platter. And I don't know to this day how it got out. Furthermore, I received no help whatsoever from my President. I went to see him and he talked about Watergate blah blah blah, can't risk the program blah blah blah, lots of luck."

Lockhart came to rest opposite Keyes, one foot up on the bench of the picnic table, arm resting on his knee, pointing his cigar at Keyes.

"I'm not one hundred percent sure of this. Say ninety-five percent. I mean, there's a certain amount of normal, illegal political loyalty: guys help each other out. In fact, I think I got less than nothing. I think I got shoved."

Lockhart absently bit into a danish, cigar smoke dribbling out of the corner of his mouth.

"You weren't part of the Indiana crowd, were you?" Keyes said. "You were a latecomer."

"Yeah," Lockhart said. "Anyway, I woke up at three in the morning a month ago and it was there, right in my own head. Been there all along. I'd forgotten it because I was suddenly fighting titanium, with lawyers and reporters and assistant attorney generals. Spending *days* trying to figure out how to shift the blame onto someone else."

Malcolm Keyes couldn't help smiling. He was starting to like this right-wing maniac. But he was more than a drummer; he was a one-man band, pedaling the drums with his feet and strumming on a guitar while blowing a horn—no, a bugle—suspended in front of his face, his elbows taking care of the cymbals. In Washington they had called him the Icepick, for the way he had chipped away at the federal budget. He was like Chuck Colson from the Nixon days; he'd have run over his own grandma to shrink the budget by fifty bucks and make his President look good. But maybe it wasn't just Lockhart and Colson? Maybe they'd all run over Grandma? He blinked his eyes; he was wandering. He couldn't afford to miss a word.

"I think now that my troubles began the day I spotted some unusual expenses going on in Agriculture," Lockhart was saying. "I'm talking big bucks. In itself not surprising. Agriculture has huge farm payments, so it's a good place to hide money. I know a little something about how to bury a billion here, a billion there. I've done it often enough for the CIA, NSA, others. But *I* didn't know what this was. *Me*. OMB director. Somebody was slipping real money past me, something like ten billion, at the same time I was slashing aid for child cancer victims."

46

Keyes sat there with open ears, waiting for the climactic chord. "What was it?"

"I don't know," Lockhart said.

Fizzle. The conductor tapping the podium with his baton in midperformance. Lockhart was standing in the middle of his cell looking deflated. "I could *not* find out," he said, hardly able to believe his own ears.

"Did you try?"

"You bet."

That was either shocking or ridiculous, depending on how you felt about Lockhart's reformation. The steel trap didn't understand something? The renowned eater of data, cruncher of numbers, couldn't figure something out?

"I mean, my guess is that it's the military. Only the military spends money like that. It was the orgiast's quality of military spending that I sniffed out at first."

Keyes was sitting there trying to think like Doc Halliday. "Tell me what you did about it," he said. "Everything."

"I went to the President, of course. He pretended to be concerned."

"Pretended?"

"I'm eighty-nine percent certain."

"Anybody else?"

"Sure. That's why I'm here. I made a pest of myself. I think my ego was wounded. I think I went a little overboard and made enemies. I badgered Rubens, Philpott, McKay. I guess I thought they thought I couldn't be trusted with it, and I couldn't stand it. But I know I was getting close to something. That was around the time the *Titanium* sank, and I still don't know who pulled the plug on that one."

It was interesting; it was suggestive; it was nothing. Was this worth a Get Out of Jail Free card? Keyes didn't know. But he knew about Halliday's reputation for being insatiable for information. He could never get enough. He always had one more question than you were in a position to answer.

Keyes stalled for a moment, emptying his coffee cup; the stuff wasn't half bad. "I'm trying to think of a nice way to say this," Halliday's surrogate said.

"You don't have to beat around the bush," Lockhart replied. "I mean, considering where this conversation is taking place, I'm in no position to put on airs. Fire away."

"It's forty-three percent interesting."

47

Lockhart pretended to pull a knife out of his heart.

"I just don't see what Halliday can do with it."

"It seems to me that knowing there's some kind of mammoth military project going on in the government is worth a *little* something. They kept it a secret from OMB. That's *crazy*. Maybe they'll keep it from Halliday. You know, when the military go supersecret like this, there's no telling what they've got up their sleeve. Right now, they're getting a lot more money than Star Wars is. It's got to be monumental."

It probably was worth something, Keyes was thinking. He personally would have been satisfied. But Halliday wouldn't. He was searching for that last Halliday question.

"Did you go down into the middle ranks at all? Somebody dealing with the nuts and bolts? There's got to be nuts and bolts to this."

Lockhart thought, and then his eyes got wide. Then a great smile dawned over his cherubic face, starting at the chin and rising straight up to his hairline. He hit his forehead with the flat of his hand.

"I talked to George Hofstader at USDA. He knew *something*, but I forget what it was. It was something a little nutsy."

"How can I get in touch with him?"

Lockhart was already moving toward the only private inmate phone in the prison. "He was caught fooling around with the soybean forecast; he's in cellblock C." He was dialing happily. "You know, you can make big bucks in soybeans if you know what you're doing."

Soybeans, Keyes thought. There were all kinds of ways to make money. Crop predictions. The "flash" estimate of GNP. Someone in McKay's administration had tried to make money on bond futures based on advance knowledge of the flash estimate. *That* guy had decided the Department of Commerce to discontinue the flash estimate. There was endless military-industrial hanky-panky. Some of these dealings had terminated in special prosecutors, indictments, jail cells. Some ended as consent decrees, or pleas of *nolo contendere,* which meant you didn't do it and you promised never to do it again. The real problem was that the Office of Government Ethics was underfunded and had an absurdly small staff. It always seemed as though the odds were terrific that you could get away with it.

George Hofstader walked in with a plastic bowl that had two apples and a small bunch of grapes in it; it was from the warden's secretary. Hofstader and Lockhart immediately went to work on the apples.

48

"What's happening?" Hofstader said, eager for any event that was not routine. He was tall and wide, with receding black hair and a big friendly grin.

Lockhart suddenly got formal.

"Like you to meet Mr. Malcolm Keyes. He's a representative of the Halliday administration."

Hofstader looked at Keyes while chewing away.

"You doing some recruiting? We got some pretty good guys in here."

Keyes smiled. He wanted to be nice to them. The whole thing was like spending an afternoon on Mars, being in a place that he could leave any time he felt like it, but they couldn't.

Lockhart was rubbing his hands together like Shylock. "He isn't here to recruit," he said. "He's here to pick your brain."

Hofstader got serious. He sat down on top of the picnic table, his feet on the bench to Malcolm's right, suddenly managing, in spite of everything, to look like a formidable bureaucrat.

"What can I do for you?"

Lockhart held his hand out toward Hofstader's face. "Think," he said. "About a year and a half ago, you and I had some hot words about budget figures. We discussed it several times."

Hofstader was searching for bits of apple on the slender core.

"I'm at a loss without my phone log. Attorney General has it."

"Now I know you must remember it," Lockhart said, getting a little testy. "You were being cagey about it. I may have gotten a little, *a little,* nasty."

Hofstader thought. Hofstader brightened. Then Hofstader darkened.

"What about it?" he said suspiciously.

"Tell Mr. Keyes here all you know about it."

"Who is he again?"

"He's with the Halliday transition team."

Hofstader looked at Keyes. He looked at Lockhart. He tossed the minute remains of the apple into an ashtray. He looked at Keyes again.

"I never heard of him. What clearance do you have?" he said.

"Oh, for God's sake," Lockhart said.

"I don't think I have a clearance," Keyes said.

Hofstader looked offended. He was looking off to the side, as though disgusted. "I don't think I like this," he said.

Lockhart flopped down on his one chair.

"This man is an intimate of the President-elect. They're going to be running the *country* in a couple of months."

49

"But there are rules," Hofstader said. "National security is involved here."

"Hofstader security and Lockhart security are also involved here."

"This really goes against my nature," Hofstader said. "Are you an American citizen?"

"Oh, Lord."

"Yes, I am."

"Born here?"

"Yes."

"Where were you educated?"

"Columbia University."

Hofstader seemed to relax a little. He slumped a little. He was shaking his head a little from side to side as though debating with himself. Impossible stupid situation. He smiled a little, shrugged his shoulders a little.

"It was part of the CIA budget," he said.

"In case you didn't know it, Malcolm," Lockhart put in, "the Department of Agriculture is a wholly owned subsidiary of the CIA."

Keyes had his fingers bunched up pressing against his lower lip. He wanted to tread lightly and not scare Hofstader, but the inner Halliday voice was urging him on.

"I don't want to step over any bounds," he said very carefully, "but could you tell me what they were spending it on?"

"No."

"George," Lockhart said.

"I do not know."

Keyes looked at him. He was an accountant. A savvy accountant with long experience. An artist really, since accountancy was the great unheralded art form.

"Guess," Keyes said.

Hofstader smiled.

"It's going to sound nuts," he said.

Lockhart brightened. "That sounds right. That's exactly the kind of stuff we're looking for, something off the wall."

"This certainly is," Hofstader said. "Somehow or other I got the idea it had to do with *cosmetics.*"

"Cosmetics," Lockhart said.

"Cosmetics," Keyes said.

"I told you."

"How did you catch on to this secret ten-billion-dollar cosmetic operation being run by the CIA?" Lockhart asked.

"The few vouchers I got to see always seemed to have something to do with dermatology and skin care. There was a lot of dermatology equipment bought. Big numbers."

The three of them sat staring at the walls for a moment. Hofstader was looking down at his lap. Then his head started to come up very slowly and when it was all the way up, there was a suppressed smile on his face.

"I know somebody who might know something."

The phone rang. It was Lockhart's broker. Hofstader ate the last grape and Keyes strummed on the table while Lockhart decided to sell five hundred shares of Southwest Colonial Goldshares at the opening of the market on Monday.

"Who?" he said across the room to Hofstader.

"Armstrong."

Lockhart shook his head. His hand was still on the receiver. He dialed the paging operator.

Kevin Armstrong had been a civilian executive accountant working in the Pentagon. But he had been working a little too well with an aerospace company. Cost mischarging, product substitution. Conflict of interest. Gratuities. Labor mischarging. False statements. DEPFU caught up with him. Defense Procurement Fraud Unit. Indicting him had taken some of the pressure off the Pentagon for its eternal slackness about bookkeeping. Armstrong had gotten fifty-two weekends in Danbury, and this was Saturday.

Armstrong was fifty-five, mostly bald, with a wizened face that made him look like a professional poker player. A green eyeshade would have been the perfect hat for him. He couldn't remember a thing.

Lockhart as well as Hofstader, who'd gotten on the team, were trying to jog his memory, and Keyes sat there quietly watching and listening. They were really trying. These people were part of the reason Halliday had won the election; there had been too many of them who had been caught with their hands in the cookie jars. At one time they had all been intensely loyal to McKay; but, time flew.

"Oh, *that* one," Armstrong was saying. "Now I know what you're talking about. That was the time I was on temporary loan to Agriculture. That was a peculiar one. The security was *insane*. I spent almost as much time dealing with security matters as I did setting up a new bookkeeping department, which was what they wanted me for. It was a crazy situation."

"How crazy?" Lockhart asked. "Why crazy?"

Armstrong scratched his nose while trying to untangle the thing in his head.

"All right. The usual deal is this. When the Pentagon wants really tight security on a project they request 'black' funding. Black is when they tell Congress they need so-and-so many billions but they can't say what it's for. As a rule they end up telling a couple or three important committee chairmen, if they feel they can trust them. Nothing new, been going on for decades. These days black funds are averaging thirty billion a year. *This* project was *blacker* than black."

Lockhart looked at him. An eyebrow went up. The lights in his eyes went on low-beam. There must have been a billion neurons popping simultaneously. He'd been taken by surprise.

"Blacker than black?" he said finally.

"Yeah."

Lockhart made three slow silent circuits of the picnic table. That mighty ego had been challenged. The Icepick didn't know something. Somebody had been slipping something past the Icepick, which was inconceivable. He stopped in front of Armstrong.

"You mean like when the CIA buys, say, seventy-five million worth of weapons on the international arms market but they pay a hundred million and get back twenty-five under the table to fool around with? That's blacker than black, right?"

Armstrong shook his head, waved an arm, scrunched up his face.

"That's another shade of black. That's not blacker than black."

"Blacker than black," Lockhart repeated. Armstrong nodded. Lockhart was showing no energy. The manic stuff was all gone. He was in a state of being nonplussed, and he was fighting for his life.

"Oh, of course," he said with fake bonhomie. "It's fuel, right? Say OPEC has a fight with itself and they all start going over their allowances, they pump too much oil and prices go down. Now the Pentagon has leftover uncommitted fuel money. If prices go up they ask for more money; if prices go down they stash away the surplus for black projects. That's it, isn't it?"

Armstrong yawned.

"You're getting close, but that's still another shade of black, that's not blacker than black."

Lockhart was standing there rubbing his chin. Lockhart was beginning to transcend his ego problem. There was an aesthetic aspect to all of this. Lockhart was totally amoral himself. To have been skunked by someone more amoral than he was provoked an intellectual fascination. What was so subtle and so underhanded and so devious that he, Dewitt Lockhart, hadn't spotted it? How could they possibly have slipped billions past him? It had to be so subtle as to amount to genius. He was simultaneously intrigued and humiliated. It would have to be something totally illogical, so that he would never have conceived of the possibility.

"What is blacker than black?" he whispered with the relish of a connoisseur.

Armstrong climbed up on the picnic table and sat down alongside Hofstader. He had a dirty grin on his face.

"You're not going to like this," he said.

"I don't expect to," Lockhart replied. "On the other hand, I'm always willing to learn. Educate me."

"They do it with inflation."

"Inflation?"

Lockhart looked insulted. Lockhart looked mortified. Lockhart looked mystified. Something as gross and obvious as inflation? He'd been deceived by inflation?

"The Pentagon uses inflation the way Rembrandt used brown," Armstrong continued. "They always overestimate the coming year's inflation rate. That's how they end up with billions of formally appropriated funds that are not committed to any particular project. It's available for anything."

Deflated, Lockhart went to the one chair in the cell and flopped down. He stared at the end of his nose, his mouth covered with a coiled left hand.

"I would have said this was impossible," he said. "It's too obvious, for God's sake. How could I not have seen it?"

"If it makes you feel any better," Armstrong said, "blacker than black backfired on the Pentagon. This project started in the first Reagan administration. Reagan made them give the money to"—Armstrong's lips got prissy, as though he were savoring an especially fine Bordeaux—"the Central Intelligence Agency. That was one of my jobs. Transferring the funds to CIA accounts."

"There's no honor among thieves," Hofstader put in.

Keyes was recording. Trio for saxophone, violin, and one-man band,

53

slightly off-key, and the instrumentalists weren't first-rate, but they were communicating nicely.

Lockhart was sitting there still nursing his wounds. *Inflation*. He was not accustomed to being incompetent; it was an alien emotion. He had never been incompetent. He'd even been terrific at toilet training. He was the toilet star of a large, extended family, having figured out the complexity and inner meanings of bowel movements when he was only nine months old. After a minute of deep self-analysis, he smiled ruefully.

"I think I see it," he said to them. "This has to be it. There is no other possible explanation. It was self-deception. Would have been too messy. I apparently couldn't face the complexities and dangers of seriously challenging the Pentagon. I actually allowed my emotions to interfere. The nonrational side of me foiled my intellect in the interest of self-preservation. There's a moral here. Even *I* am not perfect. Well, we learn something new every day, don't we?" He looked at Armstrong, chastened, subdued, nicer.

"Pray continue," he said.

Armstrong shrugged his shoulders.

"Suddenly the whole thing seemed to go blooey."

"What, what?" Lockhart said. "How, when, where, why?"

"I'll tell you what I think happened. It was a supersecret project on which they had had some kind of disaster. About a year and a half ago, work on the project seemed to come to a halt. But then they started spending money in a totally different way, which is where I came in. We had to handle a *flood* of travel vouchers. Living expenses, hotels, motels, rental cars, plane fares, meals. Colossal. It looked like the travel expenses for an army."

"Where were they traveling to?" Lockhart asked.

"All over. All over the U.S. Parts of Europe. Nova Scotia. Central America. South America. Philippines. Hawaii. Alaska."

"But you don't know the purpose of the travel?" Lockhart said.

"Not the slightest."

Lockhart took two slow turns around the picnic table.

"I think we're getting very close to what I would call a negotiable favor," he said, looking straight at Keyes. He was still looking at Keyes when he asked Armstrong the question. "Was there somebody in charge of this army of travelers?"

"Oh, sure. I talked to him any number of times."

"The name please," Lockhart said, still eyeballing Keyes.

"Albritten. Alexander R. Albritten. Big man at CIA."

Lockhart flopped down on his straight chair, totally relaxed. His cigar had gone out. He was happily relighting it.

"You know, there's something else I remember about that thing," Armstrong added. "I don't think I was supposed to know it, but I saw it on a file folder somewhere."

"What's that?" Lockhart asked, happily puffing away, dreams of parole running through his brain.

"The name of the project," Armstrong said.

Lockhart dropped the cigar. Then he picked it up with absurdly elaborate casualness so as not to look excited and scare Kevin Armstrong.

"Oh? What was that?"

"Are you ready for this?" Armstrong told them. "It's called the GOD Project."

Lockhart looked at Keyes.

"What do you think?" he said.

Keyes smiled. The inner Halliday was satisfied.

5

IN SEARCH OF GOD

THE MOOD IN the room was pathetic; they had all been pushed to the limit. The room—the Room, it was called, deep in the bowels of the Company—reeked of exhaustion and frustration and anxiety, and there was a whiff of defeat in the air. The Room was where, of late, the emotional tone tended more and more toward anxiety and frustration, to which, in Albritten's case, could be added a profound physical exhaustion. Albritten had gotten there late. The others were already seated at the monster conference table, not conferring. Albritten trudged in apologetically and put his attaché case on the table where they could all see it. Albritten had been flying incessantly for almost a year. Back and forth across the U.S. plus excursions to Hawaii, Latin America, Europe. He could barely keep track of where he was anymore. He had a chronic case of jet lag; he had become the man without a time zone. Now he sat down four chairs away from Nye—Nye was not exactly in good odor these days—facing Jessup and Carmichael. The grandiose spaces separating them seemed appropriate for four men who called themselves the GOD Group. Albritten was beginning to think of Elmer Jessup as Zeus, which would probably make Albritten Mercury. But he didn't feel

56

like Mercury; he felt like lead. He was praying he wouldn't fall asleep during the meeting.

"Let's start with the FBI," Jessup said right away. "Are we getting any better cooperation?"

Nye was handling liaison with the Bureau and also running the War Room for the GOD Project. Nye was laboring under a serious disadvantage, and Albritten was slightly surprised that he was still on the job or even alive: He had pulled *the* biggest intelligence blooper in the Company's history.

"They've finally distributed the sketch," Nye told them. "Every agent in the Bureau now has it on him at all times. Even off-duty they can keep their eyes open. However, in point of fact, we're getting only a thousand agent-hours a week out of them. I mean, we're talking fifty states. Know where they're spending most of their time? They're *still* investigating organizations like CISPES."

Jessup was looking into space, his frustration obvious. Of all the places to screw up, they had screwed up on the GOD Project. It was too much to believe that it had been accidental, and he refused to believe it, but he had no evidence to the contrary. He came back to the present.

"There's the hair problem," Jessup said to them.

"Sure," Nye replied, but he was one step ahead, which was where you lived if you wanted to work for Elmer Jessup. "We've supplied overlays for the basic sketch. They show what he'd look like with a mustache, a goatee, a mustache *and* a goatee, and then a full beard."

Jessup thought. "Braids," he said, puffing on his Churchill. There were dutiful smiles around the table.

"This is the kind of man who grows them," Jessup continued. "Goes through basic training just fine, we couldn't have been happier with his performance. And then, because his unit is going overseas, he quits, he runs. Damn coward. Braids."

"But if you *could* talk to the Director?" Nye said tentatively; he was living twenty-four hours a day on thin ice.

"Damn right I'm going to talk to the Director. In the Oval Office with the President sitting next to me. I'm going to ream him. Fucking CISPES. I want ten thousand agent-hours out of him. No, twenty thousand, goddammit," he added, pounding on the table.

Albritten stirred. He had started to slide away but Jessup's pounding woke him up, which was probably why Jessup had done it.

"Next," Jessup said. It was Albritten's turn. Albritten was overjoyed.

It was listening that was the anodyne. You could stay awake if you kept talking.

"I'm averaging two hundred candidates a week now," he said.

"Last time it was one hundred and seventy, I believe."

"Yes, sir."

"That's very good, Alex." Jessup was proud of Albritten. Albritten was his protégé. He was hardworking and might even have the strength of character to become DCI someday. "I realize that travel must be sapping you, Alex. Is there anything we can do," he asked Nye, "to make his travel any easier?"

Nye, as always, was prepared. But he was nervous and excited, especially nervous. When Nye was nervous his tongue tended to hang out. It always fascinated Albritten to watch Nye when he was over-wrought. Fascinating and disgusting. Now Nye stood up and went over to the map board, tongue drooping. He pulled down a map of the United States. There were lines running every which way between the major cities. Once Nye started talking, his tongue disappeared. And now Nye had a piece of good news to report, which was always good therapy.

Nye had started out to be a mathematician. And he remembered enough of his college math to realize there was something familiar about Albritten's travel schedule. He'd noticed it right at the beginning, as he moved pins around the map in his War Room, keeping track of Albritten. To simplify Albritten's travel schedule—so that he would spend the minimum amount of time in the air and on the road—was virtually identical to one of the most difficult problems in all of mathematics, usually referred to as the Traveling Salesman Problem.

What Albritten had to do was move around the country to various cities, testing candidates. That is, young men who could conceivably be Henry Patrick. The question was, how could Albritten test the maximum number of candidates in the minimum amount of time? While apparently an everyday problem, it had enormous mathematical implications. It was similar, for example, to the problem of how to most efficiently route a telephone call across the continent, and many other matters. Nye had managed to get one of the National Security Agency's best mathematicians assigned to CIA on temporary duty.

The mathematician had used tons of computer time, trying everything: linear programming, the Khachian algorithm, the Dantzig algorithm. He'd gone at the problem from every possible angle. Hamiltonian cycles. Probabilistic analyses of heuristics. Branch and bound methods.

"We've settled on Karmarkar's algorithm," Nye said intently. "It is *the* most efficient way to schedule Alex and to provide him with minimum travel time and maximum sleep time. Things are going to be better. Trust me. We're now turning out what we call OFP, Optimum Flight Plan."

Nye stood there with his tongue hanging out.

"All contributions cheerfully accepted," Albritten said wearily.

"That's damn good work," Jessup said, genuinely pleased, not noticing that Nye almost fainted with relief. "Alex, how long does it take you to do a candidate?"

The question made no sense to Albritten. Some candidates took much longer than others. But Jessup was a quantifier. He was an imaginative bureaucrat but he was still a bureaucrat, with the instinct for quantizing what essentially was unquantizable. It was the way the Johnson administration had managed to delude itself for years into believing it was making progress in Vietnam. But Albritten was a bureaucrat too.

"Twenty minutes," he said promptly, unconsciously looking at his attaché case standing on the table. It contained the Book of Mark. He had strict orders not to let the case out of his sight, including john time.

"Twenty minutes," Jessup said. He was thinking, looking-at-ceiling, scratching the space between his lower lip and his chin, puffing on his cigar. "That's not bad. That's damn efficient. You getting that good at it?"

"Well, yeah. I mean, I've checked out thousands of them by now." Now was the time to complain. Albritten had a big one, and *this* was the place to make it known. He glanced over at Carmichael, seated to Jessup's left, knowing that it was also the way to make a lifelong enemy. However, it was also the way to survive.

"I don't like complaining," he said. "I understand the problems involved. It's a difficult situation, no getting away from it. Nevertheless, the quality of the candidates is bad and getting worse. Some of them don't even look like the sketch. With some of them, I don't even have to take out the book. I'll fly to Montana, for God's sake, and there's two candidates and neither one of them is close. It's a terrible waste of time and energy." Albritten was now totally awake. He had just thrown down the gauntlet before Carmichael. He didn't even look in Carmichael's direction until Carmichael spoke.

"What about it?" Jessup asked.

Carmichael, like Nye and the U.S. Marines, also believed in *Semper*

Paratus. He knew that you could get out of almost any corner if you answered decisively, if you were ready.

"I've been flying around the country too," he said. "I've been speaking to them in small groups. There is a natural tendency for agents to go for production. Especially the overage types we're using. They like to bring us candidates. After all, they don't have an easy job. They have to *seduce* the candidates into going to see Alex. At a particular time and place, no less. If they can't seduce them, they have to use *force.* Guys who are sixty-five, seventy years old. But they love to bring in candidates. It shows they can still function. The message I've been bringing to them is: good candidates or no candidates. We are not interested in fluff. We want production, yes, but we want young men who could plausibly be Henry Patrick."

Jessup was actually smiling. "Don't forget, Alex, we're using retired agents exclusively on this. They're all wearing trifocals."

"It *would* be rather nice if they could see," Albritten commented.

"We're stuck with it," Jessup replied. "I know it's ridiculous, but there it is. We can't drop the workload of the Company to concentrate on this thing. I would *like* to. If it were up to me, that's *exactly* what we'd do, because this is the number-one priority in the establishment. But it's not up to me."

"You know," Carmichael said almost wistfully, "we've got this problem of his appearance. He's about the most ordinary-looking character I've ever seen."

Albritten laughed. A little too loudly and out of control. It was verging on the hysterical. He thought of terrible images to get himself to stop laughing; a chain-saw massacre in a church choir finally did it. It was also time to start winning Carmichael back, to atone for being critical.

"I can see features of Henry Patrick in everyone at this table. He should have been named John Doe. So I sympathize with the problem. It's just that there are only so many hours in the day."

"You've got to keep going," Jessup said to him, his voice husky with desperation. "I know you're tired, but I can't let a second copy of the Book of Mark off these premises. It would end up on '60 Minutes.' Hang in there, Alex." A sudden thought hit Jessup. "Who watches it while you're asleep?"

"Haas and Mancuso."

"Is Haas any good?"

"Very good."

60

"Alex, you need a good night's sleep," Jessup said.

"I construe that as an order, sir."

"If he moves, we'll find him," Jessup said to them. "In nature, that's the way the predator gets the prey. The prey reveals itself by movement. Sooner or later Mr. Henry Patrick has to move."

"Would it be any easier if you could use the CAT?" Carmichael said.

"Not really," Albritten replied. In point of fact it would have caused impossible logistical problems, but he refrained from saying it.

"Doesn't make any difference," Jessup put in. "We do not use the CAT under any circumstances. Nor do we use BEAM or NMR or the PET. *Nothing*. We use nothing that fires rays into the brain. We use only the Book of Mark. Am I being clear?"

Jessup was back in the mood he had been in at the start of the meeting: incomprehension, suspicion, frustration. He looked at them.

"Henry Patrick, trained to be a killer, for Christ's sake, a Ranger, an American Ranger, with a wonderful record in training, starts talking like a commie, I mean out of *nowhere,* and then he goes AWOL. The solution to the Vietnam Syndrome goes AWOL. There is something wrong somewhere. Have you picked up any trace of Russian yet?"

"If they're in this thing," Carmichael replied, "they're being subtle."

Albritten took a nanosecond look at Nye. He wouldn't be Nye for a billion dollars. Nye was the one who had lost Henry Patrick. Which was roughly on a par with the guy who forgot to tell Pearl Harbor about the approach of the Japanese fleet. Nye, with a five-man team to run, had lost track of Henry on a three-day pass.

Jessup was mashing out his cigar. It was time to get on to other matters. He eyeballed the three of them, ending on Albritten.

"I want Henry," he said. "I want him in my possession. I want that son of a bitch. And I want him before that other son of a bitch takes office in January. Find him, get him, bring him." Jessup's voice softened. "It's a tough job, Alex, I know that. It's like the way some theologians have tried to define God, by eliminating all who are not God. But that's all right, there's nothing wrong with that as an investigative method. Get the son of a bitch."

Alex Albritten, who was now totally awake and wouldn't be able to get to sleep for another twenty-four hours, picked up the Book of Mark and headed for the airport.

6

DEBRIEFING

A<small>ND THEN HE</small> said, 'I hope this will be of some small use to our President,' and I said, 'I wouldn't know,' and he said, 'Hey, Christmas is coming,' and I said, 'I hope you have a merry one,' and he said, 'Oh, by the way, send me a copy of the White House phone book when it comes out, will you?' and I said, 'Certainly,' and left."

There was no response. Akers was sitting on his bed, stone-faced, still listening even though Keyes had finished talking. Halliday was standing by the fireplace watching the flames. Madeleine Smith was sitting on a small brown wooden chair, polishing her spectacles.

All at once, Keyes felt like an intruder; he had delivered his message like a good cassette recorder and now he was wondering how to get out gracefully. Doolittle's chauffeur had gotten him back to Mohonk in no time; Doolittle's chauffeur didn't seem to like hanging around prisons. And now he was in Akers's bedroom at Mohonk Mountain House with a gorgeous view of the lake and the cliff behind it, which they were all ignoring. In fact, only the Secret Service seemed interested; he could see them patrolling along the top of the cliff.

Halliday finally smiled at Keyes.

"Good job, Malcolm."

"Didn't leave anything out, did you?" Akers asked, making a small attempt at humor.

"I could describe the cell he's in."

"No," Akers said quickly. "I'll find out soon enough."

"Uh," Madeleine Smith said.

"The GOD Project," Halliday said.

"Yes sir."

"G-O-D God?"

"Yes sir."

"I wonder what those screwballs are up to this time?" Halliday said to no one.

"What's hard to believe," Madeleine Smith said as she put on her glasses, "is that the director of Management and Budget wasn't in on the deal, whatever it is. Did they really think they could slip it past *him?* The Icepick?"

This was the first time Keyes had met the new Vice-President; Madeleine Smith had only been a talking head on television to him until now. She was tall and slim and looked much sexier in person than on the tube, which was a lucky break for her. Some flaw in skin color or bone formation made her unphotogenic. She was close to forty and looked it, but she was still too sexy for politics. She habitually dressed down, trying to throw it away; she had a practiced dowdiness in her choice of clothes. With her big brown eyeglasses, she managed to look like a librarian, but a librarian you didn't fool around with. You got your books back in on time. On the other hand, her small, delicate face was framed by honey-brown hair that was unpolitically long, reaching well below her shoulders. But to Keyes, her most striking feature was her hands, which were long and slender; they were so slender they seemed almost transparent.

"It's plausible," was Akers's reaction. "They probably figured he'd take the hint and look the other way. But he wasn't rational about it. He said so himself."

"He isn't one of the Indiana gang," Halliday said. "It's very possible they wouldn't have trusted him with something superdelicate. Come to think of it, they were right."

"You know what I think?" Madeleine Smith started to say.

Akers cleared his throat.

The President-elect and the Vice-President–elect both looked at

63

Akers. Then they both looked at Keyes. Halliday left the fireplace and went to Keyes with his hand outstretched.

"Malcolm, I want to thank you for a job well done. That was yeoman service; I appreciate it."

"Thank you, sir; happy to be of assistance. I think I'll be going."

Halliday walked him to the door. "I don't suppose you could forget all this, huh?"

"I'm afraid I'll never forget it," he said, smiling, going out the door. He went back down the long corridor in a dazed state. He couldn't bear to wait for the elevator: His nervous system required movement. He went down the central staircase slowly, savoring the experience he had just had. On the ground floor, he found Doolittle in the coffee shop not drinking coffee; he was poring over the *New York Times*.

"Well, was it dangerous?" Doolittle said in his know-it-all tone of voice.

"Nope. It was fascinating."

"Let's go home. On the way, I want to review some thoughts I've had about Hackenlauter."

They wandered back past the candidates who were still streaming in and out. After the first cut, the survivors would be investigated by the FBI. Keyes stopped and took a last look at the crowded Lake Lounge. There were at least twenty interviews going on at once in there. Who would be picked? Who would be tempted? Who would end up in a cell down the corridor from Lockhart?

7

PRESS CONFERENCE

MOODY WAS SLUMPED across the podium watching the animals drift in, trying to mobilize himself like a diver poised at the tip of the board. The Democratic National Committee had rented one of the banquet rooms in the Willard Hotel, and Moody's big moment had arrived: his first Washington press conference. Four TV camera teams had shown up. That was ominous. They thought they were going to get something; it was his job to see that they got nothing.

It was Moody's damnable luck to be giving his first Washington press conference at the moment of a crisis in the goddam Philippines. The goddam Philippine countryside even *looked* like Vietnam. Moody had done well back in Albany. He'd had eight years to hone his skills, and he'd managed most of the time to stay three questions ahead of them. But with this bunch, he had a feeling of dread. This was the challenge; the league didn't get any bigger than this.

He was going to have to hold all options open, without committing to any course of action, while at the same time not seeming to be waffling. But they'd worry it, torture it, have fun with it, in their endless search for a headline to sell papers, or twenty good seconds of tape to sell soap;

they'd kill for twenty seconds of good tape. He tapped the microphone to get their attention.

"The Secretaries of State, Defense, and Commerce will be named by Mr. Halliday later today at the Slocum place. At that time, brief biographies of the three nominees will be distributed to the press. That's all I have; I'll take your questions."

Q: Can we take it as an article of faith that these new cabinet announcements will be made in time for the evening news?

A: You can take it as holy writ. Four-thirty P.M. Forgive me for neglecting to mention it.

Q: Is the McKay administration keeping Mr. Halliday up to speed on the Philippines situation?

A: Yes.

Q: Uh, now that Clark Field has taken a mortar attack from the Philippine communist guerrillas, does the incoming administration still plan to stick to its platform promise of not intervening militarily in Third World countries?

A: We didn't say we wouldn't intervene. We said we'd minimize it. You obviously can't rule it out entirely. Who knows what's coming down the pike?

Q: Does that mean intervening or not intervening in the Philippines?

A: The situation there hasn't matured enough yet for there to be talk of intervening.

Q: If any Americans should die in the near future as a result of communist gunfire, would that constitute maturing?

A: That would certainly influence the administration's thinking.

Q: The McKay administration is publicly acknowledging the possibility of intervention.

A: They're not talking about intervention as I understand it. As I understand it, they're talking about retaliation. I mean, we *do* have troops at our bases inside the Philippines and as long as they're there, they should be allowed to defend themselves.

Q: Are you talking about sorties out of the bases to strike at the communist guerrillas?

(Careful, Moody told himself. He'd done okay so far. But don't make policy and don't shut off options.)

A: No. Not necessarily.

Q: How can they retaliate if they stay inside their bases?

A: You should be addressing these questions to the McKay administration. I remind everyone that we haven't taken office yet.

66

Q: But hypothetically.

(Moody was sweating. He'd have to change his clothes after this one. But that's what his job was—dancing across a minefield.)

A: We never answer hypothetical questions. You can take that as a given for the next eight years.

Q: You think there'll *be* an eight years if Halliday loses the Philippines?

A: As he said in the campaign, the Philippines are not his to lose or not lose. Nor are they President McKay's to lose or not lose.

Q: Then you see losing the Philippines as a possibility?

(Moody started to slap his hand down on the podium, but caught himself. Then he took a long breath.)

A: I have a tape recording of this entire press conference just in case we have to disprove any stories that come out about us losing the Philippines. Is that clear, gentlemen?

Q: Okay, okay.

Q: We're only doing our jobs.

A: I realize that, Mr. Eichmann.

Q: Ooooooh.

Q: Boooooo.

Q: Low blow.

Q: So the bottom line on intervention in the Philippines is, uh, what?

A: We ran on minimum intervention. That principle will be applied to the Philippines. However, we will make no statements now that might compromise the actions or statements of the McKay administration.

Q: You also ran on open and honest answers to the press.

(What might be described as general laughter, Moody thought. These sons of bitches were sharp. But you couldn't show the thin skin. Worst possible mistake. They'd bait you forever.)

A: Hey, I think we're getting off to a terrific start. I like you guys. I hope you manage to hold on to your jobs.

Q: Recently, the Bolivian army was defeated in pitched battle by the Bolivian tin miners. Does the new administration plan on giving aid to the Bolivian armed forces?

(A trap; obvious. Moody had learned a long time ago that it was fatal to fake it. Especially when it came off the wall like that. Who the fuck knew what was behind a question like that? Bolivia? He didn't even know Bolivia *had* an army.)

A: Uh, I'll have to get back to you on that one.

Q: It's been pointed out recently that a great deal of the maintenance

67

done on American military equipment is performed by civilians, who, of course, aren't required to accompany the military in time of war. What does the American military do for maintenance in time of war?

A: Uh, we haven't actually gotten into that yet. Uh, I'll have to get back to you on that.

Q: I understand that the World Freedom Institute, using its own funds, is sending military trainers to assist the Salvadoran army, thereby legally exceeding the statutory limit on American advisers in El Salvador, which, as you know, is limited to fifty-five by Congress. What will the Halliday administration's position be on this?

A: Hey, give me a break.

Q: Is Mr. Halliday really going to allow the Bolivian army to go it alone?

A: That's still under study.

Q: But you're going to get back to us?

A: Is this what you guys do to every virgin?

Q: The word from Albany is that you're a long way from a virgin.

A: To think that I'd ever hear a journalist commenting on someone else's chastity.

Q: What does chastity mean?

Q: Does the incoming administration plan on buying the Metz Mark IV Water Cannon for use during riots in the capital?

A: Yes. It's to be used at press conferences.

(Moody crossed the small stage and left by the side door, drenched. His armpits gave him away every time. The bastards had drawn blood the first time out. This was the front lines. This was kill or be killed. He was going to have to be relentless with Akers and everyone else. He had to know about *everything*.)

8

THE BOOK OF MARK

IT WAS DOOLITTLE'S suet theory of politics, and he was making the standard speech about it—about how many pounds Hackenlauter was going to have to lose. A politician oughtn't to look as if he was living off the fat of the land; only a safe-seat politician could be fat.

"And give me a couple of thousand sit-ups while you're at it. It's a small price to pay for holding on to a seat in the U.S. Senate."

It was still a little early in the morning for Keyes to do any serious thinking. He was sitting on Doolittle's couch, off to the side, studying Hackenlauter's long farmer's face. There had to be a streak of Quixote in him to begin with. A liberal in Nebraska. It was a testament to humankind's indomitable spirit. He'd spent all of the previous afternoon in the company of the senator, talking to him, dining with him, finding out about him. As a liberal in a conservative state, he was bound to be bland; he had to hide his liberalism behind a strong facade of anticommunism and anti-black-mothers-on-welfare-with-a-color-television-set.

But behind that political camouflage, Hackenlauter was authentically bland. It was a miracle that he'd managed to get elected the first time. Keyes was now stuck with the problem of making Hackenlauter's advertising seem to be authentic Hackenlauter—as opposed to slick media man's hype, which would be unconvincing. Which meant the commercials would have to look bland, while holding the viewer's rapt attention for thirty costly seconds. He was going to have to be dull in a fascinating way. You couldn't say Hackenlauter wasn't a challenge. Suddenly, Keyes tuned back in: Doolittle was doing something unprecedented. Doolittle was actually giving Keyes partial credit for the Halliday campaign.

Keyes smiled weakly; he wasn't used to praise from Doolittle. Doolittle wasn't even that nice to his mother. It was power. God, was power powerful. A smidgen of an atom of it had rubbed off on Keyes, and now Doolittle was beginning to treat him like a human being.

"Would Malcolm be doing my spots?" Hackenlauter asked.

"Absolutely," Doolittle replied. "You'll be his number-one assignment. I want you to know we're both sincerely committed to keeping you in the U.S. Senate. The country needs you."

Hackenlauter was looking impressed. After all, if you could elect a liberal like Halliday President of the United States (Liechtenstein *maybe,* but the United States?), you could elect anybody to anything. Doolittle had even been approached by an Ethiopian diplomat because they were thinking about maybe having an election there someday. He was just getting to the part of the speech where he tells the candidate that he, Doolittle, controls the campaign strategy—it was the price they had to pay to get him to work for them—when he was interrupted by the intercom buzzer.

"The President's on the line," his secretary said distractedly.

Doolittle made a mental note to chew her out. Was it the President or the President-elect, goddammit? At the same time, it was rather lovely getting a presidential call in the middle of a new business pitch.

"Good morning, Mr. President," he said into the phone, making sure Hackenlauter was listening, then getting flustered again because the President wasn't on the line and he had to wait a painful twenty seconds before saying it again. "Good morning, Mr. President."

By and large, Doolittle handled the situation rather well, Keyes thought. He attempted to look like the proud father or the teacher doting on his best pupil, winking at Hackenlauter as he handed the phone over to Keyes. For a poor anhedonic slob, it wasn't a bad performance.

"*One* more job," Halliday was saying in his ear. "I know this screws up the routine, but you're going to have plenty of time to be bored by

Hackenlauter. If it'll be of any help, I'll campaign against him when the time comes."

Keyes counted eight lame ducks on the shuttle for Washington: three senators, five representatives. They had probably been to Wall Street or Grumman, job hunting. He watched the flight attendants pushing the drink cart uphill. More politics: flight attendants. Those weren't flight attendants; those were *girls,* girls with *balls,* mere girls who weren't afraid to *fly.*

Politics. Images. Now you see it, now you don't. The presidency was something like a flight attendant. The image came across clearly. Reassurance. If I can do it, you can do it. It isn't as risky as it looks. Trust me. Everything's going to be all right. The President had more power than anyone else in the world had, or had ever had. On the other hand, Keyes found himself wondering what Halliday's childhood had been like, what his neuroses were. He had to have them. No well-balanced individual would *want* to be President of the United States. Liechtenstein, *maybe.*

When he got to the Slocum mansion in Georgetown, it was the same as Mohonk, people streaming in and out; only this time it was the establishment. In the entry he passed Jimmy Carter, who was the man some people had referred to as the Last Democrat because he'd done such a bad job he'd spoiled it for everyone else. Halliday's secretary, Phyllis, took him straight to Slocum's den, but he had to pass through the big living room. He noticed at least one Rockefeller, two Kennedys, a Udall, a Byrd, a Jackson, two Mondales, a Brown, and Art Feeny. Poor Hiram, he thought; had they done it to him yet?

Halliday was seated behind Slocum's monstrous mahogany desk, which no doubt converted at the press of a button into a pool table. The room was about what you would expect of a centimillionaire's private den: walls of books and paintings and photographs of the mighty, a floor you sank into.

"I hope you didn't get a hotel room," Halliday said. "I want you to go to Wisconsin for me."

"Wisconsin? You mean Wisconsin Avenue?"

"No. Wisconsin."

"O-kay," Keyes said haltingly.

"You did such a good job picking Lockhart's brain, I felt you were the right man to follow up on it this one more time. I want you to talk

71

to that CIA guy, Alex Albritten. Informally. Akers has set up an appointment."

Keyes was standing there thinking.

"What's the problem?" Halliday asked.

"No problem. Glad to do it."

"You're looking funny."

"Well, I do wonder about something, sir."

"Okay."

"You said you didn't want to 'know' about this thing. If I talk to Albritten, the CIA will know that you know something. Won't they?"

"Sure they'll know. But I won't have been informed officially. There'll be no paper. Even if Albritten tape-records you, it won't matter. I can disown you."

"I see."

Halliday was eyeballing him, sizing him up, doing some mind reading. Keyes felt transparent under that gaze. The tonality was definitely minor. The orchestra was tuning up, but there was an ominous, brooding quality to it. It was Brahmsian. The *Tragic Overture,* say. The woodwinds were going to be strong, the strings muted, drums along the Potomac.

"Sit down, Malcolm. Let me put you in the picture. I don't want you to think I'm being off the wall about this."

Halliday sat back in the luxurious swivel chair, hands clasped behind his head, eyes drifting slowly around the room.

"Doolittle tells me you think your memory is freakish. Well, we're birds of a feather. I'm a political freak. President McKay doesn't even accept the results of the election. He thinks it was a fluke and not a true expression of the popular will. He could be right. He's already setting up what they're referring to as Operation Grover Cleveland. Grover Cleveland was the only President to serve two terms with a space in between.

"Now, I have to figure there'll be plenty of people in the bureaucracy and the establishment who'll be eager to stick a foot out for me to trip over. Think about it. The military-industrial complex knows I'm against them. And they're in every state. Almost every congressional district. They're omnipresent. An awful lot of people and institutions have a major economic stake in preparing for war. I'm the last one they want to see in the White House. What it all comes down to is that I am simply not ready to make a decision about this GOD Project thing. If I am officially informed about it, I'll either have to accept it or reject it.

72

Either way could be politically dangerous. In any case, I don't want to have to rush my decision. So first, let's find out what the hell it is."

"What do I say to Albritten?"

"Ask him how it's going."

Five hours later, Keyes was getting out of a cab in the parking lot of the Blue Moon Motel in Racine, Wisconsin. One look at the place and he felt as if he were back in Danbury. They were making no attempt at salesmanship; separate little boxes around a small parking lot. You got a slot for your car and a bed with a piece of space around it for your body. It was dark and cold and Keyes was tired, but he was on a mission for Doc Halliday. He went up to number 4 and knocked on the door. A man with real shoulders opened it. He frowned at Keyes. He seemed puzzled at finding Keyes alone: He looked around the parking lot for signs of anyone else.

"My name is Keyes."

The man nodded and stepped aside, then looked out at the parking lot again before closing and bolting the door. The place was like a museum, basic fifties plastic preserved for posterity. A large TV, a small bathroom, a chest of drawers, a small night table with a phone, lamp, and ashtray on it. The bed had been pushed against a wall, and there was a folding massage table set up in the middle of the room. Alex Albritten was standing next to it.

Albritten looked totally out of place. He looked like an intellectual dandy, intelligent face, blue striped double-breasted suit, blue shirt, knit tie with a tightly knotted Windsor. His arms were folded and he was studying Malcolm's face. He seemed to be doing it a feature at a time—eyes, nose, mouth, chin. A look of what seemed to be something like awe was gradually stealing over Albritten's face.

"Mr. Halliday sent me," Keyes said.

Albritten smiled weakly. "I can see why," he said slowly.

"You can?"

Albritten's eyebrows knitted together. His face had now gone from awe to befuddlement in seconds.

"On the other hand, I can't understand it at all."

"You can't?"

Albritten shrugged, baffled; there were some things in life that were inexplicable. Disharmonies in the natural order that one simply had to live with.

73

"Who brought you here? How did you get here?"

"I took a cab from the airport."

Albritten almost sneered; he didn't believe it.

"You took a cab? From the airport? You? Just you?"

"What's so strange about that?"

"Nobody brought you here?"

"I'm old enough to travel by myself."

Albritten's eyes narrowed.

"How old *are* you?" he asked.

Keyes looked at him. And then at the wide man leaning on the cottage door. He was back on Mars. What kind of craziness had Halliday gotten him into this time? Albritten, of the CIA, looked fatigued, terribly fatigued. His eyes and the surrounding tissue were a mess. They'd been open too long for too many days or maybe months. He was so fatigued that he looked fed up and dangerous. He was not a man to be trifled with. He looked like a man who had long since run out of patience and was living on the edge; in that respect he reminded Keyes of the typical Manhattan bus driver.

"What's my age got to do with anything?"

"Oh, it's got to do, all right." Faint smile, intense look in the eyes, which were continuing to search the features of Malcolm's face, one at a time.

"I'm thirty-one," Keyes said.

"You're a very young thirty-one," Albritten said.

"I've had an easy life."

"Your wrinkle picture is not typical for a thirty-one-year-old. You look more like twenty-one."

"What do you know? That soap company was telling the truth."

"How do you feel?"

"Okay. Until I walked in here."

"What are you feeling now?"

"Look, what the hell is this? You *are* Alex Albritten, aren't you?"

"Oh, you're in the right place," Albritten said.

"I'm from Richard Halliday. You know who he is, don't you?"

"What's amazing," Albritten replied, "is that Halliday found you on his own and sent you here on *your* own. Extraordinary. I can hardly believe it. Strip. We've got a presidential special, Mancuso," he said to his colleague. "*Strip*," he said to Keyes.

"I guess I didn't hear you right," Malcolm Keyes said, looking for a way out of the place.

74

"Mancuso," Albritten said in a bored, fed-up voice, "cause his clothes to be removed."

Keyes didn't put up much of a struggle. Mancuso had muscles in his earlobes. And Keyes liked the suit he was wearing. It was his best one, which he saved for meetings with Presidents. What the hell *was* this? In two minutes he was lying naked on the massage table and Albritten was coming at him with a red grease pencil in one hand and a metal tape measure that had the look of a precision instrument in the other.

He reached out and felt Keyes's left shoulder, his fingers searching around for some part of the bone. Then he made a short red line there with the grease pencil.

"Hold your left arm absolutely straight down your side."

He then proceeded to measure from the red line down to the tip of the middle finger. Albritten had the intensity of a surgeon preparing for an operation, trying to locate the exact site of the tumor. He went over to the bed where there was a thick bound volume. He opened it and leafed through a few pages.

Albritten straightened up and looked over at Keyes with a smile on his face. "Mr. Halliday seems to have a good eye."

He came back and took hold of Malcolm's left calf and pushed in on it, bending the knee. He very carefully drew a red line laterally across the knee.

"Hold your leg straight," he said.

Albritten had a cigarette in his mouth, and warm dead ashes kept fluttering down on Keyes as Albritten measured from the red line on Malcolm's knee to the tip of his big toe. Then he went back to the book.

"Eureka," he said calmly. "The plot thickens."

Keyes was scared out of his wits. The thing was totally beyond his experience or comprehension. This was the GOD Project? He watched Albritten proceed to make a total of eighteen measurements and observations. Hair color, both places. Eye color. Length of eyebrows. Length of penis, plus angular deviation from plumb, measured with a high-tech protractor. Lengths of thumbs and big toes. The thought of taking evasive action was drifting slowly across Malcolm's brain. It was insanity. It was like a rape, and the rapist was getting more and more excited after each new measurement.

The eighteenth measurement was the distance between nipples. He's right-handed, Keyes was thinking. Albritten's suit coat was open and

75

Keyes could see a revolver in a holster on Albritten's left side, butt end facing forward. It was an idle observation at first. A mere statement of fact. It took a few seconds for its significance to sink in.

Albritten was leaning over him, cigarette ashes falling, considerable intensity, eyes wide, the mad scientist incarnate, his hands trembling with excitement. Malcolm Keyes, who was not a man of action, who was a fast man at the typewriter, who could compose a political slogan while waiting for the carriage return on his old IBM Selectric, realized that he no longer had any excuses for passivity; he had fallen into the hands of maniacs and had to do what he could do, whatever that might be. And he *had* gotten a good basic course in mayhem from television shows; it wasn't as though he were a *complete* amateur.

As Albritten was measuring nipple distance for the second time, just to be certain, Keyes reached across his chest with his right hand, pulled Albritten's revolver out of its holster, and then rolled off the table to his right. Crouching naked on the floor, he pointed the gun alternately at Albritten and Mancuso.

"Don't do *any*thing," Albritten said quickly to Mancuso. Albritten's demeanor had changed. He was no longer the superior dandy; he was terrified; he was cringing. "This man has skills," he was saying to Mancuso as he backed toward the bed. He picked up the book and held it against his chest. For the first time, Keyes could see what was written on the cover. One word. Mark. The basic text for the GOD Project was the Book of Mark. Perfect.

Keyes was standing there naked, holding a .38 on two CIA agents, wondering what to do next. He was trying to work out the problem of how to leave. How many other agents were outside? And what about the Mancuso problem? He would be following. Keyes would have the job of eluding Mancuso plus X number of other agents in a town he had never been in before. That was *assuming* he could get his clothes on without getting shot.

"It's possible to be reasonable about this," Albritten was saying.

An obvious way out would be to call the police, but Halliday probably wouldn't be too enthusiastic about that. He would have some kind of weird screwball scandal on his hands before he even took office.

"Why don't you just put your clothes on and leave?" Albritten said. "That fair enough?"

"You could follow me."

Albritten was being sincere and intense about ending the incident. He didn't want the police either. "Then take the gun with you. Mancuso has another one. He can take it out very slowly and carefully and lay it on the floor and walk away from it and you'll have two guns and we'll have none."

Keyes was edging around to the night table, maintaining the .38 pointed at a spot roughly midway between Albritten and Mancuso.

"It all requires trust," he said, shaking his head.

He picked up the phone and called the Slocum mansion, having first to get through an exceedingly dense motel switchboard operator. Pope answered.

"I want to speak to Halliday," he said.

"Impossible. He's in with a gaggle of senators. He's trying to find out who, if any, are his friends."

"Now listen to me, Norman. I am in a life-threatening situation and I have to talk to Halliday. This is more important than anything he's doing right now. The scandal could be a disaster. Get our leader on the phone. Now."

There was a long pause. Keyes could imagine the Pope looking at the receiver in bafflement. Malcolm Keyes, the guy who was holding up the totem pole, was talking big?

"Hold on," Pope said.

Albritten was still clutching the Book of Mark to his chest. "This is not necessary," he said.

Madeleine Smith was suddenly talking into his ear.

"What's the situation?" she was saying.

"I'm holding a gun on Alex Albritten and a colleague and I don't know how to end it. I don't know how to get *out* of here."

She sounded something like Akers in the way she replied; it was a pure, objective request for data without any sign of emotional coloring. "Why are you holding a gun on Alex Albritten?" she said.

"He assaulted me. I'm convinced that I'm in a life-threatening situation."

There was silence on the line. Madeleine was thinking. He had to admit it was an odd one.

"I want to talk to him," she said.

Keyes put the receiver down on the night table and backed away from it.

"The Vice-President—elect of the United States of America wants to talk to you," he said.

Albritten was still clutching the Book of Mark and in a state of shock as he picked up the phone. After a moment, he spoke.

77

"Yes, madam, I recognize your voice." Then he did some serious listening for about three minutes, never taking his eyes off the .38. "That would be entirely satisfactory, madam," he said finally. He put the phone down on the night table and backed away from it. "She wants to talk to you."

Keyes was feeling chilled and exhausted when he picked up the phone.

"It's all set. Give him his gun back and leave."

Keyes looked over at Albritten. Albritten was looking serious and somber and somewhat ridiculous, the way he was clutching the Book.

"That's not a good idea," Keyes said. "I know what I'm talking about."

"Trust me," she said.

Malcolm thought about it. He considered the alternatives. "I'll take the bullets out first."

"No, no, no, don't do that. You might shoot yourself in the toe. Just hand him his gun and leave."

"Madeleine," he said, forgetting formalities, "you're not here. You don't know what it feels like in this room."

"I've cut a *deal* with him," she said. "It's all right. There's nothing to worry about. Do it. Then get back here right away."

"O-kay," he said reluctantly, hanging up the phone.

He looked at Albritten. It was an act of total faith in Madeleine Smith. He held out the gun, butt first.

9

DEBRIEFING

E WAS LOOKING at me in a sort of feverish way. His face kept changing as though going through an entire chromatic scale of emotions starting with nothing less than *awe,* then proceeding on to *love* (I'm serious), then pain, anxiety, loss, fear. It was all in his face. The fear appeared as I handed him his gun back and he took it and put it away, backing away from me, never taking his eyes off my face. He was still holding the Book of Mark clutched to his chest."

Richard Halliday and Madeleine Smith were sitting riveted on one of Slocum's maroon leather sofas; Keyes was sitting on a matching ottoman, facing them. It was two in the morning.

" 'I want you to know that there's no way in the world I would ever hurt you,' he said, and I said, 'I'm glad to hear that,' and he said, 'In fact, I guarantee your safety,' and I said, 'That won't be necessary, thanks anyway,' because I didn't like the sound of it, and he said, 'At least let me give you an escort to the airport,' and I said, 'I'll take a cab.' "

"What was the other guy doing during all this?" Halliday asked.

"I don't think he knew what was going on. He never looked at the book. In fact, he seemed to avoid it, as though he wasn't cleared for it."

"Heh," Halliday said.

"Were you edging toward the door now?" Madeleine said.

"No. I was putting my pants on."

Halliday shook his head in disbelief, and Madeleine giggled.

Keyes still hadn't gotten accustomed to Madeleine's unexpected beauty. No matter how much she played it down, in person she was distracting. It was a fortunate piece of politics that Halliday's wife was good looking too, and she was two or three years younger than the Vice-President. Throughout the campaign, Halliday had kept his distance from Madeleine; there were very few pictures of the two of them together. And on his travels, Halliday always had at least one daughter with him. Now Keyes was finding that it took monumental concentration and control not to look at Madeleine's legs. They were slender, like a model's, although he was seeing them now eidetically, keeping his eyes at all times above her shoulders. Where was he? Oh yes. Albritten's motel room.

"Next thing I was looking in a mirror tying my tie but watching him sitting on the bed, and I said, 'Mind telling me what's in that book?' and he replied with a low, boozy kind of laugh. There was a degree of despair in that laugh, self-pity maybe, or even helplessness. 'It's classified,' he said, looking right at my reflection, and I said, 'The President sent me,' and he said, 'The President-elect,' and I said, 'That's not good enough?' and he said, 'Of course it's good enough. What is your clearance?' "

Keyes shrugged. The confounded credentials question.

" 'Goddammit,' I said. I was getting over being intimidated. I realized I was not in fact alone in that room. I had the Halliday administration behind me. 'I take it that means you're *not* cleared,' he said, and I said, 'Yes and no,' because I didn't know what to say. He took a long look at my reflection this time, sort of treating me like a child. 'Yes *and* no,' he said. 'That's what I said,' I said. 'He forgot the formalities. He isn't used to this stuff yet.' Albritten got up from the bed and slowly drifted over to the massage table and plopped down on it, exhausted, disgusted. 'He isn't. Used. To this stuff. Yet.' "

Keyes was embarrassed about that one; he didn't know if Halliday was used to this stuff or not. In any case, he had no business speaking *for* Halliday; he was an ear only. He looked at Halliday and Halliday wasn't picking up on it, so he went on.

"Finally, I sensed something happening. I could see it in his face. After all, he was caught in the middle. He's a career man; McKay is going out; Halliday is coming in. I felt a little sorry for him, sitting there slumped over his precious book. 'Give me something so I don't have to go back to Halliday empty-handed,' I said, and he didn't sneer; he sat there thinking. I could read his mind. He had to have been in situations like this before where you cut a little corner here, a little corner there; before you know it, you've saved your—uh . . . .' "

"Ass," the Vice-President said. "Don't stop now, Malcolm."

"I was pressuring him. I put on my overcoat. This was his last chance to buy a little grace, if he needed a little grace, and what bureaucrat doesn't? 'I'm talking about a word or two,' I said. 'It doesn't have to be anything too extensive or revealing.' He circled around the massage table, wondering how far he could go. He stopped. Long pause, looking at the wall. When he turned to look at me, there was a messianic look on his face, which I thought was appropriate for the GOD Project, and he said, whispering, 'The strategic implications of this thing exceed even the Manhattan Project. This thing solves everything; the whole ball of wax. This is what we've been looking for for a hundred years.' I thought that was generous. It was more than I expected. I didn't want to be a pig about it, so I said, 'Thank you,' and held out my hand. He looked at me as though he couldn't quite believe who I was or what I was and why I was there, but he shook my hand. His was clammy."

Halliday was drumming his fingers on the arm of the couch. Madeleine Smith was staring at Keyes.

"So *that's* what happened," she said. "I absolutely could not come up with a sane scenario that ended with your pointing a gun at a high official of the CIA."

"And, indeed, it was not a sane scenario," Halliday put in.

"Malcolm, how do you understand the measuring?" she asked. "What was that about?"

"I haven't the faintest idea. That's why it freaked me out. I would never have touched his gun otherwise. I hate guns."

"I'm sorry about that, Malcolm," Halliday said. "You must have had a few bad moments there. Totally unanticipated, I assure you. But you did yeoman work again. What do you think, Madeleine?"

"The whole ball of wax?" she said. "I'll tell you, Richard, I wouldn't even speculate on it." She laughed. "They keep fooling me. My imagination isn't up to the job. I'll say one thing, though—I don't like the messianic tone. Messianic tones in government always mean trouble."

"Appropriate name, though, huh?" Halliday said. "The GOD Project. It solves everything. God is on our side after all."

"The whole ball of wax," she repeated.

"What amazes me," Halliday said, "is that the CIA could be so blatantly illegal. They are forbidden by law to operate inside the U.S. Those measurements made of Malcolm constitute operations inside the U.S."

Madeleine cleared her throat. Keyes looked at her. She seemed to be struggling with something. He realized later that it had to be a common problem for her. She took her glasses off. Recrossed her legs. Absently scratched a knee. She was deep in concentration. She was probably even more reluctant to correct Halliday because Keyes was present.

"Richard, that isn't quite the situation anymore. Reagan slipped a fast one through some years ago. It got very little publicity."

She didn't have to worry. Halliday had an ego. He could deal with competence. All he wanted was information.

"Really? Tell me about it."

"Reagan's Executive Order 12333, dated 4 December 1981, allows the CIA to operate in this country. It gives them *carte blanche*. Americans haven't been immune to the CIA since 1981."

"I'll be damned," Halliday said. "You sure of that?"

"Yes."

Now Halliday had the fingers of both hands pressed against each other and his face was leaning on them. Keyes was sitting there watching the two of them, waiting to be told to leave. Halliday was thinking; Smith was thinking. Neither was a believer in precipitate action. Then Halliday surfaced, and Keyes saw that his stock had risen considerably.

"Akers is holding an executive jet for you at National Airport. When you land at La Guardia, there'll be a limo waiting to take you home. Tell Doolittle I said to give you a raise."

10

CLEARANCE

KEYES HAD GONE back to Manhattan and reality. He was spending his days boning up on Nebraskan politics, which were positively Byzantine. He was also getting up to speed on a possible Senate race in Texas, where state politics were totally bananas, even moronic. Keyes consoled himself with the fact that it was much more interesting than dog food. And then the telephone calls started. First from family, then friends. Then people he had worked with in the advertising business. As the days went by, he was hearing from people farther and farther back in his past, all the way to his freshman year at college. The FBI was checking up on him.

He had a dual reaction. For one thing, it meant that Halliday was thinking of using him again—which was intriguing—and this time Halliday was doing it by the book; he was getting used to this stuff.

On the other hand, it felt like a burglary; strangers were picking over the details of his life. Keyes was experiencing it as a massive intrusion and exposure; he felt stalked. He even learned a few things about his chief stalker from people he had already spoken to: Russell Vandervanter IV. Everyone was giving Vandervanter high marks for deviousness.

He seemed to be something of a cross-examiner and was skilled at finding contradictions in people's statements. Worst of all, anything negative he picked up from one of Malcolm's friends he passed on to all the others, trying to gauge their reactions. One night the doorbell to Malcolm's Third Avenue apartment rang at 11:30. When he opened the door, there was a man standing out in the hall, a bulging briefcase in one hand, his dangling FBI credentials in the other: Russell Vandervanter IV. The son of a bitch had gotten past the doorman without being rung up.

"It's a little late for this sort of thing, isn't it?" Keyes said to him.

"That's not inconsiderateness. I like to take people by surprise."

"How did you know I'd even be here?"

"We followed you home."

Keyes looked at him for a moment. Then he stood aside to let him in.

"It's a little tic of mine," Vandervanter said, strolling into Keyes's living room, making himself at home. "I like to observe the victim before sitting down to talk. When someone is unselfconscious, there is the possibility that a bit of truth will emerge."

"Did it?"

"More or less," Vandervanter said, sitting down, opting for a straight chair over an easy one. "A confirmation, actually. You have an odd way of walking, did you know that? You're sort of random. You speed up; you slow down. You wait at a street corner for the green light and then forget to cross. Then you cross against the light dodging traffic. You look in store windows a lot, which is normally suspicious: looking for a tail." Vandervanter smiled.

"And you say that confirms something?"

"That you're a problem. You're unorthodox. Inconsistent. A mixed bag, I guess is the kindest way to put it."

Vandervanter had an elfin, puckish face. There was intensity all over it, friendly intensity verging on charm. His forehead was advancing up across his head, but he still had a lot of sandy hair that was a little too long. He struck Keyes as the kind of college professor who invents new jokes each year. Keyes sat down at the far corner of his couch and watched Vandervanter flipping through his briefcase, which was bulging with files.

"You're a special case in all ways," Vandervanter said. "Normally, we'd never torment the appointee directly. We'd go behind his back to family and friends, give them all a chance to pay back old scores. But you didn't even fill out a Form 86."

"I'm not an appointee," Keyes said, "I do not have a job with the new administration."

"I see you have a Bachelor of Arts," the special agent replied, getting down to business.

"Yep."

"Married once."

"Eight months."

"What happened?"

"She started talking."

Vandervanter put his files on the seat of his chair and started to wander around the room.

"Why did you go to Cuba?" he asked.

"To cut sugar cane."

"Why did you want to cut sugar cane?"

"I needed the exercise."

"Aha, an uncooperative witness," Vandervanter said, smiling.

"It was a protest against American policy toward Cuba, which is mindless."

"Noted."

Vandervanter paused to look at a poster hanging on the wall. It showed a young woman holding a baby in her arms while the U.S. Navy was firing practice rounds onto her island paradise. *¡Fuera Yanki de Marina Culebra!* it said.

"You seem to be against American foreign policy in general," he said over his shoulder.

"You might say that."

"Why?"

"I think the idiots are leading us down the road to nuclear winter."

"Really?" He seemed surprised.

Keyes was trying to forget the entire scene as fast as it was taking place, but he couldn't help himself. Vandervanter was a piano trio. Very classical. He lived in his own perfect world—orderly, neat, yet with sharp modern edges, a Bartók violin singing in wide leaps, the cello ominous, the piano nervous. He was bending over his files again.

"Now, I can't reveal the sources of my information, but one person said you were a quasi-pseudo-radical. What are we to make of that?"

"That's Uncle Phil," Keyes said.

"I can neither confirm nor deny," Vandervanter said, sounding pompous for the first time. He had been caught off guard, and that probably didn't happen to him too often. This was no heavy-handed

85

flatfoot they had sent. Keyes had the feeling the man was always mobilized, ready, eyes moving in all directions, his head swiveling around like a tail gunner's turret.

"What is a quasi-pseudo-radical, if you don't mind my asking?"

"You mean you didn't ask him?"

"Sheer incompetence. I can't be everywhere at once."

"In any case, you've got it backwards. It's pseudo-quasi-radical, which is someone who has radical criticisms of the system without having any proposed alternatives."

"I see," Vandervanter said, scratching his chin. "But then somebody else calls you a chicken liberal."

"That's my brother," Keyes said, watching Vandervanter's face for signs of surprise, but Vandervanter was ready now. "He's called me that for years. To be liberal is, ipso facto, to be chicken. Or more precisely, Chicken Little. The sky is always falling. The liberal spends ninety-five percent of his time protecting his flanks, the other five percent being liberal. He clings to the center of the road and every once in a while races two inches to the left, makes a stand, and then scurries back to the white line."

"Is that you?"

"I'm not a politician," Keyes said quickly, a little too quickly, given the circumstances.

Vandervanter just looked at him for a while.

"I guess you aren't," he said, and then resumed his wanderings. He stopped at Malcolm's bookcase, which was thirteen feet long and took up one entire wall. Vandervanter shook his head and smiled. "It's as I suspected. An intellectual. There's game afoot! M, M, M, M, M, M, M," he said, running a finger along the shelves. "Ah, here we are. I like the way the Germans say it: *Das KapiTAL*. The Book of Marx. Have you read it?"

Keyes avoided reacting, or tried to. He also tried to stay away from a stone face, as well as seeming too deliberately casual. "The Book of Marx" was a provocative statement, all things considered. He checked out Vandervanter's face, looking for a hidden agenda, but he couldn't read Vandervanter's face.

"No, I haven't read the Book of Marx," he said.

Vandervanter went to his files and read in them, bent over.

"Your old piano teacher loves you. Says you have musical ability."

"Nice guy."

"Let's see now. You seem to be connected with a whole *raft* of malcontents. Center for Defense Information. Institute for Policy

Studies. A few of Ralph Nader's spin-offs. Union of Concerned Scientists. Bulletin of the Atomic Scientists. And, of course, the old standby, the American Civil Liberties Union."

"One could also describe all of those organizations as the loyal opposition," Keyes said, as though explaining it to a child.

"*Touché*. It's not my place to editorialize; I take it back. But tell me, do you consider the *Beijeng News* and *Granma* to be in that same category of, uh, the loyal opposition? By the way, did they give you a subscription to *Granma* as a reward for cutting their sugar cane?"

"There's nothing wrong with keeping informed about the world."

"You're absolutely right," Vandervanter said absently, going through the files again, coming on like a friendly, evil therapist. "People tell me that I have a tendency to cross-examine. If you feel that way, stop me before I kill again, okay?"

"I'll bear that in mind."

"Ever been to the Soviet Embassy?"

"No, I've never been to the Soviet Embassy."

Keyes was rubbing his eyes. He had had a long day with Doolittle, and it was late. But he anticipated Vandervanter.

"Or the Cuban," they both said simultaneously, although with different punctuation marks.

"Ever been a member of the Party?"

"Don't even waste your time."

"I get paid to waste my time."

He left the files and wandered over to Malcolm's easy chair, staring at the rug. He sat on the arm of the chair, legs crossed, arms folded, lithe, coiled, preparing to strike.

"One of your so-called friends—I'll disguise the language this time—thinks you're a man of questionable loyalty to your country. He thinks you're a potential security risk. He says that—"

Keyes was shaking his head in disgust. "Herbert," he said. "My ex-brother-in-law."

"No comment."

"You have to remember I divorced that guy. He hasn't gotten over it yet. He's carrying a torch." Keyes shook his head again in amazement. "I should never have married that woman. We had nothing in common. Except her thighs. Which were rather good."

"Well, I guess that disposes of old Herb," Vandervanter said. "What about those fund-raising letters you wrote for Americans Against Intervention in the Philippines?"

"What about them?"

"Did you believe what you wrote?"

"Of course."

"Why of course? It's politics."

"That was volunteer work. I don't lie on my own time."

Vandervanter nodded good-naturedly. He stood up and paced the length of Keyes's bookcase. He spotted *Capitalism's Dead End* by Novokof, took it out, and glanced at it to be sure Keyes saw. He looked over at him, said nothing, put it back, and resumed a slow pace as though searching for the perfect destructive question.

Then he stopped and went back to his files, which were on the seat of his chair. He spent about two minutes bent over, reading, flipping from one to another, nodding his head, going "tchk" every now and then. Then he stood up and was off on his loping pace.

"Stephanie McGillicuddy," he said.

"Yes, I know her."

"In the biblical sense?"

"You go too far, sir."

"All right, we'll be gentlemen about this. You don't answer the question and I assume the answer is yes. We'll call it a relationship, how's that?"

Keyes was still on the couch, his elbows resting on his knee while his hands were holding his face up.

"Yes we have a relationship," he said in a monotone.

"She is executive director of the Hands Off the Philippines group?"

"That's no secret. Her name is on their letterhead."

Vandervanter couldn't possibly have missed Stephanie. She was the one who'd given Keyes the Book of Marx, and a few other anticapitalist tracts, which he hadn't gotten around to reading yet.

"She's been in Managua for the last two weeks," Vandervanter said, shaking his head, amazed at the flakiness of people. "So we haven't been able to ask her about you."

"She probably wouldn't have cooperated," Keyes said. "She hates the FBI. You guys have already burgled their headquarters, let's see, three times is it?"

"Four, I believe."

Vandervanter was standing there, grinning.

"Incredible," Keyes said.

"You going to marry her?"

"None of your business."

"I beg to differ. You go to work for the President of the United States and then you turn up married to Mao Zedong's widow?"

Keyes flopped back against the couch. Stephanie McGillicuddy was his all-time favorite woman. She was a radical and critical of Keyes's life-style. He lived on the Upper East Side of Manhattan, for example, which was the abode of conspicuous consumers, as opposed to the Upper West Side, which was intellectual country. And he made good money selling phony liberals to the suckers. She accused him of being uncommitted, of being a drifter, not knowing what he wanted to do with his life. Keyes agreed with her. He didn't know who he wanted to be. None of this stopped her from being loving and sexy and adorable. Although she regularly disappeared for weeks at a time, doing things like touring farm cooperatives in Nicaragua.

"The correct answer to your question is that I don't know if I'm going to marry her."

"I can live with it. I can even understand it. Although I frankly don't understand how you can even entertain it, given your political ambitions."

"I do not have *any* political ambitions. If I can be of some help to the President from time to time, fine. But that's it."

"Well, I wouldn't exactly call that a Sherman statement. But what the hell."

Then Vandervanter pretended to remember something. "Oh, there's one grungy little thing I wanted to ask you about. It came up several times in conversations with your college chums. It seems that you wrote a paper at college which you called 'The Commiest Manifesto.' "

Keyes's face fell. He flopped back against the rear of the couch. He was amazed. Not that they had unearthed "The Commiest Manifesto," but that they cared.

"This is absurd," he said to Vandervanter, who was now pacing back and forth between the upright piano and the bookcase, looking as if he was having a hard time containing his glee. "All anyone remembers about it is that in it you called Richard Nixon a card-carrying commiest."

"You mean you haven't read it?" Keyes said.

"There are no extant copies."

"I'm not surprised."

"You don't even have one."

Keyes looked at him, then around at his apartment.

"You sons of bitches," he said mildly.

89

"Look, fella, you're moving in pretty fast company these days. We can't have you disgracing the First Gentleman. Tell me about 'The Commiest Manifesto,' Malcolm."

Vandervanter flew back to his perch, the arm of the easy chair, and coiled up with arms and legs crossed.

"It was a joke, son," Keyes said. "I created a new category for American politics. The commiest. The commiest is one who calls other people commies. That immediately creates its opposite, the anticommiest."

"How dialectical," Vandervanter said.

"How satirical," Keyes replied. "The idea is that now, in addition to the standard categories of communists and anticommunists, you have the brand-new categories of commiests and anticommiests. The stage has been set for total obfuscation. Any liberal suspected of being soft on communism can loudly proclaim himself an unrelenting anticommiest. The American public wouldn't know which end was up and the left would be liberated. The liberals would grow a pair of balls. See?"

"I see."

Vandervanter was pretending to be deep in thought, but Keyes was getting wise to him. There was a zinger coming.

"Somebody did remember *one* other statement you had in there. It goes something like this: 'The anticommunists are an even bigger pox and plague than the communists.' Is that right? I mean, to the best of your recollection?"

For the first time, Vandervanter took a notebook out of his inside jacket pocket. Then he took out a pen. An ink pen. He made a bit of business out of unscrewing the cap. There was a kind of interrogator's ecstasy on his face: The prey was trapped.

"Is that right?" he repeated. "Do you really feel that way? Perhaps I should call it youthful exuberance?"

"I can't believe this."

"If it got out, it could hurt your man. A pox and a plague. That's pretty strong stuff."

Keyes had been very neatly painted into a corner. He could no longer tell if Vandervanter had a copy of "The Commiest Manifesto" or not. The line had been in there. A worse pox and plague. He personally believed that the anticommunists, in their maniacal pursuit of communism, would end up killing humankind. He thought it over. He had exaggerated for the makers of consumer goods, which was a de facto lie. He had lied for politicians, including Halliday. Why not lie for himself?

He could get away with it *if* there weren't any copies of "The Commiest Manifesto" lying around. Keyes was weighing it. The chance to work for Doc Halliday now and then, who was the only politician in America worth a damn, balanced against the pleasure of telling Russell Vandervanter IV to go fuck himself. He hated to lie; that's what politicians did. And his own opinion of himself wasn't all that good to start with; lying was bad therapy.

"I never said that," he said. "Someone's memory is playing tricks."

Vandervanter was standing there, notebook open, pen poised. "You left out 'to the best of my recollection.' "

"Yeah, right. Include that too."

"Very *good*," Vandervanter said. "I find that encouraging. A real sign of maturation." He put the notebook and pen away. "You've got political potential *after* all! You're willing to tell a little . . . *white* lie . . . shall we call it?" He was stuffing the files back into his briefcase now. "It's not much, Malcolm, but it's something. Nourish that little trait, will you?"

11

THE MEASURE OF A MAN

JESSUP WAS BELCHING out great clouds of smoke while contemplating the big map, its voodoo pins sticking in three continents: cities, international airports, ports, Cuban embassies, Soviet embassies. Jessup was accustomed—in business and the stock market as well as in government—to deploying his forces and then pushing buttons; you applied sufficient pressure to the right spot at the right time and you made it happen; something soft in the situation gave way and you punched on through. But he had an army out there and it hadn't been able to find Henry Patrick.

He wondered what Henry might be thinking. Henry, of course, would have no way of knowing that he was the solution to the politics of counterguerrilla warfare. What did he think about, then? Not much of anything, probably. He was quite ordinary, intellectually speaking. It was a cosmic irony that as grand and profound an enterprise as the GOD Project was, it could be delayed or even, ultimately, destroyed by a second-rater like Henry. No, he wouldn't be thinking big thoughts; he'd be thinking about girls.

Jessup turned away from the map in disgust and sat down at the big table thinking small dark thoughts. Whenever something went wrong—

was inexplicable—there had to be sleight of hand somewhere down the line. Or up the line. There was an unseen hand, somewhere. Not only had Henry escaped from the army, he—or someone—had made off with all of his service records. They didn't even have a photograph of him. Or his fingerprints. Nothing. They'd had to settle for an artist's sketch.

Jessup had often wondered about old Bill Casey from back in the Reagan days. The GOD Project had been set up under Casey, and Casey was a good man, he knew what he was doing. Jessup had met him early in his own career and had always thought of Casey as a role model. But you had to wonder about that brain tumor he died of. How long had he had it? Could it have caused him to make some basic slip back then? Allow a damn traitor into the GOD Project? Tumor humor, that's what it could have been. That damn lump in his head getting him to betray his country. How could you trust the actions of a man with a bump *inside* his head?

Nye and Albritten drifted in, Nye bright-eyed and bushy-tailed, Albritten looking like something the cat dragged in.

"Anything?" Jessup said to Albritten.

"Nothing," Albritten, trying to repress a yawn, failing, said.

"I'm getting discouraged," Jessup said. "This thing is taking too long."

Nye was sitting there quietly, contentedly, giving off a peculiar kind of vibration which Albritten couldn't identify but which he knew he didn't like. He was getting resentful, feeling unappreciated; they couldn't possibly know what he'd been through.

"Has Halliday said anything about me yet?" he said.

"No."

"Don't you think that's odd?"

"Odd, hell, it's downright fascinating," Jessup replied.

"What the hell is that man up to?" Albritten said.

"He's being cute. He plays it so close to the vest that sometimes he literally cannot see his own cards *and doesn't want to*. If I told him on the record what GOD really was, his liberal principles would be put to the test. The truth of the matter is, Halliday has no principles. He does what's best for Richard Halliday. As it stands now, if the news about Henry Patrick ever got out, Halliday would be clean as a whistle."

Albritten was rubbing his eyes. He wasn't trying to conceal the yawns anymore; it was impossible.

"Then how do you explain this?" Albritten said. "Halliday doesn't know what's going on, but he sends me someone who turns out to be the best candidate I've ever seen and who then goes on to pass the first eighteen checkpoints. No one's ever come close to that before. *Eighteen checkpoints.*"

There'd been a touch of hysteria in Albritten's voice, with trace elements of petulance, resentment, frustration.

Jessup shook his head. It was pathetic, actually.

"It's a coincidence," he told Albritten. "We've checked out Malcolm Keyes all the way back to the moment of his conception. He can't possibly be Henry. Put it out of your mind."

Albritten wasn't even trying to hide his impatience. Eighteen checkpoints? The odds were starting to get colossal. He needed only two more to be certain. In point of fact, he didn't need two more. He was already certain.

"Is there any way I could possibly run those last two checks?"

"Malcolm Keyes is off-limits. Is that clear?"

"Yes, sir."

"These people are about to take power. I don't want unnecessary problems with them."

"Yes, sir."

"Sooner or later someone is going to have to tell Halliday about GOD, but it can't be while we're vulnerable, while Henry is on the loose. If Halliday finds out too soon, he could blow the whole thing out of the water and make us all look like a bunch of idiots. Which some of us undoubtedly are."

Nye cleared his throat.

"Well?" Jessup responded, sounding mean. Nye, after all, had *lost* Henry Patrick.

"I know where Henry is," Nye said.

Albritten emitted a neurotic-sounding spasm of a giggle. Jessup broke his cigar in two.

"What did you say?" Jessup said.

Nye was trying to look cool. He couldn't possibly have made such a statement loosely; that would have been insane.

"I know who he is," Nye said.

Jessup and Albritten leaned into the table. Jessup said it very slowly.

"Who is Henry Patrick?"

Nye opened a black file folder and scaled two 8×10 glossies across the great plain of the conference table, one for Jessup, one for Albritten.

Albritten was tickled; it was nothing. It was a photograph of a young

94

man's face, but the features were obscured by a full beard. It was nothing, a mess. This was the big candidate? This was Nye's big triumph?

"One big hair ball," he said contemptuously, not willing to give an inch.

Nye was ready.

"I had an anatomical retoucher give him a shave," Nye said, scaling two more glossies across the big table. Albritten's hand shot out and pounced on the picture. He picked his hand up off the thing and threw it a contemptuous glance, and almost fell off his chair. It looked like the artist's sketch of Henry. Albritten immediately saw that Malcolm Keyes, as a candidate, was now running a distant second. Jessup seemed to be having trouble breathing.

"Who the hell is he?" Jessup said quietly. "Where the hell is he? *How* the hell is he?"

Nye looked at them. He was in never-never land, between elation and a nervous breakdown.

"He's become a preacher," he said. Then he giggled.

"A *prea*cher?"

It sounded as though it had been spoken from the bowels.

"A *prea*cher," Nye replied, trying to sound plausible and reasonable and maybe even sane. "His name is John Burns and he's with a religious organization called the Twenty-fifth of December Movement."

"I'm damned," Jessup said.

"It's barely possible that you could be before this is over," Albritten said dryly, still defending his candidate, Malcolm Keyes.

"What the hell kind of preacher?" Jessup said. "What are you talking about? The what movement?"

Nye's tongue was hanging out.

"John Burns is a fundamentalist, left-wing preacher. Left-wing! Henry, you will remember, had been talking funny right before he went AWOL. Lecturing his barracks mates about *peace*. About understanding. Goodwill. *Love*."

"Love," Jessup repeated, puffing on his cigar. "Goddam love again. What is this, the sixties?" He brooded for a while in some deep frozen cave and then said, "How did you get the picture?"

"The Twenty-fifth of December Movement has a cable television program one night a week. I tuned in to it accidentally one night. I don't know why, but something about him got me excited. I decided to tape it."

Jessup was thinking out loud. He looked at Albritten.

"Is this thing worth an operation?"

Nye jumped in, nervous, twitching, eager.

"I've already taken a rough set of measurements," he said quickly.

Jessup's cigar had an inch and a half of ash. He pointed it petulantly at Nye, the ash flying off and exploding into gray dust along the tabletop.

"Now how could you do that without getting prior permission from me to conduct an operation?"

"I did not conduct an operation," Nye replied. Then he produced a cardboard cylinder that he'd left out of sight leaning against a leg of the table. He took out a rolled-up photograph, went up to the wall in back of Albritten, and tacked the top of it to the wall, allowing the rest of it to unroll.

"Gentlemen," Nye said, voice shaking with something that must have approximated bureaucratic orgasm, "meet Henry Patrick."

Jessup jumped out of his seat. Albritten wearily, cynically, turned around to see what it was. It was a life-size photograph of the preacher. In his fatigue, Albritten missed the significance of it, but Jessup didn't. Jessup got his eight hours.

"You took measurements from a *photograph*," Jessup said.

"Yes!"

Albritten had never seen Jessup this excited.

"What did you get?"

"There are eleven measurements you can get with clothes on. He's within tolerance on all eleven."

"*No.*"

"All eleven."

Jessup almost danced over to the photograph.

"I don't believe you," he said, but his tone was ravished, carefree, delighted. Albritten could hardly believe his ears. "Get out the Book, let's try it."

Albritten sat there, watching Nye open the case and take out the Book of Mark. He couldn't bring himself to watch them measure a photograph. It was absurd, measuring in two dimensions. The two of them were like a couple of kids at a party. Jessup was acting like Scrooge on Christmas morning; *everything* was funny. Nye was ecstatic. He was getting out from under his cloud, but his tongue was still hanging out.

Albritten's fatigue had turned him into something like a resentful drunk. He'd been traveling all over the country for well over a year, testing candidates, doing yeoman work, and now Nye had eleven checkpoints off a photograph of someone named John Burns and Jessup was giggling like an idiot. Whereas Albritten had gotten *eighteen* in *three* dimensions.

Jessup went back to his chair finally and lit another Churchill. He was tickled. He was chuckling under his breath; a Jessup chuckle was not a nice sound. Then he looked over at the unhappy Albritten.

"I know, you still think it's Keyes."

Albritten started off with his thumb.

"One. He has virtually no relevant experience." Index finger. "Two. He has total entrée to Halliday." Middle finger. "Nobody knows what his job is."

Pause.

"Maybe they're lovers," Nye said, and then he and Jessup looked at each other and exploded with adrenaline-consuming laughter. It was as though a ductal dam had opened up in them, allowing all the pent-up juices of frustration and confusion and anger to go roaring through their bloodstreams like a tidal wave. The two of them were pounding the table with glee. Nye proposed somehow getting a penilethysmometer on Keyes to find out what aroused him. To do it covertly would be the supreme test of the company's skill. Nye couldn't keep himself from drooling. When the humor had run its course and they were both back in reality, Jessup gave the order.

"Set up John Burns," he said.

12

THE WHITE SAFE HOUSE

THE SECOND SECRETARY saw it as a probable end to his service in the United States and, therefore, a bad setback to his career. One of the best ways to rise in the Soviet bureaucracy was to get solid U.S. diplomatic experience. They badly needed people experienced at dealing with the strange characters who ran the U.S. state. But he had less than three years in and now his superiors back in Moscow seemed willing to sacrifice him.

It was so unorthodox that at first he refused to believe it. He put the message back in the red dispatch box and went downstairs with the courier to the communications complex and demanded that it be decoded again.

Then he sat at an empty desk and waited while they put it through their magical apparatus, realizing that it was a waste of time. The crypto people were good. They rarely made mistakes; they were obsessive types, all of them. His own survival apparatus began to work. How could he possibly execute such an order without being compromised and ordered out of the country? As soon as he began thinking constructively about it, ideas began coming. By the time the message was decoded a second time—it was unchanged—he had a plan.

The Second Secretary had decided that being surreptitious wouldn't work. The FBI was *good* at that. He always went on the assumption that whenever he left the embassy, the FBI wasn't far behind. It was hard to believe they had *that* many agents available full-time for following Soviet diplomats around town, and there were moments when he had what had become a strange feeling—the feeling that he *wasn't* being followed. But, on the other hand, some of them were better at it than others.

He arranged for the larger of the limos, but he didn't go downstairs to the garage; he had it brought around front and he left via the main lobby, carrying the package himself. He even chatted with the driver for a moment out on K Street before getting in. That way the FBI got enough warning so they wouldn't have to scramble and be obvious about it. He thought of it as Russian courtesy.

In minutes they were threading through the speed barriers near the West Wing of the White House. The guards at the gatehouse perfunctorily inspected the package: The Second Secretary and his package were expected. Better yet, President McKay was back in Indiana nursing his political wounds, and the security blanket went where the President was. There was hardly anyone in the White House now. The big aides were with the President; the little aides were lying comatose, getting blessed relaxation after a year of trying to run the country and an election at the same time.

Except for Wheeler. Wheeler and a staff of three had been given the job of cataloguing President McKay's achievements in his four years so that McKay could make a ringing farewell address. There was even behind-the-scenes talk about an Operation Grover Cleveland; let Halliday make a mess of it for four years—maybe even help him along a little, a little push here, a little shove there—and McKay could be resurrected for a second term. The politicians here would have good survival abilities in the Presidium, the Second Secretary thought.

The lobby receptionist in the West Wing smiled sweetly and nodded him on. He went directly to Wheeler's office. The package contained two bottles of Yaroslavets flavored vodka and two tins of caviar, fresh out of the diplomatic pouch. He had promised the stuff to Wheeler six months earlier and then forgotten about it. When he had called several hours before, Wheeler had been overwhelmed. Wheeler was on his way out, after all; his résumé was all over town. And here he was getting a present? Maybe the Russians weren't such bad guys after all?

The operation didn't begin until he left Wheeler's office. Wheeler and his three assistants were using the corner office of McKay's Chief of Staff. It was four doors away from the Oval Office. He should have turned left when leaving. He turned right. Left would lead out toward the press section and the exit. Right led toward the Oval Office and the Cabinet Room.

The 12:30 P.M. tourist group was running right on time; they certainly were efficient in the White House. For added confusion, there were half a dozen painters plastering and painting the corridor. It was the kind of job they didn't schedule when the President was around. He casually joined the tourist group, which was standing in the corridor outside the Cabinet Room. The door was open, and there was a velvet chain barring entry. He inched toward Gavril, who was feigning interest in an anecdote about someone named Coolidge. They spoke quietly in English.

"Well."

Gavril shook his head.

"This thing is extremely secure. They have that funny building in Colorado. The big circle with the diameter? We can't get near it."

"Any thoughts?" the Second Secretary said.

"The circle suggests some kind of cyclotron or other atomic research device. One theory is that they're working on a clean bomb. A usable hydrogen bomb. Another theory is that it's an advanced light source."

"An advanced light source," the Second Secretary repeated. He wasn't technical.

"It's an experimental device for making computer chips smaller. Highly advanced technology."

The Second Secretary pretended to be looking at a portrait of Thomas Jefferson. Smaller computer chips could conceivably be the Strategic Computing Initiative. The American attempt to build a sixth-generation computer superior to the fifth-generation computer the Japanese were working on.

"The question is," he said softly to Gavril, "what about the strategic implications?"

"The political purpose of the project has to do with the exporting of counterrevolution," Gavril replied.

The Second Secretary's eyebrows leaped.

"How on earth do you know that?"

Gavril looked contrite and small.

"It cost me ten thousand dollars."

The Second Secretary bunched up his lower lip with thumb and

100

forefinger. This was the big secret project? Pax Americana? What else was new? They had more than they could handle as it was. El Salvador was a total mess. Nobody knew what was going to happen in Nicaragua. Honduras was smoking; Guatemala already on fire. The U.S. didn't even *know* what they'd gotten themselves into in Afghanistan. Then there'd be the Philippines soon. Chile maybe, Mexico maybe. They were already in Bolivia, and could Peru be far behind? The Americans had been exporting counterrevolution since before there *was* a Soviet Union.

"How can I justify ten thousand dollars for that?" he said disgustedly.

"Help me, Anatoly," Gavril said. "I thought I was going to get a specific. I was fooled."

The Second Secretary let out a long, slow breath.

"As the Americans say, I'll try to bury it."

The group was moving a short way down the corridor to the Oval Office and the guide was telling an anecdote about Lyndon Johnson that sounded in bad taste to Second Secretary Anatoly Malenki. It would never happen on a tour of the Kremlin. If there were tours of the Kremlin. Gavril and he trailed along.

"Gavril, I have a new instruction for you," he said. He pronounced the name very carefully. "Mal-colm Keyes. Mal-colm Keyes. He's a new aide to Halliday. He comes out of nowhere and has very little relevant experience. He's been engaged in some peculiar activities lately. There's reason to believe he has something to do with this project. You are authorized to take whatever actions you believe are necessary."

Gavril didn't even answer. He turned toward the guide and pretended to be titillated by some stupid bit of Americana. The Second Secretary slipped away from the group and zipped past Wheeler's office. Wheeler's secretary didn't even have time to look up. Then he slowed down and casually strolled out past the lobby receptionist, smiled at her, kept walking, and went on out to the limo waiting in the driveway, leaving behind the best safe house in Washington.

13

HALLIDAY'S PIMP

IT WAS INCREDIBLY crude from beginning to end. Disgusting, actually. Crude, disgusting, obscene. Outrageous summed it up.

It happened right after he had left the Doolittle offices at the totally fake official quitting time of 5:00 P.M. for the first time in weeks and was going down in the elevator, bemused, switching back and forth from the problems of reelecting a dozen congressmen to the headier action around Doc Halliday when at the twentieth floor something went very wrong.

There were two other men in the elevator, well-dressed, average-looking businessmen, typical of the building's populace. But one of them had the other by the back of his collar and his belt and was shoving him out of the car, concluding with a kick to the rear. As Malcolm's brain was returning from faraway places, he was looking at it in a dim-wittedly rational way. He was trying to figure out why one well-dressed gentleman would be manhandling another well-dressed gentleman. And in a fancy midtown office building that was good enough for the likes of Roger Doolittle. It was the total lack of dignity that was shocking.

As the doors were closing, the man took out a key ring with one high-tech key dangling from it. He opened the control panel and started throwing switches; the elevator was now an express. He turned around and faced Keyes. Then he opened his overcoat and his suitcoat and exposed himself. He was wearing a shoulder holster.

"I don't like questions," he said in a very quiet voice.

When the door opened in the basement, Keyes was looking into the backseat of a tinted-glass Caddy limo, drawn right up to the elevator. The man simply nodded. It was degrading; he didn't even bother to take his gun out. He looked mean and competent, with no trace of anxieties or inhibitions.

"You've made a big mistake," Keyes said. "It isn't too late to undo it. I'll go back upstairs and we forget the whole thing."

The man already had a hand on Keyes's shoulder, urging him into the car. He sounded almost kindly. "There's no mistake, Malcolm."

The man behind the wheel had to have some solid New York City cab driving experience in his background. He was bulling his way through rush-hour midtown traffic from Fifth to Madison with astonishing ease. Even pedestrians were getting out of his way; they recognized the style. Then he turned left on Madison and was speeding north, dodging buses.

This was the second time violence had been done to him, Keyes was thinking. The other one was getting raped by a tape measure in Albritten's motel room in Wisconsin. Keyes had lived in New York City all of his life and he had never been mugged. But now he had touched power, and the American presidency was the intersection of all power everywhere, and anything could happen at that intersection.

"What is this about?" Keyes asked.

"Be patient," the man replied in that soft tone of voice, that conciliatory pitch that was all the more frightening because it wasn't stereotypical; this guy hadn't learned his lines from TV.

Keyes sat there meekly, deterred by the power in the other man's armpit. If he was going to get out of this, he would have to pay attention to the details. Survival was usually a fine point, a subtlety, somewhere way out in the sixth decimal place. When they reached 72nd Street, Mr. Nice Guy put a blindfold on Keyes, and from there on it was just traffic sounds, and then finally the sound of the engine magnified in the enclosed space and a garage door closing.

The man reminded Keyes of Nikita Khrushchev, who had been something of a cliché Russian himself, a type anyway: short, fat, cunning, ebullient, earthy. He was chattering out orders in Russian to his two agents and seemed to be having the time of his life.

103

"Call me Joe," he said, slapping Keyes on the knee.

It was a comfortable but ordinary living room in what looked like an Upper East Side brownstone, and they were sitting on opposing sofas. Keyes found that he wasn't as frightened as he had been in Wisconsin, the land of the mad scientists.

"One thing I ought to tell you," the Russian said. "It's true that you could jump up and leap across the room and crash through the window like Superman. And it's only one story down. A few broken bones maybe, unless you landed on your head. But that isn't movie-grade sugar-candy glass. You'd be cut to pieces. All right? Can you forget such nonsense and concentrate on the matter at hand?"

Keyes glanced back over his shoulder at the window.

"You think I'm crazy?" he said.

"Good. A sensible man. I like that. Sensible men are much easier to deal with. God save us from fanatics, eh?"

"*God* save us?"

"Why not?" He shrugged, laughed, slapped his own knee. "Now listen. We have a few questions to ask you. That's all. Answer them and we'll take you wherever you want to go."

"Who is *we?*" Keyes replied.

"No, that's not the issue; that's not relevant. Who is *you?* That is the question."

"You know who I am."

"I don't know what you do."

"I write political advertising for Roger Doolittle."

Joe laughed. His belly shook like Santa Claus's. He was very Russian. His voice reeked of fish and folk music; East European, faintly oriental, uninhibited, rhythmically tricky. Keyes was hearing a balalaika, which was obvious, but there was another strain in there that he couldn't quite identify, an alien tonality. Maybe there'd been a Mongol somewhere along the line?

"You're no longer talking like a reasonable man."

"No comment," Keyes said, amazed at his own impertinence.

"I'm not a journalist, my friend."

"You're not my friend, either."

Keyes was trying to analyze his own effrontery. He was scaring himself. Where did he get off talking like that? He had nothing going for him. Where did this bravado come from? Was it the admiration he felt for Doc Halliday? But it was more than admiration. Keyes believed that Halliday was the most qualified human being in the country to head off

104

nuclear war. And in becoming Halliday's tape recorder, Keyes had encountered a situation that was bigger than he was. There was no way he was going to embarrass the man who could, maybe, save the planet.

"Who am I talking to?" Keyes said.

The Russian leaned forward, friendly, avuncular, patting Malcolm's knee. "The man who can save your life."

Keyes looked into those wily, jovial peasant eyes, which were also hard. The man had grown up killing chickens and cattle and eating them. Was it a big leap to killing a man? Probably not. People made that leap all the time. Sometimes people killed you for looking cross-eyed at them.

"You don't seem to understand your situation," Joe said. "At some point naiveté becomes idiocy, becomes self-destructive. You are mixed up in big affairs. This isn't the sandbox anymore. There are major issues of state here. Basic issues of power. Don't think for one moment that your puny life counts for anything."

Joe stood up and wandered around the room, thinking. Then he said, "Nobody knows you're here. As far as the outside world knows, why, you just disappeared one day. You want to be the next Jimmy Hoffa? This can be arranged."

Joe had a big smile on his face, and he also had a silenced automatic in his hand, which he now placed at Malcolm's temple.

"What do you do for Richard Halliday?" he asked.

"I line up women for him," Keyes said.

"*Really?* Well, at last communication is taking place. We're getting somewhere. So, you are Richard Halliday's pimp."

"Yes."

Keyes had selected a lie that would have the least credibility to the press. Halliday was very close to his second wife and was known to be a rarity in politics: a politician who didn't fool around. It was the only thing he could think of; there was no way he was going to tell the stupid truth.

"How do you get them?" the Russian asked.

"Who?"

"The girls, the girls. How do you get them?"

"I've got a black book locked in my desk at the office. Dozens of names. There are plenty of high-priced call girls in New York City. I know the ones who can be counted on to be discreet."

"How often do you arrange these things?"

"At least once a week on the average."

105

"Where do the assignations take place?"

"I know a number of sexual safe houses. They all have secluded private entrances. I've got apartments in New York, Buffalo, and Syracuse. Places where Halliday and the girl, or girls, can slip in and out without being seen."

"He's really a sex maniac, eh?"

"Insatiable."

The Russian pulled the trigger.

Keyes screamed.

The Russian laughed. He threw the gun on his couch.

"As a liar, you're hopeless. But I detect a certain resolution in your character." He shouted something in Russian. "I said resolution. I might have said stupidity. Obstinacy. A refusal to admit when the what is up? The jig?"

The one door in the living room opened, and one of Joe's agents entered with a large suitcase. He put it on the couch alongside the Russian. The suitcase scared Keyes even more than the gun had. It looked big enough to hold all the parts of a body. He stared at it horrified, then realized it wasn't deep enough to take his head. Keyes had a big head.

"I'm sweetening the pot. This is your last chance at the American dream. Open it."

The Russian was sitting next to the suitcase loading the clip of his automatic with real bullets as Keyes flipped the latches and lifted the lid. He was confident it wasn't going to explode; Joe was too close. It was jammed to capacity with money.

"It's half a million in twenties, which is an unobtrusive denomination."

The money wasn't in neat piles with paper tape around the middles. It was much more inviting than that. There were thick rolls of bills tied with rubber bands. There were thick rolls that weren't even tied but were held together by the pressure of other thick rolls and stacks. They were dirty twenties. They had been well used. God knew what those twenties had bought.

"You can walk out of here with it or you can take delivery in Geneva," the Russian was saying as he rammed home the ammunition clip. "Or, we can open up the account for you so you never even have to touch it."

Keyes was still looking at the money. He was feeling weak. If power was an aphrodisiac, then so was money, which was power in its purest form. Staring at all that power in its purest legally tender form, Keyes felt sexual stirrings. Joe was standing next to him now admiring it too; the two of them gazed at it the way they might at a sunset or a great mountain. The Russian nudged Keyes in the ribs.

"They all say 'In God We Trust,' " he said. "It should be 'In Greed We Trust,' eh? So? Take it to your money market and market it. Have fun. Wallow in corruption like the others. What are you thinking?"

Keyes went back to his sofa and sat down heavily. Joe moved with him. He was standing directly in front of Keyes now, the gun held loosely in his right hand.

"What do you do for Mr. Halliday?" he said.

Keyes weighed it all in the balance. The right wing was leading the country down the garden path to nuclear war. The right-wingers were not rational; they had learned to stop worrying and love the bomb, and they had dominated foreign policy for fifty years. Halliday would be *the* first President to seriously try to defuse the nuclear age. There was no way he could betray Richard Halliday; Halliday was too important to the future of the species. Keyes was in something that was bigger than he was, and he couldn't escape the consequences. And as he was thinking about those consequences, he began to hear that alien note again as Joe continued urging him to talk. It was a Russian dance, all right, orgiastic, fueled with vodka and a wild Russian talent for abandon. But there was something off-key, a dissonance he had been hearing the entire time. It wasn't only peasants dancing madly around the campfire. It was as if there were some Apaches there too. It might have been something that Charles Ives could have written: "The Apaches Do the Wisotska in Yankee Stadium." He sat back on the couch and looked at the Russian and his pistol, and he said it mildly, although with a definite tinge of contempt.

"You were born in the Bronx, you son of a bitch."

The Russian slowly blinked his eyes. "What are you talking about?"

"Who set this up? Akers? Is that fat bastard on the premises?"

There was a pause, a stage-wait actually. Joe was speechless. Then the near door opened and Russell Vandervanter IV walked in and slumped down on the far side of the half million dollars, looking nonplussed.

"I'll be a son of a bitch," Vandervanter said.

"You *are* a son of a bitch."

"Don't be a sore winner."

"I could sue."

Vandervanter grimaced.

"Now you just ruined the whole impression you made. I mean, that's a dumb thing to say, Malcolm. You're going to sue. You've been hanging around the American Civil Liberties Union too much." He even managed a giggle. "They could dine out on this thing for months. But you know that your friend Doc wouldn't like that."

"That's all you've got going for you, baby. I could hang you for this."

Vandervanter softened. It was as though he realized what Keyes had just been put through and therefore was possibly owed something.

"Look, I don't know what it is that you *do* do for Halliday, and I don't think I want to know. Maybe you are his pimp. But you've got to understand that politicians at Halliday's level usually only trust people they've worked with for at least one decade."

Keyes was massaging his temples. "You guys play rough. I don't know if I belong in this league."

"Better make your mind up fast," Vandervanter said. "I think he has a little job he wants you to do."

14

THE PRINCE OF PEACE

KEYES HAD FORGOTTEN what floor he was on—sixty-something. He had never been that high up in a building before except for the one time he had visited the Empire State Building when he was seven. He had been sitting there for twenty minutes in the plushest reception area he'd ever seen, except possibly in old Raymond Massey movies. Rugs, sofas, real flowers, views of Upper New York Bay, what seemed to be real paintings on the walls, mostly seventeenth- and eighteenth-century. He thought of Lady Macbeth hiding the signs of carnage. Risk arbitrage was the roughest, riskiest form of investing there was, yet everything on the sixty-somethingth floor seemed cool and serene.

The receptionist finally came out from behind her eighteenth-century French writing table.

"He'll see you now," she said, leading him down a corridor that looked like the Metropolitan Museum of Art, South. The receptionist at least was twentieth-century, but she was very much in tune with the furnishings: plush, subdued, a place for everything, everything in its place. There was a handsome bronze nameplate on the door: Charles C. McKendrick, one of the most redoubtable of the arbs, as well as a part-time corporate raider.

Akers had made the appointment.

"One more little job," Akers had said.

Keyes was just too convenient. They couldn't resist using him. He was the politician's dream machine. How had they gotten along without him until now? In this case he was also geographically convenient. Keyes could get from Doolittle's offices on 53rd Street and Fifth Avenue to Wall Street in downtown Manhattan in half an hour.

"What's it about?" he'd asked.

"I'd rather not discuss it over the phone," was the reply. "You'll see."

Now the door was swinging open and Keyes was looking at the most grandiose office he had ever seen. He ambled into the huge room shaking his head, chuckling, thinking: You can't keep a good man down. Lockhart was sitting behind the desk. Lockhart had even lost his prison pallor; he had obviously done a little time on a beach. Now he seemed to be handling his usual workload, roughly that of five and a half normal humans. He had two phone consoles and a smart terminal on his desk. The New York Stock Exchange tape was zipping by on the terminal while Lockhart was talking fast into a phone, fingering quarterly reports, winking at Keyes, sipping coffee from an exquisite eighteenth-century French teacup. Lockhart wasn't a whole lot to look at, but he had a power source inside that unimpressive body that was metabolic fusion power.

"I'm only on parole so far," Lockhart said, gesturing to the door with McKendrick's name on it. "It wouldn't look good for an ex-con to be working on Wall Street. There are plenty of pre-cons around here, of course. They're doomed. I can spot them a mile away. Once I get my pardon, I'll be cleansed, baptized. I can surface."

"The papers haven't picked this up yet, have they?"

"No. They will. I'll be Halliday's first scandal. But I mean, it's ridiculous to waste me; I'm a national asset."

Keyes was getting ready to take notes. It would be bugle calls and drumbeats of self-aggrandizement, along with some heavy-handed work on the glockenspiel, a one-man military band doing a time step down Fifth Avenue.

"Why am I here?" Keyes asked.

"You're working on my pardon," Lockhart said, taking out a key that opened the bottom drawer in his desk. He took out some sheets of paper that were clipped together and tossed them on his desk. "It's a little thing I picked up for our President. It's got to do with the GOD Project."

It's got to do with the GOD Project, Keyes heard, remembered. The

110

one-man band had suddenly, miraculously, produced the crashing chord from *Thus Spake Zarathustra*. Keyes would never forget the moment; he would even remember exactly how the office smelled.

"What is the GOD Project?" he asked, awestruck.

"Hey, look, I'm only shooting for a pardon, not the Congressional Medal."

Keyes stayed in his chair. He was delaying the moment of education, whatever it might be. He was the connoisseur salivating over the fish for a moment before digging in. But how could Lockhart have so many pieces of paper on the GOD Project without understanding it?

"Summarize it for me," he said.

Both of Lockhart's phone consoles were lighting up, but his secretary was holding his calls, which was dangerous for an arb: Stock prices could plummet or soar, like the blood pressure of a hypertensive when corporate raiders were on the prowl. Worse yet, it was triple witching Friday, when stock options, stock index options, and stock index futures all expired. So there could be a lot of movement, especially during the last thirty minutes of trading, and it was now 3:30 P.M.

But Lockhart was relaxed. He had his priorities straight; he knew what was really important in his life. He was leaning back in his cozy swivel chair, hands behind his head, gazing at the ceiling, big smile on his face, relishing the situation.

"It's delicious," he said. "You'll love it."

"Stop torturing me," Keyes said.

"It's a beauty. I mean, this has to be a rarity. This one belongs in the Museum of Natural History. They are no longer searching for the man they've been looking for for a year or so. The operation's been called off. They are now using quite a few agents to keep a *religious* organization under *quite* close scrutiny. I have to admit that it strikes me as crazy— although it might not strike someone else as crazy—that the GOD Project actually has something to do with religion. I'm not even touching on the question of the separation of church and state."

"What religious group?"

Lockhart was sucking in his cheeks, trying not to smile.

"It's called the Pentagonal Church of Christ. They're a fundamentalist peace movement. Their church building in the District is five-sided. They *claim* that this is modeled not after the Pentagon but after the Star of Bethlehem. The church is part of a larger group called—why aren't you taking notes?—the Twenty-fifth of December Movement."

"Where do you find these things out?" Keyes asked.

111

"Don't ask."

"Are they the ones on cable TV?"

"Wednesday evenings at nine."

"The Twenty-fifth of December Movement," Keyes mused. "The Prince of Peace. God, this thing is strange. What the hell could be going on?"

"The Twenty-fifth of December Movement does vigils at Pantex in Texas, where they make the bombs. They try to interfere with the white trains that deliver the bombs to military bases. Now and then they raid a submarine base. They managed to dent a B-52 once. They participated in Nevada Desert Experience VII. That's the Nuclear Test Site. They are left-wing fundamentalist Christians." Lockhart's smile was at its seventy-five-watt maximum. "Communist fundamentalists. Can you beat that?"

Keyes went over to the desk, bent over, and started reading.

The report was twenty-three pages long. It was a complete account of everything that was known about the Twenty-fifth of December Movement. Officers, finances, history, planned activities for the near future. Salaries. They didn't pay themselves all that much. Their expenses were low, too. For things like trips to the Newport News shipyard to throw blood at nuclear submarines they were spending considerably less than the government agents following them. It took Keyes twenty-three minutes to get through it. He wandered back to his chair, taking the sheets with him. Lockhart was still coining money over the phone.

"We'll have to burn this," Keyes said.

"I'll call you back," Lockhart said to someone. "Hey, that thing wasn't too easy to get. I had to spread a few promissory notes around. Now you want to burn it after one reading?"

"Did you make any copies?"

"No."

"We burn it."

"Listen, Malcolm, my pardon is riding on this thing."

Keyes tossed it back at him.

"Ask me something."

Lockhart's eyes narrowed with ostentatious suspicion, but he was still smiling. He opened the report to page 13.

"What's the annual interest payment on the mortgage for the church in Washington?"

112

"Twelve thousand nine hundred and fifty-eight dollars and seventeen cents."

"Screw you."

"Oh, and it has an asterisk. The note at the bottom of the page says that this is expected to rise by approximately seven percent for the next fiscal year. The mortgage is being renegotiated."

"Son of a bitch," Lockhart said, leaning back in his chair, looking at Keyes with different eyes. "Oh, man, you're dangerous."

Then he pulled out a metal trash basket from under his desk that was typical Lockhart: It was empty. Nothing Lockhart dealt with was trash; it was all data, all vital.

Keyes started balling up pages and tossing them into the wastebasket while Lockhart produced an eighteen-karat gold cigarette lighter from a desk drawer. The two of them fed the fire until it was nothing but ashes and sparks. Lockhart was pouring in ice water from a cut-glass carafe when his secretary walked into the room, sniffing. They apparently went back a ways and didn't mince words with each other. She looked in the wastebasket and then at Lockhart.

"Are you in trouble again?" she said.

15

THE PENTAGONAL
CHURCH OF CHRIST

ALBRITTEN WAS STANDING on the roof of the van with Captain
George Fisk of the District of Columbia police. He was peering
through his field glasses at the Pentagon's north parking lot. The plan
didn't seem to be working.

"They're not moving," Albritten said quietly. "They're staying legal.
They're not even moving onto the grass. They're just kneeling on the
asphalt, praying."

"I was afraid of this," Captain Fisk said.

"The dirty rats," Albritten said, a warped smile on his face. "What's
happened to the peace movement? They used to be good for a fight once
in a while. They had moxie. God save us from pacifists."

There were about three thousand people between Albritten and the
demonstrators. Or Mourners, as they called themselves: Mourners
mourning the cause of peace at the place they considered to be the cause
of war. But it was an uneven contest. The Pentagon vs. the Pentagonal
Church of Christ. There were only twenty-five actual demonstrators;
the rest were bystanders. The movement always demonstrated in units
of twenty-five, symbol of the birth of Christ.

They'd been law-abiding from the beginning. They'd come to the Pentagon via the Metro. The Metro subway stop was in the Pentagon itself, but they'd all filed out quietly without revealing any of the signs they were carrying. It wasn't until they emerged from the Pentagon and crossed the road to the parking lot that they'd revealed themselves.

"Arrest them anyway," Albritten said now.

"On what grounds?"

"Praying on government property," Albritten replied, still watching through the glasses. "Violation of church and state."

Fisk looked at him. It would set a bad example for the men, who had trouble remembering the legal niceties as it was. But he had his orders. And anyway, not one television station and only one of the print media had expressed any interest in the demonstration, and they had been able to talk the one out of covering it. The Twenty-fifth of December Movement was blacked out temporarily, and you could get away with a thing or two under those conditions. He went to the rear of the van and climbed down the ladder.

Albritten watched the operation proceed. It wasn't even taking candy from a baby; the baby would at least have kicked its feet in the air. The crowd parted politely for the police and the Mourners were marched off without even going limp.

Albritten had seen Nye's research on the Twenty-fifth of December Movement. They had started out as a storefront ministry, but they were essentially street Christians who operated on the principle that if people didn't go to the church, then the church would go to the people, bringing its message of salvation.

The Twenty-fifth of December Movement had gotten popular fast. They were tapping into a basic longing in the American people, a longing for peace and for an end to the weapons race. After only five years they had churches in thirty-five states, churches to which people flocked. And four hundred cable TV stations were carrying the weekly program broadcast from the Pentagonal Church of Christ in Washington, D.C.

There was, of course, a close resemblance between the words "Pentagonal" and "Pentecostal." "Pentecostal" was from the Greek, and it meant fiftieth, referring to the fiftieth day after Easter. But these church fathers were not Pentecostals. They did not believe in talking in tongues or faith healing. Instead, they'd called it the Pentagonal Church, which came from the same root, pente-, five, and was symbolic of the Star of Bethlehem, which had announced the birth of the Prince of Peace. It had the added advantage of being perceived as the good pentagon, as opposed to the Pentagon, which was the bad pentagon.

John Burns had become the church's best preacher and was the star of the Wednesday evening program. Burns was odd no matter how you looked at him, even in fundamentalist terms. While he was a fundamentalist who believed in the inerrancy of the Bible, he did not stress doctrine. He resembled the Pentecostals in that he stressed personal religious experience. But unlike the Pentecostals, he didn't believe in faith healing, prophecy, glossolalia. He was unique. He was also magnetic. He had filled the Los Angeles Forum, the Washington Convention Center, Madison Square Garden in New York. His rise had been phenomenal. And, as Nye had learned, he had turned up at the Twenty-fifth of December Movement at the same time that Henry Patrick had disappeared from the army base in Texas. Now Albritten climbed down the ladder and waited by the entrance to the van while the cops were marching twenty-four of the Mourners toward a bus. The twenty-fifth Mourner was being hustled toward the van by Captain Fisk himself on one side and Mancuso on the other.

Albritten was torn. He had the normal bureaucrat's competitiveness. He wanted *his* candidate, Malcolm Keyes, to be Henry Patrick. Why should Nye get the credit without having paid his dues in the field? He was torn between hoping that John Burns wouldn't measure up and wanting to be *done* with the godforsaken project. He resolved to be as objective as possible and make good measurements. He was already making mental measurements as they approached. In spite of the full beard, he could see that Burns was the right age, early twenties. Roughly the right height, five feet ten. He had good shoulders, and there was a stalking animal quality to his walk. A good candidate. Albritten was beginning to feel an academic interest.

"Are you in charge of this operation?" Burns said as they came up.

"Yes."

"Why am I being treated differently from the others?"

Albritten took a good long look. No panic. No fear. No anxiety even. Very self-possessed. Albritten had the feeling that he had never met anyone quite like him before, which was a good sign. How did a young kid like this become a preacher, a wise man? That was improbable and, therefore, another good sign. Albritten nodded his head, and Mancuso hustled John Burns up the steps into the van.

*   *   *

116

Albritten gazed at his latest candidate. Any negative emotions about John Burns's being a better candidate than Malcolm Keyes were dimmed now; professionalism was asserting itself. There was a delectable possibility here. Without all the facial hair, John Burns looked like Henry Patrick. Was Albritten's Ahabian odyssey coming to an end?

He circled around the man. Burns still wasn't frightened, which was peculiar and therefore encouraging. He wasn't even outraged. Was that what being a fervent believer in Jesus Christ did for you?

"For your information, I just gave myself the Miranda warning," John Burns said. "So you're wasting your time, whatever this thing is."

"Miranda doesn't exist here. The Constitution doesn't exist here. Get that straight."

Burns nodded, understanding the situation. This was a tiny bit of territory where the rules didn't apply. He looked at Mancuso. Mancuso was the power. Mancuso looked like one big muscle. Mancuso was an irresistible force.

"Take your clothes off," Albritten said.

Burns did a slow eye blink.

"See no evil," Albritten said.

"What is this?"

"Don't ask questions; just take your clothes off."

John Burns backed away from Albritten. *Now* he was looking frightened. He looked up at the ceiling of the van. Then along both walls and finally the floor. He sighed. He was looking around like a trapped animal. "Being powerless in an enclosed space. Forced to disrobe. Not knowing what's ahead. This is what it felt like. The Holocaust."

"This is not Auschwitz. We're not going to gas you. *Strip.*"

"I have a request."

"Anything you want."

"I want time to pray first."

"Later. We'll have a nice pray together. A real gang pray."

"You're blasphemous. We're both human beings. We're both facing eternity."

"Put off thy shoes from off thy feet; for the place where thou standest is holy ground: Exodus three, five," Albritten replied.

John Burns nodded. He was reading the look in Albritten's eyes. He began to undress.

Burns was wearing jeans and a khaki shirt along with industrial safety shoes, a sensible precaution for demonstrators, even Mourners.

"You're not the police," he said.

117

"No."

"You're government."

"Yes."

Albritten was raping him with his eyes as the clothes came off; there was an almost lascivious look on his face. He was as eager to find flaws as he was points of agreement.

"What do you want with me?"

"We have to give you a physical."

"Why?"

"We're concerned about your health."

"This is inhuman. You've sold your soul to the devil."

"You're right. Shorts too."

Albritten got out his black instrument case and removed the tape measure and the red grease pencil. Then he put the Book of Mark on a small table alongside the wheeled stretcher.

"Climb on," he said.

Albritten began the measurements. Shoulder to index finger. Neck. Waist. Inside thigh. Carefully consulting the Good Book after each measurement, always careful to shield the book from both Burns and Mancuso. Lying there passively, John Burns began to recite from the Bible.

"He that believeth on the son hath everlasting life . . ."

It was dizzying. Albritten was feeling confused; he'd gone for a year without a decent candidate, and now within weeks he had gotten past ten checkpoints with two different candidates.

". . . And he that believeth not the son shall not see life . . ."

Eleven, twelve, thirteen, fourteen, fifteen. Albritten's hands were trembling. He was having difficulty getting the measurements. He was repeating some of them three and four times.

". . . but the wrath of God abideth on him."

Albritten was vaguely aware of the way Burns was looking at him. It took him back to the time when he had first begun checking candidates. He was feeling stupid. It had to look stupid or mad or evil. He was feeling stupid, all right; stupid and excited. Sixteen. Stupid and ecstatic. He was bracing for disappointment, but he was profoundly concentrated on his work. Every millimeter was significant. Seventeen, penis length, flaccid. Good. He got the protractor out of the black case and took penis angular deviation from plumb. Good. Eighteen. John Burns had tied Malcolm Keyes. He got ready for nineteen. Nipple to nipple. The sweat was rolling off him. He'd forgotten that Burns was Nye's candidate. He was so involved in his work that he didn't notice the swaying of the van. Mancuso called to him; Albritten didn't hear. He kept after the measurement and got it, turning convulsively to the Book.

"Hey," Mancuso said. "We've got problems."

Nineteen was good. Nineteen! Albritten surfaced. The swaying was already getting precarious. He could hear chanting now.

"*John Burns, John Burns, John Burns,*" the crowd was saying.

"We're surrounded," Mancuso said, jumping between portholes on either side of the van. Albritten looked out. The crowd from the parking lot had drifted over to the van and learned that Burns was inside. There were no cops in sight, because Albritten had sent them away; he didn't want any witnesses. Once again, there was a failure of law and order; only this time it was on the other side.

There were easily enough people to push the van over; it was top-heavy to begin with. They wouldn't even know they were doing it until it was too late; they had the intelligence of a mob, which was that of a retardate. Albritten had to face the fact that John Burns might get hurt. It was damnable that he couldn't get the twentieth checkpoint, but he couldn't risk it. If there was anything that was of cardinal importance to the GOD Project it was the physical protection of Henry; nothing else mattered, *nothing*.

"*John Burns, John Burns, John Burns.*"

"How about a shot over their heads?" Mancuso said.

"Don't even think it."

"Why don't we all pray?" John Burns said from the stretcher.

"Get your clothes on. You're free to go," Albritten said to him. "Open the door."

Mancuso looked disappointed. Mancuso had not yet begun to fight.

"*Open the door.*"

The swaying stopped.

"Your friend will be right out," Albritten called to the crowd. Then he moved quickly to the rear of the van, shoving past John Burns, to pick up the Book of Mark. He clutched it to his breast.

The preacher's look was one of infinite contempt.

"You think you've got a tremendous secret in that book? Some tremendous government secret cable that's a thousand pages long and you've read it and you know something that I don't know, the rest of us don't know? There's no way I can let you down easy. I don't even want to look at your silly book. Your book is worthless. It's not going to help you. There are too many important things you don't know. All the secrets are in *my* book."

119

As he reached the top step outside the van, the crowd applauding, Burns turned to Albritten.

"Do you believe in hell?"

"No."

"Good."

"Good?"

"The surprise will be exquisite."

16

THE 24TH OF DECEMBER

KEYES HAD MADE the mistake of looking in the mirror; he couldn't find himself. The man he saw in the mirror was wearing a cummerbund and a shirt with ruffles. His bow tie was a fake and he was wearing a tuxedo jacket with felt lapels. Only Doc Halliday could have gotten him to rent such a collection of oddities and then go to the extreme of actually wearing them in public. Pearl cufflinks, shirt studs. None of it was Keyes, whose tastes ran to tweed jackets and loafers. He hustled through his hotel lobby straight out to the cab stand.

In minutes he was sitting in the plush lobby of the Four Seasons Hotel in Georgetown listening to Christmas music filtering out from a piano bar. He was beginning to feel some Christmas spirit, which he had run low on in recent years. He even liked the Christmas tree standing in the center of the lobby. For years Christmas trees had looked like hookers to Keyes, standing there brazenly flashing their lights at you, all baubles and tinsel and ropes of beads and false promises.

The Secret Service had gradually seeped into the lobby. That was the only word for it—seepage. He was suddenly aware that there were four, maybe five, agents in the lobby, their detached retinas coldly scanning for instability as people in fancy clothes came and went carrying Christmas packages.

An elevator door opened and Madeleine Smith stepped out. Keyes jumped to his feet, then remembered it wasn't a good idea to make sudden jerky movements in the presence of the Secret Service. He sauntered in her direction, and they met near the long registration counter.

"Thanks for this," she said.

"My pleasure, Madam Vice-President."

"My dates call me Madeleine." Her husband was off building a pipeline in Peshawar.

Keyes gave her a superfast glance. It was a mere flick, but he took in all the relevant data. Her clothes were totally political, with a number of reasonably good compromises. Her evening gown wasn't too tight or slinky, although it was black and nicely complemented her honey-brown hair. Her earrings never dangled; they were always nestled all snug on her earlobes. She was wearing one rope of pearls, no bracelets, one engagement ring, one wedding ring. All humbly concealed by a black cloth coat—a must for a liberal ecologist—and terminating in brown galoshes made in Akron.

While Madeleine Smith dressed down when going out into public places, she was, however, uncompromising about perfume, which didn't photograph. It was extremist stuff, and Keyes started ignoring it as best he could; it would not have been seemly to have lustful, carnal images of someone who was a heartbeat away from becoming the Nuclear Princess.

The agents were giving each other hand signals. Two of them went out through the revolving door while the one in charge had his hand on Madeleine Smith's arm. When he took it away, she spun through the revolving door with Keyes right behind her. Outside, it was snowing heavy slow flakes that filled the night. They commenced their walk through Georgetown toward Doc Halliday's Christmas party at the Slocum mansion, two agents patrolling ahead, two forming the rear guard, a fifth available to criticize. It had been deemed the minimum required operation for a walk in the snow on Christmas Eve.

Keyes had been invited to the party as a reward for services rendered; Halliday was depending on him more and more. Doolittle was less and less thrilled about the time taken away from Hackenlauter and company, but how could you refuse the President-elect? Keyes had to work nights and weekends to make up for time spent away from the typewriter. On Christmas Eve, it turned out that he was convenient for another reason. Madeleine Smith and her husband were totally alienated from each other, although he'd agreed not to divorce her until the end of her second term as President of the United States. In the meantime, there was the never-ending problem of who escorts the Vice-President. Keyes— as usual, an unlikely choice—got the job because the Vice-President liked him.

"It would have been criminal to waste this going in a car," she said now. "The last time it snowed for me on Christmas Eve was eight years ago in Buffalo. But what else is new in Buffalo?"

They were walking along slowly, arm in arm, absorbing the charm of Georgetown, which looked like the standard Christmas card: small houses, narrow streets, Christmas trees in the windows, wreaths on front doors. Keyes looked at her. Her beautiful small face was wreathed by her long beautiful hair, which—according to the Pope—had been worth a million and a half votes. It was because of the debate between Smith and Vice-President Dunbar. Dunbar had made the mistake of alluding to his opponent's tresses.

"A lot of people," Dunbar had said, "see the length of your hair as symbolic communication. It's a subtle appeal to the aging hippies of the nation, the Vietnam War protesters, the draft-card burners, the pot-smoking conscientious objectors. Your hair, in other words, says: Don't worry, folks. We're not going to go into the Philippines to protect our bases from the communists."

Madeleine's reply had a Fala-esque tinge of Rooseveltian wit, but it was spoken with a deadly bitchy sweetness.

"Mr. Vice-President," she purred, "are you playing Delilah to my Samson? Is there any chance of getting back to the economy? Or maybe *that's* what's too hairy for you."

The League of Women Voters had been unable to stanch the volley of applause and laughter that followed. Even the panel of journalists had broken up. For about three weeks, Dunbar was Mr. Delilah and Smith was Mrs. Samson. What better duo could there be for defending America than the combination of Doc Halliday and Mrs. Samson? A million and a half votes. There wasn't a peep about hair after that.

They could hear from far off a mixed chorus singing "It Came upon the Midnight Clear," the words floating through the narrow Georgetown streets.

"*Peace on the earth, goodwill to men . . .*"

"Malcolm, did you order those carolers for me?"

"I wish I'd thought of it."

They were going up 29th Street toward N Street. Window shutters were apparently compulsory on the two-story red-brick buildings they were passing, as well as wrought-iron gates. Brick sidewalks seemed to be another requirement. The carolers were still singing about peace on earth, and Keyes finally said, "Peace is like the weather. Everybody talks about it but nobody ever really does anything about it."

"That is true," she said slowly, nodding. "The biggest problem with peace, of course, is that there isn't any money to be made out of it. Peace is a money-losing proposition. Peace is like one great big base-closing. It's bad for everybody."

Keyes figured she was playing some kind of weird, convoluted Pirandellian game: the cynical politician playing the cynical politician. Money was everything. It wasn't surprising that politicians would think along those lines; they spent most of their professional lives raising the stuff.

Keyes was looking around at wreaths in windows, at blinking colored lights, at images of Santa Claus and silhouettes of miniature reindeer, at the occasional crèche. The snow wasn't sticking.

"Peace is a money-losing proposition," he said.

"Malcolm, *must* we discuss peace on Christmas Eve?"

Madeleine was holding her face up to the snow, taking the flakes on her brow, her lips, her hair, loving the informality of taking a walk on Christmas Eve with the bare minimum of retinue. An ambulance was trailing along behind them. Depending on where along the route the need might arise, there was George Washington University Hospital (they'd been put on alert) at 23rd and Washington Circle, behind them; or Columbia Hospital (also on alert) at 25th and Pennsylvania, ahead of them.

"Okay," she said. "War and peace are concerned about one of the following. Democracy. The rights of humankind. Freedom. Cash flow. Pick one."

Now Keyes was holding his face up to the snow.

"I have a sinking feeling about cash flow," he said.

"You now have a solid grounding in the basics of American foreign policy. We intervene in Third World countries to protect cash flow. That's why we have nuclear weapons too."

Keyes's eyes narrowed. He was pretending to be suspicious of her. He *was* suspicious of her. After all, she was a politician. A *professional* politician.

"You know," she said, "Christmas is just another day for most of the people on the planet. They have no net worth. Eventually they decide

124

they're not exactly thrilled with the status quo. That's when the peasant takes to the hills with an AK-47 he's probably stolen from the local army who probably got it from the U.S. Army. Now, if the peasant wins, he's not going to go back to the status quo, is he? And *that's* bad for cash flow. Bad for corporate bottom lines. Had enough?"

"What about that bomb you dropped a minute ago? About nuclear weapons helping the cash flow."

"Nuclear weapons keep the Russians in line. We have superiority. So we're able to fight a major war right on the Russian doorstep—Afghanistan—without any serious complaining from them. We used surrogates of course. The mujahedeen seemed more than willing to die. But we supplied them. It was our war. Our weapons. Our strategy. We ran it. Because a left-wing government in Afghanistan—or anywhere else—is bad for *cash flow*. The Russians took it. They retreated. Pulled their army out. That's called nuclear intimidation, Malcolm."

"Joy to the World" was ringing triumphantly down N Street and getting louder; the carolers couldn't be far off. It was impossible to sing that one badly. Keyes sensed that the advance guard had drifted back and the rear guard had advanced. They were turning onto N Street and some Christmas revelers were approaching along the sidewalk. There were two couples, and they didn't recognize their next Vice-President, which was just as well. The agents had rather casually drifted into four different, preplanned firing positions.

"Think of the American establishment as King Midas," she said. "And nuclear weapons are magical devices. They have the power to turn everything into cold, hard cash. Isn't that gorgeous? Think of it! All the cold, hard cash you want! Except that even the king's beloved daughter turned into cold, hard cash. An authentic golden-haired girl, alas."

Keyes looked at the almost golden-haired Madeleine Smith. He was waiting for her to relate a golden-haired girl to nuclear weapons and cash flow and the Russians and grand strategy and peace on earth.

"Nuclear weapons are the Midas touch. They are a supreme torment for the rich. The ultimate temptation, the forbidden fruit. Use them to eliminate the Russians, who are bad for cash flow because they assist countries like Cuba and Nicaragua. Use them, pluck the forbidden fruit, and you will own everything because there will no longer be any opposition worth a damn. Midas will be satisfied at last. The cash will flow, oh, will the cash flow! A torrent, Malcolm. The cash will flow worldwide.

"But, of course, if you use nuclear weapons, everything will be

125

worth precisely nothing. The golden-haired girl all over again. God, what a conflict that must be. They keep holding on to them, hoping they can find a way to use them without committing suicide. Satan certainly knows what he's doing." Pause. "Or is it God?" She smiled sweetly.

"I don't think I want to talk anymore about peace on Christmas Eve," he replied.

"Well, you started it," she said.

The singers had switched to "It Came upon the Midnight Clear":

> "Peace on the earth, goodwill to men
> from Heav'n's all-gracious King.
> The world in solemn stillness lay
> To hear the angels sing."

To hear the angels sing, Keyes thought. He was listening to an angel sing, all right. He was listening to a politician talking straight. This was strictly back-room stuff, not speakable in public. He was also cognizant of the fact that as a senator from California, she'd supported the Trident II—the best first-strike missile in the world—because a major system for it was manufactured in her state. The vote had also made a flaky liberal look solid on defense. In a real sense, Madeleine Smith herself was part of the military-industrial complex. He decided not to point this out to her.

The carolers had begun singing "Hark! The Herald Angels Sing," and in spite of the conversation he could see that Madeleine was moved by it, the words bouncing off the red-brick walls of Georgetown.

> "Peace on earth and mercy mild,
> God and sinners reconciled!"

Madeleine Smith was an authentic politician, which is to say that while she had ideals and goals and beliefs, she could tolerate and live with the fact that many of the things which she believed were unjust and cruel existed and would go on existing, and she didn't rage at fate. She could live with and accept the status quo while at the same time trying to undermine it.

As they climbed a small hill, they saw them, up ahead, several dozen carolers standing across the street from the Slocum place, serenading the President-elect and his friends. The two Secret Service agents in the lead were already conferring with their colleagues in front of the

126

mansion. There were more Washington cops standing around than there were carolers. Oddly, there was no press around.

"How the hell did they manage to find out about the party?" Madeleine wondered. "My God, the administration is leaking already."

As they approached, the group began to sing "O Little Town of Bethlehem." Keyes and the Vice-President—elect stood there in the snow-filled night listening to the closing words.

> "Yet in thy dark streets shineth
> The everlasting Light,
> The hopes and fears of all the years
> Are met in thee tonight."

Then they saw the sign. One of the singers was holding it up. It was lettered in a beautiful flowing script: *The Twenty-fifth of December Movement.*

"This must be their big night," she said, awestruck.

"Are you thinking what I'm thinking?" he said.

"You mean that the GOD Project may have something to do with God? Why yes, that thought did cross my mind."

"That's exactly what I was thinking," he said.

"Do you think it's possible the CIA has figured out a way to get Him on our side?" she said.

"But isn't He supposed to have *been* on our side all along?"

"I wouldn't know."

"Can I quote you on that?"

"Uh-uh. Not for attribution. Nothing's for attribution, Malcolm; everything's on deep background. Burn, baby, burn."

"I don't think I understand politics," Keyes said.

"I think I want an eggnog, straight up, hold the eggs," she replied.

He watched a snowflake dissolve on Madeleine's high cheekbone.

"Merry Christmas, Madeleine," he said.

"Merry Christmas, Malcolm," she said.

127

17

INAUGURATION

WINSTON CHURCHILL SLEPT badly for an entire decade—the 1930s," Halliday was saying. "He was worried about Adolf Hitler. Then his turn finally came and he went to the palace and the King named him Prime Minister. Churchill went home and had his best night's sleep in years; now *he* was in charge and *he* knew what to do. I maintain that night's sleep was Churchill's finest hour." Halliday looked at himself in the long mirror. "Myself, I didn't get a wink last night."

The President-elect was still in his shorts, sitting on an ottoman in front of a mirror, a towel around his neck to protect his frilly white-on-white bulletproof shirt from his television makeup.

Doolittle was wandering around the room smoking one of his little cigars. "I think I ought to remind you that *you* are *not* in charge. *You* didn't get tapped on the shoulder by a king. You got in by a nosehair. The entire right-wing establishment is out to get you; you'll be lucky they don't take Air Force One away from you."

"That's not the problem," Halliday said reasonably. "That's the challenge. I don't expect it to be easy but, by God, I got myself a Rose Garden."

Malcolm Keyes was standing by the drapes, trying to fade into them, afraid that if they remembered he was there, they'd kick him out. To Keyes the scene was all anthems, drums, glockenspiels, pomp and circumstance. The end of an era, the beginning of an era. Halliday was standing now, putting on his trousers, and doing it one leg at a time, while also trying out his inaugural address.

"The New Direction," he said to the mirror, orating. "No, that isn't it." He was still polishing. "*A New Direction*." Pause. "Nope. New Directions. There it is." He cleared his throat. "New Directions will be the theme of my administration. This is not a time for bold new programs. I have not been given a mandate for that. This is a time for transition. A time for preparing for the future, a time for dropping old, discredited, irrelevant attitudes. From war toward peace, from confrontation toward negotiation, from economic atrophy toward prosperity." Pause. "What do you think?"

Doolittle giggled. This was the third giggle Keyes had heard from him in three months, an unprecedented streak of merriment.

"I couldn't have done better myself," he said to Halliday. "In the act of saying you don't have a mandate, you propose major changes. Masterful. It's in the finest tradition of American politics."

Halliday looked at him, cocked an eyebrow, decided not to respond, and turned back to the mirror. He resumed his inaugural.

"It is foolish and dangerous to continue to stride the earth with a chip on our collective shoulder. Indeed, the chips are down now, down on the table, bet in the never-ending gamble that life is, and in which we must neither ask for nor expect guarantees. The quest for perfect security is not only foolish; it is less than rational and, indeed, is antilife. Huh? How about *that?*"

"Wonderful," Keyes said.

"Not half bad," Doolittle said.

"How about this? The word 'disarmament' has been transmuted—by means of nuclear irradiation, I might add—into the Orwellian phrase 'arms control.' I am not interested in this 'arms control.' I am interested in nuclear disarmament, and I will strive for it from this moment on."

"Lots of luck," Doolittle said.

"Yeah, well, who knows." Halliday was adjusting his bow tie. "It'll be a high-wire act no matter what. It takes a thousand hours of truth to erase one minute of lies. So we're way behind. It'll be catch-up ball all the way."

Doolittle sighed, which for him was even rarer than laughter.

"If you try too hard for peace, they'll say you're working for the KGB."

Halliday smiled at himself in the mirror. Then he shrugged. "Test of leadership," he said. "How do you get Americans to see that *we* are not threatened, that *we* are the threat? How does the psychiatrist tell that to the patient? That's the magic act I have to put on. Now you see it, now you don't, the hand is quicker than the eye. You might call me the Prestidigitator of the United States."

Keyes was all ears. He was like a kid who overhears his parents talking dirty. Politics was cynicism and manipulation. He was getting it straight from the top. Listening to them was like hearing a duo for oboe and flute. Doolittle the oboe, the ill wind; Halliday the joyous piper. Pessimism contending against *joie de vivre,* anhedonia vs. the eternal optimist, the oboe fading away into triple pianissimo as the flute triumphs on a sustained note of pure joy at being President of the United States.

Halliday was staring down at his shoeshine, thinking.

"I'm stealing Malcolm from you," he said.

"For how long?"

"The duration."

"What's he going to do?"

"I just made him a special deputy assistant adviser to the White House. I need him, Roger."

Keyes had been expecting it and so had Doolittle, but Doolittle had to make some trouble.

"Special assistant deputy what?"

"Special deputy assistant adviser."

"Deputy to whom?"

"Deputy to nobody. He can't be a special assistant to me because it would look funny."

"What are his duties?"

"He's going to be my tribal historian. My archivist. My interim Presidential Library. He's going to save me from the copying machine. He's going to save me from the leakers. I've got four electoral votes worth of political capital, and I can't afford to spend any of it. Did you know that Malcolm's memory is infinite?"

Halliday had tossed it in, as though casually talking about the horsepower of a new car or, maybe, the passing ability of the New York Jets' quarterback.

"It is?" Doolittle said, amazed. He glared at Keyes. "I didn't know that."

"This administration is going to leak like a sieve," Halliday continued. "But a *lot* of things aren't going to be on paper. They'll be leakproof. That way I can hoard my capital until I can build a bigger base out there. Until the next congressional election at the very least—which I hope to turn into a Halliday popularity contest, by the way—I can't take risks."

There was a knock on the door. "Two minutes, Mr. President."

"He'll be played down," Halliday said to Doolittle. "He's going to be self-effacing," he added, turning to Keyes. "That is, to the extent that the author of 'The Commiest Manifesto' can be self-effacing. In my personal opinion, you're one of those people who are too clever for their own good."

"Yes, sir."

"Fortunately, you're working for the right people."

"Yes, sir."

Halliday was putting on his morning coat.

"Malcolm," he said, "I have just saved you from the task of reelecting Forbes Hackenlauter."

"I appreciate that, sir," Keyes said, looking sideways at Doolittle, who had stopped pacing but was still on his eternal search for bleakness.

"Listen, I can get along without him. The question is, can you two get along without me?"

Halliday was admiring his morning coat in the mirror. Then he reached for his topcoat.

"I'm not going to risk freezing to death," he told them, alluding to those Presidents who had taken the oath coatless on cold January afternoons. "Subtle conveyance of non-macho attitudes. No mindless posturing and flexing of muscles. We've got to get the hardness out of politics. Hardness is the word that unites sex and violence. *I've* got to be sexy and *soft*. Now there's a challenge."

Keyes was holding the door open as the President-elect sailed out to take on the world.

"Come see me in three years," Doolittle said after him.

"Thanks, pal," Doc Halliday said.

PART II

The Trouble with December

18

THE WHITE HOUSE

THE WHITE HOUSE operator had awakened Keyes at 6:30 A.M. on a Sunday; there was a scramble on. He had been working in the White House for a few months now, and he was used to it; he always set his clothes out the night before and he always had two peeled hard-boiled eggs in the refrigerator so he could eat on the drive to the old Executive Office Building. Five minutes for a shower, three for teeth, and he was in his car. He shaved, by ear, en route.

Keyes was still feeling in a kind of subleased limbo. Akers had arranged the deal. An agent from the FBI had been transferred to the New York office; they had switched apartments, temporarily. Keyes wasn't that sure he had a future in government, so he hadn't completely broken his ties to New York City and Stephanie McGillicuddy.

Keyes had even made out on the deal. Square footage in Washington wasn't quite as expensive as it was in Manhattan: The rooms were bigger. Not that he was able to enjoy the extra space; he was always working. His only lingering question about the deal was the impact Stephanie McGillicuddy would have on the FBI agent. It intrigued him. What would happen when a special agent of the FBI came up against the Book of Marx?

The White House parking lot had once been a through street—West

135

Executive Drive—that ran between the White House and the EOB. It had been preempted for security reasons as well as convenience. Having a parking slot there now was a major perk. When Keyes got one it was scandalous. Outrageous. He was nobody. His office was on the fourth, or least prestigious, floor of the EOB, an interior cubbyhole with no windows. His official title was "secretary." Akers, Chief of Staff, had been besieged by complainers. Getting the parking spot was so exciting, Keyes had gone out and bought a car.

Keyes clipped his White House badge on the lapel of his sport jacket and started up the long flight of steps. The badge had been another outrage. There were blues, oranges, and browns. Keyes got a blue one, the best; it gave him total access to the EOB and the White House. There were zones that the oranges and browns couldn't enter, and most of the oranges and browns ranked considerably higher than a secretary; a lot of staff people looked at Keyes strangely. But when he got to the entrance, the uniformed Secret Service guard barely looked at him at all. Even guards on duty Sunday mornings at 7:00 were familiar with his face. Halliday was forever hauling Keyes in on nights, weekends, holidays.

Up on the fourth floor he could hear Norman Pope's voice ringing down the corridor. Pope was shaving. Pope had a black and evil Nixon beard and shaved at least twice a day, relentlessly working at looking unsuspicious. Pope had discovered an odd fact about himself. A well-wrought English sentence could thrill him and make his beard stand up.

"I have very sensitive, delicate arrectores pilorum muscles," Pope had explained to Keyes. They were the muscles attached to the hair follicles. An excited mental state could trigger the autonomic nervous system, which activated the arrectores pilorum, which then hoisted the strand of beard to a vertical position, the ideal target for a close shave.

"There is a tide in the affairs of men," Pope was saying now with considerable force, "which taken at the flood leads on to fortune"; now getting softer, regretful, "omitted, all the voyage of their life is bound in shallows and in miseries."

Padding down the corridor, trying to wake up, Keyes had to give Pope credit. He was managing to sound a hair like Olivier.

"On such a full sea are we now afloat, and we must take the current when it serves, or lose our ventures."

As Keyes entered his office, Pope was working fast on his left cheek.

"What is it this time?" Keyes asked.

Pope was still looking in the mirror he had installed on Keyes's wall,

136

since he didn't have an office of his own. He was not on the White House payroll.

"Play the *man* Gridley," he said. He started to move the razor but backed off. "We shall light such a fire this day as I trust shall *never* be put out." Pope started slicing away, from down to up. "There's a crisis in the Philippines," he said. "That's all I know."

Keyes sat behind his desk. Except for the telephone, it was an empty slab of glass. He had three filing cabinets against one wall, but they were empty too. His wastebasket was also empty; Keyes never made garbage.

"You say my nose is large? 'Tis a crag—a peak—a cape! I said a cape?—'tis a *peninsula.*" Pope peered into the mirror, which was the magnifying kind, poised at the end of a quivering extension.

"I'm wearing out my material," he said. "I'll have to let Cyrano rest for a while."

Keyes felt like the glass on his desktop, vacantly returning reflections. Politics was getting to him; the stuff he was taking in was polluting his brain for life. He was sitting in on endless meetings: congressmen, political bosses, generals, bankers, labor leaders, businessmen, bureaucrats, think-tankers. The realities of government were grim.

When U.S. early warning systems picked up something that could conceivably be a threat to North America, the military held what they called a Missile Display Conference. They were now averaging three thousand Missile Display Conferences per year. Keyes was staring blankly at his glass desktop. Some of the stuff was hard to believe except for the fact that it came from unimpeachable sources. Fifty-five cents out of every tax dollar went for national security. As compared with 2.5 cents on education, 2 on housing, and 7 on health care. The U.S. was slowly turning into India. New York was Calcutta, people sleeping in the streets, others walking around mumbling to themselves, Hare Krishnas chanting, the beggars and the homeless and the crazies everywhere. The sacred cows were the automobiles. The only thing they were missing was cholera.

The stuff was coming at him from all sides. He'd be stuck with it for life.

The Rapid Deployment Forces were regularly trained in fighting tactical nuclear war. The U.S. had more than a thousand military installations around the world, compared with the Soviets' one hundred. Four hundred people were currently on the Secret Service list of poten-

137

tial assassins. Thirty thousand more got occasional checking. Keyes's brain kept jumping across categories.

Seventeen industrialized nations had lower infant mortality rates than the U.S. Only two industrial countries didn't have a universal health care system: South Africa and the U.S. The Pentagon was relentlessly burning down forests all over the U.S. and then measuring sunlight, trying to prove that nuclear winter wouldn't happen. The navy was testing homing pigeons to see if the electromagnetic impulse that accompanies nuclear explosions would wreck their homing instincts. It was as though they were preparing an environmental impact statement on nuclear war, although they weren't bothering to find out what the effect would be on pacemakers. At the same time there were over 140,000 bridges in America that were structurally deficient. Water supply systems were deteriorating. While black men were only 6 percent of the population, they were 50 percent of male prisoners in all the lockups of the country. The country seemed to be madly tossing its wealth away pursuing nuclear superiority while everything else was going to pot.

"I hope it's a short crisis," he said to Pope. "I'm supposed to have the day off tomorrow. I need it."

"Theirs not to reason why, theirs but to do and die!" Pope replied, getting off to a good start on his right cheek. "Now that's commitment. Do *and* die. You don't see that kind much anymore. What gave you the idea you've got a day off?"

"The President's taking a trip. He doesn't need me."

Pope was smiling at himself. Tenderly. Wistfully. "I'm nobody," he said. "Who are you? Are you nobody too?"

He had just managed to police up the mustache field when the phone rang.

Moody fell in alongside them as they entered the West Wing. Moody's adrenaline was flowing; he was going to have to face the jackals, as he called them. Moody tended to see international crises as his own personal problems. As the least-informed member of the White House staff, Moody was omnivorous for data of any kind.

"The mystery man," Moody said to Keyes.

"Who, me?"

"Nobody seems to know what you do."

"Really?"

138

"What do you do?"

"I'm a secretary."

"You're Secretary of what?"

"No, I'm a small s secretary."

"To whom are you a small s secretary?"

"I'm a small s secretary without portfolio."

Moody didn't seem to realize that he was rapidly turning into some- thing of a jackal himself. And the armpits of his light spring jacket were giving him away again. He never knew enough. He held out his thumb at Keyes.

"You don't know anything," he said.

The index finger.

"You don't have a background at anything."

The middle finger.

"How can you rate a blue-badge job in the White House?"

"I don't have to know anything. I'm just a secretary."

"Even secretaries in the White House know something. You don't know anything."

"Okay, ask me something."

Moody flashed a big grin that was simultaneously jovial and sharkish; it was the hustler's smile and the dueler's smile; it conveyed the signal that you could have it either way with Moody; you could be friends or enemies, and either state was okay with him.

The President's desk was roughly at one focal point of the Oval Office. Akers was sitting on a couch at roughly the other focal point, staring off into space. Pope, Moody, and Keyes sat down near Akers, and they all sat there quietly waiting for Halliday to get off the phone.

Keyes was still intrigued by the Oval Office, starting off with the fact that it was an oval. That was off the wall to Keyes. How many rooms in the entire country were oval? Octagonal, maybe, but oval? It was strange.

It looked unfinished to him, and underfurnished. The style was American traditional, but it didn't hold together for some reason. It lacked something; it was a kind of typical political statement in that it was aimed at the blandest common denominator. There were no sharp, clean lines; it was as though hedging and compromise and the avoid- ance of confrontation had been built into the very shape of the place. The architect of the White House had been a political genius. He had created a room that, properly furnished, was the most boring place in America, which was precisely what the political leadership wanted to do to the public. Who wanted to have a nervous, agitated, attentive public? But there was history in that room. Keyes paled at the thought of remembering everything that had gone on in this room. It would be Sodom and Gomorrah and would probably send him over the edge. Then, suddenly, the Vice-President was swishing in and the President was off the phone and they were all sitting around having a tea party at 7:15 A.M. of the day when even God slept late.

"Start," Halliday said to Akers.

Akers was sitting at one end of the couch with a clipboard on his lap. It being Sunday, he was wearing a sport shirt and slacks, along with his fat, judicial, blank, noncommittal expression.

"The New People's Army in the Philippines mortared Clark Air Force Base five hours ago. Twelve dead, three F-16s destroyed."

"Ouch," Pope said.

It would be the first major test of the new administration. They had gotten through three months without anything serious happening, which was more than they had expected.

"We'll need to establish a policy line," Akers continued. "State is in Mexico City and Defense is in Israel, but they're both flying back. State should get here in time for the evening news. I recommend that he make the major response with perhaps Moody here delivering the bad news in a couple of hours after people have been up and around for a while."

Halliday didn't have to think a whole lot about it. "*This* is the policy line. Get the word out to everybody," he said. "We're going to make the response technical in nature. We talk about measures to be taken to prevent it from happening again in the future. We're already in touch with the Philippine government and we've made substantial requests for better protection of the bases. By the way, have someone at State call the ambassador and have him do this immediately so it'll be true. What time is it in the Philippines? Never mind, I don't care what time it is. Wake someone up. Keep in mind that we don't even know yet if this is communist policy. It could have been the action of a local commander and has no long-term meaning. Let's not dig a pit for ourselves. I don't want any McNamara-style press conferences with training aids showing the exact path three nineteen-year-old guerrillas took going from Bataan to Clark Field. For all we know, the Philippine army itself could have done it. I wouldn't put it past them for a moment."

Halliday stopped abruptly. He sat there looking into his own eyeballs.

140

"That's not a bad thought," Akers commented.

Akers and Halliday looked at each other. It was total mutual mind-reading.

"Make up a scenario showing how the Philippine army did it to get us to go in. If necessary, at some point, we can leak it. Have someone you trust do it. Whatever you do, don't use State Department people. I'm giving this a rat-poison classification, everyone."

"Yes, sir."

"Be a lousy way to go, folks."

"Yes, sir."

"Let's see, what else?"

Akers, Moody, and the Vice-President were busy taking notes. Keyes sat with his hands clasped on the top of his head.

"My trip tomorrow will go on as normal."

Keyes couldn't help it. It went out uncensored. He sighed. Noticeably. He glanced over at Pope; Pope was surreptitiously taking his pulse.

"Everything will go on as normal. There will be no upset. I don't even want to see anyone on the White House staff *walking* fast."

"Norman," Akers said.

Pope reached into his jacket pocket and took out a crumpled piece of paper. The calls had gone out the previous night as they did every night, 150 or more to randomly selected homes in the United States from coast to coast. He had taken the nation's pulse, and now he was reporting the reading.

"In regard to intervening in the Philippines, it's holding at sixty-five percent against, thirty percent for, five percent undecided. That's still landslide stuff. The five percent undecided is incredible. Most people actually have an opinion about the Philippine Islands. Now the next time we touch on the subject, we're going to find out if people know where the Philippines *are*. They still don't seem to know where Nicaragua is."

"They know enough not to go in there looking for a fight," the Vice-President said.

"The Vietnam Syndrome," Halliday said absently.

Keyes was watching Akers, who fascinated him. Akers was a clinical model of psychological detachment. He was sitting on the edge of the couch deep in thought.

At times, Akers played it close to the vest, secretive, suspicious, wily. At other times he was affable, amiable, hail fellow. But he seemed to have trouble juggling his moods, which led him into occasional bouts of silence. It was as though he needed time to figure out who he was being, to catch up with himself. Akers's silences were stunningly inept and yet he got away with it because once he did figure out who he was being, he was terrific at it. You tended to forget that awkward moment of transition when Akers was trying to figure out who he was. Now he emerged from the coal mine where he did his work.

"Maybe you ought to get started on your end of this thing," he said to Moody. "Rough out the schedule. Figure your own appearance around noon. Just give the nuts and bolts. Slough it off on State, who'll appear around four-thirty P.M. in time for the evening news, which will keep all the TV types happy."

As Moody left, clutching his notes, glad to get away, he said, "That goddam country even looks like Vietnam." He'd need time to prepare for the knives. Akers waited until the door was closed; it was dangerous to let the press secretary know *too* much.

Akers sat there for a while on the edge of his seat, smiling to himself. "Look," he said, "isn't the GOD Project supposed to solve the Vietnam problem?" He said it in a flat tone of voice, totally devoid of emotion or side-taking, a mere statement of fact. He didn't even smile; not for about forty-five seconds anyway. Keyes spotted a gleam in the President's eye which he didn't love. Politicians were prone to take the easy way out, because most of their problems were so intractable. Halliday took out a cigar.

Halliday didn't seem to realize that the cigar was a ploy, and a rather obvious one. He lit a cigar whenever he was stalling. But he always managed to look thoughtful and sagacious as he struck two wooden matches simultaneously and played them over the tip of the cigar.

"The GOD Project," he repeated, squinting, thinking, manipulating. "Malcolm, where do we stand on the GOD Project? What do we know?"

It wasn't a question of remembering; it was purely a matter of organization, presentation.

"About a year and a half or so ago, a young man escaped from a federal establishment of some kind," Keyes told them, "and took a major military secret with him. The secret of the GOD Project. At least one person thinks the secret has something to do with cosmetics. The CIA—with questionable legality—conducted an extremely intense search for him. The search ended abruptly several months ago. They seem to have decided that John Burns, of the Twenty-fifth of December Movement, is their man."

Madeleine's right eyebrow was almost up in her hair. Pope was sitting there on his boring couch with a radiant look on his face.

"It's a beauty, whatever it is," Pope said.

"Now apparently," Keyes continued, "the only way they have of identifying the man is to make a series of bodily measurements which must agree with, presumably, some master measurements listed in a rather thick volume with the word 'Mark' on its cover."

"The Book of Mark," Halliday repeated, making smoke like a frigate trying to conceal itself, nodding his head absently.

"I did some research on the general subject of body measurements. As a matter of fact, I called up my newfound friend at the FBI." Keyes paused a moment to let the sarcasm sink in; he was alluding to the rough treatment he'd gotten from Russell Vandervanter IV.

"If you'll look carefully," the President replied, "you'll see that I'm not blushing. Only people who are totally shameless run for office in this country. Proceed."

"I put the question to him entirely out of context. I asked him if there were any methods of law enforcement that involved measurements of the human body."

"Malcolm, next time check with me before going that far. Fortunately, you did it right. Continue."

"He replied that there were two known methods. There was the Lombroso system of body measurements used to *predict* criminal behavior, long since discredited. There was also the Bertillon method, in which body measurements were used to identify individuals. This system was generally accepted, but it was rendered obsolete when fingerprinting came along. Conceivably, the CIA could have gone back to it for unknown reasons."

"Heh," Halliday said.

"I've come across one other possibility," Keyes added, "that is in use *today* at the Pentagon." Keyes could see he had their attention; they were all sort of leaning at him. "This isn't going to sound too relevant, but the irrelevant seems to characterize the GOD Project. The U.S. Navy has a system of bodily measurements for carrier pilots."

"Fantastic," Pope whispered.

"They measure people before they go to pilot training. Seems the cockpits have gotten a bit odd. They have regulations about such matters as 'sitting height,' 'buttock to leg length,' 'functional reach,' and so forth. The idea is to find people with shorter torsos and legs but longer arms. For what it's worth, this sounds right to me."

"It sounds like reverse evolution to me," Madeleine commented.

"Carrier pilots?" the President said. "The GOD Project needs carrier pilots who have been okayed by the Book of Mark? And John Burns, a left-wing fundamentalist preacher, is one of them?"

Keyes shrugged, threw his hands in the air, decided to throw himself on the mercy of the court.

"For what it's worth," he said, "in the navy, men of the cloth are known as sky pilots."

Pope exploded with laughter, clapped his hands together, stamped a foot against the floor a half-dozen times. Halliday and Smith and Akers were all staring off into space trying to conceptualize.

"You know something?" Akers finally said, reaching for his briefcase. "In a weird way, *everything* seems to be converging on John Burns." He took out a videocassette. "And I mean everything." Akers was moving toward the VCR. It was on a low table in front of the fireplace at the far arc of the oval. "Consider this an input," he said, shoving the cassette into the machine.

John Burns was not the usual television evangelist. He was astonishingly precocious; he couldn't have been more than twenty-one or twenty-two. He seemed to know more than a twenty-year-old should know. He was worldly and experienced. In one respect he was a throwback: He looked like a sixties hippie. He had a full beard, although it was not very biblical; it was too scraggly. It looked like the kind of beard a man grows on a three-week fishing trip, so that rather than bearded he looked merely unshaven. He had on a wool shirt, a Scotch plaid, khaki pants when he wasn't wearing denims plus the usual industrial safety shoes.

John Burns was looking straight into the camera, and the camera was tight on his face, his unimpressive beard, his friendly, intense expression. The beard disguised his youth to some degree, but he was still shockingly young for a preacher. It was obvious that he was thinking on his feet; sometimes his eyes looked outward, other times they were unseeing as he searched within for language.

Burns prowled around the stage a lot, the way evangelist ministers usually did, and he carried a Bible, which they usually did but it seemed more spontaneous when Burns did it. He was theatrical but not studied. There was a large illuminated wooden cross attached to the wall behind him. Underneath the cross was a large five-pointed Star of Bethlehem that bore a definite resemblance to the Pentagon.

144

"Before concluding tonight," he said, "I want to make a confession to you."

The audience was about seven hundred people seated in folding chairs. The Pentagonal Church wasn't in the same league with the churches of the other fundamentalist stars, some of which could hold seven thousand. The Pentagonal Church of Christ in Washington could squeeze in a thousand. Burns had stopped pacing and was standing at the forward edge of the stage.

"I have to tell you that not all that long ago I sold my soul to the devil and I lived a wicked, evil life. I was a sinner. I fornicated. I lied. I cheated. I stole. And I did not care for my fellow man. None of you here tonight has ever been as bad as I was, as base as I was, as *abased* as I was."

All of this had been spoken in a low key. The tone remained the same as he spoke of coming to Jesus. The way he said it made it sound something like meeting an old friend on a street corner.

"Then Jesus showed me the way. He showed me how selfish I'd been. He showed me how *joyless* I'd been. He showed me how I was wasting my time on earth. And most of all," Burns said, looking around through the arc of the audience, "He showed me that I was indifferent to my fellow man."

("He doesn't seem to have a microphone," the President remarked. "It's in his beard," Akers replied.)

Burns was pacing the length of the stage, talking to the floorboards.

"Now what do you do in a case like that?" he asked his audience. "You've sold your soul to the devil and you're sorry you did it, you regret it, you'd like to undo the whole terrible mess. What do you do?"

He said it quietly, no fire and brimstone; the answer was obvious.

"Why, you buy your soul *back* from the devil."

He looked around the church, smiling. And the responses came and he heard hallelujahs and Praise the Lords and Christ the Kings.

"But I have to tell you it's a painful process. I'm not offering any easy outs. I'm not a salesman on television selling you something that's quick and easy. Buying your soul back is no piece of cake, the way selling it was. No sir, when you buy your soul back from the devil the price comes high; it's a seller's market; he's got a monopoly. So you pay in the currency of perspiration and fear and depression and anxiety, and when you get it *back,* what have you got?"

Burns was getting deeply into something. He was starting to move funny. He was starting to get spasmic in his arms and legs.

145

"You've got a used, secondhand soul on your hands, and I'm not talking about one that's only been used by a maiden aunt on Sunday afternoons; no sir, you've got a wreck on your hands, baby, you're ready for the *scrap* pile."

Burns was strutting. It was the invariable sign that something big was coming. His arms and legs were moving spasmodically, seemingly out of his own control.

"So I worked and I sweated and I got my secondhand soul functioning again and I became human again, thanks to Jesus, and I cherish my secondhand soul; it's *mine,* do you hear that? It's mine and it's not anybody else's and I'm not going to sell it again, ever, not for anything, not for anybody." Burns was strutting high and fast across the stage. "Not for the Pentagon, not for Congress, not for the President of the United States. There is no way *I'm* going to go across eight thousand miles of God's blue ocean to the Philippines and kill innocent peasants and lose my soul a *second* time."

Seven hundred people were going bananas. Hallelujahs. Praise be the Lords. God is goods. Burns gave them what they came for, and they loved it. Burns also knew when to get off. He stood up straight, then bowed to his rampaging audience. Then he went right into his standard sign-off.

"Peace on the earth, goodwill to men. And women. And the children. And the land. And the air. The water. The seas. The lakes. The rivers. The living planet given to us by the Lord. Goodwill to it; may God and man preserve it. Amen."

"Jesus H. Christ," Halliday said as Akers slammed down on the stop button.

"Relax," Madeleine Smith said. "He's too young. You'll never have to run against him."

"That kid knows how to do it," Halliday said.

Akers was pointing to the blank TV screen.

"He represents something that's going on in this country. These sermons of his get syndicated. His audience is growing. The Twenty-fifth of December Movement is springing up all over the country. John Burns has to be factored in when we're thinking about going into the Philippines or anyplace else."

Halliday nodded. His head went up and down for a long time as he thought it through.

"It's the most fascinating problem in American politics," he finally said. "For a Democrat, anyway. If you go in you're a kid killer. If you don't you're a commie."

"But you just heard the alleged solution to the Vietnam Syndrome talking," Akers said.

Pope giggled.

"The GOD Project seems to have real problems," the Vice-President said. "Offhand, I'd say God is in hot water."

"*I* am the one who is in hot water," Halliday replied, "and all of *my* problems are converging on that preacher. The man who has the solution to the Vietnam Syndrome, which would allow me to intervene quietly in the Philippines and thereby get the establishment off my neck. I'm going to get a lot of pressure to go in."

Halliday's eyes wandered around the room, looking for answers. Then they settled on Malcolm Keyes, as though searching *him* for answers. Keyes experienced the look as clinical in nature, as though a pathogenic organism were being observed under a microscope, or anyway an exotic one. His mind went back to the motel room in Wisconsin, and Alexander Albritten. That was the kind of look he was getting. Then the Vice-President started doing it. He switched back and forth between them, and they were still doing it. Then Akers started doing it. Pope, getting more radiant by the moment, joined in.

"You know, Malcolm," Halliday said finally, "if you gave John Burns a shave, he would look an awful lot like you."

"The resemblance is remarkable," the Vice-President said.

Akers turned on the VCR again and froze the frame on a close-up of the preacher.

"Gee, this is interesting," Pope said.

"All of my problems are either converging on John Burns," the President said, "or they are converging on you, Malcolm."

"Gulp," Keyes said.

"Malcolm, I know you need a day off," Halliday said. "But take it next week sometime," he added vaguely. "I think you'd better come with me tomorrow."

"Yes, sir," Keyes said, trying to get a little eagerness into his voice, failing, sounding hollow, insincere, political.

"If it makes you feel any better, we're going to go in search of GOD, Malcolm," Halliday said.

19

THE ESTABLISHMENT

KEYES WAS STANDING there looking at the sweep second; at precisely 5:00 A.M. he touched the President on the shoulder. Halliday was awake instantly.

"Is Marine One here?"

"Yes, sir."

"Anything new from Manila?"

"The CIA daily is in. Nothing new."

Halliday didn't spend any time in the twilight state. He was on his feet and heading for the shower while Keyes let in the steward with breakfast. Keyes promptly started drinking coffee for dear life; he had already had his two hard-boiled eggs while driving to the White House. It was going to be a long day. It was going to be a taxing day; he expected to be pushed to his limits. What he didn't know yet was that he was going to put two and two together and get eleven and would figure out what the GOD Project was before the day was over.

"I had brief biographies of everyone prepared. You can read them on the way to Andrews. I figure you'll remember the conversations better if you know some background."

Halliday was talking through the open door of the bathroom. He was standing in front of the mirror shaving, wearing a towel around his waist.

148

"I may never have another opportunity like this again if I live to be a thousand," Keyes said to him.

"The President has no clothes on," Halliday replied. "My daughters tell me that all the time."

Halliday always took out time for a serious sitdown breakfast; it was necessary for the grueling days he had to put in. Even World War III would have to wait while Halliday put a protein powder and lecithin into a tall glass of orange juice, believing that the lecithin would cancel out the cholesterol in the scrambled eggs he was about to have.

When they got downstairs, Akers, Pope, and Moody were waiting. They moved out onto the lawn without the usual photo opportunity; it was too dark. The only people there were the firemen and the emergency medical people who were always present when Marine One landed or took off from the White House lawn. You never saw them on TV; they were always off camera as the President waved jovially to the staff people who had been dragged out of their offices to provide an audience for the cameras.

On the flight to Andrews Air Force Base, Pope gave his daily state-of-the-people report, based on the previous night's telephone calls.

"It's a funny situation," Pope said in a vibrating voice, talking across the narrow aisle of the helicopter. "Given the kind of questions we asked, I don't think the numbers are all that important. Qualitatively, what I'd say is this: When it comes to the Philippines, the public is going through a period of contemplation. It's yawning. It's scratching its balls. It doesn't know if it's angry or depressed—angry at the commies and hot to trot, or depressed about another round of mayhem."

"Heh," Akers said.

"That's with a possible polling error of plus or minus four percent."

"Ah, precision," Akers said.

"Norman, that doesn't help me very much," Halliday said.

"Yes, sir, I'm aware of that, sir. You are in a difficult situation, sir."

"Stop sirring me to death and tell me where I stand with the American public."

It was a mortal admission for the infallible one to have to make.

"I don't know," he said. "The numbers are still in favor of peace, but it could go either way, depending on how the right wing orchestrates it. Americans are very touchy people. They're God-fearing hip shooters. For example, sixty-five percent are against going into the Philippines in force. But sixty-five percent also don't want to lose the bases in the Philippines. You are sailing in muddied waters, Mr. President."

149

"Could we see the numbers?" Akers said.

Pope handed over copies of the survey.

Halliday was looking out the window at dawn, thinking. "When we get to Air Force One, call State and remind him again that I don't want any of the usual State Department cage-rattling on this Philippines thing."

"Yes, sir," Akers said.

Halliday hated the State Department. He had always hated the State Department. He thought of them as an advertising agency that had one account: Anticommunism, Inc.

Halliday was suddenly giggling. "The kind of stuff that comes out of our State Department can't be called disinformation. That isn't a big enough category. There has to be a better word. Chemical powder on doorknobs in our Moscow embassy, so the Russians can keep track of wherever our people go. Yellow rain in Cambodia. That one turned out to be bee feces," he said in an aside to Keyes. "Agca. A right-wing Turkish terrorist takes a shot at the Pope—the legit one, Norman—and the State Department turns it into a commie plot It's really the Department of Cage-Rattling. I do not want the animals stirred up. Be sure and tell State that. He needs reminding."

"Yes, sir," Akers said.

Keyes was enjoying the harmony. These people were old-timers with each other, going all the way back to Halliday's three terms as mayor of New York City. They could talk in shorthand; they could level with each other. They were all familiar and comfortable with Halliday's law: Do not tell me what you think I want to hear, give me the bad news. As a consequence, they had a pronounced tendency to sound Brahmsian to Keyes. The Brahms who was the deliverer of bad news: This is the way it is, folks, without the sugar frosting, but maybe there's hope; don't give up yet. Being a Brahmsian, Keyes loved it when these three got together; it was the best musical experience in the White House.

At Andrews Air Force Base, they picked up 145 newspeople, some of whom would fly on Air Force One. Another hundred would join the entourage along the line. Air Force One left first so the photographers and cameramen could shoot the departure and the takeoff, but then Air Force One would stooge around for a while to allow the cameramen's plane to get to La Guardia first so they could shoot the arrival.

The ostensible purpose of the trip was for Halliday to make several major speeches laying out basic policy positions of his administration. But the real purpose was to sample the establishment, meet with major

150

players at every opportunity throughout the day. The first was Senator James "Dutch" McCracken of California.

McCracken was one of the more liberal senators; it was a good way to start off the day—he wouldn't be a challenge. McCracken was courtly and smooth and very much the aristocrat, in contrast to his politics. Off camera, Republicans referred to him as the Red Count. He was also one of the last members of Congress to still be smoking cigarettes. He even carried something in his inside jacket pocket that was a total anachronism: a gold-plated cigarette case. There was a slim matching gold-plated cigarette holder in his handkerchief pocket.

"You've taken over at precisely the wrong moment in history," he told Halliday, without requesting permission to light up; after all, he was chairman of the Intelligence Committee. "The crunch has finally arrived. There's no escaping it. Quite frankly, Mr. President, the best I have to offer you is pretty bad: rots o' ruck."

They were sitting at the fold-down teak table in the President's office on Air Force One. The President was sipping from a hot bowl of chicken noodle soup. Keyes was on his third cup of coffee; McCracken smoked.

"How do you define the crunch?" Halliday asked.

McCracken regally tapped his ash into the ashtray.

"If you go into the Philippines, you're LBJ all over again. If you don't—and the New People's Army marches into Manila—guess what the Republicans will do with a People's Republic of the Philippines?"

"Yeah," Halliday said.

"One thing the Sandinistas did for Jimmy Carter was not call it the People's Republic of Nicaragua. He was able to 'lose' Nicaragua without being crucified the way Truman was for 'losing' China."

"Yeah," Halliday said.

"One possible ray of light is that not even Reagan was able to get the public excited about Nicaragua. He called it a Soviet base in Central America and only Ollie North got excited."

"Hell, we've been invading Nicaragua since before there *was* a Soviet Union. It's got nothing to do with the Soviet Union. It's got to do with making the world safe for corporations."

"Now if you could get *that* point across, you'd be doing a major educational job," McCracken said.

"I'd also be alienating my own party. It isn't only the Republicans; most Democrats want to make the world safe for corporations too. You're a rarity, Dutch."

"Don't let that get out—you'll ruin me. By the way," he said, leaning

151

across the table conspiratorially, "would you like to hear my oriental theory of American politics?"

"By all means."

"Uh, who did you say this gentleman was?"

"My executive secretary."

"I see."

"Pray continue."

McCracken put his hands together in the praying position and looked at Halliday.

"American politics is extremely oriental in nature. The oriental notion of saving face is deeply embedded in American politics. The funny thing is, you rarely hear oriental governments talk about saving face, but *we* do all the time. We always have to prove that our word is good. That our commitments are firm. That our allies can rely on us. That we're not a paper tiger. I actually believe that's why we were in Vietnam. To save face. Well, we didn't. We lost face in Vietnam. But it continues to be an all-purpose *raison d'être* for doing absurd things, and the people *seem* to buy it. One way or another, you'll have to deal with orientalism in Washington."

"Interesting," Halliday replied, tossing out the test question. "Well, at least we've got God on our side."

McCracken passed the test.

"I wouldn't count on that if I were you," he replied suavely, reaching for his cigarette case. "I have a funny feeling that God is a Republican."

"As you go down the steps," Akers said when they got to La Guardia in New York, "the cameras will all be to your left. Look to the right of the last camera farthest away from you and wave. Moody will be standing there so you'll have someone to relate to."

A Rockefeller was along for the limo ride from La Guardia to Columbia University.

"There's one word I want to leave you with, Mr. President," the Rockefeller said. Keyes, in the jump seat, was trying not to look alert.

"Manganese," the Rockefeller said.

"Manganese," Halliday said.

"We have to import ninety-nine percent of it."

"I see what you're getting at."

"We have to import *all* of our colombium. *All* of our rutile titanium. *All* of our beryllium. Ninety-six percent of our tantalum. Ninety percent

152

of our chromium. Ninety-three percent of our aluminum. all of which means you can't hesitate to intervene in Third World countries. It's a geopolitical necessity; don't fight it. It's an imperative."

"What about the Vietnam Syndrome?" Halliday asked mildly.

"What, we can't intervene anymore? Anywhere? Because of Vietnam? We'll go down the drain. Talk to your military. Ask them about Low Intensity Conflict. It's the wave of the future. Hell, it's the only way out. It's your end run *around* the Vietnam Syndrome."

"Of course, I did run on a policy of *not* intervening," the President replied, staying low-key.

"So did LBJ in '64; that's *no* problem. He turned it around between election day and the inaugural. You can do it, too. All you need is an outrage or two. You milk it, you hype it, and you get your war. Get some more American blood spilled; twelve dead isn't enough. Not nearly enough. We need a massacre."

Akers, sitting in the other jump seat, had been listening to the Rockefeller expressionlessly.

"How do you feel about the nuclear test ban treaty?" he said quietly, inoffensively, not looking for a fight, just asking.

The Rockefeller closed his eyes momentarily.

"Look, I know you ran on that," he said to Halliday, "but you can't do that. That would be our ruination. We need the bomb. Think of manganese every time you think about getting a test ban treaty."

Halliday was leaving this one to Akers.

"I'm not sure I see the connection," Akers said.

The Rockefeller spoke like a professor to an especially clever student, explaining the facts of life to someone who was green and wet behind the ears, a rube from Albany, but you could see he had possibilities if you worked with him.

"What do you think the purpose of nuclear weapons is?" the Rockefeller said. "It's not to deter a nuclear attack by the Soviet Union. All we need is a hundred and fifty warheads to do that; that's all it takes to destroy the Soviet Union. We've got seventeen thousand strategic nuclear warheads. Why?"

They were on the Triborough Bridge now, which the Secret Service preferred to the Midtown Tunnel because it was less constricted. The caravan was moving smoothly, because the New York City police department had done some counterinsurgency along the route.

"Why do we have seventeen thousand nuclear warheads?" Akers asked.

153

"Because it gives us nuclear superiority over the Soviets, and what that translates into is that we can intervene anywhere in the *world* without having to worry about the Soviets interfering back. They wouldn't dare. It would bring about a nuclear confrontation, and that's the last thing they want. You saw what we got away with in Afghanistan, didn't you? *We* kept the mujahedeen in business."

"Mmmm," Akers said.

Keyes couldn't tell if Akers was learning something new or not; he could have been playing the respectful pupil.

"Okay," Akers said. "Just to clarify this in my own mind. The nuclear arms race allows us to keep escalating the weaponry so that we stay ahead of the Russians, which allows us to intervene in Third World countries. It's a protective umbrella."

"That's it. Stop nuclear testing and you can't keep escalating. You can't keep coming up with new weapons. You won't be able to stay ahead of them. They'll expand their existing systems—for which no tests are necessary—until they catch up to us. The important thing to remember is that the arms race is an imperative. You have to keep going. You must never stop."

"But then where does it all end? Is there a bottom line to the arms race?"

"The Soviet Union goes broke trying to stay in the ball game and gives up."

"Ah, I see what you're saying," Akers said. "Tell me, how do the Soviets give up?"

"What do you mean, how do they give up?"

"How would that work?"

The Rockefeller thought about that for a while. Halliday was waving to a few votes out on East 96th Street. Keyes wasn't moving a muscle.

"As a practical matter, it would happen gradually," the Rockefeller said. "We'd invade Cuba, say. The Russians wouldn't be able to do anything about it because they'd get clobbered if they tried. Then maybe we'd roll back Nicaragua. The Russians wouldn't be able to do anything."

Akers was down in his coal mine, working. When Rockefeller stopped, there was a considerable pause. Then Akers floated out one of his patented innocent questions.

"You're assuming the Russians will behave rationally," he said. It wasn't even a question. "You're assuming they'll look at the number of nuclear weapons they have and the number we have and they'll say something like 'Oops, they got us.' "

"If they don't behave rationally, they die."

"What do you figure it'll cost us?" Akers said.

"If we handle it right, it should be acceptable losses," the Rockefeller said.

Akers kept boring in.

"What would you recommend as an acceptable figure?"

The Rockefeller was looking cornered and testy. This sort of thing didn't sound too good when spoken out loud.

"I would say forty, fifty million."

"Dollars?" Akers asked.

It sounded innocent. It could have been honest confusion. But the Rockefeller looked testy.

"No, not dollars," he said.

Halliday took a good look at the Rockefeller's face and didn't like what he saw; the Rockefeller was looking offended. Halliday decided the situation called for oil upon the waters, and he did something unprecedented. He had Akers call the Secret Service limo ahead of them to change course: The presidential motorcade was going to drop off the Rockefeller at his office on Third Avenue. It was an operational nightmare and caused chaos throughout all of East Side Manhattan, but the Rockefeller was practically kissing Halliday's hand as he got out of Lincoln One in front of his office building.

Keyes didn't have to listen to the speech at Columbia University; it wasn't worth remembering, Halliday had told him; save the RAM memory for more important things. His only instruction was, as usual, to avoid photographers and journalists; Keyes was simply too awkward to have to explain to the news media.

So Keyes wandered around his old alma mater not thinking about anything in particular, enjoying the moment away from politics and reality.

And then he heard them.

The campus was crowded because of the President's visit, and he couldn't see them until he got to 116th Street. Somewhere up ahead there was a group of people singing Christmas carols in March. He ambled through the crowd in front of Low Library and got to the curb. They were on the other side of 116th Street, behind police barricades: the Twenty-fifth of December Movement.

He went down the line of faces. They looked identical to the same bunch he'd seen in Washington. Young, old, middle-aged. All economic classes. Random ethnic groups. They'd reached "Peace on the earth, goodwill to men," and it was a jarring contrast to the conversations Keyes had been recording all morning. Keyes was beginning to feel strange. Spaced-out. He was at the center of the world at the moment the crunch was coming, when forces were going to clash, when change was going to take place. For better or for worse, it was plain that things were not going to go on as they had.

On the ride back to La Guardia, Charles T. Hubbard, CEO of Citibank, was the passenger.

"Did Rockefeller talk about manganese?" Hubbard asked, as the motorcade proceeded down Broadway.

Halliday was waving at people.

"Yep," he said.

Hubbard put a hand on Halliday's knee.

"He's got a point, but he's a bit obsessed with it. There are more pressing issues. For example, you don't want to be President of the United States when the American banking system collapses."

The entire banking system was teetering on disaster, according to Hubbard. It was even worse than the savings and loan fiasco of the late eighties. Because of bad loans to Third World countries and bad oil loans and bad farm loans and bad real estate loans. They had recycled Arab petrodollars too quickly. They had wanted to push out that money and get it earning interest.

Halliday was playing him the same way as the others; he was a respectful listener who appreciated their experience and their expertise and their power. These were the people he was going to have to keep reasonably happy if he expected a shot at a second term.

Hubbard didn't look like a banker. He was small, with straight white hair. He kept a ballpoint pen in his right hand, as though ready to quote a rate at a moment's notice. He was a backslapper. He would have made a good car salesman. And he didn't seem to have any ego hangups.

"I tell you, we've got ourselves into such a pickle, it's unbelievable. There is *nobody* as stupid as a banker. There is nobody as *driven* as a banker. We get all this money and we've got to lend it *out*." He laughed uproariously. "We can't hold it. We're losing money every *second* that we hold it. The depositors we get it from don't take risks. *Their* money is safe. *We* take all the risks. I mean, who would want to be a banker?"

Halliday wasn't laughing back. Halliday was listening. He was getting one of his problems laid out for him.

156

"What do you think we should do?" he said.

Hubbard hit the flat of his hand with the flat of his hand.

"You have to squeeze the bastards. Don't ask me how. They've got to pay. They've got to scrimp. They've got to pay their interest; otherwise, we're all going to go bust. You don't want that. You don't need that. You don't want to be the second Herbert Hoover, or the second George Bush for that matter. You have to understand that most of the major banks in this country are in point of fact bankrupt. Your banks are bankrupt. It's because of the foreign loans, which are uncollectible. And the domestic loans, which are also uncollectible. Now here's the way I see it. *We* keep the country going. Your bankers keep this country *going*. Banks are the ball bearings of society. A country moves on credit. Without credit everything grinds to a halt. So therefore if something goes wrong with the banking system, it's entirely justifiable to bail us out with taxpayer money, because without us there'd be nothing to pay taxes *on*. See what I'm saying?"

"Certainly."

"Without taxpayer money it's all over. It's only because FDIC doesn't insist on seeing our loans for what they really are—total losses—that the fiction of solvency is maintained. Only an accountant's fantasy is keeping us alive."

Hubbard sat there laughing to himself while Halliday was waving to crowds. Hubbard was a man who spent his life on the edge of the abyss and had come to terms with it, more or less, in his own peculiar way.

"We've got to do something about it. Don't ask me what. We're turning into Brazil, for God's sake. We're going *bust.*" Hubbard laughed some more. "Do you remember what Confucius said? Beware of what you desire because you may get it? *We* desired Reagan." Then he was off again, giggling and smacking his knee.

"Well, now, Charles," Halliday said—they knew each other going back to Halliday's days as mayor of New York City—"balancing the budget won't be easy."

"Of course."

"Unless we cut military expenditures to the *bone,* we've got to raise taxes."

"I know. Certainly."

"But that means taxing the rich. Everybody else *has* nothing. We'd have to get it from the rich."

"Not from the rich. No. The rich have problems. The rich have terrible problems. You've got to get it from everyone else. You've got to *squeeze* them. Pry it out of them. It's the only way."

It was time for the test. Charley Hubbard was plugged into the entire establishment. He knew everybody. He knew everything. Nothing got past Charley Hubbard.

"Well," Halliday said, drawing it out, low-key, the picture of innocence, "maybe we'll have to fall back on God."

"No," Hubbard retorted promptly. "Don't count on Him. You make it happen. You can do it. You've got the power, not God. The Power. *Use* it."

Keyes was all over him. He could find no dissembling. The man was at the end of his rope. He couldn't possibly have been hiding anything. GOD meant nothing to him. Nobody knew *anything* about GOD.

The schedule called for them to eat lunch on board Air Force One while still parked at La Guardia. That would give the venerable financier and investment banker Harlan DeGroot time to say his say. DeGroot, sitting in his wheelchair, was hoisted up on a lift to the rear door of the plane, then wheeled into the dining compartment by his nurse.

DeGroot looked a hundred years old, but he was only about ninety-two. He was totally bald, surprisingly unwrinkled, and he had a child-like quality about him, although he was not senile. And he was worth a couple of billion. He couldn't eat anything that Air Force One was serving, but his nurse had his lunch in her medical bag: salt-free saltines, a salad of romaine lettuce and string beans without any dressing, and a small jar of salt-free applesauce. It didn't matter; DeGroot wasn't in the mood to eat anyway, he was in the mood to talk. Although he couldn't talk any better than he could eat. It came out in gasps.

"You have to hit them everywhere," he said to Halliday and Akers. He was the only one to totally ignore Keyes. "Central America is an unholy mess. A catastrophe. Central America is out of control. They're running amok in Central America. Nobody's at the steering wheel. The Huns are pounding at the gates!" DeGroot looked confused for a moment. "Is Mexico part of Central America? Hell, I don't give a damn where it is, it's sliding downhill. It'll *be* Central America before long. Then South America'll be next. Spanish dominoes, that's what that place is. Listen to me: World War Three has already started and we had damn well better win it!"

He sat back in his wheelchair gumming a string bean, looking swiftly back and forth between Akers and Halliday like a bird checking out the terrain.

"Well, Harlan," Halliday said after a moment, pausing to get his thoughts straight while cutting a piece of veal piccata. "It isn't as easy as all that, you know. The public isn't too thrilled about the idea of getting involved in a war. The Vietnam inheritance."

"Who cares about easy?" DeGroot said. "Nothing worthwhile is easy, you know that as well as I do. You've got the power; now you've got to figure out how to use it. That's what presidential politics is all about, isn't it?"

Keyes repressed a smile, but Halliday caught him at it. DeGroot had managed to sound exactly like Halliday himself, who was forever saying: "I am not interested in the word 'impossible.' I want options for *doing* the possible."

"We're working on it, Harlan," Halliday said.

DeGroot pointed an ancient, wrinkled, liver-spotted finger at the President.

"I know when I'm being talked to like an old man. Don't talk to me like an old man. I own an appreciable piece of this planet, and I deserve protection."

"I assure you we will do our best."

"That's too vague," DeGroot replied, sucking on the applesauce. "I think you'd better wait outside," he said to his nurse.

She looked at him suspiciously.

Akers spotted it. Akers missed nothing. He was the perfect Chief of Staff. He smiled at her.

"We'll see that the dietary rules are observed, madam."

"Also no cigars."

"The point is conceded."

The nurse left.

DeGroot was leaning forward against the safety belt of his wheelchair; the discussion seemed to have drained him of what little energy he had.

"This is plain as I can put it," he said, barely audible. "Most of the planet's people have a zero net worth, and we'd damn well better keep it that way. That's the mission of the Pentagon. That's the mission of CIA. That's your mission."

Halliday didn't seem to be enjoying his meal.

"Now, Harlan, we do live in a democracy. We have to take the wishes of the majority into account. We have to at least give it some serious thought."

DeGroot was suddenly moving with the agility of a second baseman.

159

His arm shot out and he snared the brandy that Akers had been sipping. DeGroot poured it down in one flick of the wrist; he was lucky he didn't swallow the glass. The drink transformed him. He suddenly looked as if he weren't a day over eighty.

"The hell this is a democracy. That's what it says in the Constitution. But that isn't the way we run things. It's an oligarchy is what it is. And I'm one of the oligarchs and I say we go into the Philippines."

"Well, Harlan, you certainly know how to express your point of view concisely, and I hear what you're saying."

DeGroot was still cruising high and fast on the brandy. His voice even got conciliatory. Now he was talking as though Halliday were the old man.

"The perfect model for our government is the Mafia," he said in quiet, reasonable terms. "That's the way you have to look at it. Some other gang starts horning in on our turf, we don't just sit back and take it. We rub out the *other* guy. The leader. That's what we have to do. Every generation. Get the leaders; everyone else is sheep. We got Lumumba. We got Che. Allende. We got Maurice Bishop in Grenada. We got Samora Machel in Mozambique. We got Torrijos in Panama. We got Thomas Sankara in Burkina Faso. *All* you've got to do is get the leadership of the New People's Army. Send out a hit team. If that means three thousand paratroopers, fine."

"Well, that's pretty serious advice, Harlan, and I'll take it under advisement," Halliday said, pushing a button under the table.

The nurse came back in. As she wheeled DeGroot out he was saying, "Do it with a good slogan. That's all you need. Remember the Alamo! Remember the *Maine!* Remember Pearl Harbor! Give them the right slogan and you can get away with *anything.*"

Halliday threw down his knife and fork. He hadn't even remembered GOD, not that he believed anyone would trust Harlan DeGroot with it.

"Can we get this thing moving to Detroit?" he said to nobody in particular.

It was getting to be too much. How much could you take? For the first time, Keyes went to a presidential men's room, which looked as if it was the place they made the $800 toilet seats for.

He stood over the sink splashing cold water in his face. Instead of saying "Ah," which had been his intention, it came out as a groan. Government 101 at college was never like this. The black attendant—

160

who was a master sergeant in the air force—was standing there expressionlessly. Sticking your head under water, no doubt, was the usual reaction to spending a few hours with the President of the United States.

Keyes held his cold, wet hands against his face, pressing against his eyes. The crunch was coming. The crunch was gonna getcha. Unless you assassinated all the leaders. Had the government learned that from the Mafia, or had the Mafia learned it from the government? You had to kill all the leaders so you could keep those supplies of rutile titanium coming in. Titanium made fighter planes, and you had to be willing to fight for it. Of course, fighting for titanium was fighting to defend the ability to fight. And if you *didn't* fight, the crunch was gonna eatcha.

The most amazing thing of all was that the GOD Project solved all this. The GOD Project took care of the *crunch*. And what was astounding was that nobody knew anything about it. What could solve the crunch and yet be so subtle that nobody would know anything about it?

Keyes held out his hand and the attendant put a towel in it. He was especially careful about drying behind his ears.

On the flight to Detroit, Halliday got to hear what Lieutenant General Lamar Pickering, deputy chief of staff of the U.S. Army, had to say.

Pickering had a distinctly simian face: deep-set eyes, close-cropped hair, ears that projected sideways, deep lines in his forehead. Thin lips, drooping off at the ends. He had been a paratrooper, and he looked as though he'd be ready to jump out of Air Force One at a moment's notice. He had an intense and disciplined look, and he glanced from side to side frequently, with his eyes only, not moving his head, which gave him a besieged, furtive look.

"Well, General, I'm getting a lot of pressure to take action overseas. What do you think? Should I start a war?"

"I hope not," Pickering said, sipping at a weak scotch and soda.

"At last, a man of peace." In order not to go into the Philippines, Halliday was going to need support from *somewhere.* "Why not?"

"You don't have public support for it. Nobody in the Pentagon wants to hit the beaches without being sure that the American public is behind us."

"I like hearing that. Because, so far, the public doesn't want to go in."

"Then don't go in."

Every now and then the general's eyes flicked toward Keyes, and then away. Keyes was trying to cultivate a feeling of arrogance, as a short-cut

161

way of giving off the impression that he really belonged on Air Force One; he wasn't an outsider; mind your damn business.

"It isn't that simple," Halliday said. "A lot of people will be very upset if I lose the Philippines."

"I didn't say you had to lose the Philippines," General Pickering said.

It sounded like something for nothing. Halliday asked the question as though talking to a three-card monte dealer.

"How do I save the Philippines without going in?"

"Well, you go in a little bit. It's a little bit of a rape."

"Aha, you're going to talk about Low Intensity Conflict."

"That's it."

"What does Low Intensity Conflict really mean, General?"

"It is not a deceptive phrase," Pickering replied. "I know that some of our acronyms are two hundred percent phony, but this one is straight. LIC is perfect for this era. It obscures the distinction between war and peace. As far as we're concerned, World War Two never ended; the enemies changed, that's all. I mean, just look at Latin America. You've got the Shining Path and the Tupac Amaru Revolutionary Movement of Peru. The Farabundo Martí National Liberation Front in El Salvador." Pickering's Spanish accent was exquisite. "You've got the Banera Roja in Venezuela. That means Red Banner. The Alfaro Vive, Carajo of Ecuador. Colombia is a total mess. M-19, or the April Nineteenth Movement. The Popular Liberation Army. The National Liberation Army. FARC. The Revolutionary Armed Forces of Colombia. You've got the Battalion America. The Quintin Lame. That bunch is all Indians."

"Stop it, I can't stand it," Halliday said. "Let's start with the Philippines. Talk about the Philippines. That's the one that's on the front pages."

"We go in at battalion strength; at the most, brigade strength. Those numbers simply aren't big enough to justify levitating the Pentagon. *And* we go in early. We solve the problem before its potential to become a quagmire has been realized. For example, Guatemala. Guatemala could explode at any time. The Guatemalan army is totally incompetent. If we could send in a small force now—call it an exercise—it would save us a lot of grief later. Right now there's a Special Forces unit at Fort Lewis in Washington State. They're ready to go. They're combat-ready. They already have a battalion on Okinawa. They could be in the Philippines in no time."

162

"Climb on and climb off, huh?" Halliday said.

"That's about it. It's officially known as U.S. Army Operational Concept for Low Intensity Conflict, TRADOC PAM 525-44, 10 February 1986."

"Sounds like something for nothing," Akers said.

"Not nothing," the general replied. "Something for something. But not a lot. Something for a little. Small-unit tactics mainly. Special Operations teams to take out the enemy leadership. A lot of Psy Ops."

Keyes leaned forward.

"Excuse me, I didn't get that last phrase."

He was like a court reporter breaking in on the testimony to be sure he got the record right.

Pickering actually turned his head to get a good look at Keyes. The man talked!

"Psy Ops," he said. "Psychological Warfare Operations. We accept that *some* political legitimacy is necessary for successful counterinsurgency. That's why we get into economic aid. That's why the Department of Defense has an Office of Humanitarian Assistance. We also tell them about the godless commies who are trying to take them over. We do a *lot* of that. The U.S. Information Agency feeds material to local newspapers and TV stations all around the world. We have the Agency for International Development. That *looks* like a foreign aid program. It's actually a part of Low Intensity Conflict. Strategic hamlets. Refugee resettlement. Food distribution. Civil Defense. We're working on this thing constantly. The Southern Command, for example, has a good bunch of guys at SWORD. That's Small Wars Operations Research Directorate. It's a think tank. They're covering every angle. I mean, everything's in place and ready to go. Push the button, Mr. President. You'll get results. You'll solve your problem."

"Red-baiting," Akers said.

"What?"

"Red-baiting. It seems to be an important part of Low Intensity Conflict. The commies are coming."

"We prefer to call it Psy Ops."

Akers was fiddling with his swizzle stick.

"I mean, I'm just asking," he said, "but do peasants, who don't have anything in any case, buy that line?"

General Pickering sipped his scotch and looked around the compartment without moving his head and put the glass down and said, "It works in this country, doesn't it?"

163

"You certainly have a point there," Halliday said. "And anyway," lightening the mood, being friendly, easygoing, "we've got God on our side."

Pickering smiled for the first time.

"I make it a point of never counting Him in the order of battle."

Halliday and Keyes exchanged a look. Zip. The army didn't know about the GOD Project.

Back in the car going from the airport to Michigan University—where Halliday was going to give his second policy speech of the day—the guest was a liberal congressman from Arizona, Joe Crowley.

Crowley had gone past sixty, but his six-foot-four-inch body still looked rugged and rural, and he spoke with the confidence of a man who doesn't have to worry about reelection. Keyes, on the jump seat again, found that Crowley was friendly but totally uninterested in him, which was perfect.

"I'll tell you what I think about this Low Intensity Conflict, Mr. President," Crowley said. "It's bullshit. They're kidding themselves. One thing conservatives are good at is kidding themselves. Conservatives, you know, have an awful need for simplicity. Conservatives are antithought. They don't want anyone to think, not even themselves! Better dead than red. Urine tests for *everyone*. The bomb. They have a loathing for facts. They run like hell from facts. Because facts keep contradicting their beliefs. They're refusing to face the reality that the crunch is here. It has arrived. It is in the station, blowing off steam."

Akers, on the other jump seat, threw out one of his unloaded questions.

"Why is Low Intensity Conflict bullshit?"

Crowley smiled and stretched his legs, which reached all the way to the back of the driver's seat, not an easy feat in the roomy Lincoln One.

"Well, because all of these wars we're fighting are about one thing. What I call SOP. Share of pie. That's what most wars are about. But the rich and the middle class don't much like shouldering rifles. So it mostly comes back to 'our' poor boys fighting 'their' poor boys, whether it's our own men or surrogate armies from the Third World. Ever heard of the old pacifist slogan? A bayonet is an instrument with a worker at either end of it. Now 'their' poor boys know what they're fighting for. They're fighting for SOP, share of pie. Nobody ever gives up share of pie voluntarily; it seems to be an iron rule of human nature. So if you don't have any pie, and you want pie, you've got to fight for pie. You've got to *kill* for pie. That's what the poor know. *Their* poor boy. *Our* poor boy is fighting to defend the rich. He's fighting to protect the landholdings of the rich. The bank accounts of the rich, the fine houses of the rich. Now who do you think is going to have the better fighting morale? Who do you think is going to make the superior warrior? This is why we lost in Vietnam."

"You just took away my ace in the hole," Halliday said. "I'm back at square one."

"I'm sure as hell glad you recognize that, sir."

"I'm back with the crunch."

"Yes."

"I'm going to have to come to a decision."

"I know that must be loathsome, sir."

"You know," Halliday said, "Lyndon Johnson was a master of consensus politics. A master at parceling out the perks. The farmers get this much, labor gets that much, business gets so much. Kept everybody on the team that way. But he came up against something that couldn't be parceled out. He couldn't parcel out the Vietnam War. You were either for it or against it. He didn't know what to do with that. It ruined him. I don't want that to happen to me."

"You're going to catch holy hell either way," Crowley replied. "Why not go with what feels right?"

The motorcade was speeding along and Halliday was sitting there thinking about the crunch and GOD and how Crowley would be the last one in Congress to know anything about GOD when the other one, God, intervened. The phone rang. Akers picked it up. His face was absolutely flat. Then he said, "Okay," and hung it up.

"Richard Nixon just died," he said flatly.

Nixon had really fucked things up. To his last gasp the man had been a spoiler. They were going to cancel the Texas leg of the trip, where Halliday had been scheduled to address Southern Methodist University. Akers already had the two emergency writers they had brought along with them at work on a public statement that Halliday would incorporate into his remarks at Michigan University.

But Keyes had another breather. The Michigan University speech wasn't worth remembering either, so he was free to wander for an hour. He strolled along pleasant undergraduate pathways, thinking about Doc

Halliday's problem. One part of the conservative establishment wanted to obliterate the Soviet Union. Irradiate it. Wipe it off the map. Others preferred spending it to death. Still others were willing to coexist and even do business with it. It was the coexisters that Halliday had to win over; the others were hopeless.

He was feeling an occasional buzzing in his head. It was the kind of buzz that he sometimes felt right before getting an idea for a political slogan. This time it was different; the buzzing was persisting over a long period, as though his brain needed time to assemble the components and make the connections, as though it was going to be a Big Idea. He tried to grasp it, to hold his mind loose so the idea would feel welcome, no matter how outrageous it might be, but he was interrupted by something.

Singing.

Peace on the earth, goodwill to men.

The Twenty-fifth of December Movement was behind its usual barricades, singing Christmas carols in the springtime. The same signs, the same clothes. Maybe even the same faces. They might have been fiendishly transported from the Columbia campus to Michigan. Keyes could hear a spectral voice saying: Set up Michigan University.

They were the other side of the equation. Peace was developing a constituency. Maybe a considerable constituency. But what in hell did the Twenty-fifth of December Movement have to do with the GOD Project? His head went on buzzing, even as he felt a finger tapping on his shoulder. It was Moody.

"I know exactly how long the speech is. We've got forty-seven minutes to play with. I'm buying the coffee."

There was a coffee shop on campus which was mobbed, but they managed to grab a tiny table that wasn't much bigger than the two coffee mugs.

"You fascinate me," Moody said.

"I'm really very boring," Keyes said.

Moody flashed his big friendly shark grin.

"I ran into the porters who were supposed to move you from the fourth floor of the EOB to the first floor. Now, apart from the fact that it's preposterous that you are getting a first-floor office, there was nothing to move. No records, no documents, no files. Nothing. They took your nameplate off the door and carried it downstairs. Now what the hell is going on, Keyes? Who the hell are you?"

"I'm nobody; who are you?"

166

"You've been listening to Pope shave."

"It's better than the radio."

"Answer the question, please."

"Do you mean to tell me that you even grill the White House *porters?*"

"Are you kidding? Porters and cleaning ladies are among my best sources. What can you tell me?"

"About what?"

"Anything. Anything."

Keyes sipped at his fourth coffee, and it felt restorative. He needed restoring. His mind was being permanently polluted with every hour that went by.

"The crunch is coming," he said to Moody.

"What crunch?"

"The war over pie."

"Pie, huh? What kind of pie?"

Keyes thought about all the movements in Latin America that the general had talked about earlier. He tried to get his best Spanish accent into it.

"Madre's apple pie," he said.

"The war over Madre's apple pie is coming, huh? I can really use that in a press conference. What the hell are you talking about?"

"I shouldn't have told you that much. Forget I said it, will you?"

"I never forget a thing," Moody said.

"How awful for you," Keyes said.

Plans were changing even as they were driving back to Air Force One. Akers spent the entire trip with Lincoln One's telephone against his ear, making arrangements for Halliday to view the remains of Richard Nixon, console the widow, touch a few conservative bases, be magnanimous, consider the possibility of laying out Nixon in state in the Capitol. But the networking continued.

This time they were picking the brain of Arthur Holland, professor of nuclear physics at UCLA. Halliday valued him because he was one of a small but growing group of scientists who were refusing to work on defense projects and therefore could be counted on to give an opinion about current military research without the usual salesmanship.

"I want your opinion about the Strategic Defense Initiative," Halliday said. "I mean, what the hell is that damn thing? It's supposed to be

167

on the back burner, and yet they want twelve billion for it next year. I could certainly use that money elsewhere."

Holland had done original work on laser fusion, and there was a postulate named after him. He was good enough to be still teaching and doing research at a university that made quite a bit of money from military projects; he attracted students and faculty both, so he was tolerated. Holland was small and slightly built. He had almost vanishingly thin blondish hair and an easy smile and manner.

"Star Wars makes no sense as a defensive system. The Bush administration was the first to admit it publicly, but it was obvious all along. The surprise is that the thing didn't get laughed out of existence long before."

Holland grimaced as though pained by the perfidy of fellow scientists.

"Star Wars doesn't even respond to submarine-launched cruise missiles," he went on. "And it requires the *cooperation* of the Soviets to keep their total number of missiles small, because it can easily be saturated by a lot of warheads and decoys. The first head of the program admitted that publicly. So as a defensive system, SDI is preposterous. If the Strategic Defense Initiative is anything, it's an offensive system."

"That's my Law of Slogans and Acronyms," Akers said from his jump seat, hand over the mouthpiece of the telephone. "All slogans and acronyms conceal their opposites. Which makes it the Strategic Offense Initiative."

"That sounds about right," Holland said.

"How is it an offensive system?" Halliday asked, waving and smiling at a crowd of people lining the curbside.

"If you can hit an ICBM shortly after it comes out of its silo," Holland said, "you can hit it while it's still *in* the silo. That makes it a first-strike weapon, which is the Pentagon's specialty. You can hit other things too, for that matter. Like the Kremlin. Command and control centers, and so on. The right wing thinks it's going to have Zeus up in orbit hurling thunderbolts down at any commie who doesn't salute the American flag."

Halliday was right on it.

"Zeus, huh? I thought the word was GOD?"

"Exactly. Hell, the right wing thinks it's God in any case."

Halliday and Keyes eyeballed for half a second. Nothing.

"Nonfanatics call it Keynesianism," Holland continued. "Which is probably what it really is."

168

"Keynesianism," Akers said expressionlessly.

"Military Keynesianism," Holland said.

"Military Keynesianism," Akers said.

"I guess the more common term is pump-priming. Plus pork. You know, this thing started during Reagan's watch, and fifty percent of the money goes to California companies. The most accurate name of all for it is the Strategic Pork Initiative. Star Pork."

"But if it's anything at all, it's an escalation of the arms race," Halliday said, "disguised as a defense system."

"That's it."

Halliday was wiggling his fingers at a baby a woman was holding over her head.

"But that isn't what bothers me," Holland said.

"What bothers you?" Akers said innocently.

Holland was trying not to sound mysterious and conspiratorial and paranoid, but in dealing with the U.S. government it was getting harder and harder not to sound mysterious and conspiratorial and paranoid.

"What bothers me is that the Pentagon and the U.S. establishment rarely back off from pushing an offensive system. No matter how improbable or expensive it sounds—like the B-2 bomber—they stick with it until they get it. Sometimes it takes a decade to get funded, but sooner or later they go into production. And yet they quietly backed off from this one and put it on the back burner without a real fight. I wonder about that."

"*Why* do you wonder about that?" Akers said.

"It's not a defensive system. It's an offensive system. And yet they've quietly deemphasized it. Unusual. Untypical. I wonder."

"What do you wonder?" Akers said, his cool slipping slightly.

"I wonder if it might be something else altogether. Something that we don't know about."

Keyes, Akers, and Halliday all sat there quietly, nodding their heads up and down. Keyes was feeling the buzzing in his head again. Some kind of idea was percolating. He looked over at his President. His President was scratching his balls. His President was looking bemused. What the hell else could Star Wars be? Could Star Wars be the GOD Project in disguise?

Akers had dug up a bonus. He had gotten Shelby W. Gutteridge to agree to fly in Air Force One if they would drop him off at Bowling Green,

Kentucky. It was out of the way, but it would be educational. Halliday needed to be exposed to the likes of Shelby W. Gutteridge, by way of knowing your enemy. Gutteridge was *the* most right-wing senator. He was *the* dirtiest fighter in all of Congress. His political career was strewn with corpses, foolish politicians who had thought they could take on old Shelby.

Gutteridge looked at Keyes as if at a spirochete.

"I'd like you to meet my executive secretary, Malcolm Keyes."

Gutteridge sipped at a bourbon.

"What the hell kind of title is that for a man?" he said. "Secretaries are girls. Unless you happen to be the Secretary of Defense, although I happen to think the current one *is* a girl."

"What would you recommend, Senator?" Akers put in.

"Well, give him a manly title, anyway. Say, executive assistant."

"I like it," the President replied. "Malcolm, you're now my executive assistant."

"That was a fast promotion," Keyes said. "Thanks, Senator."

"You have to speak up in this world," Shelby Gutteridge replied. "Passivity never got anyone anything. Passive is what a woman is when she's getting fucked."

Gutteridge reveled in his reputation for being a below-the-belt fighter. As a campaigner, he was hell on wheels. Some people said that the entire state of Kentucky still smelled from the negative advertising he had used on his last opponent.

"Too bad about Dick," he said, "but to tell you the truth, I never completely trusted him. Deep down he was pinko."

"Nixon?" Halliday said, unable to control his right eyebrow.

"Yeah, Nixon."

"How come?"

"That damn policy of détente. Him and Kissinger both. Set us back years."

"Set us back at what?" Halliday said.

Now it was Gutteridge's eyebrow that went up.

"I'm new at this," Halliday said, shrugging.

"Turning it into a capitalist Russia," Gutteridge said. "A capitalist Russia or *no* damn Russia."

Keyes had divided the right wing into two groups: fanatics and cold asses. Gutteridge was a fanatic, a true believer. It was good vs. evil. The followers of the Lord against the followers of Satan. Accommodation was impossible; war was inevitable. The cold asses were right-wingers

170

who didn't feel it in the gut but who adopted the same line because it was good for the career; you automatically had a major part of the establishment behind you.

"Now the question is, how do we keep the suckers in line," Gutteridge told Halliday. "That's the basic problem of every guvment. Different guvments use different methods. In this country, it's a little tricky because we have these goddam elections all the time."

"They are a bother," Halliday said, but the irony was lost, lost.

"Now, I'm not the wild man people think I am. I well understand that you're going to have political problems going into the Philippines. You're going to have to finesse it. Go in sideways. Call it a drug bust. You can get other countries to do a lot of the dirty work for you. Israel, the Saudis, South Africa. We have good friends, and you can count on them. As long as we can lord it over the peasants in the Philippines and elsewhere, we can lord it over the peasants in *this* country. You can't have the latter without the former, and that's what the arms race is all about. The nukes give you the umbrella to go in under. The Russians won't dare screw around. After that, it's all domestic politics. How good are you at it?"

Keyes spotted Halliday's right hand moving toward his inside jacket pocket. The cigar, and therefore the question, was imminent. The usual two wooden matches were struck, and just before touching flame to cigar, Halliday said lightly, "Well, at least I've got God on my side, huh? That's worth something in the balance."

Gutteridge's eyes blinked once, slowly. He was working on Halliday's face, but Halliday was blithely concentrating on his cigar. Gutteridge looked at Keyes and Akers. They were the picture of innocence.

"Uh, yeah, sure. God. Right. He's on our side."

Bingo, Keyes thought. There really was a GOD.

Keyes stuck his head under the shower nozzle and turned COLD to the extreme clockwise position. He briefly considered holding his face up with his mouth open, drowning in a standing position. But the attendant who was holding his shirt, T-shirt, tie, and jacket would probably have saved him. They probably held drowning drills on Air Force One all the time.

The conflicts seemed intractable. Nothing gave an inch. General Pickering: Low Intensity Conflict is the answer to the crunch. Joe Crowley: Low Intensity Conflict is bullshit. Go in and you're a kid killer;

171

stay out and you're a commie. And always, the likes of Shelby Gutteridge breathing down your neck. Gutteridge, that unholy son of a
bitch, knew what the GOD Project was. And GOD made the problems
go away. What a nice GOD, a benign GOD. *All* the problems!

And then there was that professorial little man from UCLA with his
funny questions about Star Wars. Was that thing the GOD Project? But
how could missile defense solve the Vietnam Syndrome? There was no
apparent connection unless Star Wars, too, was bullshit. But what else
could it be? What high-tech device could solve the Vietnam Syndrome?
The whole thing was a mess. Keyes began to feel a buzzing in his head
that wouldn't go away. It was a feeling that was one step below a
headache. He sensed that his tired brain was working on an idea. *The*
idea. The solution. Nothing less than the meaning of GOD.

Keyes turned COLD to extreme counter clockwise and toweled off.
Then he stood there feeling like a poodle while the attendant blow-dried
his hair. They were getting to the end of the trip. New Jersey and
Richard Nixon weren't too far off, but there were miles to go yet.

Akers, who tried not to miss any possibilities, had managed to line
up George Rothweiler, getting him flown to Bowling Green, Kentucky,
by the time Air Force One arrived to drop off Senator Gutteridge.
Rothweiler was yet another improbable quest for Halliday, but Halliday
wanted to hear the bad news, and he was sure to get it from Rothweiler.
There was almost nobody who would turn down a ride on Air Force
One and an opportunity to tell the President of the United States how to
do his job.

It was improbable, because Rothweiler was an arch-right-wing think-
tanker. A theorist. A man who spent his days at the Free Market
Institute, looking at the harsh realities, gazing into the abyss, thinking
thoughts; in Rothweiler's world, the unthinkable was thought even
during coffee breaks.

Rothweiler's appearance was as severe as his intellectual approaches.
He was about thirty-five and mostly bald. Rimless eyeglasses, iron-gray
mustache, a hard nose, a firm chin, a trim hard body. He had an unusual
physical presence for someone who spent his workday thinking.

"There are certain imperatives that you're stuck with," he said to
Halliday. "This is what every new President has to learn and adjust to.
There is nothing you can do about it."

The day was starting to get long, and Halliday was having his first
scotch off the rocks.

"What's the bad news?" he asked.

Rothweiler smiled. It was obvious that he was searching for words that would let the new President down easily. How did you tell a child about hell and damnation?

"I don't know how far you've thought these things through, so suppose I start at the beginning?"

"Fine."

"The first thing you'll have to take into account is capitalism's dirty secret. It's the skeleton in the closet and there's no way you can get around it. I mean, if you want to be realistic."

"What would that be?" Akers said, his eyebrows revealing a *soupçon* of emotion.

"That capitalism doesn't work," Rothweiler said. Then he giggled. It was probably a nervous giggle. After all, he was talking to the Big Cheese and the Big Cheese was looking rancid. And yet it was a basic proposition. Elementary, my dear Watson. Any President who didn't face up to it would walk into a buzzsaw.

"Capitalism doesn't work, that is, without a big military budget," he added. "The more advanced the capitalism, the more military budget you need. Otherwise you get a recession or a depression. *We* need a *big* military budget."

Halliday started feeling for a cigar. Akers had become a total blank. Keyes was tuned into the music, which was atonal and grating and minimalist. Rothweiler continued to elaborate on the obvious.

"With all his liberal New Deal programs, Roosevelt was unable to end the thirties depression. It took nothing less than World War Two to do that. Truman had the Korean War. Then Eisenhower tried to keep military spending down and had three recessions in eight years. Kennedy and Reagan both understood the situation. They both spent Pentagon budget like money was going out of style. They both had booms. But you need boom-boom to get a boom."

Rothweiler smiled perfunctorily and sipped chastely at his Perrier. Rothweiler neither smoked nor drank. Rothweiler thought. Rothweiler pursed his lips. Rothweiler unconsciously made a kiss sound.

"The reality is," he went on, "that military spending soaks up excess GNP which otherwise would just lie there. Know what I mean? It funnels the money to corporations that hire workers. That's capitalism. Now, you might argue, since I realize, sir, that you're a liberal, why not use that excess GNP to build homes for the homeless and so forth?"

"That's a thought," Halliday said noncommitally.

"But you'd be undermining your own premise. That is to say, the capitalist premise. You'd be competing with the private sector. That, sir, of course, is socialism. Mixed economy stuff at a minimum. That's the sort of thing they do in Nicaragua." He dismissed Nicaragua with the fluttering of a few fingers.

"Worse yet, you'd create a well-fed, educated lower class that begins to make demands for even more redistribution of wealth downward. One person one vote, remember. These people might start *voting*."

"You make things sound bleak," Halliday said, searching absently for his wooden matches. The frigate wanted to "make smoke" and disappear.

"It gets worse before it gets better," Rothweiler replied. "Your other major imperative is that we must have constantly expanding markets abroad. We cannot consume everything we make at home. Try that and you're back on the recession slash depression slash socialist route.

"*But*. Every time a Third World country goes socialist we *lose* market opportunities. We lose more control. We lose the ability to buy and sell at good prices. So we cannot survive as capitalists in a socialist world. It's impossible. Fortunately, there's a bright side to all this."

"There's a way out of this mess, is there?" Akers said.

"You need an enemy, of course. To justify the Pentagon budget. Okay, you've got a beauty. The Soviet Union. The communist devils. *And* there's the added advantage that anytime a country goes socialist we can call it Soviet expansionism. So we can use the Soviets not only to justify the Pentagon budget but to also justify going into the Philippines or anyplace else that tries socialism. But of course there's a problem here too."

"Peace keeps threatening to break out," Akers mumbled.

Rothweiler sipped thoughtfully at his Perrier, eyes squinting, deep in concentration. The think tanker was floating in concepts, making connections.

"This is going to sound like a funny way to put it," he said. "Possibly even paranoid. But you could view these persistent Russian attempts at disarmament as a communist plot to destroy capitalism in America."

He sat back and looked around for responses.

Halliday made smoke, thought, worked a tic through his body. He was waiting for Akers to say something brilliant. Akers didn't say a word.

"You realize," Halliday said finally, "that politics is a world of perceptions."

"Absolutely."

174

"Many Americans believe the Russians are being peaceful. That they're genuine."

"West Europeans too," Rothweiler said. "You've got big problems with NATO."

"And they do in fact seem to be genuine."

"That is true," Rothweiler said slowly. "Peace is a serious obstacle to preparations for war."

"So what do you recommend?" Halliday said.

Rothweiler actually looked indecisive. He was squirming. Reluctant to speak. Embarrassed.

"We can take it," Akers said.

"Okay. I guess it comes to being a test of leadership. Perhaps the supreme test in a democracy."

"Okay," Halliday said evenly, trying to encourage him.

"For what it's worth," Rothweiler added, "I thought George Bush was rather good at it. He always solemnly welcomed the Soviet moves, but he quietly downplayed their significance. 'This looks like real progress.' 'We're taking a very serious look at this.' 'This seems to represent a real departure from the usual Soviet line' etc., etc., etc., lose 'em around the bend. But getting him to cut the military budget was pulling teeth."

Rothweiler looked at them. He looked wary. He knew whom he was talking to but it was open and shut. This is the way it was: heavy military spending or socialism.

"I take it then that you're for Star Wars?"

"Definitely. It's a wonderful opportunity to use up GNP. In a capitalist fashion. And if you get boxed into a corner and have to cut some military programs, you could take up some of the slack with space exploration. You can't spend *real* bucks on space, but it can plug a hole. Bush started that ball rolling back when he wasn't sure what kind of disarmament proposal would come winging at him next."

"And you're in favor of going into the Philippines."

"Definitely. Negative reinforcement. Wear them down. Never give up. It wouldn't be the first Hundred Years War. It's just going to have to go on and on. That's what it takes to defend our system. It's the task of each generation."

"A hundred years' war," Halliday mused.

"It has to be fought on the sly, I'll grant you," Rothweiler said.

"Well, maybe with the aid of God we can succeed."

Rothweiler didn't answer. He just sat there.

175

"You mean you don't believe in God?"

Rothweiler smiled.

"I haven't made up my mind yet."

At Newark, Bishop John Chandler joined them for the ride in Lincoln One to Nixon's home. Keyes had expected someone with a miter and purple robe, but Chandler showed up in a dark conservative business suit with a power tie.

·Bishop Chandler was a Methodist and a member of the United Methodist Church. But he had the look of a Mississippi riverboat gambler about him. He was smooth and charming and totally at his ease. Keyes was beginning to be amazed by the number of people who were not intimidated by the President of the United States.

It was dark now and there was no one to wave at, so Halliday was able to pay full attention.

"What do you think, Bishop? What have you got to tell me? The floor is yours."

"Drop the bomb," the bishop said, eyeballing Halliday for any possible reaction.

Keyes wanted to break in; he saw it and Halliday didn't. But it was out of the question.

"On whom?" Halliday asked.

"On no one. Walk away from the damn things. Get us a test ban treaty. *End* the misery, for God's sake."

"I agree with you, Bishop, but that's easier said than done."

"May I speak frankly?"

"The kind I like."

"The warheads are nuts."

"I agree."

"So does the American public."

"Yes."

"Then why do we still have the bombs?"

"They have a significant constituency."

"As far as I have been able to see," the bishop said, "the only people on the *planet* who want to keep the bombs are the elites of the Western democracies."

Halliday nodded up and down for a few seconds.

"I agree," he said finally.

"The Soviets would fall all over themselves to get a test ban treaty. Their GNP is half ours. Maybe only a third. They don't want the arms

176

race. They can't possibly win an arms race. It must be bloody murder trying to stay in the arms race. Well, hell, they've quit."

"Certainly."

"Then what can be done about this constituency of the bomb?"

"Believe me, I'm working on it."

"I have, frankly, come to the conclusion that the nuclear hawks in this country are, at a *minimum,* a bunch of goddam fools. And I have not taken the Lord's name in vain if I have influenced your thought processes at all."

"I'm in a position to say that you have not taken the Lord's name in vain."

"The Catholic cardinals are starting to come around too, and *that's* like raising the *Titanic.* If you can get a test ban treaty, you will have a lot of popular support, and you can count on the Methodist bishops to support you from their pulpits. That is a promise."

"Bishop, I'm going to hold you to that promise," Halliday said. "I'm going to get a lot of flak getting a test ban, and I'll need every rifle I can get on my side."

"Onward Christian soldiers," Bishop Chandler said.

Nixon was laid out in the dining room of his New Jersey home.

Halliday and Akers and Bishop Chandler were off somewhere paying their respects to the widow. Keyes was sitting on a folding chair watching the coffin, and the two marines standing guard over it, one at each end, and at Henry Kissinger, who was looking down at his old boss, and who had probably always looked down at his old boss, but who had to be having funny feelings about the meaning of it all; Tricky Dick and Tricky Henry were going to end up in the same place. Then Kissinger turned away from the casket and hurried out of the room, not even noticing Keyes.

Keyes wandered over to the casket. He looked in and shook his head. Nixon didn't even look sincerely dead. He looked as if he were faking it, still working on his rehabilitation, one final play for public sympathy before getting up and running for Congress again. To Keyes, the mood was pure Prokofiev, the *Lieutenant Kijé Suite,* the tongue-in-cheek death march for an empty coffin.

"Did he wink yet?" Halliday said, coming in.

Keyes glanced at the nearest marine. His face was a total blank but Keyes had the feeling they had just ruined his life.

"I'm beginning to think he's dead," Keyes said.

177

"I'm beginning to see a measure of consolation in the human condition," Akers said. "There is something to be said for mortality. There *are* limits. You can't run forever. No matter how bad they are, sooner or later we get rid of them, all of them."

"He's shoveling sulfur in hell right now," Halliday said. "He has ten thousand years of it ahead of him. Nothing but shoveling burning sulfur, day and night. But it'll be good therapy. When the ten thousand years are up, we will, at long last, finally have the New Nixon."

Akers coughed to keep from laughing in front of the two marines.

"You've got to give the devil his due," Akers said. "What a character. The premier red-baiter in the country turns out to be the one to recognize Red China. Until Nixon, you know, China was a tiny island off the coast of Asia. On top of that, he told the Soviets he was willing not to blow up their country. Probably the only politician in the country who could have done it, except maybe for Ronnie XIV. The question is, does it take a Nixon to make peace? For your sake, Mr. President, I hope not."

Seeing Nixon in his coffin was having a strange effect on Keyes. He was feeling faint. The buzzing in his brain was very strong. He was starting to sweat. He sat down on one of the folding chairs, trying to figure out what was happening to him. Halliday's voice was only a drone in the background as the sweat poured down his face. He took a guess. It might have something to do with memory. One of the basic premises that had guided Richard Nixon was that most Americans forgot most political events within three weeks of their occurrence, after which you could proceed as though they had never happened: Only Keyes remembered, because his memory was endless and infinite.

He kept trying to focus on Nixon. What was Nixon trying to tell him? Nixon had dealt with the Vietnam problem. In his fashion. He'd managed to bomb a foreign country without any Americans knowing about it. For a while, anyway. Cambodia. It was the ideal operation, when you thought about it. *High* Intensity Conflict that was *still* a secret. Nixon had tried to solve the Vietnam Syndrome while the Vietnam War was still going on. But it all came to nothing. You couldn't deceive that much. It was too difficult. It was impossible. How could you fight a war—how could a democracy fight a war—which the people of that democracy didn't want to fight?

He was feeling nauseous now. Nixon had been right. People drank of the waters of Lethe, the river of forgetfulness—the stuff was pumped into every municipal waterworks—and they forgot things like World

178

War One and the Holocaust. It enabled political leaders to get away with almost *anything*. And Nixon had, up to a point. But there was a *limit*.

Something was happening. The nausea was fading away. He began to feel cool. The dizziness was going. Even the buzzing in his head had vanished. Halliday's voice suddenly started to tune in.

"You know something?" the President was saying. "Nixon said he wasn't a crook. He was wrong. It is impossible to be President of the United States without being a felon. And probably a serial murderer. Hell, let's get back to Washington."

Halliday started to go, then stopped, turned, looked at the coffin.

"Oh, by the way," he said, in tones of pure acid. "Give my regards to Lyndon, will you?"

Keyes stood up and followed the President and Akers out of the room. His mind was clear. The idea had arrived. He knew what the GOD Project was.

Moody and Akers had a ride waiting for them at Andrews Air Force Base, so only Keyes accompanied the President on Marine One back to the White House.

Halliday was exhausted. It was three in the morning. The day wasn't ending any too soon. He took his jacket off and simply threw it away. Then his shoes. He sat in his chair and adjusted it for maximum horizontalness.

"Make the scotch, Malcolm," he said.

Keyes opened a wooden cabinet attached to the rear of the cockpit cabin and made two straight warm scotches, giving Halliday three times as much as he gave himself. He had to touch Halliday's hand with the glass; Halliday's eyes were closed.

"You see what a mess things are," he said, taking the drink.

"It's worse than I ever dreamed. I don't think I'll ever recover from today. I'm scarred for life."

Halliday quaffed.

"You know," he said slowly, "some countries are more difficult to deal with than others. We are one of the tough ones. The Soviets are too. And the Israelis. Most Americans seem to think that we're pushovers, but we're not. We're hard as nails. We're as tough as the Israelis and the Soviets, maybe tougher. Of course, it's easy to see why the Israelis are tough. The leadership all have the Holocaust in their heads. Six million people killed senselessly. That's what you call a trauma. The Soviets

179

have the same thing. Twenty million dead in World War Two. All of European Russia ravaged, all the way to the Volga, to the southern edge of the Caucasus, to the suburbs of Moscow, Leningrad besieged for two years. That's traumatic, Malcolm. That makes you difficult."

Halliday was silent for a while, and Keyes, listening to the beat of the rotors, was beginning to think he was asleep. He wanted to tell Halliday about the GOD Project, but he was inhibited. His idea was both plausible and ridiculous. It was both outrageous and sensible. It explained things. It explained *everything*. A theory that fit the data so precisely had to be a good theory. But he wasn't quite ready to risk looking like a fool to Doc Halliday.

Halliday opened his eyes and sucked at his scotch.

"But *what* is the American trauma? What makes *us* so tough? When I was a kid I thought it was Pearl Harbor. But Pearl Harbor wasn't that big. Three thousand dead compared with twenty million. The battleships and cruisers that were sunk were obsolescent. The Japanese missed the carriers, which were at sea. *Those* were the capital ships of World War Two.

"No, it wasn't Pearl Harbor. Eventually I decided it was something that happened on the Eastern Front in World War One."

"But our troops were on the Western Front in World War One."

Halliday loosened his tie and opened his collar.

"It had nothing to do with our troops. You see, what happened was that after the Russian Revolution in 1917, the Soviets wanted to get out of the war. They called for an armistice with the Germans, who were tickled to death to get it. The Germans wanted peace with Russia so they could switch one million German troops to the Western Front to counter the Americans who were coming on line. But the peace negotiations between Russia and Germany dragged on. And while it was dragging on, the German soldier was fraternizing with the Russian soldier. But the Russians, by this time, were all Bolsheviks. The plague bacillus spread to the Germans. It was that easy. So many Germans became converted to communism that Germany never did get that million-man bonus. Those million troops became unreliable soldiers, unwilling to get themselves killed fighting for one set of imperialist masters against another. Now *there's* a trauma. That's a big one. That ranks with the six million and the twenty million. Why, the leadership in almost every democratic country of the world had to go crazy over that one. That's where the anticommunist fever started."

Keyes sipped scotch and made a face, which Halliday didn't see because his eyes were closed, and listened to the rotors to make sure everything was working right, and said, *"That's* the American trauma?"

"No."

"No?"

"I changed my mind. The American trauma is even more fundamental than that. It goes back much farther than that. The real American trauma occurred in 1791."

"1791?"

"Are you ready for this, Malcolm?" Halliday threw the rest of his scotch down his throat and dropped the empty glass on the floor of the chopper. "That's the year Congress added on the Bill of Rights to the Constitution. The Bill of Rights is the trauma. It made Americans too free. Freedom of the press. Freedom of speech. Good God. Made it difficult to fool the public. The big rich have been walking on eggs ever since, terrified that the secret would get out."

For the first time, the scotch seemed to go down well. Keyes looked at his glass with a raised eyebrow. He was really getting into politics.

"Uh, what secret would that be?" Keyes asked, watching Halliday's face. The eyes were still closed, but he was wide awake.

"That in a country where we have one person, one vote, everything is run for the benefit of the big rich. And that isn't easy to hide."

When Marine One got to the White House, the fire and medical people were waiting, as always. Once again, Marine One didn't crash. Halliday and Keyes both forgot about Halliday's shoes. He walked into the White House in his stocking feet and coatless, but he'd remembered to thank the pilots. It was 3:30 A.M.

Halliday made a presidential decision not to floss his teeth. He was in his pajamas in a minute. Keyes turned down the covers for him, and the President climbed in looking gray and exhausted.

"Malcolm," he said.

"Yes, sir."

"Did you get it all?"

"Yes, sir, I got it all."

"All the he saids and the I saids?"

"All of it."

"Good man, Malcolm. We're going to use all that stuff later on. Gonna write a book."

181

"Uh, Mr. President."

"Yes, Malcolm?"

"I know what the GOD Project is."

"What?"

"I know what the GOD Project is."

"Zzzzzzzzzzzzzzz," Doc Halliday said.

Keyes switched off the light and quietly slipped out of the room. He had the biggest secret in government and nobody to tell it to. He strolled to his big, fancy perk of a parking space and drove home.

20

TRADING HORSE

RICHARD HALLIDAY HAD finally made a tentative, noncommitting, reversible decision about the GOD Project. He was getting tactical: thinking pork, trading horse, counting vote, slapping back. Issuing invitations to seductions in the White House Rose Garden; all congressmen slavered over picture-taking in the Rose Garden. He had been in office long enough now to have the lay of the land. He had slight majorities in both houses of Congress, but the conservatives in both parties were already planning to blow his nuclear test ban treaty out of the water, and liberal support for it was weak, tentative, Jell-O, which was par.

Halliday and his executive assistant were in the office-of-no-straight-lines, waiting for the shootout to start: Himself, Elmer Jessup of the CIA, was coming for a visit and there was going to be gunplay. Furthermore, it was 4:00 P.M., close to the evening news deadline, which could hardly be called the moment of truth for politicians but which, nevertheless, was what the government aimed for seven days a week.

"Conservatives love bombs," Halliday was saying. "The bigger the bomb, the better they like it. I doubt if you will ever find so exotic a creature as a conservative dove; it would be a fundamental contradiction. Bombs give power to elites over masses; that's their attraction."

183

"I hate to hear you talk like that," Keyes replied. "You make it seem hopeless."

"Not hopeless. Never say hopeless. Challenging, Malcolm. I'm going to trade horse. A test ban for the GOD Project. Even Steven. That is, *assuming* you're right about the GOD Project. And I'll grant you it's a good theory. It seems to solve the establishment's major problems. It sounds juicy enough for the conservatives to be willing to trade their *pants* to get it. The price will be support for a test ban which will bring the arms race to an end. The nuclear test ban is the key to everything, the key to sanity, to ending the nightmare of the Cold War. But you heard what I heard yesterday. It's going to take a bit of doing."

There was no doubt that Elmer Jessup and most other conservatives thought of Halliday as a liberal wimp. What they didn't know about was the Byzantine quality of New York politics; they had never seen Halliday at work. The plan was to have Halliday and Jessup sitting in opposing easy chairs, with Keyes in a mean, subservient straight chair facing both of them, but closer to Jessup. That way Jessup would have to break eye contact with Halliday in order to look at Keyes. Conceivably, he might even forget Keyes was there; there was an organizing principle involved when Richard Halliday went to the bathroom.

Halliday personally opened the door of the Oval Office at his secretary's knock, anything to catch the son of a bitch off guard: a presidential hand suddenly outthrust, big smile, pat on the back. Jessup and Halliday were natural enemies. Jessup was a hard-line, right-wing hawk who, left to his own devices, would have nuked the Soviet Union long since. *Then* he would have taken on black welfare mothers with color television sets, whereas Halliday would have tried to get them federally subsidized service contracts concealed as Technological Upgrading for Urban Areas.

Jessup promptly refused coffee, brandy, and sherry. Jessup was there to be fired, and he was going to go out with good, conservative dignity, not parleying with the enemy. He had stayed on for a few months to enable Halliday to canvass the field, but now his time had come.

"Well, Elmer," Halliday said, "you and I have to be classic exemplars of that old saying. We are *strangest* bedfellows, wouldn't you say?"

Jessup refused to concede that there had been any graciousness in Halliday's approach.

"That is certainly true," he said bleakly.

"Nevertheless, I have a favor to ask."

"I'll be glad to assist in the transition as best I can," Jessup said flatly, no conviction, no emotion, rote, reciting his lines according to the standard script—the doomed man about to walk the plank.

Halliday was playing with him, dragging it out, making the torture exquisite. There was absolutely no point in being easy on Elmer Jessup.

"Quite frankly, I was thinking about something more than a transition. The truth is, there's no surplus of able candidates to fill your job. So I was hoping you could stay on for a year or so. That would give me stability and experience in an important position, and who knows, we might make a team."

Jessup was suffering from cognitive dissonance. Halliday had achieved total military surprise. Keyes was seeing wheels within wheels in Jessup's eyes. Jessup's psyche—which had to be a veritable funhouse—was probably firing off all kinds of laser rays and particle beams. But the tone of his voice suddenly changed. It struck Keyes that he was suddenly listening to a Princeton cardsharp who has just been asked by a rich widow lady if he'd like to play poker.

"Well, I *had* been planning on going back to the private sector, make a little money, but if you think I can still make a contribution, I'd be glad to help out."

Halliday smiled graciously and leaned across the gap between them and offered his hand to Jessup, who managed to get his own hand up without taking too long a time. This was one of Halliday's specialties: making nice with mortal enemies. He was good at supping with the devil, and with the shortest kind of spoon. Halliday regularly offered deals which the other guy grabbed at hungrily but which usually ended up bringing home the bacon for Halliday; he'd been pulling that stuff for years in New York. But Keyes saw that he was rubbing his hands again, which was a bad habit. It made it look as if ownership of a famous bridge had just changed hands.

The reality was that a flaky liberal President needed a rock-solid conservative in a spot like the CIA. It gave the liberal credibility. It reassured the right wing. It took the pressure off a bit. But there was a price to pay. Money, in this case.

"McKay's last budget called for a budget increase of three point five percent plus inflation," Jessup said. "Is that agreeable with you?"

"I thought it was two point five," Halliday said.

"Three point five," Jessup said, and Keyes was covertly nodding his head up and down for Halliday's benefit.

Halliday started feeling for a cigar.

"Why do you need that much?"

Jessup thought. He hadn't expected substantive questions.

"For one thing, the price of European politicians has gone way up. Italy, France, Germany, Britain. As the U.S. gets more unpopular with different populations, the price goes higher and higher. *And* we've got major covert efforts all around the globe. Nicaragua. Honduras. Guatemala. El Salvador. Angola. The Philippines. Chile. Mexico. South Korea. The Middle East." He had rattled the names off almost as though they were election districts in the U.S. All around the globe there were people trying to rouse local populations to revolt against law and order, against the status quo. "Maintaining the status quo is the most expensive project there is," Jessup said. "The only thing more expensive is not maintaining the status quo."

"But we're rapidly going broke doing it."

"Three point five percent," Jessup said.

Halliday nodded and thought and said, "Three point five percent." Then he gestured with an eyebrow at Keyes, who promptly went to what looked like a proper Chippendale sideboard but which a flick of the wrist turned into a wet bar. It also contained a concealed shredder. Generally speaking, Halliday's bar was an all-purpose problem solver. Keyes ostentatiously opened a bottle of Soave Bolla they'd had on ice to make Jessup's wine spritzer, Southern-style, with lime instead of lemon. Coming back with the tray, Keyes caught Jessup looking at him. For an undercover type, Jessup had a remarkably transparent face. Who is this guy? Jessup's face was saying. What the hell is he doing here? He doesn't contribute anything. He doesn't even take notes. What is his purpose?

"Let's see, now," Halliday was saying. "Moody can make the announcement in time for the evening news, if that's all right with you?"

"Fine," Jessup said.

As the President and his Director of Central Intelligence clinked glasses, Jessup tried to smile. It was pathetic. He couldn't do it. From a geniality point of view, the man was impotent; he could not get the corners of his mouth up. His problem was the zygomatic major, the muscle that pulls lip corners up. Jessup's was a runt, atrophied, dysfunctional. Whereas his triangularis muscle—which pulls the lip corners down—was an athlete. He spread his lips in a last-ditch attempt, but he ended up looking like a snarling wolf with big teeth that could chew anything.

"Now tell me about the GOD Project," Halliday said. It was offhand,

186

friendly, curious. A President having a tête-à-tête with a top aide. But there was a landslide on Jessup's face. The cardsharp with the funny deck was suddenly looking at four aces, which sort of preempted the four he had up his sleeve.

"Who is this man?" Jessup said.

"Malcolm Keyes. He's an aide of mine. My executive assistant."

"I know he's Malcolm Keyes, but who is he?" He swiveled his head around for a good look at Keyes. "I saw the FBI report on you," he said accusingly.

"They gave him a top secret clearance," Halliday said, sneaking a wink at Keyes.

"How about letting my guys vet him?"

"Elmer, he has my complete trust and confidence. Can we continue?"

Jessup had gotten what he wanted anyway. Time to recover. Time to build his face back up, get his mask back in place. And he had a terrific comeback.

"You've already been completely informed about the GOD Project," he said.

. It was Halliday's face's turn to fall.

"I believe it was the briefing you were given at Langley two days after the election."

"I don't recall that," Halliday said weakly.

"I distinctly remember the occasion. Of course, I could always check the tape of the meeting. As I recall, you didn't seem to be too interested in the technical details."

It was two heavyweights stalking each other, both agile, both counterpunchers, no glass chins here. Jessup had taken good care of himself; Halliday hadn't known the meeting was taped. Halliday glanced involuntarily at his human cassette. *Touché.* Jessup didn't know *this* meeting was being taped.

"We probably started off the briefing with the program's formal name, SCI, for Strategic Computing Initiative, and then you tuned out on the technical details."

"Okay, tell me about the Strategic Computing Initiative."

"It's an unusual operation," Jessup said. "I mean, there are aspects of this operation that are unparalleled in the history of covert operations. SCI has a cover story, plus it has its own reality. But in this case the cover story happens to be *true.* You can't get more plausible than that. When you're hiding behind the *truth,* you're invulnerable."

187

Halliday smiled a connoisseur's smile, in appreciation of the deviousness of the covert mind.

"Tell me how you hide behind the truth," he said.

"The cover story is that it's the Great Leap Forward. An attempt to beat the Japs. They're trying to come up with a fifth-generation computer and screw the world. SCI is going for seventh-generation. It's being developed by a consortium of private computer firms, ninety percent federally funded. The director of the project is Dr. Theodore Monk, who's an artificial intelligence expert. DARPA—Defense Advanced Research Projects Agency—is the federal entity involved. All CIA is doing is providing security. I don't know a whole lot about it."

"That's the cover story and it also happens to be true."

"Yes."

"And what's the real story?"

"It's the brains of the Strategic Defense Initiative. That's what they're really working on."

"Star Wars?"

"Yes."

"A computer for Star Wars? That's the GOD Project?"

"Computers are the major problem. In fact, computers aren't good enough. You need nothing less than artificial intelligence. That's what the GOD Project is."

Keyes was trying to do ESP so that Halliday would ask the right question, and Halliday asked it.

"Does GOD stand for anything?"

"Games of Defense," Jessup replied.

"That's more modest than I expected," Halliday said, deflated.

Keyes had the opposite reaction. These peaceful acronyms of the Pentagon. The most deadly first-strike missile in the inventory was called the Peacekeeper. It should have been named the Peace and Quiet Keeper, the peace and quiet of the graveyard. There was also Peace Is Our Profession, under the aegis of which the Strategic Air Command was ready to destroy the planet on fifteen minutes' notice.

"Games of Defense," Halliday said.

"Yes," Jessup said.

"That's not very godlike."

Jessup shrugged.

Halliday had only one zinger left. He sat back in his chair, hands clasped behind his head, not even looking at Jessup, confident that Malcolm Keyes would be touching that base.

"Who is Albritten looking for?"

Jessup sat there nodding. Thinking and nodding. He had to have been prepared for the question; Keyes himself had been one of the candidates.

"This is embarrassing," Jessup said finally. "I said before that the Strategic Computing Initiative was assigned to us for security reasons. The fact is, we fucked up. Badly. Someone from SCI absconded with significant data, and we're conducting an intensive search for him."

"Really?" Halliday said solicitously. "How unfortunate. Significant data, huh?"

"Yes."

"What is this person's name?"

Jessup looked as if he were sitting in a dentist's chair.

"Henry Patrick."

"Who?"

"Henry Patrick."

"*Henry* Patrick?"

"Yes."

"Henry *Patrick?*"

"Yes."

Halliday nodded. Halliday was having fun. You didn't get opportunities like this too often.

"Found him yet?"

"No."

"Keep me informed, will you?"

Doc Halliday was finally lighting up his cigar, while working a tic through his body. He scrunched up his nose, pursed his lips, jutted out his chin, twisted his neck. The tic was slowly working its way down to his toes while he held two wooden matches to the cigar.

"Games of Defense," he said, puffing. "The way these things usually work out, I suppose, it'll turn out to be Games of Offense. Now there's an acronym for you. GOO. Which is what the military turns people into. Did you get it all?"

"I could draw the shape of his front teeth."

"That guy is dangerous. He slipped it past me and I never knew it."

Halliday sat there, making smoke and finishing his drink.

"It's plausible and implausible at the same time," he said. "Henry Patrick? Games of Defense? The GOD Project is led by a Monk? At the same time, his basic proposition *sounds* reasonable. It's barely possible

189

the son of a bitch is telling the truth. I'll tell you, frankly, Malcolm, I'm inclined to believe Jessup rather than you."

"Yes, sir."

Halliday was still in his chair, drumming his fingers on the armrest, considering possibilities, testing for political balance.

"Okay," he said. "You and the Vice-President will have to test it out. God, how I want you to be right."

21

IN THE PRESENCE OF GOD

AIR FORCE TWO was bumping along the hot, flustered air of the Midwest and Keyes was sitting alone in the press section with a cup of coffee and funny thoughts. In the first place, he was thinking about stealing the cup and saucer, because they had the vice-presidential seal on them. In the second place, his job was too exciting and too educational. It was even painful. He was finding out too much about how things really worked. He was stuck for life with stuff that he didn't want to have anything to do with. How did politicians handle it? And Keyes was only a tool, a mechanism. Halliday and the others had to take responsibility for their acts. Was it possible to be a President and be a moral human being?

He looked over the mimeographed sheet of the day's schedule. Vice-presidential time was precious; the day was ladled out minute by minute. Being this close to power concentrated the mind; *nothing* that Keyes gave his time to was paltry; it was *all* vital, crucial, global, and frightening. Given the importance of the material, it was criminal to feel sorry for yourself. Which Keyes now believed was one of the reasons people bothered going into politics in the first place; you tended to forget about dying, and temporary immortality wasn't to be sneezed at.

He was gazing fondly and greedily at the coffee cup when Osgood came in. Osgood was Madeleine's press guy. Osgood waved him in.

Keyes moved slowly, taking in as much of Air Force Two as he could. It was still only a 707 and ancient; the Vice-President hadn't gotten her 747 yet. He went through a conference room with a long rectangular table, followed by a galley—it could serve eighty meals at once—a sort of living room/den, then a communications center that looked like the combat control center of a guided-missile cruiser, and finally a door with a seal on it.

The first thing that hit him was the hundred-proof perfume. It made his nose crinkle; he was going to have to blow it sooner or later. She had promptly cut through a lot of accumulated Washington air pollution straight to the sinuses, to the erectile tissue in the nose that caused heavy breathing. Then he noticed that while he had been daydreaming and planning the heist of a cup and saucer, the Vice-President had been working. Her white plastic fold-down desk was strewn with memos and documents. Then he noticed Madeleine.

Since they weren't seeing the press that day—they had actually managed to get Air Force Two off the ground at Andrews without half the world finding out about it—Madeleine didn't have to dress down. In order of his gaze: violet silk blouse, gray contoured skirt that didn't hide the figure and went a scootch below the knee, partially dangling earrings, medium-high heels, bracelets on all wrists, a rope of pearls around her throat, and clear nail lacquer. He must have held the gaze a hair too long.

"I'm supposed to charm him, remember?" she said.

"You would have in any case, Madam Vice-President."

"Sit."

Keyes sat on an unpromising looking chair made of metallic tubing with leather thongs connected to the tubing via small springs. It was comfortable. The chair had a tendency to give; however Keyes moved on it, the chair gave; it was an accommodationist chair; it didn't seek confrontations. He rested his arms on the armrests and they gave a little; he crossed his legs and the whole chair worked with him. He tried to assume a mien of appropriate seriousness; in point of fact, he was feeling like Stan Laurel; he was already recalling the scene as "An Interview with Vice President Madeleine Smith at 35,000 Feet," in three sharps.

"What are we looking for, Malcolm?"

"I don't know."

192

"Malcolm, I am passing up an important base-building meeting in Cook County because of this trip."

"Quite frankly, I'm sorry I said anything."

"Malcolm, you're chickening out. That's the worst thing a politician can do. You have to learn to be brazen. Defy logic. Believe that two and two makes five. Or three, depending on the circumstances. Eventually, everybody will agree with you."

"I'm only a tape recorder, not a politician."

"You don't have any idea what we're looking for?"

"It's going to be subtle."

"Why?"

"They agreed to the visit too quickly. That means they're not worried. That means I'm completely wrong and my idea is idiotic. Or."

She was reading a memo.

"Pray continue, Malcolm," she said, not looking up.

"Or we're going to get a guided tour through a Potemkin village."

"Meaning you can push your fist through the scenery."

"Yes, ma'am."

"You don't have to call me ma'am in private."

He looked at her. He smelled her.

"What should I call you in private?"

"I answer to the name of Madeleine."

"I believe I can manage that."

Keyes had surprised himself. He was beginning to forget something. He was beginning to forget that he was only Malcolm Keyes. He was getting accustomed to close proximity to power. After all, these people were only people. Although on the other hand they weren't only people. They were extraordinary people. Energy. Stamina. Curiosity. They were interested in everything. They were people whose lives coincided with their jobs; they never stopped politicking. The country was too big, there was never enough time to touch all the bases, but they tried. Keyes was getting an education. He personally disagreed with most of Halliday's decisions, plus the few that Madeleine made, but he understood why they made them now. There was very little improvising in politics; almost all decisions were overdetermined. There were a *lot* of reasons for everything they did, although the reasons could get tawdry.

"Can you take ridicule?" the Vice-President was saying now.

"You mean if I'm wrong about the GOD Project?"

She nodded.

193

"I'll tell you exactly how I feel at this moment. It is inconceivable to me that I could be wrong."

"Wow."

"It's in the cards, Madeleine. It's the only thing that makes sense. It's like what the man says; it's an imperative."

"I only want you to remember one thing, Malcolm," she answered. "The most important thing you can do today is not make me look like an idiot."

"I have little fear that such a thing could possibly happen, but I'll certainly watch what I say," he said smoothly.

It turned out to be the most badly advanced vice-presidential trip in history.

Air Force Two landed at Durango Airport in Colorado on time. Waiting for them were two Secret Service limousines plus the battlewagon, which had been flown in on a cargo plane. The battlewagon looked like a bloated limousine, and was a kind of mutant crossing between a hospital, a communications center, and a tank.

What they hadn't looked into was the nature of Route 550, which would take them from Durango to Ouray, where the Consortium was located. They had known that the weather made it bad helicopter country; the route led across the San Juan Mountains, one of the Rockies' stormiest ranges. Which was why the Consortium had selected Ouray to begin with: It was virtually unapproachable for eight months of the year because of heavy snows and high winds. The avalanche danger along Route 550 from Durango to Ouray was severe. It was April and still dangerous. Anderson, leading the Secret Service detail, recommended aborting the trip; the Vice-President would have none of it. Anderson commandeered a Colorado state highway department snowplow, just in case.

The safari started off for Ouray with the snowplow in the lead, the battlewagon second, then the Vice-President's car; the troops were in the second limousine at the rear. There was a top speed of thirty-five miles per hour. The route was dangerous, since a sudden avalanche could sweep a car off the road and into a chasm. Anderson was a jittery mess dealing with it; he spent most of the trip in the cab of the snowplow. They got to the Consortium two hours late. It appeared suddenly as they rounded a bend in the road, a monstrous four-story building that covered 460,000 square feet, big enough to hold any

194

number of football fields: The GOD Project was a house of many mansions.

The Secret Service went into their routine. The team in the battle-wagon got out and covered the front entrance, while Anderson entered the building alone. The team in the last car got out and surrounded Madeleine's car before she and Keyes emerged. It seemed a little over-done to Keyes, since they were in the middle of nowhere, but that was the drill.

Inside the entrance of the huge yellowish-brick building there was an array of security portals that looked like telephone booths. The things were capable of weighing you, checking your magnetic identification card, photographing your retina, and comparing it all with computer files before opening. In front of it there was a massive console that was all television monitors and switches and phones. It was manned by three armed guards, and there was bureaucracy.

"That's ridiculous," the Vice-President was saying.

"I'm sorry, madam, but only you and Mr. Keyes are on my list."

"The Secret Service is cleared to go anywhere," she said, as though talking to a five-year-old.

"This project has a special security classification, madam. I'm very sorry, but those are my orders."

"You people might have said something about this before we came here," she said in amazed anger. "Can you believe this?" she said to Anderson.

"I don't like this whole thing," Anderson said. "I recommend that you don't go in. This situation is totally out of control."

One of the telephone booths opened quietly, and a man stepped out. It was the Monk, the director of the Consortium. He approached the Vice-President shyly with his hand outstretched and a small smile on his small mouth.

"I'm Theodore Monk. I'm terribly sorry about this," he said to her. "You have no idea how security-conscious Director Jessup is. I'm in trouble with him as it is over security matters, and I daren't break the rule without getting his permission."

"Then call him," she said.

"I just did. They don't know where he is, if you can believe that. He's airborne somewhere. The Director moves around a lot. However, I can assure you that this is one of the safest installations in the country. You will be completely secure in here."

Monk was very softspoken. You had to lean into him to get it all.

Madeleine's lips were twisted and her nose was wrinkled as she thought it over while checking her watch. They were already two hours behind schedule, and the day was in danger of being wasted.

"How do we make arrangements for my Secret Service people to have lunch?" she asked.

Monk was probably one of the few people, maybe the only person, who could have run the Consortium. He was one of the fathers of artificial intelligence. He was close to seventy and he looked extremely frail. He was thin and gave the impression of a man who had been drained totally and had no reserves to draw on. Yet he went on, year after year, performing prodigies of research and development and administration. He had close-cropped grizzly gray-and-brown hair, and when he walked, his arms didn't move; Monk gave the impression of being the eternal convalescent, someone who's never quite up to par and needs a lot of bed rest. He had been a full professor at Berkeley for decades and was a past president of the American Association for Artificial Intelligence. From his physical state, it was difficult to believe that he had been administering the Consortium for sixteen years, handling the endless and inevitable difficulties involved with a group of competing computer companies who had banded together to achieve the impossible.

Monk had the day laid out. He never brought up the matter of being two hours late. His manner wasn't guarded; in fact, he seemed excited at the chance to show off his installation to the Vice-President. The government was picking up 90 percent of the cost, and this was his bureaucratic shot at justifying a colossal budget. The first thing he did was give her a briefing book that was four hundred pages long and was guaranteed to be unread. The Vice-President handed it to Keyes. He glanced down to see if it was the Book of Mark. It wasn't.

After leaving the Secret Service stranded behind the telephone booths, Monk took them to an anteroom where they were issued white gowns and white masks and white hats and white slippers. The Vice-President had to roll up her long hair into a bun. Computer chips were delicate; they enjoyed the best environmental conditions in the United States.

The Consortium consisted of two buildings. The one they were in was the main building. It was *surrounded* by the second building, which was mostly underground and had been built in a circle; the main building was a diameter of that circle. Monk was very proud of his circle, and he

196

took them there first. He called the place an advanced light source; it had made the Strategic Computing Initiative possible.

At the mere mention of "advanced light source," the Vice-President's eyes began to glaze over, but Keyes was avid for data, for clues; Keyes was listening, recording. And Monk was playing to Keyes. It had started right from the beginning; Keyes had been getting exceptional vibes from Monk. Monk seemed to have the same fascination with Keyes's face that Alexander Albritten had shown at their meeting in a Wisconsin motel.

The advanced light source was also known as a synchrotron radiation facility. Electrons ran around the circle at close to the speed of light. At one point in the circle, the electrons emitted X-rays, which was the point of the exercise. Monk seemed to sense the Vice-President's indifference as well as Keyes's intense interest, and he directed his remarks more and more to Keyes. They had gotten down to the fundamental limitations of nature itself; the miniaturization of computer chips had reached a dead end imposed by the wavelength of light, which had looked like an inescapable limitation for years.

The problem was that chips were initially drawn on a large scale and then reduced photographically, the amount of reduction being limited by the wavelength of light. By using X-rays, which were shorter in wavelength, they could make chips that were a lot smaller. Small enough to make new things possible, small enough to engineer new possibilities. X-ray lithography; it was yet another cusp.

After circumnavigating the advanced light source, they returned to the main building. The main building was where they had to put on the masks. It was eerie; all you could see was eyes. Eyes were the basic communicators, *the* most basic. But not seeing the whole face was a serious loss of information.

The main building was like being inside a monstrous Patek Philippe watch: Precision was everything. It was where Keyes expected to find something incriminating. He could feel the filtered air pressing against his eyes; that colossal piece of space was at higher than atmospheric pressure so that no impurities could drift in from outside the building. There were dozens of superclean rooms, and everybody was in lint-free gowns and caps and masks. Keyes found it alienating; there was intense cooperation coexisting with extraordinary distancing; it was as though every human being in the place was a pathogenic organism. But Monk, in his neurasthenic way, was having a ball showing off his toys, justifying his budget.

There were all kinds of indescribable machines. Scanning tunneling

197

microscopes with television outputs so workers could see what was happening at the atomic level. Trays of silicon wafers cooking in ovens everywhere. There was little automation; it was a research center, and most jobs were done by hand. The engraving of chips, the cleaning of chips, the deposition of various chemicals on chips. Monk, the undiscourageable salesman and bureaucrat talking muffled through his mask, never stopped talking.

"You see," Monk was saying, "Star Wars has a *lot* of problems, but the worst one is the computer program. It needs a million lines of code, at a minimum. Maybe two million. And it has to work right the first time. This is clearly absurd. Preposterous. I would go so far as to say impossible. Everyone knows that *no* computer program of more than twenty or thirty lines *ever* works right the first time; it *always* has to be debugged. But we won't have this opportunity in the event of nuclear war with the Soviet Union."

Keyes was feeling claustrophobic with the mask on his face, but he was fascinated by what he was hearing. Even with a mask on, Madeleine looked bored; he was hoping Monk wouldn't notice. He didn't want to worry about an offended bureaucrat; he wanted data. But there didn't seem to be a problem.

"Just look at the basic parameters," Monk said, putting an arm around Keyes's shoulder. "First you have the laser beams in battle satellites orbiting above Russia. Only about ten percent of them will be over Soviet missile fields at any one time. The computer is going to have to know which of the battle satellites are available and what their best targets are. Virtually instantaneously.

"But some of the missiles are going to get through. So here's where you bring your second defensive layer into action: earth-launched mid-course weaponry, which is called the Exoatmospheric Reentry Vehicle Interception System, or ERIS. The idea is to kill the bus before it releases its progeny, maybe ten warheads per bus along with hundreds of light, cheap decoys. Once they're out, the job gets tougher, and there isn't much time in which to do it. But those that *do* get out are handled by a third defensive layer, High Endoatmospheric Defense Interceptor, or HEDI, also earth-launched. HEDI has the really tough job of distinguishing between warheads and decoys. Crucial decisions have to be made in microseconds.

"Then there's the pop-up system. The SDI people have all kinds of ways to complicate my life."

"The pop-up system," Keyes said, seeing a toaster.

"Yes. You see, now they're afraid to have the laser battle satellites orbiting over Russia on a permanent basis. Maybe the Russians will figure out a way to destroy them. So now the plan is to wait until the Soviets have *launched* their missiles and *then* the entire laser system is boosted into orbit from submarines, but fast. Very fast. Fast enough to get into orbit, track targets, and then take them out while they're still in the boost phase. This leaves even less time for decision-making. Do you see what I'm getting at? It's too complicated. No computer could do it. No computer program is up to it. Impossible. Laughable."

"But I can tell you're smiling," Keyes said, "even with your mask on. So you must have an answer."

Keyes felt Monk's hand squeezing his upper arm.

"The answer," Monk said, "is that nothing less than artificial intelligence is required for the Strategic Defense Initiative to work. That's what we're trying to create here. Which is to say intelligence that is hardwired and yet not programmed. Intelligence that has the capacity for decision-making, for evaluation, for common sense."

Keyes nodded. The Vice-President nodded. Monk kept right on talking; Monk was a bureaucrat on a talking jag. They had given up on silicon; it wasn't fast enough. They had gone to the more expensive gallium arsenide, which was much faster, and speed was of the essence in shooting down a missile. Gallium arsenide could also resist the effects of the electromagnetic pulse that accompanied a nuclear explosion; it could take a licking and go right on ticking. He told them about a program neither one of them had ever heard of: the Diamond Technology Initiative, which was a subsidiary of the Strategic Defense Initiative. The DTI was a vital activity, because *diamond-coated* gallium arsenide chips were even *faster*. And they got rid of heat better, so the components could be closer together, and that made them even *faster*. But they'd gone even further than that. They had figured out a way to make the diamond coatings *thinner,* which made them *faster*. As far as transistors went, they had abandoned the traditional transistor and were using the ballistic transistor, which was extremely tiny and, therefore, faster.

Keyes and the Vice-President were looking into each other's eyes and smiling behind their masks. Monk was rambling on about molecular beam epitoxy, advanced computer architecture, metal-organic chemical vapor deposition. When Monk started talking about accelerating dopant atoms used to spray the surface of the gallium arsenide wafer, the Vice-President was having a struggle to keep from breaking up.

Keyes was having a struggle to keep up. He was trying to take in everything he was hearing as well as seeing. He kept cross-checking things in the briefing book, flipping back and forth as the Monk went from one area of the GOD Project to another, showing off his fantastic Erector Set. And Keyes was still getting those funny vibes from the good doctor.

Now Monk was patting Keyes on the back, and lingering, moving his hand around. Keyes looked at the Vice-President and shrugged infinitesimally. He could see, above her mask, one slim vice-presidential eyebrow rising toward her white cap.

"I'm beginning to see why this thing is called the GOD Project," the Vice-President said, hoping to catch Monk off guard, which she did. His eyes panicked momentarily, and he took a deep sighing breath before answering.

"Well, yes," he said. "I guess you could look at it that way. This thing will be up in the heavens, an entity in the sky looking after us, protecting us, keeping us safe from everything. Although the acronym is much less grandiose than that. Games of Defense. We'll be gaming it incessantly, you know. Right up until the moment when, uh, we may, unfortunately, have to use it."

The Vice-President said it quietly, easily, as though puzzling it out as she went along.

"But Dr. Monk," she said, "the boost phase is when the missile is close to the ground, isn't that so?"

"Of course. Yes. That's what makes the speed of the pop-up system so impressive."

"But if the laser beam can hit missiles *close* to the ground, it can also hit missiles *on* the ground. Wouldn't that be a first-strike weapon rather than a defensive system? Wouldn't the Soviets see it that way?"

Monk collapsed onto the top of a workbench. He was looking peaked. There was no energy in his voice. His long arms hung down on his thighs, motionless.

"I suppose you could argue it that way. Yes. Although you're getting into strategy now, which isn't really my area. And policy, of course. But certainly, you could argue it that way. Yes."

Madeleine had been briefed by Halliday's arms control adviser and she was up to speed, prepared to punch holes in any phony cover story Monk might use.

"Many people say that SDI doesn't even respond to bombers and cruise missiles," she said. "Of what earthly use could it be if it doesn't respond to bombers and cruise missiles?"

Monk, besieged, had an answer, although he didn't look all that convinced himself.

"That's covered by ADI, the Air Defense Initiative. It's something the U.S. is working on with Canada. ADI will guard our northern border against the threat you mention. I have nothing to do with ADI, but the two programs do complement each other."

Madeleine was being relentless.

"What about the coasts?" she said. "What about the threat of low-trajectory submarine-launched ballistic missiles off both coasts?"

"That's not my field, actually," Monk replied, trying to be suave, failing. "The navy is handling that one. The navy tracks all Soviet subs once they put to sea. That way they can be in a position to destroy them before they can launch missiles. That's another program."

"But now that the Soviets have bought silent-propeller technology from the Swedes, doesn't that make their subs much harder to track? Maybe impossible to track? Isn't that a big hole in our defenses?"

Monk was looking claustrophobic.

"Why, uh, temporarily, I suppose. Although there's a Sonar Initiative under way to make our detection systems more sensitive. A *lot* of oceanographic research is going on."

"Has that succeeded yet?"

"No."

"Is it likely to succeed in the near future?"

"Maybe. I don't really know. No."

"Then there's a big gap in our defenses."

"You could say that, yes."

"But in nuclear warfare any gap means disaster."

"Yes."

"So isn't that yet another reason to make the Soviets believe that SDI is not a defensive system but is indeed an offensive system?"

Monk looked at her. Even with his mask on he was an open book. He looked as if he'd been on the witness stand for nine hours. He was trapped, disarmed, helpless. He had no answer. He started stuttering. He'd underestimated her, a phenomenon which Madeleine regularly encountered with men and regularly cashed in on. Monk, as a last resort, fell back on honesty.

"They would see it that way, yes. They would use a worst-case scenario. That if you *can* use a system offensively, you *will* use that system offensively."

"But *we* don't even believe it works defensively, right? The Bush administration blew the whistle on that one, isn't that right?"

"Why—uh—yes."

"So it *does* look suspicious. I mean, that we even go on funding what could be construed as an attempt at a major breakthrough in offensive warfare."

The Monk looked faint.

Madeleine tossed it off casually, a throwaway, not anything that had been seriously thought through.

"Unless it's something else entirely," she said.

Monk did the slowest eye blink Keyes had ever seen. It was a stalling kind of eye blink, in Keyes's considered opinion. It reminded him of Halliday's cigar, making smoke, looking for some place to hide while figuring out the new rules of the game and taking time to regroup. Monk sighed. Monk shrugged. He held his arms out in a gesture of helplessness that was undoubtedly genuine.

"What else could it be?" he said.

The Vice-President looked into Monk's eyes for a long moment and saw nothing there, and she relented, backed off; there seemed to be nothing to tantalize, torture, wring out.

"Yeah," she said. "What else could it be," and she promptly lost interest in Monk and the GOD Project.

Madeleine's questions seemed to have bushwhacked Monk, and Keyes didn't want him dying on them; Keyes wanted to get back to data; Keyes hadn't given up. So he spoon-fed Monk a restorative question.

"I imagine," he said, "that to have any hope of achieving artificial intelligence, you must have made some fundamental breakthrough going beyond chip technology."

Monk smiled behind his mask. He reached out and patted Keyes on the shoulder and lingered there, caressing it, then sliding down his arm before breaking contact.

"Yes," Monk replied. "We did that." The question had given him enough energy to stand up, and they resumed the tour. "What we did was throw out the diode, which is a basic component of computers. The diode was the major obstacle to developing artificial intelligence. So was the transistor, although we still have uses for it. You see, intelligence lacks the certainty of the go/no-go diode. True intelligence is emotional. True intelligence is nonlogical. You might even say irrational. Or, anyway, nonrational. So how can you possibly create artificial intelligence using logical diodes, the zero *or* the one, the go *or* the no-go. No, it can't possibly work."

"You're not using diodes?"

202

"Very few."

"What are you using?"

"We developed the heptode," Monk said, savoring it. It was going to be good for a Nobel if they ever got around to declassifying it. It would be posthumous, no doubt, but so what? "I got the idea while trying to develop a computer program for playing the board game Wei-ch'i, better known as Go in this country. It's an extremely complex strategy game for which diodes and transistors were simply inadequate. The heptode can assume *dozens* of different states. It's almost an analog device, like a clock face which gives off continuous readings, and that's what the brain is: It's almost an analog device. Previous researchers have been going down a dead end trying to make analog intelligence out of digital diodes."

"Okay," the Vice-President said, trying to get down to basics. "You've got a supercomputer."

"*Not* a computer," Monk replied pedantically. "Computers are not intelligent. The Japanese are working on a fifth-generation computer. *We* are working on a seventh-generation computer, except that the seventh-generation is no longer a computer; it's artificial intelligence."

"Dr. Monk, I'm afraid I'm a little weak on the details. What's the bottom line?" the Vice-President asked.

Monk's dull eyes flared up; it was the perfect question.

"The most common criticism you hear of Star Wars is that we're allowing machines to control our destiny. The GOD Project is a way of restoring 'man,' as it were, to the loop. You won't have a mere machine making the decision to fire. Machines are fallible. Computers are fallible. Instead, our interests will be served by an entity that is intelligent, but much faster and more precise than man would be. An entity that will be able to evaluate the situation with savvy, intuition, common sense."

"That sounds incredible," Keyes said.

Monk was sitting again, this time on an abstract data support mechanism.

"You don't know what we've been through," he said. "You've probably never heard of fuzzy sets."

"I can't say that I have," Keyes said.

"Fuzzy what?" the Vice-President asked.

"Fuzzy sets. Say the set of high temperatures. What does high mean? What is high? It's fuzzy. Intelligent thinking is fuzzy. Slightly. Tall. Usually. Expensive. They're all fuzzy. It's the opposite of two plus two

203

equals four, which even a nitwit calculator can handle. But that's what it takes. Fuzzy logic. They fought me all the way on it."

Monk's voice sounded wiped out, dead.

"Who fought you?"

"Everyone in artificial intelligence. The logical logicians. The unfuzzies. I call them the diode dopes. I resigned the presidency of the Artificial Intelligence Association and joined the North American Fuzzy Information Processing Society, which is where the action is."

"I see," Keyes said, picking up the ball which the Vice-President had dropped. "That sounds spectacularly human, fuzzy logic."

"And then there's hypertext," Monk said. "Nonsequential text. Associational thinking, actually. How to call up stored information that is not logically related but *emotionally* related. What does emotion have to do with SDI, they all told me, not understanding that it was *key* to the problem of shooting down a missile."

Keyes had almost forgotten why they had traveled to the Consortium in the first place. He was dazzled by Monk's achievement.

"And all it takes," Monk said, sounding totally spent, "is one point two billion self-replicating heptodes."

Keyes responded without even thinking about it.

"One point one five," he said.

"What?" Monk asked.

"Uh, one point one five billion heptodes. Page 372 in the briefing book."

Monk shyly took the book and slowly turned to page 372 while glancing fondly at Keyes. Then he sat down at a computer work station. Keyes could sense that behind the mask, Monk was beaming.

"You're right," Monk said fondly, almost paternally, and certainly proudly. "You're absolutely right. One point one five billion. You're quite remarkable. Did you know that?"

Keyes was being obstinate.

"I'm willing to concede that there's a bare possibility that I could be wrong," he said.

They were in the Vice-President's office on Air Force Two flying back to Washington.

"Face it, Malcolm," she said. "Look at it from their point of view. SDI is the biggest make-work project the military-industrial complex has ever had. But if you *did* believe in it, then what Monk said is entirely plausible. They're trying to put a man in space, permanently. But more than a man, faster than a speeding missile, the fastest gun in the *world*. A tin god, sort of."

"A gallium arsenide god."

"Yes, gallium arsenide. A little arsenic in space to permanently poison arms control."

Keyes sat there sipping a medium-vile scotch, not yet ready to concede defeat, looking at the Vice-President, looking at the cover of the briefing book, which was stamped TOP SECRET, thinking back over everything he had seen and heard.

"But if that's the case, why did Alexander Albritten measure the angular deviation from plumb of my penis?"

The Vice-President looked thoughtful.

"That *is* a good question," she said, still thinking, plaiting a loop in her hair, getting that fiendish look he had learned to be wary of.

"By the way, what was it?"

He looked at her.

"Seventeen degrees."

She looked back at him.

"Isn't that rather, uh, freakish?"

"It most certainly is not."

She looked disappointed.

"Too bad," she said. "I thought maybe *that's* why the good doctor was so affectionate with you."

22

THE RIGHT CANNOT HOLD

—President Richard Halliday

AND HE WAS smiling at me and he had his arm around my shoulder and he was squeezing my upper arm. And *he* took off my mask back in the dressing room. I felt as if I were being *undressed*. He looked into my eyes with an intensity of affection that was embarrassing. What did I do to deserve this? I'd like to see that look on a woman's face someday. I didn't know what to do. The Vice-President saved me. I forgot what she said."

Halliday's feet dropped off the desk.

"You forgot?"

"Maybe I never heard it. I figured he wouldn't have the energy to chase me around a desk, but I wanted to hide somewhere anyway."

"I told him we were behind schedule," the Vice-President put in. "That's a code phrase that communicates to bureaucrats. They know they've been dismissed."

The President got his feet back up on the desk and leaned back in his chair. He was looking almost as tired as Dr. Theodore Monk always looked. It was 10:00 P.M. and he was working on his second tepid scotch. Keyes had a premonition that the President was going to age a lot in the four years.

206

"Malcolm," Halliday said, "it looks like you were wrong. Monk's story is logical. *And* plausible, and those two don't always go together."

"Then why have they been so secretive about it?" Keyes asked.

"I figure the secrecy revolves around the fact that it isn't the Strategic Defense Initiative; it's the Strategic Offense Initiative. *That's* what they're really hiding."

"It does not explain why they are watching John Burns of the Twenty-fifth of December Movement," Keyes said.

"No, it doesn't. But that could be *anything*. Something so dumb that we are not capable of imagining it."

The Vice-President was sipping a kir, and looking remarkably fresh considering that she had been on the go for eighteen hours. Keyes marveled at the endurance of politicians. That was the first requirement of being a politician: You had to be a long-distance runner; you had to have stamina; it was even more important than good teeth.

"Richard, are you going to continue to fund the SCI?" the Vice-President asked. "Are you going to give them their twelve billion?"

"Absolutely," Halliday replied, sipping scotch with his eyes closed. "Those diamond-coated gallium arsenide computer chips are my bargaining chips."

"Who are you bargaining with?" she asked.

"The hawks in Congress. If they give me a nuclear test ban, I'll let them have their SCI. It will be a *fantastic* swindle. It will be my finest hour, screwing the right wing royally. You see, if they can't test, they won't be able to complete S*DI*, in which case S*CI* reverts to its truthful cover story and becomes merely a commercial competition with the Japanese."

Halliday was almost horizontal. His feet were on the desk, his head was lolling on the back of his chair. Keyes was worried that he would nod off and drop his glass. But Halliday wasn't asleep; Halliday never slept.

"I don't have quite enough data," he said. "I need more input. By way of touching a base."

He opened his eyes, and they were pointed precisely at Keyes.

"In your spare time, Malcolm, find out about him. Who the hell is he? Where does he come from? Why is the CIA so interested in him? Does he have a secret agenda? I think I'd better learn something about that kid, because the way he's going, he could become a political force in this country."

Keyes felt astonished, not a little inadequate, and cornered. When you worked for Richard Halliday, the notion of spare time became an archaism. It must have shown.

"Malcolm, you did a real good job at Danbury Prison. I have complete confidence in you. Trust yourself. Do it the way you want to do it. Then come back and tell me the he saids and the you saids. And this way it stays in the family."

Keyes nodded. The President of the United States had just given him an assignment for which he had no previous experience, and who would expect total performance. He felt like Elmer Jessup: He had to really work at getting the ends of his mouth up so as to look confident and efficient.

"I'll take care of it right away, sir," he said.

23

CAT AND MOUSE

KEYES AMBLED DOWN the long flight of steps outside the EOB, hands in his topcoat pockets, discouraged, having just spent six hours trying, and failing, to find out something, anything, about the TV evangelist preacher John Burns. Nobody outside the Twenty-fifth of December Movement knew anything about John Burns. Nobody inside the Twenty-fifth of December Movement would talk to Malcolm Keyes. Halliday had such a passion for secrecy that he was willing to use a totally inexperienced investigator in order to get the dividend of perfect security. It was a compliment, actually; Halliday trusted him.

But as he approached his car in the West Executive Drive parking lot, he was shocked to see a stretch Mercedes in Moody's slot, which was adjacent to Keyes's. Moody drove an Edsel which was held together with wax. Besides which, it was strictly verboten to park a foreign-made car in the West Executive Drive; it was a hanging offense.

Keyes approached it as though it were a Martian rocket ship. He couldn't see in; the windows were tinted. He went to the rear and checked the plates. Washington, D.C. As he went back toward the front, the rear door was flung open and a large pair of hands reached out and grabbed him by the lapels, yanking him into the backseat. He suddenly found himself sitting between two large muscular specimens who looked efficient, who looked deadly, who didn't have eyes; they were as indifferent as twin .50 caliber machine guns on a search-and-destroy mission. The two men were the kind that know how to take and give orders and who, furthermore, were not serious contributors to the American Civil Liberties Union. The driver paused at the gatehouse to return a temporary pass.

Then the Mercedes was speeding up Pennsylvania Avenue and Keyes was taking stock. Now that he was over the shock, he found that he wasn't frightened; he was furious. He had been through this before.

"The three of you," he said, including the driver in his benediction, "as well as whoever your boss is, are going to get the Distinguished Asshole Merit Badge Award. My complaint will go directly to the President of the United States."

He was wasting his breath. They had their orders. There was no point talking to people who took orders. Anyway, it was a short ride; they were in Silver Spring, Maryland, in no time—it was after 10:00 P.M. on a Sunday—and the Mercedes pulled into the ambulance driveway of what looked like a five-story private clinic or hospital. Keyes was hustled out of the car, through a doorway, and up three flights in an elevator. When the elevator door opened, he was quickly shoved across a narrow corridor and through a door into a room where there were two men waiting, one dressed just like a doctor.

The doctor was tall and slim and about sixty. He had a belabored bedside manner; he would have done better being a researcher. The other man, in a business suit, was in his early thirties. The doctor flashed an admiring glance at Keyes and then slowly walked around him.

"Who's in charge here?" Keyes said imperiously.

"Why do you ask?" the business suit said.

"I've already been through this stupid thing, and I *passed*."

The doctor looked surprised, even shocked.

"*I* didn't know that," the doctor said to the business suit, who shook his head slowly from side to side.

"I see," the doctor said to Keyes. "You're joking. Well, you fooled me. That was a very clever joke. You seem quite clever."

Keyes pointed a finger at him and shook it.

"Heads are going to roll," he said. "The President is going to chop heads. I'm talking about the President of the *United States*." Keyes had really gotten into Washington power nuances.

The doctor was standing there rubbing his chin, looking at Keyes,

210

thinking. He looked at the business suit, his eyebrows making question marks. The business suit said something to the two goons in what was supposed to pass for Russian, and they both took out shiny, nickel-plated .32 revolvers which looked ridiculous; they looked like cheap Saturday-night specials that not even a black teenager in Harlem would waste his time on.

"You seem to be very alert to questions of power," the business suit said. "Do you recognize what the two gentlemen have in their hands? Does that settle the issue of power in this room?"

Keyes thought it a rather crude, fascistic response.

"Those things are pencil sharpeners," he said.

The doctor flashed a weak grin, his face turned partly away from Keyes, looking off into space, pondering, confused.

"How many fingers am I holding up?" he asked.

"Twenty-three and a half."

"You're a peculiar one."

"I'm also a busy man. Could we get this over with?"

"This is wery strange," the doctor said in his fake Russian accent. "You're having an abnormal reaction. Aren't you frightened?"

"I'm bored," Keyes said contemptuously.

"Bored?" The doctor seemed amazed. "Why are you bored?"

"I'm tired of this stupid routine."

"What routine?"

"This checking up on me."

The doctor sat down on a rolling stretcher. He looked over at the business suit.

"He's evidently referring to that, uh, other organization," the business suit said, *sotto voce.* "Proceed."

"When are you people going to believe that I'm reliable?" Keyes asked.

The doctor's head fell down. He was sitting on the stretcher, elbows on knees, hands propping up his chin. Then the whole structure collapsed as he stood up.

"Reliable?" he said, suddenly outraged. "Reliable?" But then he seemed to see an absurdity in the situation, and he began to giggle. It was a trifle maniacal. He was wandering around the small room now, pacing and scratching his head and giggling. "*Reliable,*" he said to the business suit. The business suit smiled.

"You certainly get to the heart of matters," the business suit said. He was leaning against a wall, arms folded on his chest; his clothes were

211

very conservative and well pressed and well tailored to his slight, slim body. "Tell me, do *you* consider yourself reliable?" When he got nothing but a dirty look from Keyes, he added, "How about patriotic?"

Keyes rubbed his eyes. He was *not* getting to the heart of the matter. They weren't getting the message.

"Oh, am I patriotic," he said.

"That's pretty flat, Malcolm. I'm not hearing any fervor. Where's the feeling? What is it specifically? How big? When did you first start feeling patriotic?"

"The first time I touched a girl. She was wearing red, white, and blue."

The doctor bunched his lower lip between his thumb and index finger. His eyebrows had sort of concentrated over the top of his nose. He was not giving off the appearance of a superior intellect.

"Is there a problem?" Keyes asked.

"I guess I don't understand the function of wit," the doctor said to the business suit.

"It has survival value," Keyes said dryly. "It helps a man deal with dumb situations."

The doctor was shaking his head up and down, looking at Keyes.

"I suppose you're not going to answer the question about patriotism?"

There was a basic parameter that Keyes was missing. The entire conversation was off-key, atonal, maybe even pentatonic: alien to the modern ear. His right elbow was leaning on some kind of infernal machine holding up his chin as he considered his reply.

"I feel patriotic stirrings toward the U.S. Constitution, in particular toward the first ten Amendments, in particular toward the one about prohibitions against unreasonable search and seizure."

"Wery, wery smart," the doctor replied. "You're certainly smarter than I expected. I'd say your problem is that you're too smart, if you want my adwice."

"Look, my friend," Keyes replied. "I *know* this is a *test*. Do you understand? You can't bluff me."

The doctor was standing a few feet from Keyes, his hands clasped behind him, looking stumped.

"You *know* this is a *test?*"

"That's it. You've got it now. Can I go now?"

The doctor stood there looking at his own nose, thinking. Then he got a bright idea.

212

"Do you know what *kind* of test it is?"

"It's a loyalty test, of course."

"Ah!"

The doctor was suddenly very businesslike and officious. He waved to the two gorillas.

"Take him to the CAT," he said.

"The cat?" Keyes said. Bizarre images flashed through Keyes's brain. What were they going to do to him this time? The cat? What the hell was the cat? The two goons hustled him through a door into a much larger room. He was looking at a *big* machine. And it had a suspicious-looking cylindrical hole in the middle of it, big enough to hold a person. There was a man in a white coat standing in front of it.

"Take off your topcoat," the white coat said.

Keyes took a good look at the two goons, shook his head, and took the topcoat off.

"Now the jacket. And the tie. And your shoes. And your belt."

Keyes had come to understand something about power, and he was in their power. There was no alternative. He took off his jacket and his tie and his shoes and his belt.

"Climb in," the white coat said. "Feet first."

"Does it matter that you've got the wrong man?"

"In."

Keyes climbed in.

"You must remain absolutely still," the white coat said, fastening a helmetlike device around Keyes's head. "No matter what happens, you must remain absolutely still. Is that clear?"

"Why, yes, I think so."

Keyes could sense that the doctor had left the room. There was a brief silence. Keyes was watching them upside down. The man in the white coat, the two goons, the man in the suit. Then the voice of the doctor was booming out over a loudspeaker.

"It is essential that you do not move. Don't open your eyes. Don't swallow. Is that understood, Mr. Keyes?"

"I get the message."

Keyes was feeling claustrophobic. He was strapped in, and he couldn't have moved very much if he wanted to. Then the damn machine started to move. He felt totally out of control. It was rotating ninety degrees off center in either direction.

"He's moving, dammit."

"I'm not moving."

"Oh, for God's sake."

He could see that they were all looking up at the loudspeaker. In a moment, the doctor had returned.

"What is this nonsense?" the doctor said. "We're wasting our time here. Who ordered this?"

"I did," the man in the suit said.

"It was a mistake."

"You're sure?"

"Of course I'm sure. It's right in front of my eyes."

"Is the test over?" Keyes asked.

"Yes, the test is over," the doctor said.

"Will someone get me out of here?"

Keyes was watching them upside down. The white coats were coming off, the topcoats were going on. They were grabbing briefcases and preparing to abandon ship, as though they had rehearsed it thoroughly. Then, quite suddenly, they were all through the door, slamming it behind them, and Keyes and the CAT were left alone. He lay there for a few moments, not moving, still docile. Then he decided that the moment had finally arrived for pure violence.

24

HAPPY HOUR

I WAS READY TO take on the five of them. I had previously been manhandled by a maniac with a tape measure, and now they had sicked the CAT on me: computerized axial tomography. Enough was enough. It took me about a minute to get out of that infernal machine. I ran through the next office and out into the corridor. The five of them were just getting on the elevator. 'Who the hell *are* you?' I asked, grabbing the doctor's lapel. The son of a bitch smiled at me. 'You're wery healthy, did you know that?' he said, and pushed me away. I stuck my foot in the door. 'You're not getting out of this building until I find out who the hell you are,' I said. And the doctor, the *doctor,* not one of the goons, kicked my foot viciously and said, 'Father Christmas,' and the door closed and they were gone. I was standing there in my stocking feet and my pants were falling down and I didn't feel like racing down the fire stairs after them. Needless to say, nobody in the hospital knew who they were."

Halliday went to his Potemkin Chippendale sideboard and poured two scotches. He handed one to Keyes as he returned to his desk. He picked up the phone.

"I want the Director of the FBI and the Director of Central Intelligence."

215

They sat there quietly, waiting for the calls to come in. Keyes had taken a cab from the hospital in Maryland to West Executive Drive, where his car was parked. Then he had decided to take a chance and see if Halliday might still be working. Having a blue pass, he could get into the White House at any hour.

Even though it was close to midnight on a Sunday, the phone rang in about sixty seconds: The establishment never slept. The Director of the FBI had won the race. He denied any knowledge of the operation but said he would check and call back. The DCI was waiting on another line before Halliday had finished with the FBI. One more denial, one more promise to look for a wild card.

Halliday thought and drank for a few minutes and then said, "Maybe it *was* a Russian this time? Possible?"

"Wery."

"Sooner or later, the inner meanings will emerge, Malcolm; I guarantee you."

The President was looking appalled, drained, disgusted. Keyes couldn't help thinking of John Burns when he looked at the President. Was Halliday going to have secondhand-soul problems too, by the time his watch was up?

"You know, Malcolm, in a way this problem is almost refreshing. The stuff I usually have to deal with is awful. What I do most of the time is appease greed. That's what a President's job is: the appeasement of greed. They fight like tigers over it. Harry Truman had it all wrong: The buck *starts* here."

Halliday started back to his bar, picking up Keyes's glass as he went by. At the rate he was going, he was going to wear a path in the orientals; it would be like Ike's golf-shoe cleat marks in the floor tiles leading out to the Rose Garden. As he was pouring the scotch, Halliday's gray face suddenly brightened. He went back to his desk, handing Keyes a drink as he passed.

"Malcolm, how about this?"

Halliday put his drink on the desk alongside his feet and lay back in the swivel chair, hands clasped on his chest.

"When I leave the White House, you and I write a book about politics," he said. "It'll be the first nonfiction book about politics ever written by an American President. By *God*, that's something to live for. And you, my friend, are going to be my living memory, my source book, my notes, my presidential files, my library. From now on, I'm bringing you in on everything. All the bad stuff. What are you thinking?"

"It sounds very exciting," Keyes said. "I'd love to."

"I'll even put your name on the cover. After mine, of course."

"Of course."

"I mean, what passes for political discourse in this country is pure bilge, from start to finish. It always amazes me how the public lets us get away with it."

Keyes's eyes were floating around the room. He already had a mental reservation, and he felt that he should express it, even at the risk of offending the President.

"Can I believe that you will really do that?" he asked.

"I'm making you a promise, Malcolm. Now, I know the promises of a politician don't weigh too heavily in the scales. But those are the public promises. The private promises of a politician are his stock in trade. That's all he has to work with. I'm making this a private promise. You and me. Four years on the best-seller list. Deal?"

It was a ravishing idea. All previous presidential memoirs were worthless; they had all remained loyal to the cover story by which Americans were governed. Now Halliday was proposing to carry out the failed quest of Adlai Stevenson: to tell the truth to the American people.

Keyes nodded.

"Deal," he said.

"Okay, let's get back to work."

"Work?"

Keyes took a stiff swallow of scotch. It was awful, but it gave him time to collect his wits. He was still on the best-seller list. Not to mention the fact that it wasn't even Sunday anymore; it was going to one.

"Have you figured out a way to approach the Burns thing?"

"Yes, but it didn't work."

"Why not?"

"I thought a good start would be to talk to the business manager of the Twenty-fifth of December Movement. But he won't see me. I talked to him on the phone three times today. He's adamant."

"He won't see you, huh?"

"He's offended by the surveillance on Burns, which I gather is pretty obvious. I have to tell you he's very teed off at you, sir. The last time I spoke with him, he said there was no censored way he would discuss *any* censored thing with *any* member of the censored censored Halliday censored admini-censored-stration."

Still in his near horizontal position, Doc Halliday reached for the phone.

"That ought to be easy enough to smooth over," he said.

217

25

CHOCOLATE SODOMY AND STRAWBERRY GOMORRAH

THE FBI BUILDING was a cross between the Temple of Karnak and the Hound of the Baskervilles. Keyes was trying to figure out what the architect had been trying to say. The place was ugly: a huge animal with dozens of column legs sort of standing there in a crouch ready to spring. Although the repeating patterns of square columns and square windows relentlessly suggested order, which sooner or later, presumably, led to law.

Inside, the building was plush, muted, and banal. Vandervanter's office was like the exterior. It was orderly. There was so much order in the FBI Building it was oppressive. Vandervanter had three beige side-opening file cabinets, a desk, two chairs before it, and a little table with a vase that had two flowers in it. There was a law degree from Harvard on the wall. The only hint of sloppiness and human habitation was the top of the desk, which was covered with thick files, and Torquemada was sitting behind it with his thin smile.

"Preparing more interrogations?" Keyes asked. He took one of the chairs without waiting to be asked.

"Not that it will make any difference," Vandervanter replied. "When the author of 'The Commiest Manifesto' gets a top secret clearance, security is in trouble. What can I do for the man?"

Vandervanter had a pleasant *viva voce* quality to his voice even when he was engaged in the process of predation. Keyes found that he liked him in more or less the same way he liked Lockhart; they were pleasant people as long as you didn't discuss serious matters.

"I want to get an interview with a man. A private, personal interview."

"You mean *you're* checking people out now?"

"No, I'm not checking people out. All I want to do is talk to the man and maybe get some information."

"Who?"

"He's the business manager of a religious group. It's called the Twenty-fifth of December Movement. His name is Breskin."

"What's the problem?"

"He doesn't want to be interviewed. He thinks the Twenty-fifth of December Movement is being persecuted by the U.S. government."

"I should certainly hope so," Vandervanter replied.

"It's possible."

"Those people are nuts," Vandervanter said, some real meanness edging into his voice.

"Think you could, sort of, talk him into talking to me?" Keyes asked, raising his eyebrows, trying to be conspiratorial.

"I might."

"Any ideas on how to proceed when I do talk to him?"

"You've already been interrogated by me. You've had the best possible training." He thought about it a moment. "Taking the victim by surprise is always a good technique. Surprise is the high ground."

Keyes nodded. "I'll remember that."

"What do you want to talk to him about?" Vandervanter asked.

Keyes held it back for about three seconds, savoring it, tasting it, swallowing it, digesting it.

"It's classified," he said.

Max Breskin was fortyish, fattish, shortish. He was an old-time advertising and PR man who had been around. He had once had his own public relations agency, but it had gone bankrupt. He had also had a little brush with the law over the possible concealment of assets during the bankruptcy proceedings, which was the fact Vandervanter had dug

219

up to make Breskin reasonable. Keyes wasn't all that proud of the tactic, but Doc Halliday needed help; the issues were big; it was standard governmental immorality.

Breskin was staying at a moderately expensive hotel in Washington, which was not his home base. He traveled around the country a lot. The one luxury the movement had indulged in was buying a Learjet, which Breskin used when John Burns wasn't. Breskin spent a lot of time lining up new TV and cable outlets for the Burns program and getting newspapers around the country interested in running stories on the movement in general and John Burns in particular. He was in touch with every peace group in the country.

As soon as Keyes set foot inside the cocktail lounge, two large, mean-looking Christians came up. Breskin was sitting at the bar ten feet away, looking at himself in the mirror behind the bar.

"If you want to talk to me," Breskin said, still looking at the mirror, "you have to let them frisk you."

Keyes held his arms in the air, and one of the Christians went over him. The Christian nodded.

"Welcome, friend," Breskin said. "Have a drink?"

Keyes sat down next to him.

"I've never been frisked before," he said. "I didn't like it."

"You're frisked every time you go through an airport, only you don't feel it."

"Then there's something to be said for subtlety."

"I'll drink to that. To subtlety."

Considering the circumstances, Max Breskin was surprisingly friendly, even voluble. He was untense, unhostile, matter of fact.

"What do you want to know?" he said to Keyes.

Keyes decided to trap him right off, Vandervanter-style, take the high ground, rattle him, see if there was any connection between the Twenty-fifth of December Movement and a certain top-secret government project.

"I want to know if you believe in GOD," he said.

Breskin nervously glanced over at his two Christians, but they were out of earshot talking over a couple of root beers.

"That's a dirty question, fella."

He watched the eyes and the mouth and the shoulders in that order. There wasn't a twitch; Breskin had taken the question straight; he didn't know anything about the GOD Project.

"What's more important for a guy like me is that I believe what the marketing potential is."

"I see," Keyes said. "The marketing potential. The marketing potential of Jesus, I assume."

"*Fabulous. Infinite. Bottomless.* When I had my own agency I handled a few churches. Made a few connections. I spotted the Twenty-fifth right off the bat as a comer. I mean, the time was right. Why should the right wing own God? I'll tell you, one thing about me, I know a selling proposition when I see one. How many times in your life do you get a Volkswagen or a Federal Express, huh? They've got a unique product. Left-wing fundamentalism. It fills a gap in the marketplace; it's golden time. I ran with the ball."

Max Breskin seemed to have a lot of clout in the hotel; one of the Christians went up to the television set at the end of the bar and switched it from a music video to the Twenty-fifth of December Movement: It was John Burns time.

Burns was pacing up and down the stage, head down, hands in his back pockets, not talking. Burns used the longest pauses in religion and the theater. Breskin maintained that he had gotten the trick from old reruns of Jack Benny programs.

"I have a confession to make," Burns said finally. "I'm going to make it right now to all of you, and you don't have to keep it confidential; this is an open public confession of a very sinful fact about me."

"Listen to this," Breskin said. "I can tell. He's got that look in his eyes."

Burns was looking out at his audience, arms at his side, a smile on his face that made his scraggly beard look ridiculous. It was a genuine smile. John Burns didn't put on his smiles like most TV preachers. When he smiled, he meant it; Breskin asserted that the occasional Burns smile sent contributions skyward.

"Are you ready for this?" John Burns said, looking around as though assuring himself that everyone was listening. "*I have a soft nose.*" Pause. Titters. Coughs. Rustlings. "And I want you to know that I've given a lot of thought to this sin. After all, it's un-American to have a soft nose. Lord, I would think at three in the morning, how could you have given me such a soft nose? Everyone knows a hard nose is the best nose. Isn't that right?"

"I'll tell you, this kid knows how to play to the house," Breskin said, as Burns drew laughs and applause. Burns was looking out at them now and smiling again—the second time in only a few minutes. Very unusual.

221

"Jesus, why did you make *my* nose so *soft?*"

Max Breskin might as well have been sitting in the audience at the Pentagonal Church of Christ. He was giggling, lapping it up, proud of his client, pleased as punch, digging Keyes in the ribs with his elbow. "You know, he makes most of this up *on* camera. It's spontaneous. It comes to him."

"Well, this whole question of nosemanship began to fascinate me," Burns continued. "I pondered it in the late hours. Why, oh why, was I so afflicted and out of touch with so many of my countrymen? And do you know what I decided late one night? I decided that Jesus would say that *His* nose was soft too. *Is* soft. Jesus's nose *is* soft."

John Burns wasn't smiling now. He was pointing a finger out at the audience. "I tell you, brothers and sisters, these cold warriors of ours with their hard noses, these people in government who are quick to bristle, gung ho, *rarin'* to go, these people have as much chance of getting into heaven as a camel through the nostril of a *hard nose.* Thank you, Lord, for my soft nose; thank you, Jesus."

John Burns had to stop because his audience was applauding and singing and chanting. Breskin looked as if he could hear the angelic tolling of cash registers. He slapped his fist on the bar.

"Chocolate sodomy and strawberry Gomorrah—that's how I rate it. *This* time with hot fudge, whipped cream, and sprinkles. That's the rough equivalent of two ears, the tail, and *both* balls in bullfighting."

Keyes was fascinated too. He looked at Burns standing there on the tube, some combination of spellbinder, radical, and stand-up comic.

"You know," Breskin said, "most televangelists are professional wrestlers. It's all choreography. All those people are up on Stanislavsky, they can cry on cue. As a matter of fact, I wouldn't be surprised if most human interaction was professional wrestling. But *this* is no act, this kid isn't a wrestler."

"Who is he?" Keyes asked.

"Who is John Burns?"

"Yeah. Where does he come from? How did he get this way? What kind of education did he have? He speaks rather well; he must have some kind of education."

"University of Missouri, two years, kicked out."

"Why?"

"Living a life of rapine. Screwing all the girls, not studying, drinking, boisterous, disrespectful of his professors, bloodthirsty behavior in the laboratories."

222

Keyes was trying to think like Vandervanter. He wanted to pursue lines of inquiry; he wanted to narrow things down and get to the bottoms of things.

"What did he do after college?"

"Knocked around. Odd jobs. McDonald's. Department-store clerk. Then something happened. I don't know what it is and he won't tell me, but he got religion. He got tied up with the Twenty-fifth originally as a gofer, which satisfied him. But he read a lot and asked a lot of questions. It's like he was finishing his education on his own with his own syllabus. Then he started talking, and they slowly realized what they had."

"What was his family like?"

"Pious, conservative, and very poor Kansas farmers."

"Are they alive?"

"They live in eastern Kansas somewhere, on a piece of bad ground. Or they used to. I forget. He doesn't talk about them. They don't get along. They think he's sacrilegious."

"They're being shortsighted. This kid could run for President," Keyes said.

"Oh boy, would I like to manage that. I suppose this country is too conservative for him, but we would make one hell of a run for it. They would know they'd been in a fight. God, I can taste it."

Keyes kept probing.

"Has he ever worked for the federal government?" he said to Breskin, who was ordering another round of drinks.

"Are you kidding?"

"What did he study at Missouri?"

"Electrical engineering."

"Really?"

"It was his father's idea."

"Has he ever worked for a weapons plant?" Keyes was reaching for something, anything; the inner Halliday was fussy, complaining, urging.

The genial Breskin smile vaporized.

"What the hell are you talking about? You trying to get him on some kind of sabotage rap? Listen, we've all just about had this shit."

"You've got me wrong," Keyes said quickly.

"When you're for peace in this country, you've got real problems. Oh boy, what a problem. You're a peacemonger. You're strange. You're flaky. You're weird. You're soft on something. The kid's right on nosemanship. You're an unwitting agent of the KGB. Or maybe a witting one if you're for peace."

"I can't say that I blame you."

"I just want to tell you guys something. I want you to go back to your friends in government, whoever the hell they are, and tell them that we've had it. They dragged that kid into a government vehicle and *stripped* him. That's not going to happen a second time."

Keyes spilled his white wine.

"They *stripped* him? Why did they strip him? What did they do after they stripped him?"

"You're not going to believe this."

"I am in a position to believe anything."

Breskin took a long sip from an unrecognizable drink.

"They measured him," he said.

"They measured him?"

"Yeah."

"What did they measure?"

"His body. His legs. His arms. His penis."

"How many measurements did they take?"

Breskin slowly turned away from his image in the mirror and looked at Keyes. His forehead looked busy. He was thinking all kinds of thoughts and feeling emotions, and they were showing in his eyes and his mouth.

"Nineteen," he said slowly.

"How come they stopped at nineteen?" Keyes asked quickly.

Breskin still had that funny look on his face. It was as though there were two conversations going on. One conversation involving words, plus a second conversation that was all subtexts, and Breskin didn't have the faintest idea what the subtext was. But out of sheer politeness he was going along with the gag.

"Because we raided the joint, that's why. They *had* to stop. People power."

Keyes was nodding his head up and down.

"You *made* them stop," he said.

That's what the surveillance would be about, then. They wanted to grab Burns and finish the job, get that twentieth measurement. That being the case, would they try to grab Keyes himself to get numbers nineteen and twenty?

"Look," Breskin said, "I think I have to remind you people of something. This is still a free country. A man should be able to speak his piece without being attacked or degraded or submitted to some kind of phony Book of Mark."

"Jesus," Keyes said.

"So I want you to know we're taking good care of him. Spread the word. You're not going to be able to pull that shit again. Got me?"

"Got you."

Keyes liked Breskin. He had held to his part of the deal. He had answered questions. He had been open. Keyes had no complaints.

"I'd like to ask you one more question. And don't get upset about it."

"Shoot, friend."

"I'd like to talk to him. Can you set it up? You name the conditions."

Breskin was looking back into the mirror at himself, evaluating. Keyes figured Breskin must have had a fundamentally sound personality to be able to look at himself that much; it augured well.

"I can't promise it," Breskin said. "I'll try, but he's his own man. I don't control him. Nobody does. And he's *pissed* about that incident with the Book of Mark."

"That's all I can ask for," Keyes said, draining his drink. He wanted to sneak away but John Burns was on another roll, and he couldn't resist listening. He was hooked on John Burns.

"Now we all know that we have a major drug problem in this country. Why do you think that is?" Burns scanned the audience from right to left, his eyes slowly taking in the whole place. It was almost as though he really expected an answer; it wasn't mere rhetoric. "It's because people on drugs are refugees. Now, refugees are usually from *other* countries. Central American countries. Latin American countries. Asian countries. But we have more refugees than any other country on *earth*, refugees from themselves, refugees in *place*. Why do so many of us have to run away? What's wrong with our lives? Is it possible that there's something missing? Why are so many of us running for our lives *from* our lives? Is it possible that they need Jesus?"

It certainly was, anything was possible, Keyes thought, slithering out of the bar, the lion going on tippy-toes past the Christians, thinking: Torquemada would have done better, but he hadn't done half bad.

"And he said he's *pissed* about that incident with the Book of Mark, and I said I can understand that, and trying your best is all I can ask for, and he nodded and said he'd be in touch and I said good night and that was it."

Doc Halliday was looking positively majestic behind his desk in the Oval Office. He looked even more like a President than Warren Harding and Melvyn Douglas put together.

"You and Burns certainly have something in common," Halliday mused. "I wonder what the hell it is."

"Stop looking at me that way."

"Malcolm, level with me. Is there anything funny in your background?"

"Nothing that you don't know about."

Halliday was nodding his head.

"I take it back. You got the treatment from an expert. Vandervanter's conclusion was that you're flaky but serviceable."

"That's me."

"Kansas," Halliday said.

"Yes."

"What do you mean, yes?"

"He comes from Kansas."

"I *know* that. You just *told* me that. What I want to know is, how soon can you get there?"

26

THE MONK GOES TO CHURCH

IT WASN'T ONLY hard work that drained Dr. Theodore Monk; he was also prey to what he called situational fatigue, and his situation at the moment was especially exhausting. He was seated across a desk from a man he didn't care for—Elmer Jessup—and for whose profession he had acquired a loathing. Director of Central Intelligence. It sounded like a lobe of the brain, but it was totally misleading. Spooks were centrally intelligent the way the Defense Department was defensive. Director of Peripheral Intelligence, perhaps. Even better, Director of Marginal Intelligence. But even that was too good for mere spinal-cord automata.

"You let that son of a bitch get away in the first place," Jessup was saying. "I can't prove it but I know it. You or someone in your organization. My hunches are never wrong."

"I'm not going to sit here and be insulted," Monk fired back. "And furthermore, take those ridiculous tails off me. They're so inept it's embarrassing. I'm afraid everyone on the street knows I'm being followed."

Jessup looked inscrutable.

"You people *dogged* Oppenheimer. You tapped him and bugged him and followed him, and he never stepped out of line. And you missed Klaus Fuchs, who was stealing you blind."

227

"*I* didn't miss him."

"You would have."

It was the only way to have a casual conversation with Elmer Jessup; show no fear or apprehension. Then he *might* drop that intimidating act he put on for everyone, including two or three Presidents.

"Now look," Jessup said, "it's the total lack of records that's suspicious. No fingerprints, no photographs. No physical measurements or descriptions whatsoever. Forcing us to rely on that damn book. How could that have happened?"

"Why don't you ask the army?" Monk replied testily. "They're the ones who lost his records."

"Maybe."

"Oh, now it's maybe."

"We'll find out about that too, before this is all over."

Monk's anger had produced a shot of adrenaline, and he was on a brief energy high. The scientists were the ones who made things possible. There would be nothing to talk about if the scientists hadn't done their work. But then these security goons showed up, and right away everyone was under suspicion.

"What do you think about John Burns?" Jessup asked.

"I don't know. I simply don't know. I've seen him on television, and he looks right. It could be him. Although that beard causes a problem. And the long hair. Any change in facial or scalp hair can make a substantial difference in someone's appearance. And Henry was rather typical, remember. He had no outstanding physical characteristics. Plus the fact that he's been gone for over a year. Even as little as a year of living can affect a face. But it seems to me we're avoiding the issue." Monk leaned forward when he spoke, keeping his back straight. It was as though he were allowing a clear channel for his lungs to supply as much power as possible for use in vibrating his vocal cords. "Henry is no dope, after all. Why would he go on television?"

Jessup smiled for the first time in Monk's recollection, although it was more like a dog curling its upper lip. Jessup's smile couldn't possibly signify pleasure; it was amygdalic, reptilian.

"He thinks he's above the rules," Jessup replied. "That goddam commie son of a bitch is a kamikaze. He doesn't *give* a goddam as long as he can lay waste. That's what I think. But we'll change all that too."

Monk didn't bother replying. The last thing he wanted was a psychological discussion with a spinal cord.

"When are you seeing him?" Jessup asked.

"Tonight. At the Pentagonal Church."

Monk couldn't repress a giggle, which came out as a bassy, low-frequency half-sob. Whenever the Twenty-fifth of December Movement executed its symbol—the Star of Bethlehem—whether in sculpture or paintings or medallions, it always came out looking like the Pentagon. The good Pentagon, on God's side, as opposed to the bad Pentagon, which was on Satan's.

"Write a report as soon as you leave, while it's still fresh in your mind."

"Yes, of course," Monk said. "I'll do my best, naturally."

Monk got there an hour ahead of time. He wanted a front seat. He wanted John Burns to be able to see him, recognize him. He would be watching his face for the shock of recognition. It also gave him a chance to see the mechanical side of the Twenty-fifth of December Movement. The TV cameras and cables and monitors, and the special lighting effects as well as the microphones, which were everywhere above the altar/stage, all, no doubt, out of camera range so that it would look as though John Burns were speaking directly to you, without the need of electronic enhancement.

When John Burns finally emerged—there was no shock of recognition—Monk found that he was unable to listen to all of the words. He was too fascinated by the man. The man, not the message. The way the man moved, the way he looked, the way his lips moved, the carbonation in his eyes. Gradually, the words started to penetrate, and he saw there was wit, passion, unpredictability. How had he gotten so religious? How had he gotten so political? What had he gone through; what had changed him?

If, indeed, he was Henry Patrick.

He was talking about stupidity.

"I want to talk about a subject very dear to my heart tonight," John Burns was saying. "I imagine that it's one of the most important subjects in the world. Stupidity. Now what would be a perfectly wonderful example of stupidity?"

Burns waiting, using his Jack Benny pauses with exquisite effect, looking out over his audience, smiling at them, arms out, palms up, waiting for a nonanswer to a rhetorical question.

229

"How about seventeen thousand strategic nuclear warheads?" he asked. "It takes about one hundred and fifty warheads to destroy the Soviet Union, and we've got seventeen thousand and counting. Now is that stupid enough for you? Stupid could even serve as a collective noun here: a stupid of warheads."

Monk had become a spectator. He was totally absorbed. John Burns was the only fundamentalist preacher who could use wit. They all tried, of course, but preacher wit wasn't too funny. You laughed because you knew the preacher was trying to be funny. It was like the dog that walked on its hind legs; it didn't do it very well, but it was amazing that it could do it at all.

"Now, how could well-educated, intelligent people get us into this jam, where there are nuclear warheads all over the planet, and where every decade that goes by, yet another country goes to work on the nuclear rockpile, learning how to make little ones out of big ones? How could a big, dumb thing like this *happen?*"

Burns was pretending that it was hopeless. Impossible to understand. Beyond human comprehension. He was pacing around the stage, hands in his back pockets, looking down at the floorboards, trying to decipher the indecipherable.

"I mean, can you call *all* of our Joint Chiefs over the last forty or so years stupid? *All* of our Secretaries of Defense? Stupid? *All* of our Presidents? Stupid? *All* of them?"

Burns did something he rarely did. He stopped pacing and sat down on the front edge of the stage, his legs dangling in space. This was a difficult shot for the cameramen to get, and there was scrambling, but Burns couldn't have cared less; he was rolling.

"Has anybody here tonight ever done something stupid?" he asked. Yep. A lot of hands were going up, a lot of rueful smiles appearing in the audience. "Of course. And I've already admitted publicly that I, personally, have done *ten thousand* stupid things. I have been stupid, and I know what stupid is. But what do you say about intelligent people who are stupid *all* the time? Who are stupid for *decades?* Who are stupid for *generations?* Who go on making more and more nuclear bombs and spreading them all around the planet?"

Burns was starting to twitch. It was no longer possible for him to sit on the stage, calmly addressing his audience. In one fluid movement, he was on his feet pacing back and forth across the stage.

"Well, the answer is that these people are fanatics. A fanatic is someone who narrows his vision down to a *tunnel.* A fanatic is someone

230

who shuts out a *lot* of real estate. Everything that contradicts his or her cherished beliefs is shut out. In other words, brothers and sisters, these well-educated, highly intelligent big shots who run our lives from Washington are a collection of *voluntary* stupids, which is what all fanatics are."

Burns paused to look out at the crowd, and then started working them like a stump speaker.

"They've learned to stop worrying and love the bomb," he said, holding out his arms in disbelief.

Dr. Theodore Monk felt stirrings in the crowd around him that he wasn't fond of. He was a long way from the sanctity of his laboratory now; he was out in the body politic.

"They want their bombs; they don't want to give up their bombs," Burns said, arms still out in the shrugging position.

Monk was hearing a lot of "Jesus, save us," and "Praise the Lord." Some were giggling; some were crying quietly.

"They want their little teddy bombs to curl up with at night so they can feel *safe.*"

To the people in the Pentagonal Church of Christ, what Burns was saying was getting funnier and sadder simultaneously. But Burns was starting to modulate into a different mood entirely.

"I'm sorry to say that some of these people are fellow Christians, born-again, just like you and me. And *they* think that when the warheads fly, that will be the End Time, the Rapture, and *they* will fly up to heaven. For the trumpet shall sound and the dead shall be raised incorruptible! One Corinthians fifteen, fifty-two." Burns had wandered back to the podium. He now pounded it so hard it fell over. Monk almost jumped out of his chair.

"This is not only stupid; this is *sacrilege,*" Burns said. "It isn't whatever politician sitting in the White House will decide when the End Time comes! It isn't whoever happens to be General Secretary of the Communist Party in the Kremlin who will decide when the End Time comes! Jesus will decide that, thank you. And if nuclear weapons *can* end life on this planet, then *they* are sacrilegious; *they* are the Antichrist!"

Dr. Theodore Monk stood up as self-effacingly as he could, and he was a master of self-effacement. He glided up the long aisle totally missing the point, which was that he didn't have to worry about being criticized or hanged for walking out on John Burns. They couldn't have cared less. He was invisible. John Burns had their attention.

231

When he got to his hotel, he had to dial Elmer Jessup's number three times before he got it right.

"I can't tell," he said desperately. "He's wonderful. But I can't tell. He's unbelievable. But I've got to talk to him. I've got to see him up close and talk to him. It's the only way."

"I figured you'd say something like that," Jessup said.

27

IN WHICH MALCOLM KEYES ATTACKS AN ENEMY SILO

SPECIAL AGENT VANDERVANTER looked ill at ease sitting behind a desk; his natural mode of being was to pace back and forth across whatever space he had available. He didn't think well off his feet. He looked trapped sitting there, wearing his usual small smile; he was having a second meal of crow on wry, but he had enough of a sense of humor to handle it.

"You want me to help you find someone but you can't tell me who he is or where he lives," Vandervanter said.

"That's it."

Vandervanter was smiling and nodding.

"Your clearance simply isn't high enough," Keyes remarked.

"Revenge is sweet, isn't it?" Vandervanter replied.

"As a matter of fact, it's chocolatey."

"Enjoy it while you can; it doesn't happen this way often. You may look back fondly at this moment as the high point of your life."

"All I'm asking for is a fifteen-minute crash course in how to be a special agent."

"You're a fast learner, huh?"

"Okay, twenty. That's all I can spare; I've got a plane to catch."

It was too much. Vandervanter had to pace.

"Okay," he said, heading toward the door, talking over his shoulder. "You go to the locality where you think the person lives. You've got a locality, right?" Keyes nodded. "You go there and you look for the lowest level of government you can find. The town hall. The police station. Anything that sounds like a bureau of records. A municipal building." Vandervanter had reached the door. He wheeled around, headed back toward his desk, looking at Keyes, his hand rubbing the back of his neck. "Look for places that have tax records. Birth records. If that doesn't work, you go to the next higher level of government. Might be the county. Might be the township. As a last resort, you go to the state capital. Congratulations, you're now a special agent. You must come see me again sometime."

Keyes was staring vacantly out the window at the repeating patterns of the FBI building.

"You know," he said, "a letter of introduction from you on FBI stationery might smooth the way."

Vandervanter stopped pacing and looked at him.

"What the hell's come over you? A few months ago, you were nothing."

"I think power has gone to my head," Keyes replied.

Vandervanter looked at him, motionless, sort of hanging there.

"If you should have any questions while you're in the field, why, give me a ring."

Keyes nodded. He smiled politely. He was getting wonderful cooperation.

"I don't think I'll do that," he said slowly. He was guessing, but it was worth a try. "You could trace the call."

Vandervanter paced.

"That was very good. You're showing promise. But I could also check out your airline ticket, unless you used a false name and paid cash. Any form of credit would be a dead giveaway."

Keyes nodded again.

"Where do I pick up my diploma?" he asked.

Keyes stopped the car about a hundred yards away from the place. It was on a small hill, and he stopped as soon as he could see part of the roof. He didn't even know why he was doing that; it just seemed like a good idea. He could at least approach the place slowly, absorbing what he was looking at and getting into. He was still on the steep incline of the learning curve as he walked up the hill to the farmhouse.

He had gone all the way to the county level looking for a Mr. and Mrs. Joseph Burns, without turning up a clue. It was as though they had never existed. Then he had gotten the idea of checking all the banks in the area, and he had found them. The Burnses had been foreclosed years before and no one knew where they had gone. Now he was hoping he could find a picture of John Burns in an empty upstairs bedroom, *something* to bring back to Halliday. It would settle an important issue, an ambiguity.

The name was still on it, fire etched into a small board that was hanging vertically now by one small piece of chain: BURNS. There were two steps up to the porch, and then a half-open door into the house itself. The place was a blasted, empty space. A few empty corrugated boxes, broken plates, a pair of boots that looked as if they had been through the Civil War. The Burns family had been gone so long there weren't even white patches on the walls where the pictures might have been; the Kansas winds had blown in enough topsoil to make everything uniformly gray.

As he went up the stairs, he had the feeling that the Burns family hadn't owned a whole lot of things. He had the feeling they had run out of everything; the bankruptcy had been total; the place was used up; even the air seemed depleted.

In the middle upstairs bedroom he found a matchbook from the Mayflower Hotel in Washington lying on the floor.

Keyes was afraid to move. He was afraid to make a sound. He wasn't even sure he wanted to breathe. He twisted his head around and looked behind him. There was no one standing in the doorway. Keyes realized now that he hadn't gotten his degree in Special Agenting after all. He was in over his head. Someone else was looking for the Burns family. Who the hell could that be? He decided to do his thinking outside and went back down the creaking stairs as slowly as possible. On the porch, he fought off the desire to run like hell down the hill to his car. He knew what Halliday would say. You mean you didn't investigate? You didn't pursue the lead? Look for more clues?

He looked around the place. The sun was behind the clouds and everything looked gray. There was no sign of fauna, four-legged or otherwise. There were a few outbuildings—a barn, a silo, what looked like a garage, and a tool shed. He forced himself to walk to the barn, boxing the compass with his nose as he went.

The place was another wipeout. It didn't even smell. He walked past what looked like cow stalls, going very quietly. In the rear there was nothing but big spaces and a rusting plow blade.

"Was there a haymow?" Halliday would ask.

There was and there was a goddam ladder leading up to it. There was no hay in the haymow, but as he was moving lightly around the place, he heard the cocking of a pistol.

Keyes froze.

There was no one in the haymow; it had to be coming from below. There was no one standing at the top of the ladder pointing a gun at him. There was no sense staying in the hayloft; a bullet could tear through wood. But what was the point of going back down the ladder? He looked to see if there was anything remotely resembling a weapon.

The place was bankrupt.

There weren't a whole lot of options in any case. He tried to think of a good way to surrender. But maybe they didn't take prisoners. He couldn't stand the suspense. He started back down the ladder. Halfway down, he heard the cocking of a second gun. He froze again. Nothing happened. That was encouraging, because he was badly exposed: unarmed and halfway down a shaky ladder. He kept going. He was starting to feel really optimistic. He was getting close to the floor. A third gun was cocked. It was getting ridiculous. He ambled up to the door to peek out through the crack and heard a *fourth* gun cocked.

"Oh, for Christ's sake," Keyes said. It was the rusted hasp on the barn door rattling against the loop. It didn't even *sound* like the cocking of a gun. He stormed out of the place disgusted with himself and headed for what looked like a garage thirty yards away. He wrenched open the door.

There was a brand-new stretch Mercedes-Benz parked inside carrying D.C. license plates.

He stood there paralyzed, plunged into a new mood of terror. What would Halliday expect of him? How much could he be expected to do?

"Maybe there was a registration hanging from the steering column. Or in the glove compartment. You mean you didn't at least look inside?"

He went up to the driver's door thinking: Maybe I've got it all wrong. Maybe Halliday would say: You mean you didn't get the fuck out of there?

He decided he was going to have to figure it out for himself, without any assistance from the President of the United States. He opened the door as quietly as possible and sat down in the gorgeous leather smell. There was no registration, and the glove compartment was locked. He got out and tried the trunk. Locked. I have no knowledge of lock picking, Mr. President, he thought, and eased back out through the garage door.

In the tool shed, there was nothing but grass growing up through gaps in the wood floor and a rusty ax. Hey, things were starting to turn around. He picked it up, hefted it, swung it through the air. The ax head stayed on the handle. He went back out, heading for the silo, which was some two hundred feet away. He started for it, going past overgrown weeds, rusted metal objects, rotting gunnysacks. The only things missing were cattle skulls lying around and jimsonweed blowing past him.

When he was fifty feet from the silo, the door suddenly flew open and three men marched out. Keyes's jaw dropped. It was the business suit from the KGB and his two goons.

"You," Keyes said.

KGB's eyes bulged.

"You," he said.

The only thing Keyes could think of was that Halliday was right: He should have gotten the fuck out of there.

"Why are *you* here?" KGB said. He circled slowly around Keyes. "This is very confusing," he said. "I don't understand this. Would you please drop that stupid ax; you might hurt someone."

Keyes tossed the ax to the ground.

"I see you're alone."

"Maybe."

"You're alone. A veritable George Armstrong Custer charging an enemy silo with a rusty ax. You Americans. It must be in the water."

Keyes was studying their faces. They were an odd-looking bunch, standing there on a burned-out farm in a cold Kansas wind. If there was any peasant blood in any of them it wasn't showing. They were utterly urban, especially the slim, dapper, urbane Mr. KGB. But at least the confrontation didn't seem to be mortal.

"What of value can be learned from the fact that you are here?" Mr. KGB asked. "On the surface, it makes no sense. You *have* to realize this is a Potemkin farm. Or to be more precise, a reverse Potemkin. You do realize that, don't you? This whole place was manufactured by General Dynamics. It's a complete fake. At a cost of a hundred and fifty million dollars, I would guess. Aging the wood was a problem, and there were cost overruns, bribes to the city council, certain arrangements with the Department of Agriculture. I mean, this thing is USDA-approved, certified as Grade A prime bullshit."

237

Keyes was blushing in the presence of the enemy.

The Russian snapped his fingers. "Now I see," he said. "It's the only thing that makes sense. *You* don't know either, do you?"

"I have no wish to pursue this discussion," Keyes said.

"Hah! That's it; that's it! Incredible! You people play your cards so close to the vest, your left hand doesn't even know what its own middle finger is doing."

Mr. KGB was rattling off something in Russian to the other two, and they were all having a good time with it.

KGB abruptly turned back to Keyes.

"All I've got in the car is vodka. But it's American-style. Freezing. Could I make you a martini?"

"Another time, perhaps," Keyes said.

"Can we drop you anywhere?"

"Thanks, no. I'm being picked up."

They all headed for their Mercedes.

"If we find out anything, we'll let you know," Mr. KGB called back.

Keyes stood there in front of the old Burns homestead, watching them drive back down the hill. For the first time in his life, he actually felt like having a scotch.

28

THE FALLING PIANO AFFAIR

RECALLING KANSAS, KEYES was fiddling uninterestedly with his salad.

"And they honked their horn at me as they went by going on down the hill. It was mortifying."

The Vice-President was working away at a lamb chop.

"Mortifying and astounding, Malcolm," she said. "That the KGB and CIA are both fascinated by that preacher fellow. Not to mention our President."

They were in the White House mess, having lunch; Keyes was reporting to the Vice-President because the President was in Houston, mending fence. Keyes was an old hand at eating in the White House mess now; he was no longer stealing the menus. The Vice-President always had one glass of red wine with lunch. She sipped it now, looking at Keyes.

"What on earth could that *be?*"

"I told you what it is."

"It can't be, Malcolm. That's utterly preposterous."

"Since when is 'utterly preposterous' inappropriate as an adjective for a government program?"

"*Touché.*"

239

Keyes was feeling more and more at ease talking to her, being with her. He was being less guarded, more spontaneous. She seemed to encourage it. Keyes filled a need. He could think in her league. She hadn't met too many men in her life who could. It was a major problem for an intelligent woman; she referred to her husband as a dumb blonde.

"Funny thing about John Burns," she went on. "In a way, he's one of our few allies. He's a force for peace. He's drawing big numbers. And we need all the help we can get. You know, peace has no constituency in the federal government. The conservatives don't want it. They want to roll back communism everywhere, and they want to hold on to the bomb to do it with. The military-industrial complex gets rich off the arms race, and they've spread the contracts around to just about every congressional district in the country to keep Congress on the team. In effect, it's a military takeover of the government, American-style. So Richard needs people like John Burns. Just look at who's arrayed against us. Most of the establishment. Most of the bankers and businessmen. The Pentagon. Even big labor, for God's sake. For allies, we've got John Burns, a few bishops, and the peace groups."

Keyes shook his head, still picking desultorily at his salad. Keyes was depressed.

"You know," he said, bringing up a recent incident from RAM memory, "an air force general came in to see the President the other day. He claimed that Soviet warheads are simpler than American warheads and, therefore, are more 'robust' than ours. In other words, we need to keep testing to be sure our warheads still work, but the Russians don't have to. So a test ban would be a dangerous advantage for the Russians. They keep coming up with reasons for not giving up testing. The reasons seem to get nuttier and nuttier."

The Vice-President obviously had a fast-track metabolism; she was like a bear eating for winter.

"Richard calls it the Falling Piano Syndrome," she said. "You see, there's this man who's terrified of being hit on the head by a grand piano that's being lowered out of a tenth-floor window. So he walks along the sidewalk with his head up all the time, watching out for falling pianos. Not surprisingly, he's forever bumping into people and mailboxes and lampposts and getting into contretemps because he isn't watching where he's going. Well, this man gives the matter a lot of thought and eventually comes up with the perfect solution. He ends up out in the road, doing a dance along the white line, dodging trucks and buses but at long last *safe*. From *pianos*. That's what the right-wing position on the test ban amounts to. They'll claim that even with site visits and seismic detectors on Soviet territory, the Soviets will still manage to cheat. They might be able to test a one-half-kiloton warhead without us spotting it. So, because of the dangers of a half-kiloton warhead, we keep seventeen thousand of the big ones around. *That's* safer. Of course, they're going to get us all killed, sooner or later. That grand piano in the sky will eventually fall on all of us."

It was the kind of image that had a perverse appeal for Keyes. "The planet will go up in one great big lugubrious nuclear C-sharp-minor chord," he said. "How can they get away with this craziness decade after decade?"

"It's a political art form in this country. LBJ ran on a peace platform back in '64. American boys should not have to do what Asian boys should be doing, he kept saying. He won forty-five states. Then, between election day and inauguration, he orchestrated and he hyped and one month after inauguration American boys were doing what Asian boys were supposed to have been doing. That was the escalation in Vietnam. He got away with it, too." Pause, eating. "For a while."

Keyes had no appetite. He was rapidly losing enthusiasm for government. Politics. Democracy.

"You know," the Vice-President said, talking easily, eating voraciously, sipping delicately at that one glass of red wine, "there's a complex more deadly than the military-industrial complex. It's the Oedipus complex. They've plucked out their own eyes. They're self-blinded. They're not afraid of the bomb. They're willing to fight a hundred years' war. That's the real Oedipus complex. Think of a drunken blind man flailing around in a dynamite factory trying to light a wet cigar. That's the right wing in America."

Keyes sighed heavily. It was too much for him. It was too big for him. He had a sinking feeling about the future of the country, the race, the planet. Then he noticed Norman Pope moving across the mess.

Pope seemed to be in a manic state. He couldn't pass a hand without shaking it. He was saying a word here, there, patting a back, clinking coffee cups. It almost looked as though he were sampling the room: Do you think this is a good mess, a medium mess, or a bad mess, accuracy guaranteed to within four percentage points.

"Hi, folks," he said, pulling up a chair, putting down his coffee cup.

Madeleine was all business.

"What have you got?" she said to him.

"Sixty, thirty, ten on the test ban," he replied. "Sixty for, thirty

241

against, ten don't know. Ten percent of the people don't know what to do with the bomb." Pope was smiling. "Should we tell them?"

"What else?"

"Sixty-seven, twenty-seven, six on the Philippines. Sixty-seven opposed to going in, twenty-seven in favor of going in, six don't know from nothing."

"Trends?" she said.

"I think the people are beginning to realize there's such a place as the Philippine Islands," Pope said. "They're leery about it. It sounds Asian. It sounds like trouble. It sounds like body bags and MIAs. But they also don't like losing. I think. That's plus or minus one hundred percent. The fact of the matter is, I don't know what the hell is happening out there."

While Madeleine was listening to the Pope, Keyes was thinking about her. He couldn't help himself. She was so attractive. What did she do for a sex life? he wondered. Anytime she made a move, the Secret Service was there. There was no way she could possibly be surreptitious about it. So her lover would have to be someone either in the White House or the EOB. Somebody who was not only attracted to her—who wouldn't be?—but was also a master of discretion. But it would take more than that. It would have to be someone intelligent enough to think in her league. That had to narrow the field quite a bit. How did a really intelligent woman find a compatible lover? She suddenly turned from Pope and winked at Keyes. She'd read his mind. Keyes was still capable of blushing. He did. She turned back to Pope, smiling bitchily.

"Maybe you should take bigger samples," she said.

"Maybe I should. That will cost more."

"When it comes to polling, Richard is a big spender."

"I'll try it and see."

"Norman, why don't you ask them the question flat out?"

"What question would that be?"

"Would you be willing to live with a communist government in Manila in order to avoid another land war in Asia?"

"Whew. That's certainly laying it out," Pope said. "It scares me to even contemplate asking such a question."

"Then make the wording nicer. But not too nice. Let's get some real information."

Pope nodded.

"I'll do that."

He stood up and clinked coffee cups with Keyes.

242

"I hope you can go without sleep for the four years," he said, and was moving back across the mess, looking for bases to touch.

"Madeleine," Keyes said, "we should go back to the Consortium. That's where the answer is. I feel it in my bones."

The Vice-President was now starting to cancel out the glass of red wine by pouring herself a big cup of coffee from a carafe. She poured milk and sugar into it simultaneously.

"That would be premature, Malcolm," she said. "Richard wants to wait until they try something. And they're bound to. They can't afford to wait. The GOD Project is going to save the Philippines for them, right? John Burns is the center of the GOD Project, right? Something has to happen soon. Let them play their cards. They'll probably screw it up."

"Yes, Madam Vice-President," Keyes said, with an uncharacteristic tone of rebellion.

She looked at him.

"By the way," she said casually. "You have a little assignment from Richard."

29

SHERRY BREAK

OSCAR CRESPI, the principal owner of International Aluminum, had called the meeting. Things were happening. Troops were on the march, stability was at risk. Stability was always at risk, but in the past, the country had defended it, restored it, nurtured it. Now, Crespi was having his doubts. And when stability was lost, were not chaos and anarchy in the wings? Chaos and anarchy were the enemies, because they were always succeeded by communism: You went from being in the black to being in the Red. The Red red. Red was a hateful color. It made Crespi feel like a bull, and he was ready to charge.

"We're orchestrating," Farnsworth was telling them soothingly. "Everything's going to be all right. We're starting to get editorials out of the big dailies now. The *New York Times* is going to run one next Wednesday called 'Do We Want a People's Republic of the Philippines?' Jimmy Carter called on Halliday. Walter Mondale. Jerry Ford sees him next week. His own majority leaders in the House and Senate are with us. We're going to make that man go in, I guarantee it. He isn't strong enough to hold out."

Listening to Farnsworth talk was a peak experience for Albritten; it was like being in the big time; in fact, the time didn't get any bigger than this. They were in the Upper Fifth Avenue headquarters of the

Council on Foreign Relations in Manhattan, sipping drinks, quietly discussing the affairs of the nation. It was the center, the core, what might be called a meeting of the board of directors of United States of America, Inc., where they gave each other a State of the Corporation Message. *This* was the establishment.

It was the tiniest minority, after all, the minority of the rich. As a minority, the rich were like all minorities; they were conscious of how few they were. But the rich were the fewest, so they were touchy, even paranoid. The rich always had to worry about the guillotine. They felt constantly threatened by the 90 percent of Americans who had nothing, who were the unrich, but who had 90 percent of the *votes,* who theoretically were in *control.* To be rich was to be nervous, jittery, suspicious, and hypervigilant.

But to be present at a meeting of the big rich meant that you had earned trust. It was the ultimate compliment; it boded well for the career. Once you were admitted to the council, you were a potential candidate for high office in some future administration; in Albritten's case maybe a deputy secretary of defense. Possibly even DCI someday.

"But we're going to have to do some of his thinking for him," Farnsworth went on. "This Philippines thing is getting out of control." He paused for a sip of sherry. "We've had men killed at Clark Field, and the public *still* doesn't want to go in. What do we need, another *Maine?* Blow up an aircraft carrier? Will we never get past Vietnam? I must admit I was for it myself at the time, but *what* a blunder."

"We don't need to sink an aircraft carrier," the CEO of International Aluminum said. "We need a Bay of Tonkin incident. Old Lyndon would have figured out how to manage one. Richard Halliday will never do a Tonkin. The man can't be trusted."

"He thinks he's the wave of the future," Farnsworth said. "He thinks he's going to benefit from the awakening of the doves."

"The awakening of the doves," Crespi mused. "Sounds like a mural by Michelangelo."

Albritten was paying attention; he was sitting there in his leather club chair, straight and quiet, minding his p's and q's. This was power. No politician wanted these people against him. It was impossible to govern without their cooperation. Presidents came and went at the pleasure of the small percentage of Americans who took the trouble to vote; but the big rich had tenure. And when you had as much money as these people had, running the world was a must; your money was everywhere, into

245

everything. You couldn't very well put, say, $800 million into a pass-book savings account, could you?

Albritten didn't even envy Earl Farnsworth or Oscar Crespi. Having hundreds of millions of dollars couldn't possibly feel good; you had to be worrying about it all the time. All great wealth created great anxiety; that was the price of being rich. If the President of the United States fell down a flight of stairs, so would the stock market: You could lose fifteen million in an afternoon; such was the ephemeral nature of big riches. Or if some half-baked commie guerrilla general halfway around the world got ambitious, hundreds of millions of dollars in investments were placed in jeopardy. Albritten knew for a fact that Farnsworth personally had $175 million invested in Philippine enterprises, and now the New People's Army was on the march.

The redoubtable Senator Gutteridge was trying to contain his impatience.

"Look," he said, "I'm all for working over Halliday. Get him anxious, nervous, make him sweat. Make him look soft on defense; that always works. Fine. But that's only the first half of it. We get the project back on track and then present it to him all knit up, welded seams, the answer to the Philippines. We make it easy on him. We solve the whole problem for him. That's the important part. Can we talk about the project?"

Farnsworth nodded. He looked at Jessup, his eyebrows up.

Albritten sipped chastely at his sherry. He was thinking that this was a demonstration of democracy at work, but not a democracy of votes. It was a democracy of dollars; one buck, one vote. And Earl Farnsworth was a living, breathing landslide. It was actually a terrible burden, but Farnsworth could handle it, because he loved money the way a plumber loved his favorite wrench or a violinist his Strad. The pursuit and protection of big riches was a calling, an avocation, a twenty-four-hour-a-day job that required a dedicated, obsessive perfectionist. Albritten admired Farnsworth without envying him.

"There are problems," Elmer Jessup said. He was puffing on a Churchill, his white wine spritzer lying untouched on a solid oak end table.

"What problems?" Farnsworth asked.

"I refer you to Dr. Monk."

Monk had been slouched in an easy chair, staring off into space, waiting his turn. He was experiencing the usual situational fatigue. He did not care for the scene. Nevertheless, he tried to put a good face on it and sound optimistic.

"Gentlemen, we have two very serious candidates."

Gutteridge pounced on him.

"Now what the hell does that mean? Very serious? Are they or aren't they? Dr. Monk, you sound like a damn fence-straddling bureaucrat, if you don't mind my saying so."

Monk let Gutteridge's vehemence simply wash over him and then waited for it to ebb back out to sea.

"In each case," he said, "Mr. Albritten was unable to complete the series. But he got provocatively close."

"Circumstances intruded," Albritten put in.

"Who are they?" Farnsworth asked.

"One of them is an aide to President Halliday. The other is the chief spokesman for the Twenty-fifth of December Movement, a peace group."

"Good Lord," Farnsworth said. "This is really murky."

"The whole thing is preposterous," Gutteridge said, looking balefully at Monk. Gutteridge didn't trust Monk either. Monk smiled his meek, small-toothed smile.

"They're both exquisite," he said. "They're very bright. They're really outstanding individuals. John Burns is a rebel, right down to his toenails. He's the rebellious son. A classic. There's no dealing with him. He's impossible."

This was said with love and compassion. There was no animus or vituperation; he was being clinical and paternal simultaneously.

"Malcolm Keyes, on the other hand, looks even more like Henry Patrick than John Burns does. And there's something very unusual about him. He has an extraordinary memory. I saw it at work a few weeks ago. It's phenomenal. You could easily regard this as a disorder, a glitch. Perhaps linked to other disorders. To me it's a sign of pathology. Of the two, I lean toward Malcolm Keyes, but we have confirmation on only eighteen of the twenty points of comparison. Nevertheless, it is my opinion, gentlemen, that Malcolm Keyes is the solution to the politics of counterguerrilla warfare."

"I have to register my disagreement here," Jessup put in hastily. "I think it's that damn crazy preacher, who's passed *nineteen* of the twenty."

"Mr. Jessup is certainly entitled to his opinion," Monk said disdainfully, offended that mere security would dare to differ with science.

"What are we going to do about it?" Crespi asked.

Monk looked at Jessup. Jessup looked at Albritten. Albritten looked at the ceiling.

247

"There are risks," Jessup said finally.

"You got that right," Farnsworth said. "There certainly are risks. Look, I don't give a goddam about the bases in the Philippines. They can be replaced. It's the psychological effect. It would be a disaster if the commies ever managed to kick us out of the Philippines. It cannot be allowed to happen. Everybody'll start getting big ideas. The dominoes are worldwide, and they don't have to be next to each other anymore. So we've got to get the project back on track in time for the Philippines. And Central America. Maybe even South Africa. *That's* where the risks are. And what about Mexico, for God's sake? It's a time bomb."

"We're working on it," Jessup said.

"Elmer," Farnsworth said, managing to sound like a parent talking to a child.

"Too much time is passing," Gutteridge said. "You have to do it and be done with it."

"Hell, we don't have *any* more time," Crespi put in. "Gentlemen, this is the *crunch*. The irresistible force meeting the immovable object."

Albritten was moved. Shocked. Jessup was looking beleaguered. He had never seen that before. The mighty Elmer Jessup! Treed, cornered, defensive.

"The only way to speed it up," Jessup said, waving his Churchill at them, "is to take chances. I'm talking about going in harm's way. Serious chances."

"What do you call a serious chance?" Farnsworth asked.

"That Burns kid is very well protected. He's got a band of *Christians* surrounding him. This would require a very complex operation. Malcolm Keyes works in the White House. He's an intimate of the President of the United States. These are risky situations."

"Take the risks," Farnsworth said.

"What's there to worry about?" Gutteridge asked.

"You've got to make calls if you want to get results," Crespi said.

"Do you want another Watergate?" Jessup said. "Or an Iran-Contra? *That's* what I'm worried about. If we slip up. I have to tell you that the Company is not perfect. It has never been perfect."

Albritten was watching Jessup squirm and privately enjoying it; it didn't happen often. It was positively titillating. Old Elmer had to wrestle with a basic problem: As the decades since World War Two had gone by, the establishment's hidden agenda had gotten further and

248

further from what they were *saying* they were doing. It was getting tougher and tougher to explain it all away, to manage to look plausible on the evening news. Even the average American, for whom foreign affairs didn't rate alongside a hockey puck, was beginning to have doubts.

Earl Farnsworth was poised with his sherry halfway to his lips. "You're saying that if it failed, we'd end up with a Watergate or something."

"That's it."

"Don't worry about it."

"Don't worry about it?" Jessup said.

"We get a congressional investigation committee together and they drag it out for fuckin' *ever*. We *bore*. By and by they don't want to *hear* any more about it; they've *had* it. Let us worry about that, okay?"

"Okay," Jessup said. "But I think I ought to remind you that you're putting me at risk. Do you want to see a liberal Halliday flake in my job?"

"Elmer," Farnsworth replied, "that's the kind of bridge you cross when you get to it."

Albritten watched Jessup sucking on his cigar. What they were saying was that Mr. Elmer Jessup of the CIA was expendable. Which came with the territory. When you were trying to run the world out of a democracy, dirty tricks were inevitable. You couldn't possibly do things aboveboard. If the U.S. establishment kept its hands clean, Third World nations would be falling to communism all over the planet; most humans had no interest whatsoever in maintaining the status quo. The risk of disgrace was built into the system.

Gutteridge called them commonists.

"I'm telling you, without this thing working for us, the commonists are going to run *wild*. We'll be helpless."

Farnsworth, on the other hand, was being very calm. He hiked up his navy-blue gabardine trouser legs about a quarter of an inch, the sharp crease cutting through the atmosphere like a razor. He sipped. He stared off at the paneled walls of the study.

"Elmer," he said, "you're a genius at this sort of thing. You'll figure a way. Put your best people on it. I'll bet Albritten here has plenty of ideas. Elmer, you've *got* to deliver Henry Patrick to the Consortium, and you've got to do it yesterday. To delay is even more dangerous than taking action."

Monk was looking alarmed.

249

"Gentlemen, I *urge* you not to do anything rash. Sooner or later, we'll get a break. So far the breaks have gone against us, but sooner or later it'll go our way. Rash action would almost certainly be counterproductive."

"We never engage in rash actions," Jessup said, brushing him off. "We plan. What do you think, Alex?"

Albritten knew how the establishment admired the gung-ho spirit; if you could solve their impossible problems, they loved you.

"I believe it can be worked," he said.

"There, you see?" Farnsworth said.

Jessup chewed on his cigar and looked at Albritten slowly. He wasn't clear about it, whether it was outright betrayal or normal bureaucratic manipulation and survival. He took the cigar out of his mouth. He took the first sip of his wine spritzer.

"I'm putting you in charge of it," he said to Albritten. "Settle it."

30

THE WINTERS OF OUR
DISCONTENTS

THE FIRST-FLOOR corridor of the EOB, 6:30 P.M., Keyes ambling along.

"Marley was dead, to begin with. There can be no doubt whatever about that."

He had just had a hamburger at the White House mess. He and Pope would have to be at the Pentagonal Church by 7:00 P.M. at the latest if they wanted to get good seats.

There was an uncanny, otherworldly quality to it.

"In life, I was your partner, Jacob Marley."

Keyes strolled into his office and sat at his empty desk, edging away his empty wastebasket with a foot and then easing back in his chair. He was going to get a close-up look at John Burns, and then he was going to listen to Max Breskin talk and maybe learn something about the crazy confluence of John Burns and the Philippine Islands and the GOD Project and the CIA and the Joint Chiefs and the American establishment and maybe the real meaning of intervention in Third World countries as well as various fundamental implications of the Cold War and the arms race. He couldn't wait.

"Business! *Mankind* was my business. The common welfare was my business; charity, mercy, forbearance, and benevolence were *all* my business."

Pope was going along because he could provide mature political guidance and Halliday totally trusted Pope. Keyes was still an amateur.

"It is required of every man that the spirit within him should walk abroad among his fellow men and travel far and wide, and if that spirit goes not forth in life, it is condemned to do so after death."

Keyes waited for Pope to finish shaving and put his electric shaver back in its case. Then Pope sat down on Keyes's one chair with his sphygmomanometer in his lap. He had a new one. It was automatic. No more pumping up. The thing pumped up by itself and then gave a digital readout and an optional printout of systolic, diastolic, pulse, and time and date. Pope snapped open the hard plastic case, put the cuff on his upper arm an inch above the crease of his elbow, and got a reading. He didn't say anything, but he started belly breathing for dear life. He did it twenty-five times and then took his pressure again.

"Down to one fifty-five over one oh three. I can live with that."

Keyes found, once he was in the Pentagonal Church of Christ, that he was paranoid, once removed. He found himself looking at faces, the faces of the people sitting in folding chairs, waiting for John Burns to appear. Most of them had to be worshipers. But a few of them had to be CIA. The problem was that they all looked like plausible candidates. The most innocent-looking person could be the cleverest of agents. Once you got into that mode, you were ruined; anything was possible.

They had gotten there early enough to get seats close to the stage. Which is what it was; you could hardly call it a pulpit. There was only a five-pointed star attached to the rear wall and above that a simple cross. The auditorium itself was basically circular, with the audience seated in 270 degrees of the circle. The five points of the pentagon were triangular rooms, one of which was the television control room, the point directly behind the stage. Sitting there was like being in a theater waiting for a play to begin. Promptly at 8:00 P.M. the lights began to dim throughout the five-pointed auditorium, where a thousand people were eagerly awaiting the appearance of John Burns. The stage was totally black for a few seconds, and then a spotlight came up and Burns was revealed, standing there looking straight out, expressionless, holding a Bible under his arm, seemingly indifferent to thunderous applause: It was merely something to be gotten through before he could say whatever it was he had to say.

Keyes could see the similarity between Burns's face and his own. No one ever really knew what his or her own face looked like. No matter how much you might stare at yourself in the mirror, you were seeing only two dimensions, you couldn't ever see yourself the way others did. And yet the resemblance was obvious and striking, much more so than when he had seen Burns on television. Keyes had fleeting thoughts of his mother's having strayed. But it was ridiculous. She wasn't the type. The truth was, there were only so many faces. However it happened, mankind was descended from a small number of mating pairs; from only one if you believed the Bible. How did inerrantists handle the incest question? Keyes wondered.

Burns was wearing a khaki shirt with epaulets, which were a faint suggestion of the military, but his sleeves were rolled up above his elbows, which dispersed the effect. That, plus the usual denim pants and industrial safety shoes, gave him the look of a rural preacher working out of a tent. He stood silent for a moment, rotating his gaze out over the 270 degrees of audience while holding out his Bible. He was calm and self-assured, a born performer.

"Do you believe every word in this book?" he said to them.

Amens, hallelujahs, cheers, sobs.

"Of course you do. And I do too. This is God's book; this is the word of *God*. This is not a met-a-phor." He held the book high over his head, and as he said the word "metaphor," his voice dripped acid, and he had the audience right with him, ready to go, ready to go anywhere, anywhere Burns wanted to take them.

He was still holding the book over his head, and he shook it.

"This is not a po-em."

Yea brother, amen, hallelujah, praise Jesus, Christ the King.

"This isn't a book to be interpreted by interpreters who think they know more than *God*. This book is literally true word for word from first page to last, and it doesn't require interpreting. God's truth and beauty do not need lit-er-ary crit-ics."

Laughter, amens, nervous energy, a few people standing up now, emotionally incapable of remaining seated.

"Now, we speak of inerrancy in connection with the Bible. We say the Bible is not in error, nowhere in error, *never* in error. Those who believe that are inerrantists. I have to tell you that I am *almost* an inerrantist but not pure. You might call me a neo-inerrantist. You see, I've got a problem with one word. One word in the Bible.

253

"I know that must be shocking to many of you. But so far I've kept no secrets from you, and I have no intention of starting now. I am not pure when it comes to the Bible. One word in the Bible is *false* in my opinion, and I can't conceal this thing from you, so let's get it out into the open. I believe the scribes got that one word wrong; after all, they were only human, and humans err, do they not? Humans are *not* inerrant."

Total uncomprehending silence.

If this wasn't sacrilege, it was about as close as you could get. John Burns was in danger of losing his audience, probably for the first time in his career. Surely he had gone too far this time, even for the members of the Pentagonal Church, the Twenty-fifth of December Movement. He had shocked them; he couldn't possibly have expected less. But he was on the prowl, moving around his little stage looking for language among the floorboards.

"Brothers and sisters! The one word I'm talking about refers to the temperature of hell!" Burns told them. "I do not believe that hell is a hot place. I *know* that hell is a cold place. In the grand scheme of things, my friends, hell couldn't possibly be a hot place. The notion is absurd. Heat nurtures. It is cold that kills, cold that tortures. Think about it. Imagine it. Go back a few thousand years. What must it have been like in winter before there was central heating, before there was steam heat, before there were fireplaces, before there was *fire?* Numbing, inescapable cold. The scarcity of food. Helplessness against the elements. Whipsawed by the wind and the temperature and the snow and the ice and the desolation. God gives us a touch of hell every winter, a reminder that if you don't banish the coldness from your heart, then you are going to endure freezing eternity. Winter teaches."

Long arm pointing out toward the audience, index finger moving across the 270 degrees.

"When heat returned in the spring, *that* was a suggestion of heaven. The restorative warmth, the warmth of the sun returning, the warmth of the *Son*—the Son of God. Food growing. Animals abundant." He sang a line that came out of nowhere and bowled them over: "Summertime, and the living is easy." He had won his gamble; they were back with him.

"I hope somebody's taping this," Pope whispered amid the roaring.

"In more ways than you can count," Keyes whispered back.

"But how does springtime warm the coldness of the human heart?" Burns went on. "The coldness that is the little bit of hell we all carry around with us. It's what produces Satan's work, that coldness. Look at

254

the language we use: When we don't like someone, our relations with that person cool. Are chilled. Grow cold. The ultimate manifestation of this coolness is cold *war.* Cold war is hellish too. Always hating, always arming, ever more thousands of nuclear weapons. Leading to what? Leading to *nuclear winter.* Leading to nuclear winter *hell.* Hell is cold and bare and white and ungreen. Hell is stasis. Hell is paralysis. Hell is nuclear everlasting winter!"

"Jesus, Mary, and Joseph," Pope said.

"He does make some rather interesting connections, doesn't he?" Keyes whispered.

"Now," Burns said. He had animated his audience and his audience had animated him. He was strutting around the stage, arms and legs cutting through the air. "Who wants to be saved from nuclear winter hell?"

Unanimity in the Pentagonal Church of Christ.

"Does anyone here believe that Minuteman I is going to save him or her from nuclear winter hell?"

A frightening wave of sound rolled over the auditorium. Keyes could feel it physically. There was power in the room. Keyes had moved inside the circles of power, but he was only just beginning to appreciate what power was.

"Does anyone here believe that Trident Two is going to save him or her from nuclear winter hell?"

Again that awful sound swept over them.

"No!" Pope said, digging Keyes in the ribs.

"No!" Keyes said.

"Does anyone here believe that Midgetman I is going to save him or her from nuclear winter hell?"

The audience was standing up en masse now, Keyes and Pope included.

"Would you like to know what's *going* to save you from nuclear winter hell?"

The reaction was pandemic. Moaning, amening, yes brothering, talking in tongues, strutting along the aisles, writhing *on* the aisles.

"*Jesus II* is going to save you from nuclear winter hell. Jesus is coming *back,* and all you have to do is *believe* in him, *accept* him into your heart, to be saved from nuclear winter hell!"

The place was going nuts and bananas; it was a barely controlled riot, spirituality run amok. The sound level was appalling.

"Let's get the fuck out of here," Pope whispered at a hundred decibels.

"Blessed are the peacemakers: For they shall be called the children of God," Burns was saying as they were going back up the aisle. "Matthew five, nine."

Keyes and Pope left the auditorium shaken. They had experienced the reality of power, down where life was lived in the real world with no long flights of steps and tall columns—Pope's statistics come to life and expressing a point of view.

They reentered the church at the point of the star which was directly behind the stage. It was where the TV director was running things. There was the usual bank of monitors, each showing a different shot: Burns full-figure, Burns close up, the balcony, the entire hall, interesting-looking spectators, or spectators having interesting-looking reactions. The director had the luxury of being able to tape any and all of the shots he was getting.

"I know a little something about PR," Breskin said, right off. He was being low-key and friendly. "You guys aren't the only ones who know how to orchestrate. I have a lot of connections in the media. You see what I'm saying? Lay a *finger* on him and I'll blow it sky-high; you won't be able to contain it; it will be a stink bomb, I guarantee it. I'm just trying to be clear about this with you people."

"Carlos on Camera Four, zoom in on John," the director was saying into a microphone. "Three, loosen up on John. One, there's a woman sobbing in the balcony. Get a shot of her. She's in section D."

"Could you be a little clearer about the problem?" Pope said to Breskin.

"You want to be clearer about the problem?" a woman said. She had been sitting in a corner, fenced off by a video recorder; she was quite young and her name was Miriam.

"Have Camera Five go to the third row at the right end of the balcony," Miriam said to the director.

"Five, pan to the right," the director said. "Too far, back a scootch. That's it."

Miriam tapped the fifth monitor with a long delicate finger and looked at Keyes and Pope. She was pointing to a man seated in an aisle seat.

"He's one of your agents," she said.

She moved to the third monitor.

"Get up close," she said. "Left-hand side of the mezzanine. About halfway up. Aisle seat."

"Camera Three, tilt up, move in. Slowly."

"Stop," the woman said.

"Stop," the director said.

She tapped on the monitor.

"This person is an agent."

It was a woman of about fifty. She seemed to be enthralled by John Burns.

"First row, left-hand aisle seat."

"Camera One, pan left. Hold it."

It was a man of about thirty-five. He looked no different from the rest of them.

"I don't believe it," Pope said.

"We're going to publish their pictures in the *Pentagonalist.*"

"Do you know it's a violation of the law to reveal the identity of CIA agents?" Pope said.

"Reveal their identities? We're going to make them famous. Assuming your prostitute mass media pick up on it."

The girl couldn't have been more than eighteen. She was dressed in a simple frock, no makeup, flat shoes, and she knew who she was.

Keyes gestured at the monitors.

"What do you think they're doing out there?"

"You mean you guys don't know?" Breskin asked.

"I didn't say that."

"Then what did you say?"

"He said that government is complex," Pope put in.

Breskin shook his head. He even managed a smile.

"Let's look at this thing. What's the guy doing? Selling secrets to the Russians? Betraying his country? Bullshit. He's taking God back from the right wing. Is that a crime these days? He's pointing out some stupid, and I mean stu-pid, contradictions in American society. Is that a crime these days? Maybe it is. That kid gets out more news in five minutes than CBS does in a year."

"Let's not get down to basics, all right?" Pope said.

"I'll tell you what they're doing out there," Breskin said. "They're studying John's movements. They're trying to find the moment when he isn't protected so they can grab him again."

The girl stepped in front of Breskin and confronted Pope and Keyes.

"What are you going to do about this?" she asked.

"We'll have to look into it," Pope said, trying to sound authoritative, looking as if he needed his blood pressure machine.

"Tell them that it's going to be a fight," she said.

"A fight?" Pope said.

"That's right. It isn't going to be easy. He isn't a pushover." She was tapping Pope on the chest. "You're going to pay a price if you try anything. Am I expressing myself clearly?"

"Yes, ma'am," Pope said. "I hear you."

The Pope, along to supply mature political guidance, nodded to Keyes and tilted his head at the door. Keyes was still in nuclear winter hell. Keyes didn't know where power really lay anymore. Was it in the U.S. establishment of banks and corporations and generals? Or was it in the Pentagonal Church of Christ? In any case, he knew that a clash was coming, and there would be winners and there would be losers.

31

LOW-INTENSITY CONFLICT

THE UNOFFICIAL POLITICAL garbage pail of the President of the United States was tilting his chair against the wall of the Cabinet Room, cultivating self-effacement and invisibility, reels spinning behind his eyes. The transition from the Pentagonal Church of Christ was jarring. This was the other side of the coin. Or, as John Burns might put it, the hard noses.

The four principals were sitting at the cabinet table itself: the President, State, Defense, and the commanding general of the Joint Special Operations Command. Keyes was in record mode. He was also in education mode. He was John Doe being a fly on the wall, listening to his leaders level.

Decision time was rapidly approaching, State was musing. They weren't going to be able to fudge much longer. State had been around forever. He'd spent a long career working both sides of the street, alternately playing the respectable conservative for the Democrats and the respectable liberal for the Republicans. He was seventy, and his face had settled into basically friendly lines and wrinkles, and he had a soft-spoken, easygoing manner that tended to disarm opponents until they got to know him.

"You know," he was saying, "World War One was the Vietnam of its

259

day. It was a ghastly blunder any way you look at it—politically, strategically, tactically. It gave the Bolshies the opportunity to take over in Russia. It was so awful it *almost* eliminated war as an instrument of national policy. It took a Hitler to rescue the West from pacifism."

They were working on Halliday, coming at him from all sides. They all wanted to go into the Philippines. Everyone was hot to trot. A People's Republic of the Philippines was the establishment's nightmare, and they were working at wearing down Halliday's resistance.

Keyes stole a glance at Defense. It was a mistake. Defense was looking right at him, wondering who the hell he was. Keyes broke contact—he was accustomed to doing that, since he'd been brought up in Manhattan, the eyeballing capital of the world—and tried to look modestly interested in what State was saying.

State was laughing ruefully.

"Old John Foster Dulles used Hitler as much as he could. He really got mileage out of Hitler. Nasser was Hitler. Walter Ulbricht of East Germany was Hitler. Ho Chi Minh was Hitler. Stalin was Hitler. Maybe Stalin *was* Hitler. Your problem, Mr. President, is that you don't have a Hitler. You've got your World War One: Vietnam. But you don't have your Hitler. It's pathetic, really. We've got nuclear superiority and we can go in almost anywhere in the world and the Russians wouldn't dare try to stop us. But without a Hitler we are unable to commit serious forces. I believe that, sir, is the political meaning of the last election. That's why you won. The public thinks *you* won't go in."

"I'm relieved to hear you say that," Halliday said. "That's a bit of reality we all have to accept. Is there anybody here who doesn't accept that?"

"They'd be marching again," Defense said. "We'd be back in the sixties. I personally wouldn't want to live through the sixties again."

"The Pentagon does not wish to hit the beaches anywhere without the full backing of the American people," General Dander said.

It was too easy. Keyes didn't believe any of it. All three of them were champing at the bit to go in. The sell had to be coming soon.

"Now, I know you ran as a peace candidate, and you *won* as a peace candidate," State continued, "although your mandate was something less than overwhelming. But what do you think will happen to you if we lose Clark Air Force Base and the Subic Bay Naval Station?"

"But we don't really need Clark and Subic. Why should I risk American lives?"

"The psychological blow would be awful. It would encourage leftists all around the world."

There it was, Keyes thought. Orientalism. Saving face. Killing people not because it was absolutely necessary but for appearances' sake.

"But that's why we went into Vietnam."

"Sir," State said, trying not to sound too condescending, "how do you think the *public* will react if you lose Subic and Clark?"

"I don't know and neither do you," Halliday said.

"That's right; I don't know. Nobody knows. But I know how the Republicans will orchestrate it to the public."

"I guess you know," Defense put in, "that the Republican National Committee has already launched what they call Operation Grover Cleveland."

Keyes and Halliday exchanged a communication that not even the National Security Agency could have decoded: "Here it comes." Never mind that Halliday's options were getting narrow. Never mind that the crunch was coming, that history was catching up with Doc Halliday. Never mind that the public didn't want to fight and also didn't want to lose. Never mind that the issue couldn't be compromised, that it was go or no go, fight or run, that Halliday had the difficult task of acting like a dove without looking like a pigeon: Defense would have all the answers laid out neatly. Defense actually believed that he knew everything. He was now on the point of enlightening the President.

"I think, perhaps," Defense said, "that it's time for General Dander to make his presentation. This will be brief, sir."

That went without saying. Anything that Defense was involved with would be pithy, worthwhile, convincing, and brief. Everything soon would be obvious.

General Dander was in charge of the Special Operations Forces, or SOF, which was about to be offered as the solution to the Philippines problem. And the Chad problem. And the Central America problem. And any other goddam problem that cropped up any goddam place on earth. Dander was taut, nervous, filled with himself, conscious that he was getting rare presidential attention and time was of the essence. He talked like a burp gun in fast, noisy bursts. He leaned forward over the cabinet table, both hands palms down on the table, and said, "The problem we have to deal with is how to fight a war without the American people realizing it."

Dander didn't pull punches. Communication was taking place.

"That's been tried before," Halliday said. "That's how we got Irangate."

"I'm not saying without congressional approval. We'd do this strictly legit. I personally don't think we'll have a problem there. Congress understands the basic situation. The whole idea is to use surrogate armies, such as the Army of the Philippines, with little touches here and there added in."

"Tell about the little touches here and there."

"Mostly we're talking about noncombatant stuff." Dander was selling, which was all right; that was understood on both sides. "Programs to win over HAM, as we call it. Hearts and minds. We build hospitals. We propagandize against the New People's Army. Nun raping, and so on. Psy Ops. Psychological warfare. We drop Christmas presents to kids from helicopters, which gets going good associations to helicopters; the chopper got a bad image in Vietnam. We set up soup lines; we sponsor sporting events, resettlements, and so on and so forth. Winning the HAM. Low Intensity Conflict, as we call it."

"Where does the conflict come in?" Halliday asked innocently.

"*One* battalion of Special Forces."

Halliday smiled, and Keyes recorded it. They made it seem so easy. That's what was going to save the free world from left-wing revolutions: one lousy battalion.

"Does it bother you that such an action would violate the 1973 Congressional War Powers Resolution?" Halliday said.

Keyes was subtly shaking his head from side to side, but it was too late.

"I assume, sir," the general said, "that you're referring to 50 U.S.C. P1541[c], which prohibits the introduction of military forces into potentially dangerous situations. However, that resolution provides for several exceptional conditions, one of which is an attack on our armed forces, which we have here."

Halliday nodded, conceding the point. By now he'd picked up the signal from Keyes.

"What can you do with one battalion?" he said to Dander.

"Important jobs that the surrogate armies are incapable of doing. Like taking out the commie leadership. If you can get the leaders, you can really hurt them. There are only so many good leaders per generation. Surgical operations of that nature. Taking out supply dumps. Supply has to be basic to the NPA. I mean, we can paradrop; we can hit the beaches. We can hit the beaches at *night*. We can range far behind their lines. We move in; we move out. The *navy,* for God's sake, has even offered us some of its attack submarines. They have more than they need. We can use them to launch conventional cruise missiles against NPA installations. This is the ultimate in covert warfare. It will come out of *nowhere*. No headlines. No journalists. Any casualties are the result of defensive patrolling around our bases."

Defense jumped in with his little aside, a delicious little tactical bonus.

"If casualties should get too high to hide—if the battalion takes a clobbering, say—that just might tip the scales that allow you to go in in force."

"In other words, if I fail badly enough, I succeed."

"Uh," Defense said, somewhat at a loss. "Well, I wouldn't have put it quite that way, but I suppose you could say that."

Halliday's head was not moving, not by so much as an eighth of an inch. It was not moving up and down as someone else's head would to at least acknowledge that he understood what he had heard. Halliday did not give satisfaction easily. He had already given far too much satisfaction in his choices for Defense and State; they were significant compromises, made because he felt that he had to mollify the establishment and keep everyone on board; his entire administration was built on quicksand.

"I'll tell you, gentlemen, Low Intensity Conflict sounds like a scam to me."

Halliday was very skeptical of the military. They had a way of making promises they couldn't keep. He had said it to Keyes once: These people all think they can solve a complex situation with an explosion. The military mind was the ultimate in oversimplification.

"Will soup kitchens make the Filipino peasants forget about the fact that the land is not being redistributed? That's what it's all about, after all. Land. Do-re-mi. I mean, seventy percent of the population are peasants, most of them living below the poverty line. Very frankly, I feel that Low Intensity Conflict is the advertising mentality. It deals with surfaces, not with realities. It's a con job. And we're still relying on surrogate armies."

"For the major combat only," Dander insisted.

"But our surrogate army in the Philippines is getting its ass kicked. That's why we're meeting here today. I don't even think those guys want to fight. They're making a living, that's all they're doing. Why would they risk their lives defending American bases? And in the meantime, our losses are climbing as the NPA apparently infiltrates with impunity and lobs shells into our bases whenever they damn please. They've got the high morale. Our guys don't. As a famous strategist put it, the moral is to the material as three is to one. That's certainly the way it worked in Vietnam. Maybe as ten is to one."

Defense, State, and General Dander all sat back in their chairs. They exhaled, practically in unison. There was silence in the Cabinet Room. Keyes, missing nothing, recorded the duration of the silence; it was like a rest before the last dying fall of a plaintive violin.

"What else is there to do?" State asked finally.

"You tell me."

"The alternative," Defense replied in his assured way, his logic always being unassailable, "is the loss of the Philippines and divers other places around the globe."

There it was. Richard Halliday was going to have to do one thing or another; it was the end of consensus.

"But isn't time against us?" he said. "Won't we lose those divers places eventually, after a lot of bloodshed and waste of resources? Too many people want share of pie. Aren't we talking about a hundred years' war? Is there any point to this?"

It was clearly State's prerogative to respond.

"All *you* have to do, sir, is hold out for another four years. Let someone else worry about the other ninety-six. If you can hold the line for four years, you will have done your job. Taking the long view at this point would be self-defeating."

Another long pause. Defense was playing with his pencil. Defense was troubled. He seemed to be on the point of coming to a decision. Then he spoke to Halliday. His head was pointed at Halliday, but his eyes were down on the table.

"Speaking very theoretically," Defense said, "suppose you could go into the Philippines, engage in Low Intensity Conflict, and take *no* casualties. I realize that's a hypothetical proposition, but suppose you could do it. No casualties, no headlines, no fright videos on the evening news. Under *those* circumstances would you go in?"

Halliday flicked a microsecond look at Keyes. It was almost a look of embarrassment. Defense had virtually described the GOD Project, as defined by Malcolm Keyes. Keyes himself had an odd reaction. He was feeling both triumphant and terrified at the same time. It was eerie. He brought his chair forward so that all four legs were on the floor. He was feeling dizzy again, the way he'd felt at Nixon's wake. Then General Dander spoke.

"I have to interject here the thought that you cannot realistically expect zero casualties."

Keyes looked at Dander's face. There was no hidden agenda, no play-acting. General Dander didn't know about the GOD Project.

Doc Halliday was shaken and indecisive. He wasn't even looking for a cigar.

"For the sake of argument," Defense said.

Halliday was fumfering around.

"That's rather hypothetical," he said. "But I might. I'd have to know more about the details."

"Fine," Defense said. "Let's leave it at that."

"Make the drinks, Malcolm."

Malcolm made the drinks.

"Okay," Halliday said, seated on a couch, eyes closed. "Let's have it."

Keyes sat down on the couch next to Halliday, something he'd never done before; he'd always kept a respectful distance.

"What I have to say is going to sound strange. May I be frank?"

"You know me, Malcolm. Out with it."

"I'd like to request Secret Service protection."

Halliday opened his eyes. He focused on Keyes.

"I see that you're serious."

"Yes, sir."

"It's what Defense said in there."

"Yes, sir."

"Without conceding an inch, I'll grant that you could construe that little hypothetical question as confirmation of your theory about the GOD Project."

"And *if* I'm right, I'm in trouble. That thing is getting very important to them. The Vietnam Syndrome, right? That means John Burns is in trouble too. With both of us it was a case of *measurementus interruptus.* Albritten didn't get all his data. My guess now is that it's some kind of identification system."

"I'll have to think that one over, Malcolm. That's a heavy one. Be a scandal around here. I don't even know if it's legal to have the Secret Service commit resources to protecting you. You weren't elected by the people. Dammit, I was afraid you'd have some kind of bad reaction to Defense. Malcolm, don't you think it's odd that General Dander himself obviously doesn't know anything about it? After all, he's in command of SOF. If what you say is true, wouldn't he be in the know?"

Keyes took an extra-large dose of scotch and then put the empty glass down on the coffee table.

265

"Wouldn't *you* be in the know?" he said.

Halliday stood up, grabbed Keyes's glass, and headed for the bar, nodding his head up and down. Then he came back with the drinks and sat down again, still nodding his head.

For Keyes, it had to be the low point in his career in politics. The trickery built into a democracy was getting to him. The brazenness of the scheming. The endlessness of the scheming. All for the purpose of doing something the public didn't want to do. Politicians were like the navigator of a ship who slyly navigates it to a different destination than the captain thinks he's headed for. That's what life in a democracy was like. The people were in command. The people were the captain. But the politicians were the navigator.

Halliday stirred.

"I'm going to bed," he said, starting out of the room. He stopped and looked back at Keyes. "You're feeling the crunch too, huh, Malcolm? I'll see what I can do."

32

CAESAR'S GAME

THE AIR IN the room was a perfect sixty degrees Fahrenheit, 40 percent humidity, video machinery being among the most cared-for entities in society. John Burns, a perfectionist, kept tinkering with his taped programs all the way to air time.

"I look insincere there," he said, pointing to one of the monitors. "I was trying to look cute and coy, and it didn't work. Take that bit out. Cut right after I say, 'What did *you* do in the war of the rich against the poor, Daddy?' Go to an audience reaction shot. Use the one where the three middle-aged women are giggling. Know the one I mean? Then come back to me where I say, '*I* don't want to fight in the war of the rich against the poor. Does anyone here really want to blah blah blah blah blah?' "

Burns had been sitting at the console next to the editor. Now he stood up and moved around the triangular room, alive, excited, satisfied—he had found his life's work, and he was happy at a fundamental level.

"What do you think?" he asked Max Breskin, putting an arm around Miriam.

"Terrific," Breskin replied. Breskin always said terrific. And by the time Burns finished editing, it was usually a tight, fast-moving, provocative half hour of the kind that you would never find on a commercial channel. The ratings were going up; in some markets Burns was beating out movies. Breskin had been excited too; Breskin had thought that he had found *his* life's work. But now he wasn't so sure.

"You know, they're still watching you, John," he said.

"Yes, I know that."

"I have to tell you, I'm worried. I think you should at least *consider* giving up your ministry. For your own safety. For a while, anyway."

Burns smiled and hugged Miriam.

"Never, never, never, never."

"Now, not so fast. Listen to me. Think about this. Those people are still out there watching you. So I went to the FBI."

"You did?"

"You're damn right. I complained about harassment. They denied any involvement. I then registered a complaint that the CIA was doing it. A couple of weeks later they sent me the bug letter. 'As far as we can tell, Mr. John Burns is not under surveillance by any agency of the U.S. government.' "

"They're lying," Miriam said.

"That makes it even more ominous," Breskin said.

"Why do you think they're doing it?" Burns asked.

"I don't know," Breskin said. Breskin was depressed. His all-time-best account had become an enemy of the people, and he didn't know what to do about it. "You're getting stuff out there the establishment doesn't like to get out. As long as you were small-time, it was okay. They don't give a damn about small numbers. But now you're starting to get big. You're getting the word out to too many people. You're end-running the mass media. You're playing with dynamite, John."

"I'm not going to let it bother me."

"Let me ask you something, John. Is there anything in your life you haven't told me about?"

Burns went up to his business manager and put his hands on his shoulders. "Did I forget to tell you about the time I flunked algebra in high school?"

"Okay, John."

"You know what I think I'm going to do? Next week I'm going to go down into the audience. We'll have to get a mike with a long cable. I'll confront whichever of them is sitting downstairs. I'll identify him as a federal agent. I'll say to him, 'Do you know what Jesus would say about your line of work?' "

"I don't think that's a good idea, John."

268

" 'You're living a life of deception to serve the rich. Do you know that you, too, have the camel problem? That you, too, have as much chance of getting into heaven as a camel through the eye of a needle? And you're not even *rich*.' "

"I wouldn't do that, John."

" 'Tell me something, sir. Do you recognize yourself when you look in the mirror? Do you know who you are? I'll tell you, my friend, I'd like to pray for you. To Jesus. Would you like to get down on your knees with me and pray my prayer to Jesus to save your immortal soul? How about it, friend?' "

"John, you've got to understand that you're going up against forces that are simply too big for you."

"Are these forces too big for Jesus Christ?" Burns said, calmly, evenly.

Breskin didn't know what to do with that. What could you do with that? Max Breskin found himself wandering around the triangular room trying to figure out how to do an end run around Jesus Christ.

Burns was still standing there, his arm around Miriam, lithe, smiling, a man who knew who he was.

"We're the Romans," Burns said now to the business manager of the Twenty-fifth of December Movement. "We're everywhere. Our overt and covert legions are on the march. Caesar is on the march. Whoever happens to be President of the United States is Caesar."

"And do you think Caesar is going to permit you to interfere with Caesar's game? Do you think the American establishment is going to allow you to interfere with Pax Americana?"

Burns shrugged.

"Is this America or isn't it? Do we or don't we have freedom of speech?"

"No," Breskin replied. "We don't. Not if you're getting too big an audience. You only have freedom of speech if you're a small-time crank. John, you are no longer a small-time crank."

Burns liked that.

"A big-time crank, huh?"

"John."

"I am not going to change. I am doing what I want to do."

Breskin nodded. He hadn't expected to change anything; John Burns had a mission. At least he'd tried.

"All right," Breskin said. "Then I have another suggestion. I think it may be constructive. As a matter of fact, it's somewhat stronger than a

269

suggestion. I made an agreement. I agreed to let one of them talk to you. He's a big shot in government. But *we* will control the security in the situation. We will be in complete control. I can guarantee your safety."

Burns looked surprised.

"You already agreed? Without asking me first?"

"I thought it might satisfy them in some way. Maybe after talking to you, they'd lay off."

Burns sat down next to him at the console.

"You usually talk these things over with me first, Max."

Breskin was looking at a monitor, avoiding the Burns gaze.

"Yeah, I know. Well, I figured this was important and there was no way out of it. So why not?"

Burns put an arm around Breskin's shoulder.

"Okay, Max. If you think so, I'll do it. But tell me something. Is there anything in your life *you* haven't told *me* about?"

33

PRESS CONFERENCE

Moody: I HAVE a statement to make. Troops of the U.S. Army in the Philippines suffered casualties this morning while on patrol in the vicinity of Clark Air Force Base. Three dead, seven wounded. In addition, one of our helicopters was shot down, although the crew survived. An investigation is being conducted at this moment into the conduct of the patrol. When conclusions are reached, they will be released immediately. I'll take your questions.

(They'd already been alerted by an AP bulletin, and they almost blew him away. The sound of so many voices shouting questions at him was terrifying. Moody, briefly, felt like running.)

Q: What do you mean by vicinity?
Q: What are the rules of engagement?
Q: What were the NPA casualties?
Q: Is the President going to make a statement?
A: One at a time, please.
Q: What do you mean by *vicinity?*
A: Vicinity means nearby. Next.

Q: How far from Clark are American patrols permitted to move?

A: That is obviously a military secret. You don't think I'm going to tell you a thing like that, do you?

Q: Do you know?

A: Yes. No.

Q: You left out perhaps.

A: I do not know the precise rules of engagement, and I don't want to know them.

Q: Does all this sound familiar?

A: What's that supposed to mean?

Q: Isn't this starting to sound like Vietnam?

A: It doesn't sound like Vietnam at all.

Q: It sounds like the Vietcong raid on Pleiku in 1964.

A: Clark Air Force Base is not Pleiku.

Q: What's the difference?

A: If you don't know the difference between Pleiku and the Philippines you're in the wrong business.

Q: Is the Philippine army any better than the ARVN was in Nam?

Q: What's the next step?

Q: Is the President contemplating a military draft?

(Those goddam commies were going to keep him on the hot seat for the entire term. It was a crunch, all right, and, as usual, Moody was caught in the middle. His problem was that he couldn't let it appear there was a possibility of war, but at the same time he also couldn't let Halliday's response look weak, either to the American public or to the New People's Army.)

Q: The President ran as a peace candidate. Isn't this patrolling contrary to his peace platform?

A: Absolutely not. We are not starting a war.

Q: NPA troops and American troops are shooting at each other, but it's not a war.

A: Now look, Sam, the patrolling was for the purpose of protecting American troops. Not starting a war. It's the obligation of the President to take whatever steps are necessary to protect American troops.

Q: But in the act of protecting American troops, he's losing American troops.

A: Look, I'm responding to questions, not political speeches.

Q: That wasn't a political speech.

Q: How many men were on the patrol?

Q: How many NPA attacked them?

272

Q: What were the NPA losses?

Q: Is it true that the NPA are using Soviet-made weapons?

A: I have nothing on that.

Q: Can you foresee a day when the Russians end up using Subic Bay as a naval base, the way they're now using Cam Ranh Bay in Vietnam, built at considerable expense to the American taxpayer? And I have a follow-up.

A: Don't bother.

Q: You haven't answered the question.

A: You're saying that was a serious question?

Q: Here's my follow-up. Does the President regard these bases as worth fighting for?

A: An independent panel is going to be announced shortly. It will evaluate precisely that question: whether or not the bases are strategically essential. Some experts feel they aren't.

Q: You mean there's a possibility we *wouldn't* defend them?

A: I didn't say that.

Q: Well, if the panel is going to consider the question, then you must be considering the possibility of not defending the bases.

A: If you print that you're going to look foolish. I never said that. I've got a tape of this press conference. They are going to talk about the strategic value of the bases, not whether or not we're going to defend them.

Q: You mean we'd defend them even if they weren't essential?

A: I did *not* say that. *You* said that.

Q: Yes. I admit it. *I* said that. Are you going to answer that?

A: I've already answered it.

Q: Will the panelists be doves or hawks?

A: They will be objective. Just like you ladies and gentlemen of the press.

Q: Uhhhhh.

Q: Various whistling sounds.

A: That's all I know. I'll keep you informed of developments as they break.

Moody walked away from the lectern and out of the White House briefing room, wounded. But he was getting battle-hardened. The New People's Army was toughening him up. However, he was going to have to store more shirts and suits and T-shirts in his office. And maybe get darker suits, even if summer was coming.

273

34

THE OVALS

IRST SEAT, LAST row, left side. The man wasn't listening.

You could see that right off. He looked uncomfortable on the folding chair to begin with, his arms crossed in front of him, his legs crossed first one way then the other. Bored, Keyes thought. The man was bored. Which was grounds for suspicion right there. You might love John Burns or you might hate him, but you weren't likely to be bored by him—not if you were sitting in the Pentagonal Church of Christ.

Keyes was at the rear of the auditorium, leaning against the cinder-block wall, free-lancing, working on his own case; his President was attending a forgettable international conference in Cuernavaca. Keyes wasn't listening to John Burns either. Keyes was scared. He had gotten some idea of the power of power, and of the total amorality of power. When you got involved with power you were in a dangerous country where anything went; it was a bad place where there was no Bill of Rights, no Geneva conventions, no Roberts Rules. And there was no way he was going to get Secret Service protection.

Malcolm Keyes and John Burns had turned up at the center of this power universe. There were people who seemed to think that one of them was the solution to the politics of the Vietnam Syndrome. One of them was the answer to nothing less than the *crunch,* the solution to the

274

crunch! Through the instrumentality of John Burns—or Malcolm Keyes—American presidents would be able to have their cake and eat it. Or their pie. They could have their pie and *eat* it. They would be able to invade Third World countries at will, and there'd be no protests because it would be three card monte—now you see it, now you don't.

Keyes was trying his best to be clinical about the whole thing. He figured that whatever they might be doing to John Burns, they might be doing to Malcolm Keyes. So he'd gone to the church to see if he could spot what it was they were doing to Burns. He'd been studying faces for half an hour, while pretending to look for a seat. Moody referred to the Burns audience as a fringe group of flakes and snake charmers and dropouts. Moody was wrong. They looked like any group standing on a street corner in a big city, waiting for a traffic light: Burns was drawing the unfreaked, the unstoned, the ordinary people.

But in the first seat, last row, left side, there was a man who didn't look like he was waiting for a traffic light, and the man had now stood up and was walking toward Keyes. Keyes pretended to be listening to the sermon but was sizing the man up in quick glimpses. Middle aged, conservatively dressed in a sport jacket and slacks. A bit thick in the center. There was a cop look about him. The look on his face communicated law and order.

He drew even with Keyes and kept walking. Keyes decided he was an interesting possibility. He gave him a big lead before starting to move, then ambled along behind trying to look casual, knowing he was in over his head again. He pretended to be watching John Burns, who was exciting the faithful, having a ball, stiff-legging it around the platform, stirring up trouble.

After going about ninety degrees around the central circle of the building, the man stopped at the door on one of the "point" rooms, one of the five triangular rooms in the building, and went in, looking behind him surreptitiously. He didn't notice Keyes. Keyes speeded up. GOD could be behind that door, and he was willing to take chances. He opened the door cautiously and looked in. It was the men's room.

Disgusted, Keyes went over to the sinks to wash his hands so as not to look like a complete fool. While he was doing that, he noticed in the mirror two large, hairy, mean-looking Christians enter. He watched them, the water still running over his hands. He was seeing something that he couldn't believe, couldn't take in. Terror and confusion, the combination that added up to paralysis, were at work: He couldn't react. There was even a fascination to it, like watching a movie. What he saw in the mirror was one of the Christians taking out a hard rubber billy, waving it through the air, and bringing it down on the back of his head.

Keyes came to slowly. It took minutes. He was disoriented; he was seeing patterns, and he had no idea what they were or if they had any meaning. What could those whirls and swirls possibly mean? Then he realized he was staring at wood. The night air was chilling, and that's how he knew he was out of doors. He looked up and saw the moon, but not much of one; it was a fingernail clipping. He turned around on whatever it was he was lying on and he was facing the White House.

He sat up; it was a park bench. He was in Lafayette Park across from the White House, and there was a bump on the back of his head.

He stood up, testing. Everything seemed to be in its place. He tried walking. He could walk. He walked out of the park, slowly; he could feel each step pounding in the back of his head. He went along Pennsylvania Avenue like the lame and the halt, not even knowing where he was going. It took him several minutes to remember that he had an office in the EOB. He checked to see if he had his pass on him. He did. There was even a wallet. He looked at his watch. He still had one. It was after ten. Two hours had passed.

He drifted down the first-floor corridor to his office. There were lots of people around. Workaholics struggling for survival, status, power, soul. He went into his office, closed the door, and collapsed on the chair behind his desk. The enormity of the potential disaster was slowly becoming clear. He was custodian of the records, the master archivist of the bad stuff, the compromising stuff, the stuff Richard Halliday wouldn't even put down on paper. Had he been given a truth drug and blabbed? Did truth drugs work? He didn't have the faintest idea. All he knew was that the Twenty-fifth of December Movement, of all entities, might now have a lot of compromising material on the President of the United States and he was going to have to do something about it.

Halliday was in Mexico City and no doubt could be reached, but Keyes didn't have one of those funny telephones that cost thirty-five thousand dollars and took up about a cubic yard of space. He picked up his phone and dialed the EOB operator.

"I have to speak to the Vice-President as soon as possible," he said. "This is an emergency."

* * *

276

He had to wait. She was attending a diplomatic reception at the Zimbabwean Embassy. Then when she came back, she had three of the Zimbabweans with her; they wanted to see what the Oval Office looked like. Keyes sat alone and headachy in the Roosevelt Room, waiting for them to leave while thinking horrible thoughts, like Keyesgate. He was called in as soon as the Zimbabweans left.

She was bubbly. She had had one or two or three champagnes. And there obviously hadn't been any photo opportunities planned for the evening. She was dressed to the nines. A beautiful lady politician had come out of the closet for an evening: a black silk suit, pink blouse, rather high heels, and *red* fingernails. Astonishing. It was obvious that she was rather harmoniously proportioned. He had never seen her looking so sexy, and he found it impossible, if not also somewhat peculiar, not to have lustful thoughts about the second most important person in the polity. He was experiencing retinal orgasm.

She sat down behind Halliday's desk, and that was good—it concealed a lot of her. Keyes sat in a chair at the right end of the desk, the place where Akers usually sat, and told her about his adventure. When she heard about the blow on the head, she picked up the phone and called Halliday's physician, who was a major general attached to Walter Reed Hospital in Washington. He was there in twenty minutes and pronounced Keyes well, although it was too late for ice; all Keyes could do was to ignore the knob on his head. While he was there, the general took Keyes into Halliday's secretary's office and checked his arms for needle punctures. There were two—one in each upper arm. He made a third one, taking a blood sample.

After the doctor-general left, Madeleine came into the secretary's office. He wasn't entirely dressed yet.

"Let's not stand on ceremony," she said. "Come on in. We'll have some champagne. We *both* deserve it. I've been telling lies for my country all evening."

Keyes got his T-shirt back on and his outer shirt mostly buttoned. Madeleine went up to the fake Chippendale. "How do you open this thing?"

Keyes was still tucking in his shirttail.

"You twist that knob on the right of the middle drawer to the left."

The thing bloomed; doors opened and a work surface came down. "He *does* have champagne in here, doesn't he?" she asked.

"It's in that little refrigerator on the left. He's got a bunch of splits in there."

She began pacing a lot, carrying her drink, her heels tapping out something in Morse code. She looked vibrant and intensely alive.

"This is the third time you've been snatched, isn't it?"

"Yes."

"Each time by a different party."

"Presumably."

"Do you understand it?"

"Nope."

"I don't know what to say," she said. "Let's at least wait until the blood test comes in to see what they gave you. But I think it's time for Richard to take some type of action. This thing is an outrage. Richard gets back to Washington early tomorrow morning. I'll get you in to see him. You're first on line."

Then she sat down at Halliday's desk again with a fistful of telephone messages. Keyes sipped champagne and watched her. She called a fund raiser of hers in California. Then the mayor of Atlanta. The president of the Buffalo city council. The Manhattan borough president. The business manager of Carnegie Hall. The executive secretary of the Fort Worth chamber of commerce. During each conversation, she made concise notes on the back of the call slips, getting down the gist of the conversation; Madeleine was organized.

Keyes was feeling funny feelings. He had fallen into a time warp; he felt as awkward as a sixteen-year-old at his first dance in the gymnasium, but the girl he was thinking about picking up was the Vice-President of the United States. A quick fantasy flitted across his brain: a red fingernail on the Button. Was it any scarier than a plain male fingernail? Keyes didn't think so. It was shocking, but it wasn't scarier; power was asexual.

"God, there's too much going on," she said. "I don't have time to think anymore. I have to let other people do my thinking for me. I have to be in too many places and I have to talk to too many people. I haven't had any fun since Richard's birthday party back in March. You weren't at that, were you?"

"Yes, I was. It was at his vacation house in the Catskills."

"I don't remember seeing you there."

"I remember talking to you on that big triangular deck of his that juts out into the woods."

"You have the advantage of me, sir," she said, sipping champagne.

"You were wearing gray slacks and a heavy dark brown sweater. I remember how striking your hair was against that sweater. You looked to me that day like the perfect librarian. A fantasy librarian."

278

"What else?"

"I went up to you and asked what you thought about the GOD Project. It was the only thing I could think of to talk about. You said you thought it was some lunatic right-wing scheme to prove that God was on their side, and I said right-wingers would never feel the need to prove that, and you told the joke about having to be very quiet in heaven because the Catholics thought they were the only ones up there."

"Do you remember everything, Malcolm?"

"Only what I want to remember." Pause. "Along with what I don't want to remember."

She went back to the bar to get them two more splits. Those champagne bubbles had done their work. There was a litheness about her, a loose-limbed ease of movement, an abandoned quality, pure liquefaction.

"You know, Malcolm," she said, popping open the two bottles, "my husband is doing me the favor of not divorcing me until after my second term as President of the United States."

"He sounds like a reasonable man," Keyes said.

She shrugged. "It would be good for business if he were to be First Gentleman."

"I appreciate the confidence," Keyes said.

"I need somebody to talk to, Malcolm. I don't have anyone. I've got to have somebody I can trust or I'll explode."

Things were getting serious. Keyes was going to have to face up to a basic political issue. The lady was being provocative. She was radiating. He looked at her sitting behind the President's desk. She looked as if she could hold it down. She looked presidential. She also looked sexy and vibrant and taut. But how did you make a sexual advance to a Vice-President? Of the United States? It was his biggest challenge yet, and he wasn't sure he could rise to the occasion. He was going to have to get past the power barrier. He was going to have to forget that red fingernail on the Button.

"Do you know you have a complex face?" he said.

"A complex face? I don't think I like a complex face. Can you do any better than that?"

"Well, your life is in your face. It's in everybody's face. Your face contains contradictions."

Madeleine sipped champagne.

"Politics will do that to you," she said. "What are my contradictions?"

"Your mouth droops down a little at the ends. Why is that? At the

279

same time, you have laugh lines around your eyes. Merriment. Merriment and pessimism in one face. How did you get that way?"

"I don't know what you're talking about, and I'd appreciate it if you didn't talk about my *wrinkles.*"

"But they're attractive. They're sexy."

"I'm too old for you."

"You are not."

"I'm two years older than you, right?"

"Seven."

He stood up to take a close look at the earring on her right ear.

"These aren't the kind you usually wear."

"No."

"I've never seen earrings like these before."

"I got them in Mongolia."

The pattern was so interesting that Keyes touched it with his finger, tracing the filigree. "That's a really fascinating earring," he said softly. He accidentally touched her ear while doing it, and she quivered, so he traced the filigree of her ear and she sat quietly sipping champagne at Doc Halliday's desk. Then she took her wedding ring off and put it in her purse.

"Promise me you'll never write a book about me," she said.

"I promise. And that's not a public promise; that's a private promise."

He moved his finger behind her ear and caressed it. She didn't move. He went down along her neck to the far ear and caressed it very very slowly.

"Er, Malcolm, how are you on AIDS?"

"I'm in a low-risk group. I'm shy."

Without a word, she reached into her purse and took out something which she put on Halliday's desk.

It was a condom.

Keyes took out his wallet. He placed another one next to hers.

"You're faded," he said.

"His and Hers," she said.

"A drama in two acts," he replied, leaning down and kissing her lingeringly on the lips. He didn't even know how she got rid of the champagne glass but her arms were suddenly around him and she was kissing back with intensity. Keyes was feeling powerful inside himself. It was the centripetal emotion. Everything inside him was hurtling toward the center. He kissed her again and it happened again, even more powerfully. It would have to be powerful. He was going to have to overcome any inhibition he felt about scoring with the Vice-President of the republic.

280

"That was pretty high-voltage stuff," he said, breaking off.

"Really? How many volts?"

"Ten thousand."

"Is that high?"

"My insulation breaks down at eleven thousand and I arc over."

She was still sitting in the chair with Keyes bent over her. She pulled him down and kissed him a second time.

"Where?" he asked.

"Right here. Right now. The Secret Service would be impossible. The only person who would dare walk in here unannounced is Akers, and he's in Mexico with Richard." Then she kissed him passionately.

Keyes kept trying to defocus from the realities of the situation. He was out with that pretty girl he had picked up at the high school gymnasium dance.

"Who's going to do it?" she said.

"Do what?"

"Take my clothes off."

"I couldn't possibly allow the Vice-President to do manual labor."

Keyes quickly saw that he wasn't going to be able to drag out the undressing; she was in too much of a hurry. She kept giving him instructions. "Buttons in the back. Hook and eye on the side. It pulls *up.*" As he was unhooking her bra, she was clearing a place on Halliday's desk; she didn't even seem to want to wait long enough to cross the office to one of the couches. Later, he realized she had planned it; she didn't want to risk staining a couch, and by doing it on the desk, she would be in easy reach of Halliday's phone if a call came in at the wrong moment.

She hadn't needed a whole lot of foreplay either; he struck love oil—Arabian light of an extremely low viscosity—very quickly. Keyes was still tentative. Before he could forget who *he* was, he was going to have to forget who *she* was, but seeing her lying on the desk in the dim light, exposed, vulnerable, a lonely woman craving intimacy and excitement, dying to let go, already well along to forgetting who *she* was, he was able to enter the little oval in the big Oval and they both forgot who they were.

She had worn her glasses the entire time, and now they were totally awry; the lens for her right eye was up on her forehead, the sidebar for the left eye was below her ear. She had a tattoo, a dove, below her left breast. She was looking profoundly at ease, satisfied, elected; her constituency had come through for her.

And she had certainly known what she wanted. She had given Keyes, who was standing at the end of the desk, a running stream of instructions. "Higher. Screw. Slower. Faster. Now, now, now, now, now, now."

"I'm afraid I had premature ejaculation," she said.

"It was heaven," he said.

"Yes."

"Madeleine."

"Don't move. We'll part naturally."

"Madeleine."

"I'm pleased that you're not calling me Madam Vice-President. It shows that you're beginning to loosen up. I find it very intimate that you're calling me Madeleine."

"Madeleine."

"Yes, Malcolm."

"That was heaven."

Nature was taking its course; he was sliding out of her.

"Bye-bye," she said.

"Bye-bye," he said.

"Malcolm."

"Yes, Madeleine?"

"I've been meaning to ask you."

"Yes, Madeleine?"

"What are those red grease-pencil marks on the inside of your left thigh?"

35

MORNING AFTER

K EYES WAS BACK in the office of ovals at 7:30 the next morning when the whoosh of Marine One's helicopter blades could still be heard slowly coming to a stop: The President was back.

Keyes had actually blushed when he'd first walked in and seen the desk. His cheeks burned. He couldn't help feeling that there was some kind of betrayal involved, screwing Mrs. Samson on Doc Halliday's desk, which would probably end up in a library someday and be immortal. They had done it twice, because they had only two condoms. He was now carrying a twelve-pak which he had gotten from an all-night drugstore in downtown Washington.

The President had already been informed about Keyes's adventure at the Pentagonal Church, and he was outraged. He talked to Keyes about it over scrambled eggs—Halliday preferred White House cooking to Air Force One's—while Keyes ate a roll smeared with raspberry jam. Raspberry jam was the specialty of the mess; it was Halliday's jelly beans.

"Roughing up an aide of mine?" Halliday was saying. "That's nothing less than a constitutional crisis. There's no way I'm going to let this pass. Heads are going to roll. The trouble is, I don't know which heads. You turned up okay in Lafayette Park. That means you were disqualified for some reason. They raped you with a tape measure again, and for some reason, you didn't measure up."

"In that regard, it's like failing your draft physical. I have no complaints."

"Do you think you could identify those two Christians? We could go over there and grab them all, line 'em up, right under their illuminated cross."

"I doubt it," Keyes said. "There's so much hair, they all look alike. And I only saw them for about two seconds."

"Anyway, the problem is they could have been loyal members of the Twenty-fifth of December Movement or they could have been CIA infiltrated in there. Whenever there's covert stuff going on, there's endless ambiguity. It fucks the head, Malcolm."

"Yes, sir."

Halliday was tackling his bacon and eggs with relish, stoking the furnace. After a bill-signing ceremony in the Rose Garden, he would be leaving for Toronto to see the Canadian Prime Minister. Then he started laughing into his coffee.

"Working for me hasn't exactly been easy, has it?"

"I'll tell you the truth, Mr. President. The flights of steps and the tall columns and the solemn rites and ceremonies give an impression of solidity and orderliness that is not entirely justified."

"A false impression of solidity?"

It was only 7:30 A.M. and Halliday had only had orange juice with lecithin and proteins, but Keyes could have sworn it was a drunken laugh.

"You don't know the half of it," Halliday said. He was laughing so hard he spit up some of his scrambled eggs. "Let me put it this way. Washington, D.C. is like a mental institution which the mass media cover *straight*. They don't tell you those pictures you're seeing are from a mental institution. They don't give their viewers an elbow in the ribs. They don't wink. They play it absolutely straight. If my Secretary of Defense opens his mouth and makes a statement, that statement is the story. They don't question it. If Defense said that the moon was made of green cheese, the headline would be: 'Moon is green cheese, Defense says.' Way down below in the copy, there *might* be an editorial note in brackets: 'Some critics of the Pentagon assert that the moon is *not* green cheese.' "

"You're ruining my life," Keyes said.

"I haven't even started. But if you stick to the insane-asylum idea

284

about Washington, you won't go wrong. You wouldn't believe the struggle the conservatives are putting up to avoid a test ban treaty. They don't want to get rid of the *bomb*. I, personally, don't understand anybody who doesn't want to get rid of the bomb, but the conservatives don't. Why, if you brought a bomb in to my Secretary of State, he'd throw his arms around it and give it a big, wet smacker. It's crazy time on the Potomac."

Keyes was busily eating raspberry jam. Halliday's images weren't helping his concentration. The Vice-President had been giving *him* big, wet smackers; the Vice-President had been going crackers, groaning, throwing her legs around him and caressing his buttocks with her calves. He had never had crazy lovemaking like that before. She had even answered the phone at one point and was calmly able to handle the situation; Keyes had helped by slowing down. She had looked him in the eye during the entire conversation.

"Er, why do you think they like the bomb so much?" he asked.

"It's power. Pure power. Conservatives are infatuated with power."

"Why are they infatuated with power?"

"Because they're always outnumbered. Conservatism is a scam of the rich—a poor conservative is the dumbest kind of shit. So the conservative inevitably thinks in terms of power over multitudes. Nuclear warheads are to American foreign policy what tear gas is to civil disobedience."

"This is for the book."

"Damn right."

"How will I handle that?" Keyes asked, the writer already worrying about making something that sounded crazy sound plausible. "Don't they realize their assets will be blown up too? Their banks, their real estate, their corporations, their estates."

"No, they don't realize it," Halliday answered. Halliday smiled ruefully. "You know, they aren't even hawks, they're ostriches. Mutants, actually; part hawk, part ostrich. Imagine a great feathered thing crash-diving into a sand dune from five thousand feet of altitude. That's your so-called hawk."

"Damn."

"Has anybody told you that you're leaving in half an hour?"

"No. Where am I going?"

"The Consortium."

"The Consortium?"

"You and the Vice-President."

285

"Me and the Vice-President?"

"I want to find out once and for all. I'm not playing any games with them anymore. It's hardball time. Find out what the hell that thing is. Do what is necessary. Solve it; end it. Okay?"

"Yes, sir," Keyes said, rising. "Now I see why Marine One is still here."

"Come back with it, Malcolm."

He glanced at the desk as he went out. He was gung-ho, eager to please his President. But there were two long plane rides with the Vice-President coming up. He touched a corner of Halliday's desk as he went by. He was in love.

36

THE HORSEMAN

THE SECOND SECRETARY had a long lens attached to his 35mm camera, and it was pressed up against the venetian blinds. He was peering through it at the house across the way, chuckling. American incompetence at intelligence was nothing less than stunning. They had a safe house in suburban Maryland that was as ordinary and unpretentious as you would find in any suburbs inhabited by the lower middle-middle. Totally anonymous, perfect. But here comes the biggest limo in Washington turning into the driveway and out steps Elmer Jessup.

At least they knew enough to send the limo away, so as not to have it look like the opening of a summit conference. In less than three minutes, a second limo pulled up with a degree of subtlety; this one didn't turn into the driveway. Alexander Albritten was out and inside the house in a flash. It was the third one that the Second Secretary was interested in. He thought he knew, but he wanted to be sure. A third limo promptly showed up, disgorging a doddering Dr. Theodore Monk, looking exhausted, slowly making progress up the driveway, looking as though he might even make it to the front door.

The Second Secretary didn't even have film in the camera; he used it instead of binoculars, which he regarded as more suspicious. He put the camera into his big white sack and quickly went down the stairs and out through the kitchen to the driveway where his laundry truck was parked.

"I'm really sorry to hear that," Monk was saying to them. They were gathered in the living room, which had been designed to be working-class bourgeois with every cliché in the book.

"The resemblance was so close," Monk continued, a sad smile on his face. "And that *memory*."

"What about his memory?" Jessup said.

"He has an extraordinary memory. I mean, it's outstanding. It started me thinking, I want to tell you. I feel let down that it isn't him. Are you absolutely certain, Alex?"

Albritten was sitting on a cream-colored ottoman; the Book of Mark was in an attaché case sitting on a blond wood coffee table next to him.

"I had plenty of time," he said. "I wasn't rushed. I repeated the last two measurements three times. He failed both of them. Scratch Keyes."

"Too bad," Monk said, the same sad smile still on his face.

Jessup waved his unlit cigar at Monk.

"You're a scientist, for Christ's sake. What are you doing being regretful over the data? The data are the data. You accept the data. It's an unappetizing choice in either case as far as I'm concerned."

Jessup was sitting on a low easy chair covered with something that looked like faded imitation gold lamé that was starting to look greenish.

Monk didn't bother to respond to Jessup's comment.

"Can we get on with this? I have a plane to catch."

Albritten looked at his watch and jumped to his feet, crossed the fake oriental rug to the twenty-eight-inch color television set, and flipped it on.

"Last look," he said. "Decision time, gentlemen."

The very first words they heard as the picture faded in were "Elmer Jessup," and John Burns was staring straight into the camera and coming out of the picture tube looking into Elmer Jessup's blue eyes.

"Now we must try to speak kindly about this man," Burns was saying. "He is one of God's creatures, even though he has fallen. Oh, how he has fallen. We must sympathize with him. He carries a heavy burden of sin, sin which he has incurred in the service of great wealth. This sinner—who claims that he's born again, who claims that he is a Christian—has heavy going ahead in the next life. I wouldn't want to be in his shoes."

Monk was looking uptight and defensive.

"It's rebellion," he said. "Delayed teenage rebellion, that's all it is," he added lightly.

Jessup had gotten a monstrous cigar going. He blew smoke at the television set.

"How can a born-again Republican turn into a goddam commie, that's what I want to know. Are you trying to tell me this isn't an accident? This wasn't planned?"

Monk was stung.

"You probably rebelled yourself once," Monk said. His eyes squinted and he chewed a fingernail. "Or maybe that's your problem, maybe you didn't."

Before Jessup could reply he was interrupted by John Burns. Burns was prowling the stage, energy flowing, eyes dangerous, his face radiating.

"Now how can we help Elmer Jessup see the error of his ways? How can we save his soul?" Pause. Weak, sad, concocted smile. "It's such a small soul. Satan has it filed away in a very small compartment in his safe in hell, along with all the other lost souls. This soul I'm talking about is *small*. Souls don't come any smaller than *this* soul. Why, this soul is about the size of an atom! And an atom of hydrogen at that, which is the *smallest* of the atoms. Why, it's possible to think of Elmer Jessup's soul as *the* smallest soul on earth!"

"You don't know the half of it," Jessup said. "Wait till I get my hands on you, kid."

"You can even tell the state of Mr. Jessup's soul by looking at his face. He has the slowly acquired furtive look of the rich, the guarded look of someone whose hand is perpetually in the cookie jar. Unless he learns to change his ways, Mr. Jessup is going to get a face-lift in hell, a *slow* face-lift in the coldest nether regions of hell. And why? Because to Mr. Jessup, money is not expendable, but people are."

"That little son of a bitch," Jessup said slowly, with a half-giggle. "I'll say this for him. He's feisty. He stands up on his hind legs. That's a good quality. Too bad he went rancid," he added, looking at Monk.

Burns was pacing back and forth on the stage, Bible under his arm, looking down at the floor, looking for a thought there, finding it, looking out at the audience, the muscles in his face relaxing. It was a good thought, they were all going to respond to it, it would mean something to them and they would enjoy it together.

289

"You know," he said, "Mr. Elmer Jessup is a famous breeder of racehorses. And he was a pretty fair polo player in his day."

"Pretty fair, my ass," Jessup said. "The fuckin' best."

"The image of Elmer Jessup on the back of a horse is one I find peculiarly apt and suggestive and *right*. It evokes the Book of Revelation, which tells us about the Four Horsemen of the Apocalypse: Pestilence, Famine, War, and Death. *Four* horsemen."

Burns did a pretend gallop around the stage, holding pretend reins in his right hand, slapping his buttock with his Bible. He stopped suddenly, convulsively.

"But there is a *fifth* horseman in our midst, and the fifth horseman is the leader of this grim posse. This fifth horseman is the greatest of them all, because he is responsible for them all. When Elmer visits a Third World country, pestilence, famine, war, and death follow. Coups ensue. Death squads go to work. Kill all the leftists! Kill the complainers! Kill the malcontents! Kill, kill, kill! And so, for this year, I would like to present the Equestrian Award of Fifth Horseman—Greed—to none other than Mr. Elmer Jessup of the CIA."

Mr. Elmer Jessup of the CIA passed wind.

John Burns was crouched at the edge of his stage, looking out through 270 degrees of audience.

"So we have this Fifth Horseman, cantering along, trampling on the vintage where the grapes of wrath are stored, smashing, destroying, laying waste. How are we ever going to save this creature's soul?"

"I've had about enough of this."

"Brothers and sisters! Let us pray for Elmer Jessup's atomic, hydrogen, immortal soul. Jesus, we are asking for nothing less than a miracle here. We ask that you bring enlightenment and holiness to the soul of Elmer Jessup so that he may cease his evil transgressions and be restored to the human race deprived of his greed. This would be only a first step, Lord, in converting *all* of the Fifth Horsemen, and they are legion."

Jessup inadvertently bit off the end of his cigar, and he threw the whole mess into the artificial fireplace.

Albritten stirred. He was afraid of Jessup. He was, in fact, terrified of Jessup.

"I think I should point out," he said, "that John Burns has already passed nineteen of the twenty checkpoints."

Even Dr. Theodore Monk now seemed wary of Jessup's mental state.

"I have to concede that John Burns could plausibly be Henry Patrick," Monk said.

"Goddammit, get him. Do you hear me? Get him and bring him to this room. Do you hear me?" he said to Albritten.

"Yes, sir," Albritten replied.

"Yes, sir? What do you mean, yes, sir? What the hell does that mean?"

Albritten fumbled for a moment. He had no idea what Jessup was talking about.

"I mean I'll get that ignorant little son of a bitch and I'll bring him here to this room and I'll take the twentieth measurement."

Sudden mood change. The operational tone of voice.

"How are you going to do it?" Jessup said. "He's surrounded by Christians all the time. *Surrounded.*"

"Not all the time," Albritten replied. He looked at Jessup with an overacted crafty, evil, lascivious look on his face. "He's got a girl."

37

IN THE PRESENCE OF GOD

I T WASN'T QUITE 7:00 A.M.

Air Force Two was on the wing, headed for clarity, for Colorado, for the Consortium, for the secret of the GOD Project; they were running a mission because Doc Halliday would touch *any* possible base, no matter how absurd it might sound.

She was dressed in slacks for the plant visit and her hair was up in a bun, but she had the perfume on, the devil stuff. So although she was looking and sounding businesslike, efficiently pouring coffee for the two of them, there was that whiff of chaos and anarchy and mindlessness in the cabin.

"How far are we authorized to go?" Keyes said.

"All the way," she said coyly, an eyebrow arching playfully upward. "We're coming back with the news this time. We're going to find out if your crazy idea is right or wrong, once and for all."

Keyes sipped at the life-giving coffee. Vice-presidential coffee was the goods. He was still thinking about stealing a cup-and-saucer set.

"Suppose it turns out I'm right?"

"Then Richard will have four aces up his sleeve and another three up his pant leg."

"Can we be indiscreet? Take risks?"

292

"If absolutely necessary. But, Malcolm, do try to be pristine. It would be neater if we knew what it was and they didn't know that we knew what it was. That way, Richard would be in the position of being able to torture them exquisitely. And remember, I don't want you and Dr. Monk fooling around."

"I'll try to keep my hands off him."

"Now, Malcolm, I've got five Senate bills and a staff meeting to get through before we land."

"I'll have the martinis ready when you get home from the office, darling," he said, and left, taking the cup and saucer with him.

As usual, they had to leave the Secret Service behind at the entrance, but Dr. Monk was waiting right there and took them up to his office for brunch and a briefing. Keyes could see that the romance was over; Monk wasn't playing to him anymore or even touching him. He was concentrating on the Vice-President, which was the more normal bureaucratic thing to do. Monk was absolutely tickled when the Vice-President told him that the President was fascinated by the procedure for accelerating dopant atoms and wanted to know more about it.

On their first visit to the Consortium, Keyes had taken in the structure of the building and realized that the chip-making facility took up only about two-thirds of the building. What was in the other third, which was the eastern side of the structure? The place where they had gotten the lecture on accelerated dopant atoms was as close to the eastern wall as they had been; hence the Vice-President had to concentrate on keeping her eyes from glazing over. Monk was so taken with all his technologies that it wouldn't be hard.

After coffee, they strolled to the changing room, where they got surgically clean. White caps, white masks, white gowns, white shoe covers. As they approached the inner checkpoint, there were signs all over the place: MASK AREA. And Monk warned them again.

"It's bad for the chips and it's bad for you. Do not take your masks off. If you have to sneeze, sneeze right through it. Do either of you get claustrophobic with a mask on?"

Then they were going through the second layer of telephone booths, their retinas getting photographed again. Monk hated it. The party was cleared for only certain areas that were clearly spelled out; it was what they called a block clearance. After they passed through the checkpoint, Monk complained about the security people. He called them Elmer Jessup's Shiites. "They're the most fanatical people in CIA. Your CIA

Director, madam, is a pain. Security procedures constipate all other procedures."

They went strolling along the upper level of the plant, looking down at the great open space where most of the chip making was done. Madeleine was being her charming best with Monk, hinting sexily about budget increases, admiring the technology, keeping Monk in bureaucrat heaven. Keyes, the memory man, the stenographer, was ignoring the conversation; it was what Halliday had started referring to as forget stuff. Instead, Keyes was studying the lay of the land. There was an entire third of the building they were not being shown—to the right, to the east. Keyes checked his watch. There were only minutes to go before the President's phone call was due to come in; Halliday had guaranteed to keep Monk busy for twenty minutes.

Monk led them to the right, away from the big open space, and down a corridor to a room on the left, that is, to the north. Inside they found a standard piece of governmental advertising: a new working model of the Strategic Defense Initiative. The model, at least, worked; the laser fantasy of the Pentagon. It was busily blowing up Soviet missiles, accompanied by audio and visual effects, while Monk was delivering the canned spiel for visiting dignitaries. Madeleine's mask couldn't conceal the fact that she was yawning. She was saved by the PA system.

"Dr. Monk, telephone."

"I told them to hold my calls," Monk said testily. Someone was interfering with his big bureaucratic moment with the Vice-President.

"In that case, it must be a very important call," Madeleine said. "I don't want to do anything to hold up progress."

"Madam Vice-President, I can't leave you here waiting while I take a phone call. It's probably stupid."

"Dr. Monk, we won't move an inch until you come back. Please, you'll be tending to the nation's business."

Monk tottered out. He was dubious about leaving them there but too embarrassed to ask them to come with him; Halliday had figured it that way.

They waited, watching the display with its fake laser beams shoot down Soviet missiles, waiting a full sixty seconds just to eliminate the possibility of a false start by Monk. Madeleine was monitoring her wristwatch.

"Pilots, man your planes," she said.

* * *

294

They raced out the door and turned left, heading east. There was a long corridor ahead of them which terminated in a locked door. Keyes took out a ring of keys. He had gotten them from Lockhart. It had cost the President the under secretary of commerce for international trade, whom Lockhart now had the power to name. He finally found the right one and pulled open the door. Keyes and the Vice-President stepped inside, awestruck. They instantly knew they had found something, although they didn't know what. The walls and floors were all painted in stripes of vivid scintillating colors. At first sight, it looked something like a supermarket checkout counter in living Technicolor. But Keyes recognized it immediately. It was VIBGYOR, the spectrum of visible light: violet, indigo, blue, green, yellow, orange, red. There was a blank gray space between each series, and the stripe patterns were repeated as far down the corridor as they could see. It was startling and disorienting.

"Madeleine," Keyes said, taking it all in, "I have a funny feeling that we're not in Kansas anymore."

Madeleine remained the cool executive.

"You go to the left; I'll go to the right," she said.

The walls were off the wall; VIBGYOR was everywhere, with that gray stripe in between. It struck Keyes that it could be some kind of eye test, an ongoing eye test that would continually test the retina's ability to perceive color, which might be a basic indicator of brain functioning. He even had a theory for the gray stripes in-between. You could regard the gray stripes as being either at the violet end or at the red end. If they were at the red end, conceivably the gray stripes represented infrared, which was not perceivable by the human eye but which would certainly be useful in night fighting. It might be possible to *see* the heat of the human body.

Apart from the walls, everything was a brilliant white, and spotless. The place looked as if it had been painted that morning. Lady Macbeth would have had nothing to do. The whole place was so clean you could eat off of it, but then, chips were the most tenderly cared-for entities in society. The signs on the doors were crazy; going down the corridor they got more and more bananas.

VOCABULARY. HATE. TACTICS. CULTURE. CULTURES. FECAL. REPRESSION. PATRIOTISM. Keyes was going along, throwing open all the doors. They were all laboratories with nobody working in them. Among other things, the GOD Project seemed to be on hold. He didn't know what he had been expecting; he had only had weird fantasies, but now it was starting to be anticlimax time. He went into a room labeled M8. It had one workbench against the far wall with nothing but breadboard electronics on it: an engineering model of something—the wiring exposed, no neat packaging in black boxes. It looked like a pile of junk in a surplus store on Canal Street in Manhattan. Keyes turned back to the door, hoping that Madeleine had made out better. A voice spoke.

"Are you infantry or airborne?" someone said.

Keyes slowly turned around. There was no one there.

"Can't you talk? Are you missing something too?"

There was only the workbench with the electronics spread out over it. There were two things on top of metal stands that *had* looked like eyes to him, but they really didn't look like *eyes.*

"Nod if you understand me."

Keyes stood in the middle of the room with pounding temples. Plausibility and absurdity had converged on the GOD Project. It wasn't *quite* as he had envisaged it, but he was *right.* He had given Doc Halliday sound advice; he had taken a ridiculous gamble and won. He was standing at the center of the military-bioindustry complex.

"I understand you," he said, voice shaking.

"*Good.* You've got all your faculties. You must be very happy. Now tell me, are you infantry or airborne?"

"Uh, neither. I'm a civilian."

"What kind of civilian are you?"

Keyes had to work that one through.

"I'm an American civilian."

"Then you have absolutely nothing to worry about."

"Why is that?"

"I'm here to protect your interests around the world."

Keyes nodded his head slowly up and down.

"I'm very glad to hear that," he said.

"I'm a freedom fighter."

"We all owe you people a great debt."

"Thank you. I'm a Mark Eight Freedom Fighter, the latest model. As you can see, I don't have a body yet, but Dr. Monk says that before long I will. And then I'll be able to kill people and lay girls. I can't lay girls right now."

"I can understand the problem."

"You can't lay girls without a body."

"Well said."

"Do *you* lay girls?"

"Every chance I get."

296

"Is it as good as they say?"

"Better."

"Hoo ha."

Keyes stood there reveling in it. It was like landing on the moon the first time. Or finding out that you didn't need handholds in Australia. It was profoundly satisfying. Delicious. The joy of discovery. Eureka.

"Tell me," Keyes asked, "which people are you going to kill?"

There was a pause. Keyes was watching what he assumed to be the eyes, but there was nothing to see; there was no carbonation.

"Commies. *Any* commies *any*where."

"Very good," Keyes said. "Now tell me. How do you know a commie from a noncommie?"

Silence. He almost thought he had heard an electronic sigh. Mark Eight wasn't sounding all that intelligent. Which was curious. Why would they want to make oafs?

"Anybody Dr. Monk says is a commie," Mark Eight finally said.

"Good enough for me," Keyes said. "But look. What happens if they kill you before you kill them?"

Keyes was half expecting a short circuit. A blown fuse. Smoke rising above the breadboard layout.

"I'm afraid I don't have an answer to that," Mark Eight said, sounding somewhat pedantic. "I'm afraid I'll have to take that up with Dr. Monk. But I have a feeling that if that happened, I wouldn't be able to lay girls, and that would be awful."

The door opened, and Madeleine walked in.

"Hoo ha," Mark Eight said.

Madeleine threw a fast glance at Keyes. He nodded at the pile of junk on the workbench.

"You can't kid me, you're *girl,*" it said.

Madeleine's right eyebrow went up. She glanced at the workbench and then at Keyes and then at the breadboard and then at her watch and then at the breadboard and then at Keyes.

Keyes said it in a singsong delivery.

"I told you so."

There was a clearing of a voice from across the room.

"I'm sorry to inform you that I can't lay you yet," Mark Eight said. "I don't have a body."

Madeleine was not looking very feminine, with her brown horn-rimmed glasses over the high mask. It was a measure of Mark Eight's astuteness that he had even identified her as "girl."

297

"Oh, that's all right," she said, glancing at Keyes without moving her head.

"I can't get in your pants if I don't have anything to get in your pants *with.*"

"I *understand.*"

"But I want you to know I like you. I think you're a terrific girl."

Keyes knew she was smiling. She was amazing. She was already starting to swing with it.

"You're a pretty fast worker," she said seductively.

"There's no time to lose; the commies are coming."

"Well?" Keyes said smugly.

"Malcolm, I'll never question your political judgment again."

"We can never rest, you know," Mark Eight said. "It's our fate. It's happening on our watch, and we're stuck with it. We can never rest until every godless, atheistic communist is wiped off the face of the earth."

It had managed to get some real emotion into it. It wasn't kidding.

"He's a Mark Eight Freedom Fighter," Keyes said to the Vice-President.

"Don't overdo it, Malcolm," she said.

"My name is Gordon."

"How do you do, Gordon. It's a pleasure to meet you."

"You ain't seen nothing yet, baby."

"I'll bet I haven't. You're quite a man."

"You haven't had it until you've had it from me."

Even Madeleine Smith, slayer of political opponents, seemed at a loss for words. She looked at Keyes, and he knew exactly what her face looked like under the mask.

"Well, I guess I'll just have to wait," she said. "It's getting late." The twenty minutes were running out. "Shall we go, Malcolm?"

They were going toward the door when it exploded open. There was a man standing there, all in white, from his nose to his toes, holding an AK-47 assault rifle—they apparently didn't trust the M-16—and he was pointing it at the Vice-President of the United States.

"Freeze," the man said.

Keyes froze, in more ways than one. It was jarring, out of context, unbelievable. How could somebody be pointing a weapon at the Vice-President?

"Do you know who this is?" he said to the guard.

"Shut up."

"Take your mask off and show him who you are."

"Take that mask off and you're dead," the guard said.

"You're making as big a mistake as you can make in this life, my friend," Keyes replied.

"I'm not your friend. *Nobody* is cleared for this room today. Lean against the wall and keep your feet out, both of you." He shoved the Vice-President. It was entirely possible he was sub–Mark Eight and didn't know she was a woman. It was entirely possible that he was like a lot of Americans who, say, didn't know what continent Nicaragua was on and might not even know who the Vice-President *was.*

"Be calm," Madeleine whispered to Keyes. "We'll get this straightened out. Don't do anything rash."

They could hear the guard talking quietly to someone over the telephone. Keyes was trying to keep from being disoriented and panicked. The Vice-President had been caught in some kind of CIA web, her Secret Service locked outside the building, and a CIA crazy holding a gun on her. They were dealing with yet another mindless fanatic, the kind of person with a bad habit of obeying orders. The situation felt mortal. A lot of people in the establishment didn't care one iota for Madeleine Smith. The idea of Halliday's having a heart attack and Madeleine's rising to the presidency was nothing less than horrifying to a large part of the establishment. If anyone wanted to take advantage of the situation, he would have a fine opportunity now. Keyes and Madeleine had trampled on a sacred grotto; it could very easily be an innocent accident.

Madeleine had evidently been following along the same general line of reasoning.

"Maybe you *should* do something crazy," she whispered. "Do something *male.*"

Keyes nodded. He was waiting for a chance to do something male. But he didn't have the faintest idea what. The man hung up the phone. The moment was approaching. Madeleine's life—not to mention his own—might be hanging by a thread.

"You leave those Americans alone, you commie prick," Mark Eight said, "or I'm going to tear you apart. Did you hear that? Did I communicate?"

The guard was taken totally by surprise; *he* didn't know what the GOD Project was either. It was yet another example of the constipation of security. Keyes reacted without a whole lot of ratiocination. He whirled and kicked at the man's crotch, missed it *completely,* but his foot kept on going up and he caught the man underneath the chin. Both of them fell flat on their backs. But only Keyes stood up; the guard had been poleaxed. He looked like he was going to be out of it for a while.

"Attaway, babe," Mark Eight said. "Take no prisoners."

"You did the right thing," Madeleine said. "This was out of control."

Keyes was reaching for the AK-47.

"No, no, no," she said. "Leave the gun. Don't touch the gun. No guns."

"You're the boss."

"Let's go find Monk," she said.

Keyes turned for one last look at the pile of junk on the workbench. "Thanks for your help, Mark."

"Gordon."

"Gordon."

"Listen, anytime. You're my kind of people." Then he called out to Madeleine as she was going through the door, "One of these days it'll be you and me, honey!"

They had managed to lose themselves in the hidden third of the Consortium. And they had gotten a break: This part of the project was dead in the water; there was no one around. As they raced through the place looking for an exit, they found one room after another that was off the wall. There were rooms that looked part operating room, part garage. There were rooms that looked part television repair shop, part health club. And everywhere the corridors were in spectacular Technicolor—but more intense than Technicolor; it was almost as if the stripes were holographic in some way. Then they found a door with one word on it: MARK. They opened it. It turned out to be the Museum of Mark.

Keyes almost fainted. He started to sway; his knees were starting to give. He grabbed Madeleine's arm to steady himself. There were six Marks, all in glass cases, and they all looked like Keyes; it was like seeing six stuffed brothers. They were all dressed in jungle fatigues, rifles at the trail position. They walked past the glass cases, awestruck. Keyes felt a powerful urge to have a bowel movement.

"Six," Madeleine said. "We just met Mark Eight. That means they thought you were Mark Seven and now they think John Burns is Mark Seven."

Keyes was squinting at the Marks, mentally adding in a full beard. There was a family resemblance to John Burns.

300

"The odd thing is, you would expect Mark Eight to be superior to Mark Seven. But he's an imbecile."

"A virile imbecile," Keyes said. "A freedom fighter."

She smiled weakly. "Malcolm, how do we get out of this?"

"These guys are CIA goons. They know what they know. They follow orders. I don't think we can just walk out there and surrender; I don't trust them. What do you think?"

"If we could get to a phone, I could conceivably call Anderson at the gate. But what would that accomplish?" She was asking herself the question more than Keyes.

"Anderson has only eight men with him," she continued. "They couldn't possibly break into this building. They might all get killed trying, and if they knew about this situation, they *would* try. Theater of the absurd, Malcolm. The Secret Service in pitched battle with the CIA. We have to find a nonconfrontational way out of this."

Keyes was nodding his head up and down. When you were with politicians, you didn't get around to dealing with reality until you first got around to dealing with politics.

"*If* we could get to a telephone, you could call the President," he said. "He could call Jessup. Jessup could call his madmen."

"Sure, but where do you find a phone in a freaked-out place like this?"

It had been fifteen minutes since they had heard a sound. Keyes opened the door of the museum half a crack. There was nothing. A full crack. Nothing. He stuck his head out and quickly looked both ways, then ducked back in, thinking about what he had seen. There was nothing.

"Let's go," he said.

They went out into the VIBGYOR corridor carrying their shoes, moving slowly, listening at doors, trying doors. They finally found a room with a phone. The sign on the door said HEURISTICS, and it was filled from floor to ceiling with what looked like computer programs.

Madeleine picked up the phone cautiously and listened. There was an outside line. She dialed the White House.

"This is the Vice-President," she said. "Connect me to Richard immediately. This is an emergency."

In thirty seconds, she was talking to Moody in Toronto.

"I have to speak to Richard," she said.

301

"That won't be easy," Moody said. "After talking to Dr. Monk he went into a big lunch meeting. He's sitting on the dais."

"I don't care what he's sitting on; this is an emergency. Get him to the phone."

They waited five minutes for Moody to get back to wherever the telephone was.

"He won't come," he said. "There's no way he's going to walk out of that meeting. The Russians might go on alert, for God's sake. The stock market could crash. He can't risk it. But the moment he can get away, I'll have him call you."

The Vice-President hung up. She understood Halliday's problem. The politics of the thing were ruinous. The timing was rotten. The situation was hair-raising.

"The question is, how long is it going to take him?" she said. "Sooner or later, those idiots out there are going to find us."

Keyes was standing there with his eyes closed, thinking. Thinking like a politician.

"Ideally," he said, "what we have to do is disappear out of this building and turn up magically somewhere else. Right?"

Her eyes brightened.

"You understand the situation *perfectly*. Is it possible?"

"I have a thought," he said, picking up the phone. He dialed Lockhart's number.

Lockhart was in a cranky mood. He had already managed to lose four million dollars that morning. Keyes explained the situation.

"What do you people want from me?" Lockhart said. "I've already worked *miracles* for you people. The trouble is, you're all amateurs. You don't appreciate what goes into this kind of thing. You don't know what the stakes are."

"Work another miracle. You've got half an hour. That's all I can give you."

"What kind of miracle?"

"Find out how we can get the hell out of this stupid place in one piece. And without going through the front door."

"You're crazy. No. It's worse than crazy. It's incompetence. That goes double for your Vice-President. Uh, don't quote me on that."

"I'm calling back in half an hour. Have the answer." Keyes hung up the phone and looked at Madeleine as brightly as he could. "I have a degree of confidence in the man," he said.

"Get me out of here, Malcolm. That's an order."

"Yes, madam."

When the half hour was up, he called Lockhart. He could sense her watching his face as he listened. He tried to stay controlled and businesslike. Then he looked at her.

"He's got to be able to name the new chairman of the Securities and Exchange Commission." The incumbent had just had a stroke.

Keyes watched her thinking that one through. There was no time to wait for Toronto. She was going to have to make the commitment on her own, and politicians lived and died on their promises.

"Deal," she said.

"Deal," Keyes said.

He hung up.

"I'm to call back in fifteen minutes."

Laundry was a major issue at the Consortium. All those white gowns and caps and masks required significant logistics. These logistics were a slight flaw in the security shield of the place. Lockhart had to have been really well connected to have come up with the scheme, which was somewhat undignified but had the advantage of being politically sound.

They went down a corridor, made a left, then a right, then slipped into Room 98. They made it. The crazies were nowhere near them; the crazies were all back near Mark Eight and the big chip room. There were a number of empty laundry carts in the room. The laundry chute itself wasn't too large; it would be a bit of a squeeze.

"Tell me, Malcolm, do I go head first or feet first?"

He pulled open the metal drawer and climbed in.

"I recommend feet first, Madam Vice-President," he said, and was gone.

38

THE IMPERIAL LAUNDRY

IT WAS AS though Lockhart were getting some kind of tricky conservative's revenge. It was mortifying; clever, but mortifying. Lockhart's plan was based on the fact that the Consortium—like most security installations—was basically structured to prevent unauthorized *entry*, not unauthorized exit. In that sense, the Consortium—like most security installations—had a hole big enough to drive the literal truck through.

Keyes had braked all the way, pressing his rubber heels against the metal chute. When he slid out on the loading platform at the rear of the Consortium, he was moving slowly, and he casually stood up and looked around. He hadn't been noticed. He poised himself in front of the chute and caught Madeleine, who came flying out of the thing at sixty miles an hour.

A guard walked up to them.

"Anything the matter here?"

"No. She fell down. She doesn't look where she's going."

The guard glanced at their badges and ambled away.

Keyes and Madeleine started sorting laundry. Countless masks and caps and gowns and shoe covers lay on the platform.

The loading platform ran the width of the building. There were guards all over the place, but they were concentrated at the doors leading *into* the Consortium. They were defending against entry, against the suppliers, whose trucks were pulling up to the loading platform constantly. Technical supplies, food supplies, incoming laundry, outgoing laundry.

Keyes and the Vice-President were further aided by the fact that all Consortium employees on the shipping platform were wearing masks, because they were going in and out of the building, taking in supplies. As long as they had their fancy badges hanging around their necks, they were anonymous. Lockhart delivered.

The hard part was waiting for the laundry truck to arrive. Sooner or later, one of Jessup's brilliant Shiites was going to think about the laundry chute. It took over an hour, during which time Keyes and Madeleine kept their heads buried in laundry carts, sorting laundry. Keyes used the occasion to take advantage.

"Not the caps," he said to her sharply, as a guard was passing. "The *gowns*. The *gowns* go in this one."

After a lifetime, the laundry truck finally backed up to the loading platform. It was a panel truck with the name Imperial Laundry painted on the side. The driver got out and opened the rear doors. Madeleine pushed a cart into it and then dropped down onto the floor. Keyes was right behind her. As soon as he was inside, the driver slammed the doors shut.

Keyes and the Vice-President were lying on the floor looking at each other as the truck slowly pulled away from the shipping area and began to wind its way along the dirt road to the highway.

"I think this is worth the Securities and Exchange Commission," Keyes whispered.

"Best political deal I ever made," she answered. "That guy is my favorite conservative."

It was when they got to the highway that they heard the driver's assistant say, "*Spasibo.*" They were still looking at each other when the driver opened the rear doors and they got out to see a stretch Mercedes pulled over at the side of the highway. The rear door opened and the Second Secretary of the Soviet Embassy got out. He hurried over to Madeleine, bent low, kissed her hand, smiled charmingly.

"This is indeed an honor, Madam Vice-President."

Keyes's eyes narrowed. This particular Russian kept turning up in the strangest places. Lockhart had to be some kind of crazy, corrupt, amoral genius who would cut across any and all lines to solve a problem. Wall Street must have been a piece of cake for him. Madeleine was rising to the occasion.

"Why, thank you, Mr. Secretary. I'm highly appreciative of your courtesy. This is Malcolm Keyes."

"We've met," the Second Secretary said.

"Now and again," Keyes said suspiciously. "How could you possibly have gotten here this fast?"

"I happened to be in Denver when the call came in. If it hadn't been me, it would have been someone else."

"Oh, that explains it," Keyes said.

"Well then, the niceties having been disposed of, I propose that we get the hell out of here," the Second Secretary said.

The car was not very communist. It was the same stretch Mercedes Keyes had been kidnapped in and which had turned up in a barn in Kansas. Keyes and the Vice-President sat in the rear, while the Russian sat in one of the reverse-facing seats, playing bartender.

"In view of your recent adventure, is it possible that you would have need of a small drink? Or, possibly, a large one?"

"Scotch," Madeleine said. "Three fingers, one cube."

"Canadian," Keyes said. "On the rocks; fill the glass."

"Coming up," the Second Secretary said jovially. "By the way, where would you like to go?"

"To the nearest phone."

The Russian pointed to one hanging right next to her ear. "Help yourself."

"I wouldn't dream of running up a bill on the Soviet Union," she said prettily.

"Runkel's Gap is the nearest town. I could drop you there."

"That would be most generous of you, Mr. Secretary."

"Do call me Anatoly, madam. Runkel's Gap," he said to the driver over the intercom. Then he passed them their drinks. He was having his usual vodka, freezing, with a twist.

"I think the time has come for straight talk," the Russian said. "There are some obvious difficulties with this situation."

"Which ones were those?" she said sweetly-deadly.

Anatoly pursed his lips. He was trying to come up with reasonably diplomatic phraseology.

"I do *so* hope that your State Department won't declare me persona non grata as a result of today's little adventure."

Keyes swiveled to Madeleine, completely hooked by the conversation. She was sitting there calmly inhaling her scotch.

"You mean you want me to forget that you know a thing or three about a supersecret American installation."

Keyes swiveled back to the Second Secretary. The Russians were supposed to be good negotiators. Keyes waited.

"Quite frankly, the only ice I like is the kind you find in a glass. I like working in this country. But I'm not talking something for nothing. At the very same time, the Soviet Union could *totally* forget that we saved the American Vice-President from her own CIA."

Having made a delicate point, Anatoly sipped delicately at his vodka. The Vice-President didn't respond. She was thinking through.

"Anatoly, why did you go to the trouble and take the risks of helping us out today?"

The Second Secretary, getting ready to make them fresh drinks, was staring at the ice cubes in his ice bucket as though they were a reminder of Siberia. You could *still* end up there, freezing, with a twist.

"For more than one reason," he said.

"Tell me, Anatoly."

"In the first place, I paid off an obligation."

"To whom?"

The Second Secretary merely tilted his head to one side, implying that the question was clearly improper.

"In the second place," he continued, "the Soviet government would like to see the Halliday administration make a go of it. The Soviet government feels that the Halliday administration is somewhat saner than some recent U.S. administrations and genuinely seems to want a test ban treaty."

"Don't let that out to the press, will you?" she said.

"Never!" he said, smiling, drinking, laughing, nudging Keyes's knee with his elbow, enjoying the irony. "You know you're up against another basic limitation," he went on. "The first one is nuclear winter. You can't launch a first strike against us because you'll set off nuclear winter and commit suicide. Now your robots are rebelling, uncontrollable, impossible. Sometimes I think nature—dare I say God—is on *our* side."

Madeleine was ignoring him. She was thinking over the basic proposition.

"We don't tell about you and you don't tell about us, huh?"

She sounded dubious. There was no way of knowing, after all, how much the Russians knew about Monk's operation.

"I'm also willing to throw in what you Americans so aptly call a sweetener."

"That's always a sign of good faith, Anatoly. But it has to be worth something. What is it?"

The Second Secretary hesitated.

"Um, does this gentleman have a high security clearance? He *could* ride with the driver, and they can't hear anything up there. Nothing personal, you understand, sir. Matters of state."

"He has a very high clearance, Anatoly. You may proceed."

"Does he really?"

The Second Secretary was obviously as surprised as everyone else about the rapid rise of Malcolm Keyes in the councils of state. He looked him over for a few seconds before resuming.

"I'm willing to show you everything we know about the GOD Project. Some of it is hot off the copier. But you must give me your promise of extreme discretion. I could get in trouble if this got out."

Keyes couldn't help it. He had to cough in order to disguise his astonishment and failing nerve and pure eagerness about finding out what the Russian knew. He realized he would have made a lousy negotiator. Madeleine, on the other hand, was calm; it was just another back-room political horse-trading session.

"Now, I *can't* give you a copy. That would be unforgivable. However, I *can* let you read the documents. Nobody can prove that you read them."

"Malcolm, I'm much too upset to read anything. Would you mind scanning it?"

Keyes looked at the sheaf of papers the Second Secretary was holding out to her. He held his hand out. Anatoly looked dubious but he handed them over.

The Vice-President held her glass out.

"Anatoly, you've got yourself a deal."

Clink!

The Second Secretary left them off at the only coffee shop in Runkel's Gap. Madeleine promptly got five dollars in quarters and called the White House. Keyes went next door to a general store and bought a pad. He went back to the coffee shop and sat at the counter and ordered coffee.

"Put me through to Toronto," Madeleine was saying. "Oh. All right. Connect me with Air Force One. This is another emergency."

The proprietor, pouring the coffee, was listening, fascinated, spilling coffee all over the counter.

"Richard, I got separated from the Secret Service and they don't know where I am."

Richard apparently had a long reaction to that.

"Richard, I can't explain now. Would you please get in touch with Air Force Two and tell them to get in touch with Anderson and tell Anderson I'm at the Good Old Boy Coffee Shop in Runkel's Gap, Colorado."

The proprietor leaned over to Keyes and said very confidentially, "Who is she?"

"She's the weather girl for KLTV in Denver."

"I *knew* I recognized her."

Keyes took out his ballpoint. He sensed instinctively that he would have to put it down on paper. It would be too long for a recitation. It would be difficult for Halliday to give Keyes that much time. And the information was worth studying and digesting. It was nothing less than an education. Halliday could absorb it at his leisure and then consign the sheets to the shredder he had hidden in his wet bar. Keyes looked at the first blank page of the pad. Then he started to write out what he was already calling the GOD Papers.

39

THE GOD PAPERS

THE PAGES THAT the Second Secretary gave to Keyes were copies of various memos written by high-ranking members of several administrations in Washington, scattered thinly over a period of years. The first of them were dated late 1980, shortly after Ronald Reagan's first election to the presidency of the United States. Most of the memos were from Dr. Theodore Monk to Secretary of Defense–designate Casper Weinberger. A smaller number were to Reagan's DCI, William Casey, and to other scientists on the GOD Project. Still others were written during the Bush and McKay administrations.

6 NOV 1980

TO: Dr. Theodore Monk
FROM: SEC DEF DESIGNATE WEINBERGER
RE: Our "running gag"

1. Is it doable?
2. What does the scientific community think?
3. President-elect Reagan finds it fascinating.

TO: SEC DEF DESIGNATE WEINBERGER
FROM: Monk
RE: How to spend a trillion dollars

1. I realize all of this started with a few too many cocktails at the minority leader's garden party, but I'm beginning to have serious thoughts. Progress is catching up to fantasy.

2. The formula for living matter is:

$$H_{2960} \, O_{1480} \, C_{1480} \, N_{16} \, P_{1.8} \, S.$$

3. That formula doesn't really have anything to do with the counterinsurgency problem, of course. It doesn't express the dynamics of life; it's passive life stuff, content at rest. But it's provoking that you can boil life down to a string of numbers and letters, isn't it?

4. Let's get a little closer to the problem. In the human being there are forty-six chromosomes, made up of approximately one million genes. One million tiny hunks of DNA, all of it in the human zygote, the new individual, and in every cell in the body to come. All the information is there, laid out molecule by molecule, everything you need to know about life. Now suppose you could write an ordinary differential equation for each gene?

5. By an ordinary differential equation (in case you were nodding that semester) I mean an equation that would express dynamically the possibilities of the gene, its function, how it would carry out that function, under what circumstances, and so on. You would, of course, end up with one million simultaneous equations, but I'm assuming the United States of America could afford the computer. Having those equations, you would be in possession of the most powerful knowledge ever acquired.

6. You would have the formula for man.

7. And that has a lot to do with the counterinsurgency problem.

22 NOV 1980

TO: SEC DEF DESIGNATE WEINBERGER
FROM: Monk
RE: The solution to the politics of counterguerrilla warfare

1. I was able to get a fast grant from one of the think tanks and so I conducted a five-day seminar at the old Harriman mansion in Arden, New York. I had the best men and women in the relevant fields (consistent with the sobriety of their politics, of course).

2. We alternated between small working committees, which specialized in particular problem areas, and plenary sessions. Eighteen hours a day.

3. All assumptions made were on the conservative side. Conclusion? Now is the time. *Someone* is going to do it. We had better do it first.

2 DEC 1980

TO: President-elect Reagan
FROM: SEC DEF DESIGNATE WEINBERGER
RE: The Vietnam Syndrome

1. The politics of counterrevolution, including counterguerrilla warfare, have become intractable. We should be able to send in some advisers to El Salvador, but an invasion of Nicaragua is out of the question; the American people are still unbudgeable about armed intervention in Third World countries.

2. We ought to be able to get enough Democrats to go along with us in financing and organizing former Somoza National Guard people into an insurgency force. But that will only be a delaying action to make the Sandinistas feel pain. It is probably not the long-term solution; the Sandinistas are simply too well entrenched.

3. Down the line, we're going to have similar problems in Guatemala, Honduras, El Salvador, Mexico maybe, the Philippines, etc.

4. So, there's a disaster coming. Maybe on your watch. I'm talking about nothing less than . . . the loss of countries all around the globe to left-wing governments. Our options are almost at the vanishing point. How can we avert this catastrophe?

5. As you know, Dr. Theodore Monk of MIT has an idea. He's already done considerable staff work on his own. I'd like

312

the three of us to get together at your earliest convenience. We'll need at least an hour.

25 DEC 1980

TO: President-elect Reagan
FROM: SEC DEF DESIGNATE WEINBERGER
RE: Overt/covert warfare

1. Let me say again how happy we were about your enthusiastic reception of the GOD Project presentation.
2. If it is indeed doable, the SIR—or Standard Insurgency Robot—is clearly the answer to the difficulties of intervention in Third World countries by a democratic nation. Indeed, I would go so far as to say it is the ultimate in statecraft: It is the unification of overt *and* covert warfare in *one* instrumentality. Yes, it would be employed on the overt battlefield. But no, there wouldn't be any casualties. No body bags coming home. No MIA families to worry about. No one would care. It wouldn't be news. We can handle the media. For all practical purposes, as far as the American public would be concerned, it would be covert warfare.
3. GOD is the end run around the Vietnam Syndrome.
4. I most urgently recommend immediate funding.
5. If the Israelis ever got this thing, you *know* they'd be planting trees all the way to Hoboken.

31 DEC 1980

TO: SEC DEF DESIGNATE WEINBERGER
FROM: Monk
RE: Presidential objections

1. I was disappointed to learn that the President changed his mind. It was sheer rotten luck that he saw Frankenstein on the Afternoon Movie on Wednesday, and there's no getting away from it: There are similarities.
2. The real problem, of course, is the belief barrier. The barrier that stands in the way of anything that truly departs from current beliefs. Remember when the four-minute mile was beyond the reach of humans? Same thing: The President can't believe that man could reliably be created by mere scientists.

313

3. Between us: This is magico-religious thinking—that man was created by some magical godlike process that is beyond our ken. In point of fact, life on this planet is the product of a lot of bad concepting but some damn vigorous field testing. The brain? A twenty-watt computer and data handler made out of meat. The real achievement is the twenty watts. Spectacular power efficiency. DNA? A phenomenal storage and data transmission system. About a billion years of experimenting went into it. The eye is a fabulous achievement, and the pituitary and the thyroid and that great crapshooter the sex organs. I know the President is a religious man, but it is necessary to convince him that these achievements were done *blindly*. Thesis by accident. Postulate by accident. Lab work by accident. Testing by accident. The monkeys pounding away at their typewriters turning out *Hamlet* (us). And therein lies my answer to the President's objections. It won't take *me* a billion years. *I* know what I'm doing.

15 JAN 1981

TO: SEC DEF DESIGNATE WEINBERGER
FROM: Monk
RE: The GOD Project

1. I've begun making preliminary staff selections and will shortly submit the list for your approval and vetting.
2. I think that shipment of Soviet tanks for the Sandinistas is going to turn out to be the worst mistake the commies ever made.

27 FEB 1981

TO: SEC DEF Weinberger
FROM: Monk
RE: SAUSAGE

1. First, congratulations on being installed in office. We're all hoping this administration can make a difference to the world.
2. I can understand your chagrin over the use of an acronym you never heard of. In point of fact, it's a gag acronym used by some of the people on the project and it evidently turned up in a memo somewhere.

314

3. SAUSAGE stands for Semiautomatic Unitized Self-Propelled Antiguerrilla Entity.
4. Boys will be boys!

16 JUN 1985

TO: Dr. Heilmann
FROM: Monk
RE: Hate

1. In re your group's proposal that we program the SIR to hate Russians: I hate it. History demonstrates that it would be foolish. We no longer refer to Japanese gentlemen as "Jap monkeys." We no longer refer to German gentlemen as "Krauts" or "Jerries" or "animals to be stamped out." They are now distinguished allies. Surely we must learn from history.
2. I am not denigrating the importance of hate. An eighty-year-old man can still hate like a tiger; this bears out the contention that hate is stronger and more satisfying and more essential to survival than sex. But it's atomic, so we have to watch our step with it.
3. Once we program the SIR to hate, he's going to hate other SIRs to some degree as well as himself. We're going to have occasional race riots, suicides, God knows what. But that's a price we have to pay. We're stuck. We don't know which way the historical winds are going to blow. So we can't simply program in hate for our *current* enemies, or to any particular racial, ethnic, or ideological prejudice. We want *pure hate*.
4. Always remember that man is the best possible model, one designed by a far tougher taskmaster than the Pentagon. There were no sweetheart deals, no altering of the test data, no rigged field trials, no revolving doors between government and industry. Man is authentic, the primal killer.
5. I predict, however, that a new branch of psychology may very well come into being: sirchiatry.

16 NOV 1988

TO: President-elect Bush
FROM: Monk
RE: SIR unit costs

315

1. I urge you not to make long-term judgments about SIR unit costs based on present expenditures. The installation here in Colorado is purely a pilot plant. And not a very good pilot plant at that. It's one big improvisation. Every step we've taken, after all, has been into the unknown. So inefficiencies have piled up and everything is costing vastly more than it should.

2. But once we go into mass production, it will be mass production (and it will be that in every sense of the word). Unit costs will approximate that of a two-door Toyota.

3 FEB 1989

TO: Director Jessup
FROM: Monk
RE: The Book of Mark

1. To only be allowed to have one copy of the Book of Mark, as we call it, throughout the entire project, is absurd. Some of the very accomplished scientists on this project are wasting time *standing in line* waiting to refer to it. I hereby request that we be allowed to make five additional copies of the Book of Mark.

3 FEB 1989

TO: Dr. Monk
FROM: DCI
RE: Book of Mark

1. Not on your life.

3 MAY 1989

TO: SEC DEF Cheney
FROM: Monk
RE: CIA

1. Isn't there some relief you can give us from these maniacs? Our CIA protectors are hard-nosed, beady-eyed fanatics. Security people as a general thing always manage to screw up the works.

2. Security and scientific progress are mutually exclusive. They keep compartmentalizing us. They shut us off from each

other with this moronic need-to-know doctrine. Security and science are incompatible. Can you get us any relief from these people?

4 MAY 1989

TO: Monk
FROM: SEC DEF Cheney
RE: Security Procedures

    1. My best advice: Live with it.

20 FEB 1990

TO: Dr. Caruthers
FROM: Monk
RE: Running hot

    1. The way things are now, the SIRs are all going to be feverish. It looks as though they'll be running at about 106.8° F. I know that I've said we want to be able to fling a bunch of hotheads out there on the world, but I didn't mean to be taken literally.
    2. High temperature not only reduces service life, it violates our fundamental principle of verisimilitude. SIRs have to be able to take the standard physical (except for X-rays, of course).
    3. I've decided therefore to switch to sprayed-on superconductors for the memory chips. According to my calculations this should eliminate enough heat to bring design center temperature down to 98.6° F.
    4. The really efficient killer is cool.

13 MAR 1990

TO: President Bush
FROM: DCI
RE: The Pentagon and GOD

    1. The possibility of field trials in the not too distant future raises a few questions. I am worried about the Pentagon in general, the army in particular.
    2. Interservice rivalries in the Pentagon are worse than professional hockey. The U.S. Army's most dreaded opponent, to

317

take one example, is the U.S. Marine Corps; they're terrified of marine glamour.

3. The U.S. Navy is a little universe all by itself, with its own army (the marines) and its own air force.

4. The U.S. Air Force would like nothing better than to have one great final dogfight with naval aviation to see who rules the skies.

5. Given this situation, who is to run GOD? It will be the worst shoot-out of all time.

6. Therefore, I urge you to instruct SEC DEF not to tell *anyone* about GOD and leave it as a division of CIA. We know how to keep secrets. And we have vast institutional experience in running armies in Southeast Asia, Central America, and Afghanistan.

7. I know this inevitably has to sound self-serving, but I believe it to be in the interest of national security. If the Joint Chiefs ever started feeling insecure, this thing would be leaked all over Washington.

11 OCT 1990

TO: Dr. Maselli
FROM: Monk
RE: Our deepest, darkest secret

1. I have come to the conclusion that we have been unable to acquire ballistic transistor technology. Our transistors are simply not fast enough.

2. At the same time, it is quite obvious that the Japanese production-line ballistic transistors are exactly what we need.

3. For the first time I feel the need for security! Let's try to bury this in a memory hole, but Mark Seven is not going to be 100 percent made in America.

15 APR 1996

TO: SEC DEF Eagleburger
FROM: Monk
RE: Field trials

1. We're very excited out here. This is the culmination of another Manhattan Project. But that one was only four years. This one has taken fifteen.

318

2. I now know what Oppenheimer must have felt shortly before the Trinity test.

3. When Henry Patrick leaves here and enlists in the army, the world will have begun to change. Irrevocably. American politics will begin to change. The problem of intervening overseas from a democracy/one person one vote base will be on its way to solution. American power will be liberated!

4. It's highly possible that the war/peace issue will vanish from the front pages, from the evening news. This and future administrations will not have to manufacture outrages in order to get society's agreement to intervene. In a very real sense, this is of greater significance than nuclear weapons.

5. There is, of course, the potential fly in the ointment: that the Soviets get the SIR. We'll have to put the think tanks to work on that one. But I continue to believe that our technology will be superior and that our SIR will beat theirs every time, man for man, from Indian wrestling to marksmanship.

29 JUL 1996

TO: SEC DEF Eagleburger
FROM: Dr. Monk
RE: Henry Patrick

1. I cannot account for what happened. I'm at a loss. I'm desolate. You can have my resignation anytime you want it. I will say all the right things before any congressional committee I might be called before. The loss of Henry Patrick is inexplicable; I cannot account for it; and I accept the responsibility.

29 JUL 1996

TO: Director Jessup
FROM: Monk
RE: Henry Patrick: test procedures

1. In every measurable parameter, Henry Patrick was design center. The perfect engineering model. He was a paragon. I couldn't possibly have felt prouder when he left here to join the army.

2. My guess is that you're going to have a hard time finding

him. He's a clever fellow. And he has a *very* strong sense of survival.

3. We have begun a series of simulations here in an attempt to discover the nature of the problem.

4. *Please* bear in mind that recovering Henry is not the highest-priority assignment. Recovering him *intact* is. We have to find out what went wrong. We have to be certain about that. Otherwise, how can we go into production?

5. Therefore, you must prevent your people from using any kind of X-ray device, CAT scanner, etc. Any of these devices could change Henry ever so slightly and might obliterate the source of the problem.

6. I realize the records on him have been lost, and I simply can't account for that. Perhaps you can tell me. But because his identification records have been lost, the only way you can safely identify Henry is by using the Book of Mark.

7. Find the man who is composed only of the basic parts in the parts list. His arm must be one of the sixty arms we have in stock. His leg must be one of the eighty-four legs in stock. And so on. Fingerprints don't work here because we made them random, as they are in nature.

8. There are a total of twenty tests that will determine it for sure. Now, I say "for sure." Strictly speaking, there's a giga maybe—what you might call a faint possibility. But it is extremely faint. The probability roves out to the millionth decimal place and beyond, out near where the sun comes up and the tides ebb, out there with death and taxes. Whoever is "constructed" of twenty basic parts that can be found in our catalog is assuredly Henry Patrick.

9. If you have any interest at all in the success of the GOD Project, do not test Henry in any other way.

40

DEBRIEFING

AND HE SAID, 'It's a pleasure to have served you, madam. The Union of Soviet Socialist Republics will always extend its warmest hospitality to such a gracious, and may I add a personal comment, beautiful, member of the U.S. government,' and the Vice-President replied, 'A deal is a deal, Anatoly. You don't have to overdo it.' The Second Secretary smiled. Then he shrugged his shoulders. 'You people are so much easier to talk to than that last bunch,' he said, and the Vice-President replied, 'Enjoy the pizzaburgers, Anatoly,' and the Russians drove off and we went into the coffee shop and the Vice-President raised you somewhere over Lake Michigan."

The President was sitting in his favorite chair. His secretary, Phyllis, was holding his calls. He was looking appalled; there had been a whiff of political assassination about the entire affair.

"My sense of it," Madeleine said, "is that it was a series of blunders and not a conspiracy. But you've got to do something about Elmer Jessup. He has too much power; he's got everybody terrorized."

"I can assure you, Madeleine, he won't be able to sit down for a week."

"And, of course, you're in debt to that mad genius Lockhart."

"I accept the terms of the deal," Halliday said, smiling for the first time. He looked at Keyes.

"Malcolm, you regularly come back with some of the worst stuff I hear. I keep having to apologize to you for getting you into these scrapes. Believe me, I never expect these things to happen. Who could?" He worked at making a straight face. "How did it feel going down the laundry chute, Madeleine?"

"Oh, just another day in politics," she replied.

"This is what tight security does," Halliday said. "It confuses everything. The right hand doesn't know what the left hand is doing. The Consortium is a classic. The guard couldn't recognize the Vice-President of the United States because she was wearing a mask, and then he was taken by surprise because he didn't know what it was he was guarding."

Halliday was holding up his chin with his thumbs, the web of his laced fingers pressing against his nose.

"You were right all along, Malcolm," he said. "I must say I lacked the imagination to believe it. Now it seems inevitable. Historically inevitable. It's a way out of the crunch. The solution to all of the problems. *Any* problem *any*where. It's the wet right-wing dream. Anywhere poor people rise up to take a bigger share of the pie, GOD will smite them. As long as American boys aren't coming home in body bags, you can get away with almost anything. It's the way for a democracy to be an imperium."

"Not with Mark Eight it isn't," the Vice-President replied. "He's a jackass. He's amazing, but he's a jackass."

Halliday smiled at her.

"Maybe that's what you need," he said. "A jackass. Somebody who accepts the basic situation without question. A real team player. No fragging of officers. No morale problems. One hundred percent gung ho. When the people get too smart in a democracy you have to have something like a GOD Project. Otherwise, the peasants will win."

Halliday sat there musing, fantasizing, working through some geopolitical riffs. "It's terrifying when you think about it. Suppose everybody got it? Suppose there was GOD proliferation? The Germans could resume the *Drang nach Osten*. The Japanese could go back to work on their Greater East Asia Co-Prosperity Sphere. Only the Chinese would find it superfluous."

"The South Koreans could become a superpower," Madeleine put in.

"Along with Taiwan. You just *know* they could make them better and cheaper."

"Drink time," Halliday said, promptly making three warm scotches.

"It's easy to see why they tried to keep it from me. I ran on nonintervention, after all. They were afraid I'd blow the whistle."

Keyes and Madeleine exchanged glances.

"Uh," she said, "Malcolm and I have concluded that this thing is inherently unleakable. You can't leak it, Richard. Any leaker of such a story would look like a maniac."

"You've got a point," Halliday replied. "But, you know, right-wingers wouldn't see it that way. Right-wingers are always terrified of the truth. Because what they're doing is always so far away from what they're saying they're doing—it's the one percent manipulating the ninety-nine percent, remember—that they're always terrified of bits of truth leaking out. They have to work overtime at disinformation."

Keyes stopped being a tape recorder for a moment. It was uncharacteristic, even presumptuous, but they weren't mentioning a certain item.

"What about John Burns?" he asked.

Halliday nodded.

"Of course," he said. "If *you're* not Mark Seven, then *he* must be. Or at least they'll think he is. Which means the CIA will go after him. And what do we do about that? What is our ethical obligation to John Burns, alias Henry Patrick, alias Mark Seven?"

"Hoo ha," Madeleine said.

Halliday worked at his scotch, taking one prolonged gurgling swallow.

"The irony is that I might even use the damn thing if I thought it would *work*. The answer to the Vietnam Syndrome? You think I'd look down my nose at that? But we're forever spending billions on weapon systems that don't work. If John Burns turns out to be Mark Seven, then he is the typical product of the military-industrial complex. He's a trillion-dollar toilet seat."

Halliday was looking at his nose, thinking.

"What did that thing say SAUSAGE stood for?"

"Semiautomatic Unitized Self-Propelled Antiguerrilla Entity."

Halliday looked lost.

"Self-propelled," he said. "What? Uniformed?"

"Semiautomatic, Uni*tized,* Self-Propelled, Antiguerrilla, Entity."

Halliday drank.

323

"I might point out, sir, that it's not all that far from the Census Bureau definition of a robot."

"Which is what?"

Keyes rattled it off.

"A reprogrammable multifunctional manipulator designed to move material, parts, tools, or specialized devices through various programmed motions for the performance of a variety of tasks."

Halliday was nodding his head.

"You know, you could read 'citizen' into that. Even the reprogrammable part. That's something you accomplish with slogans. Unfortunately, the conservatives have us beat in that department. They have superior slogans. There's a slogan gap."

He wandered back to his bar and made one scotch, since he was way ahead of Keyes and the Vice-President.

"The point is," he said, padding back to his overstuffed chair, "that a Mark Seven SAUSAGE hired killer has turned into a pacifist Jesus freak. That's if they're right, which I doubt. In any case, John Burns is in hot water. I don't want to lose him. If he could take the stink off left-wing words and ideas, he can help make American politics a little more rational. He balances off a lot of the fire breathers. I'm going to do what I can for him, Malcolm."

41

LIBERAL SEX

H E HAD TO adjust to the situation each and every time. It was
necessary to reduce her to woman, not the pulse beat away from
being the Nuclear Princess, the Amazon leader of Western civilization,
Madeleine the Great. The fact that she wore her tortoiseshell glasses all
through it helped. And that brave lonely dove tattooed beneath her left
breast; her *left* breast: Madeleine never missed a trick. He kissed the
dove and could feel that he was breaking through the power barrier once
again; he could feel the centripetal emotion of love, the flying inward
toward his center.

"The member from New York is voting aye," she said. "This is
clearly a case of big government."

He rolled onto her.

"You can't kid me," he said. "You're girl."

Congress was in session.

Sex was Madeleine's opportunity to lose control, safely. Sex was when
she made up for playing life close to the vest, eternally watching every

syl-la-ble, touching all bases, remembering the polls, remembering the taboos, remembering how far Richard wanted her to go and no farther. Sex was the antithesis of politics and an antidote to politics, which was why there was need for a constitutional amendment that automatically forgave politicians their sexual transgressions; it was what gave them a hold on sanity.

It was worse for liberals than conservatives. Being on the right side of politics was inherently safer than being on the left. A conservative politician could err on the side of conservatism, take a position more right-wing than he or she usually took, and it wouldn't be a serious mistake. But if a liberal politician strayed too far to the left—out in the general direction of socialism and communism, which were virtual curse words in the United States—it could be fatal.

For this reason, liberals had to be more careful; they had to repress more, play it closer to the vest, they had always to be on red alert. Liberals were so guarded in their professional lives that they tended to be much more concupiscent in their personal lives than conservatives were.

The situation was even worse for women politicians, who had the additional burden of having to be constantly aware of accidental sexual meanings in what might be perfectly innocent circumstances. Therefore, a female liberal politician would be the most straitlaced and repressed of all and, consequently, would be the most unrepressed in bed. And a female, liberal *Vice-President* had to be the best lay in Washington.

Madeleine's arms and legs were wrapped tightly around him, and she was giving thrust for thrust, talking a blue streak, letting it all hang out, unguarded, totally vulnerable: the politician on a rampage of honesty, saying fuck you to the entire electorate. Keyes was the beneficiary of a thousand interviews with the press, of doing time on "Face the Nation," of fencing with anchorpeople and ambitious reporters, of being nice to potential contributors and pretending she cared about their greed, of always walking a wavy line between conflicting interests. Keyes was getting it all. Keyes was hanging on for dear life, purging her of political frustrations until the consensus finally arrived, unanimity, the measure passing by acclamation, demonstrations in the aisles, bands playing, shouting, laughing, crying, tumult, there's a hot time in the old town tonight!

* * *

326

Her snores sounded like groans. They were heartrending soul snores. He hated it when she snored that way after love; the snores seemed to contradict what had gone before. It sounded as though some great disappointment or loss were being described, and each and every snore was a stab at his heart. What had he done to deserve this? He much preferred her sneezes. Her sneezes were very feminine, high-pitched grace notes that always reminded him of her physicality as well as the baroque period, say Bach, stealing time, slipping in his extra little curlicues.

He looked at her, glasses askew, the dove still in flight, everything else exhausted; the bedclothes had vanished. She was totally wiped out.

He thought of the problem of the brain—that IBM PC made out of meat—dealing with sex. The end of logic, reason, the reciprocal of Erasmus. The crotch—she called it Headquarters, Supreme Headquarters—teaching the brain how to be illogical, irrational. Sex was the slot machine that didn't turn up lemons or bells but bananas, the machine going bananas every time you played it except when you got too logical, too Erasmusian, and then it broke down; then it came up lemons.

He could feel her eyelashes against his shoulder; she had opened her eyes.

"Where am I?" she asked.

"We're in heaven."

"I like it here."

"You have to keep quiet, though. The Catholics think they're the only ones up here."

"I don't have the strength to make noise. Malcolm, we seem to be getting along extremely well."

"I think so."

"You've got to promise never to write a book about me."

"I promise."

"I'm probably worth a million dollars to you."

"That's just for paperback rights."

"That's going to be a terrible temptation, Malcolm."

"I don't kiss and write."

"You'll have the opportunity to change history. It might appeal to your male vanity."

"Madeleine, you don't know me too well as yet. I don't *want* to change history. I'm not like you in that respect. *You* want to change history."

"That is true."

"I want history to go on its own way as though I didn't exist. I don't want the responsibility."

"Then why are you going to write Richard's big book for him?"

"That's his responsibility. I'm just the three-by-five file cards."

"That's an evasion. It's slick but it's unconvincing. I don't believe you. You are not as self-effacing as you think you are."

"You really think so?"

"Malcolm?"

"Yes, Madeleine?"

"Do you have any more condoms?"

42

JESUS VS. THE LAUNCH OFFICERS

Dr. Theodore Monk left his CIA escort behind and slowly went along the sand of Virginia Beach, arms barely moving, head down, taking careful steps along the damp, hard-packed sand, his footsteps dissolving in water behind him. The Twenty-fifth of December Movement was making him walk a mile—which was probably his physical limit—to make sure there wasn't anyone accompanying him; no doubt there were fierce Christians lurking behind every sand dune.

The ocean was calm, but there was still enough winter left in the air to bite a little. Up ahead he could see a small group of people waiting near the shore. When he got closer, he could see that it was indeed John Burns, with four of his Christians. It was like a spies' meeting on a bridge between East and West. He stopped about ten feet away. That average face, that design center of American faces; they had spent quite a bit of supercomputer time arriving at it.

"Hello, Henry," he said.

"My name is John. John Burns."

"Okay. Could we talk alone?"

"You have to let them search you first," John Burns said.

329

"Certainly."

Monk actually smiled faintly while one of the Christians ran hands over him. As if he would ever want to do anything to hurt a hair on Henry's head. He had made Jessup guarantee that there would be no interference with the meeting. He wryly thought of it—the Christian's hands now sliding down his thighs—as some sort of historical summit: the director of the GOD Project and the star preacher of the Twenty-fifth of December Movement. When they were sure that Monk was unarmed, the four Christians backed off about twenty feet, boxing the compass.

"You look very well," Monk said.

"Thank you. Tell me what you want."

"A chat. That's all."

"All right. Shall we walk along the ocean?"

"That would be splendid," Monk said warmly.

John Burns was of average height for an American male: five feet nine. One hundred and sixty pounds. Brown eyes. Shoe size $10^{1}/_{2}$. Hat size $6^{3}/_{8}$. But he seemed to have undergone a personality change, although it was for the better. He seemed positively vibrant, interested, aware. Mature was the word. He had matured. Come into his own. He was his own man, complete you might say, walking easily, liquidly, unselfconsciously. *Alive,* that's what the word was. God, was he alive.

"You're with the government, aren't you?" Burns asked.

"Yes."

"Is it because I'm for peace?"

Monk was determined to be as honest as humanly possible. And, of course, Burns was dead on target, more so than he realized.

"Yes."

"Why? Will you tell me that? Is it subversive to be for peace?"

"No, it's not subversive to be for peace." Monk was struggling, fumbling. "The situation is vastly more complex than that. Quite frankly, I don't have time to answer that question. We'd be here all day. You only gave me thirty minutes."

Burns simply nodded his head, and they walked along in silence for a few minutes.

"You know," Burns said after a while, "when it comes to the question of war and peace, I find that I invariably think of the Jews."

"The Israelis?"

"No, the Jews. Of World War Two. The six million who were killed in the ovens and gas chambers. They say Nazis did that. Nazis did things like that. I don't see it that way."

"How do you see it?"

"Those weren't Nazis. Those were people. They were human beings. Human beings did those things. Human beings sent six million other human beings to the gas ovens for no reason. Now when we look back at that we all wonder, how could human beings have done such a thing? It's hard to understand. It's so demonic, so evil, so irrational. And yet they found a way. Somehow they rationalized it. They justified it to themselves. And that's exactly what the American leadership is doing with nuclear weapons. If there are any survivors, they will all wonder how human beings could have done such a thing; how human beings could have aspired to nuclear weapons, built nuclear weapons, piled up nuclear weapons, *used* nuclear weapons."

This wasn't the way Monk wanted the conversation to go. He was interested in more personal matters; he wanted to probe into the Burns psyche.

"Who are you?" he asked Burns.

"I'm a preacher."

"Where do you come from?"

"Kansas."

"Are your parents alive?"

"Yes."

"What are their names?"

"Sarah and Abraham."

Monk looked puzzled.

"Any brothers, sisters?"

"No."

"Other extended family?"

"Quite a few cousins. Not many aunts and uncles left."

Monk plodded along the beach, confused.

"When did you first come to Jesus?"

"About a year and a half ago or so," Burns said casually.

Monk watched the waves sliding up onto the beach, smoothing everything in their path, making a *tabula rasa* out of the sand.

"Can you tell me how it happened? What the circumstances were? How you were affected? What you felt? What you thought?"

Burns smiled.

"That's a big order."

"Please tell me."

"All right."

Burns took a few steps in the sand, thinking about how he had come to Jesus.

"It started off with food," he said.

"Really? Food? How extraordinary. How do you connect food with Jesus Christ?"

"Well, you see, I'd been living a bad life. A sinful life. I was a terrible sinner. I didn't care about my soul and I didn't care about my body. I ate nothing but junk food. Fast food. Fast junk food. Fast and junk, because it didn't matter, the only thing to do was fill up that void in the middle of my body. *Fast.*"

"Uh huh."

"I can't really tell you how it happened, but one day I began to think about food. And my body. And what I was taking into my body. It suddenly seemed wrong to be putting junk food into my body, my one and only body. That suddenly didn't make sense anymore. At the same time, I imagine I got interested in what I was taking into my *soul.*"

"But how did *food* lead you to this?"

Monk watched Burns think while the waves slapped on the sand.

"I started preparing my own meals," Burns replied. "Instead of going to a fast-food place, I went to vegetable stores. I bought vegetables. And fruits. And I brought them to my furnished room and I made meals. Healthy meals. It was the shapes and the colors which caught my eye. Red round radishes. Green cylindrical peppers. Peas in the pod. You cracked open the green pod and inside there they were, lined up: good green things to eat. Don't you think that's amazing? To open up the pod? To crack a nut? To peel a banana? All those good things inside? I mean, how did that happen? Did you ever study the patterns in an onion? The layers inside the layers inside the layers? Onions defy definition. They're imponderable. You seek and you seek and you seek and then you come to the end and you find nothing, it's all vanished. The cabbage is like that too. Murky. As opposed, say, to the simple, straightforward carrot. And have you ever taken a good look at the tomato? It's *incredible.* I mean, how did that happen?"

John Burns was starting to move funny; spasms were beginning to ripple through his arms and legs.

"How did it happen that the fruits of the earth were so abundant and varied and *good for your body?* Did you ever take a good *look* at an ear of corn? It's fantastic. You pull back the green outside and then the golden threads inside and there they are: kernels, row upon row. Food! *Slow* food. From out of the earth! Food from the earth and the sun and the rain, everything working together to provide God-given food!"

332

Burns had unconsciously slipped into his strutting motion. Monk had stopped moving and Burns was almost dancing around him.

"I had never been so moved before in my life. I saw that this was no accident. This had been provided for us. God had provided this for us, and Jesus was the Son of God. Jesus was in every red radish and green pepper and slender string bean and purple round cabbage, and He was in oats and alfalfa and wheat. We *all* partake of Jesus, and not just during the rite of communion. But most of us don't realize it."

Monk was shaking his head up and down in agreement. John Burns was seeing everything as if through the eyes of a young child seeing the world for the first time. And such a bright child. His abilities were available to him; he wasn't neurotic; he was open, wide open.

"Do you ever dream, John?" he asked.

"Of course," Burns said.

"Do you remember any of your dreams?"

"My understanding is that you're a computer scientist, not a psychoanalyst."

"That is correct."

"That seems like an odd question for a computer scientist to ask."

Monk put a hand on the young man's shoulder.

"Be patient with me," he said.

"I have a recurring dream," Burns said.

Monk tried to look calm. He started to move his arms as he walked, because he knew that looked normal, but he didn't know how to do it and he ended up looking ridiculous.

"Would you tell me about it?" he asked, his voice breaking.

Burns was walking along looking down at the sand.

"It's a dream about Jesus," he said.

"Really?"

"When the dream starts, Jesus has entered a Peacekeeper silo and he's talking to the launch officers. He tells them that they are trying to usurp His power. He is the one who will decide when the End Time comes, when the Rapture begins, when the believers will rise up to heaven while the unbelievers are consigned to nuclear winter hell."

"What do the launch officers say?" Monk waited, fascinated.

"They ask Him for his clearance, His credentials. He doesn't have any. They send for the air police. They want to have Jesus arrested."

Monk waited but Burns was silent for a long time. They walked slowly along the seaside. "You have to understand this is a nightmare. I wake up sweating and trembling. Sometimes I walk in my sleep while I'm dreaming it. It's disturbing."

"I can understand that. Can you tell me what Jesus does next?"

"He points to the buttons, one for each launch officer. He says, 'You must never push these buttons. Only the Lord can decide when time comes to an end. If you push those buttons, I won't be Jesus anymore. You will have preempted me. You will have launched a preemptive first strike against Jesus, Son of God. You will be the antichrist.'"

"My God," Monk said. "Quite a confrontation. How does it end?"

Burns was taking deep breaths, trying to control his emotions.

"They call Him a commie bastard," he said, finally getting it out. "That's the way it always ends. They keep repeating it. Commie bastard."

"John," Monk said. "Listen to me, John. That was a dream. That isn't the way it is."

"Yes, it is. That's exactly the way it is. Jesus was for the poor, and that makes you a commie bastard these days. Jesus was for peace, and that makes you a commie bastard, and I don't know why I keep dreaming this."

Monk didn't know what to say. He couldn't help feeling that he, Monk, was somehow the progenitor of the Jesus symbol in John's psyche; Monk was the father, the creator, the beloved. But he was getting more than he had bargained for. He didn't feel capable of debating psycho-politico-religio-economic meanings with John Burns.

"Mark, honey," he said.

"My name isn't Mark. My name is John."

"John, then. Listen to me, John. It isn't the way it looks. It isn't that bad."

"You're kidding yourself, Dr. Monk. It is an ignorance that, no doubt, is profitable for you in one way or another. In the short run."

The two of them walked along in silence, Monk silent because he didn't know what to say, Burns silent as he once again fenced off the conflict of his dream and returned to his normal good humor.

"I love the ocean," Burns said after a while.

"So do I."

"It tells us that we're small, insignificant. It banishes the sin of pride. At least while we're close to it."

"Yes, I believe that."

There was only the sound of the waves slapping at the shore.

"At other times, I think of the ocean as a big friendly dog that doesn't know its own strength."

Monk liked the image, although he was startled by it. It was a little too good.

"Look, John," he said.

"Yes? What? Talk to me. Tell me something. Anything."

"John, you have to realize that you are at the center of powerful forces. Forces that are far too powerful for you. And you are the nexus."

"Are they more powerful than Jesus?"

"John, do not underestimate the trouble you're in. I'm telling you this for your own good."

"I'm in trouble," John Burns said quietly. It wasn't a question. A mere statement of the fact. "I'm in trouble because I think that nuclear weapons are a sacrilege." Long pause. "I talk about the war of the rich against the poor. That's it, isn't it? That's the key to everything, isn't it?"

"No. I mean yes and no."

"Jesus save me."

"Jesus is *not* going to save you," Monk said sharply, saying it before he could censor himself.

Burns smiled beatifically.

"I don't mind that you don't believe in Jesus."

"I didn't say that."

"Then you do believe in Jesus?"

Monk took ten steps in the sand alongside the ocean before replying.

"I haven't decided yet," he said.

Burns looked at him fondly. He knew that Monk was being honest with him. He respected him for that. At the same time, he checked to see that his four Christians hadn't wandered off too far. They hadn't; they were flying a tight formation.

"Jesus will be the one to decide whether to save me or not," Burns said quietly. "Not the United States government or any of its agents."

"It's hard to have a rational discussion of these issues," Monk said petulantly, "if you keep bringing Jesus into it. This *Jesus ex machina.* We've got to stay on the plane of reality."

"Oh, Lord," Burns said. "*You're* being the realistic one, is that it?"

Monk let it pass.

"Look, you are talking about the saving of your soul. Fine. That's Jesus's department. I'm talking about the saving of your life."

"I will not save the one at the risk of losing the other," was Burns's reply.

"If you will help me to help you, you will not be risking your soul. Come to Colorado with me, where you'll be safe."

"You're very strange," Burns replied. "Why would I want to do a thing like that? I like it here. I like my work here. To be safe from what?"

"I can't tell you. But I'm begging you to come with me. I am the only one who can save your life."

Monk watched him react. It was a reaction of innocence. Burns didn't know what he was talking about, and Burns didn't care. There was no communication; instead, he was solicitous.

"I think we'd better turn back now. You'll have a long walk back to the car."

Monk looked at him with sad, fond eyes.

"I wish there were something I could say to you. Something persuasive."

"I wish there were too. You have good intentions. I can see that. But I feel I have to leave a thought with you, on this practical, earthly plane of yours. The Twenty-fifth of December Movement exists on that plane too. We have lawyers, for example. Quite good lawyers. Quite good, dedicated lawyers who were born again and believe in Jesus. If I am ever attacked again by agents of the federal government, there is going to be *legal* hell to pay. I hope you'll pass that on."

"You can be sure I will. I'll tell you the truth, I'm glad to hear it. But I don't think it will work. It's not enough. They'll figure a way around it."

When they got back to where they had started, Monk took a long look at John Burns.

"Good luck," he said. "And take good care of yourself."

"God bless you," John Burns said.

Monk strolled off slowly, his arms barely moving, looking down at the sand, never looking back.

"The poor man," John Burns said to the others.

43

THE MEASURE OF A MAN

I T WAS ANOTHER little White House perk scandal; the only aircraft available for an immediate flight was Air Force Two, and Keyes got it. They flew him alone to Durango, Colorado. There the winds over the San Juan Mountains were deemed tame enough to allow helicopters to fly safely, so he got to the Consortium in no time without having to traverse a dangerous highway. The helicopter landed in the parking lot of the Consortium, in sight of the shipping platform from which he and the Vice-President had recently escaped.

Then a contrite and humbled Monk escorted him to a room with a conference table, and he sat at the head of it while Monk went out and then returned and put the volume on the table. Monk didn't say a word. He turned and left.

It was the Book of Mark.

It was a parts list.

It was a catalogue of all the basic parts available for the assembly of Mark Seven Standard Insurgency Robots.

All of Henry Patrick's records had disappeared, including his fingerprints. The identification process was further complicated by the neces-

337

sity for not using any of the modern inspection devices that would have made the job a cinch. X-rays. CAT scanners—Computerized axial tomography. PET—Positron emission tomography. BEAM—Brain electrical activity mapping. NMR—Nuclear magnetic resonance. None of them could be used: They might alter the Problem.

It was necessary to get Mark Seven back in pristine condition; radiation and magnetic fields might alter the Problem or destroy the Problem. They had to be able to test him in his present state so they could find out where they had gone wrong. Somewhere along the line, Dr. Theodore Monk had made a ghastly mistake, and he was going to have to find that mistake—or be in danger of loosing an army of pacifists on the world.

That left only one way of identifying Henry Patrick—to find someone whose body parts exactly matched the standard body parts listed in the Book of Mark, which was a Dr. Frankenstein's Sears, Roebuck mail-order catalogue for the right wing.

Memorizing the Book of Mark had been the most prodigious test Keyes had ever faced—flipping page after page, studying hues, dimensions, shapes, memorizing what the Consortium believed to be a representative range of sizes of all organs for the American male, because an army of clones would have been absurd; there were seventy-five different right arms alone. And since it was to be an army that represented a democracy, they had included black, Hispanic, and oriental parts.

Keyes had been pushed to his limit, maybe beyond; he wasn't sure yet. When you worked for Doc Halliday, you regularly worked at the outermost limit of your abilities. Keyes felt blasted. Abused. A victim. At Andrews Air Force Base, he walked back down the steps of Air Force Two in a daze, but he wasted no time. He got a cab, and went straight to the Pentagonal Church of Christ.

While waiting to see Max Breskin, Keyes slowly strolled down one of the big aisles toward the stage. He jumped up onto the platform and strolled around it, looking out at the thousand empty seats, trying to see it the way Burns would, but it was impossible. The faces weren't there. Someone like John Burns fed off faces; faces were meat and drink to him, whereas Keyes lacked the performer's mentality.

"Looking for a job?" Breskin asked, coming up behind him.

"I don't think I'd pull in the money," Keyes said.

Breskin was looking wary.

"What can't I do for you?" he asked.

"I have a favor to ask."

"A little one or a big one?"

"A real big one."

"No deal. Negative. Out of the question. Goodbye."

"You're usually so reasonable."

"I've decided that being reasonable is a bad life strategy."

There was no way to go but honesty. Keyes hadn't worked out how he was going to phrase it. It was going to sound insane no matter how he couched it. So the only thing to do was say it out straight, without trying to be a politician, without trying to conceal anything.

"I want you to persuade John Burns to take his clothes off and permit me to perform certain measurements of his body."

Keyes stopped and stared down at his feet the way Burns did, awaiting the storm. But there was no shock or outrage.

"But you've already *done* that," was the calm reply.

"I know that. That was in the Pentagon parking lot. But that was someone else."

"Who else?"

"I can't tell you."

"What the hell was that about, anyway?"

"I can't tell you."

"Naturally. You know, you guys are really weird."

"Yeah, I know that."

"I'm talking freakish."

"Yep."

Keyes had never doubted that he had a major selling job on his hands.

"John would think I was crazy if I even suggested it. And he'd be right."

"Yeah, I suppose he would."

"Will you please tell me what the hell is going on?"

"I can't tell you. Don't ask me; I can't tell you. But I'll say this. It is in John Burns's best interest to allow me to measure him. And that's the straight stuff, Max."

"The straight stuff," Breskin said, mumbling, closing his eyes, massaging the corners of his eyes with the thumb and forefinger of his right hand.

"I realize there's a chasm between us. But there must be some way to negotiate it."

Breskin quietly pointed a finger at Keyes.

339

"It is nonnegotiable."

Keyes was falling back on the inner Halliday again. What would Halliday say to someone who had used the word nonnegotiable?

"Then do me this favor. Let Burns turn me down."

Burns was in the control room editing his latest sermon. He smiled at the request.

"I'm thinking of your own best interests," Keyes said, feeling like a total phony, a con man, a scam artist, even though he believed what he was saying.

"Do you believe in God?" Burns said.

"Not really."

"That seems oddly ambiguous."

"Well, I do wonder about who made the universe. I mean, where did all this stuff come from? I do wonder about that. It's the chicken-and-the-egg problem. Who made God?"

But this was Burns country. He had no problem with a question like that.

"You're going about this all wrong," he replied. "You're being too cerebral. Forget logic. Logic doesn't work in love, and God is love. God is beyond human logic. You're locking yourself in. Or should I say you're locking yourself out? You're out in the cold, my friend. What are you doing out there? That's why you're involved with these funny people in the government. That's why you're spending your prime years doing the devil's work. Those nuclear weapons your President has at his disposal are Satan's toys. Satan *wants* us to play with them. That's what you're involved with. Why don't you accept Jesus, welcome Him, and pray with us."

Keyes looked at him. From head to toe. He was lithe and alive. Especially the eyes. They were plugged in. They gave off a readout. And he watched Burns's lips while he talked. How could they make lips talk so fast and with such facility? Lips were complicated. They had to get plugged in to the brain for a sort of intellectual double play: thought to nerves to muscles. Dozens of muscles. Maybe hundreds. What the hell, if you could believe in airplanes, you could believe in artificial lips.

"Let me put it this way," Keyes responded. "Could you possibly do this as a personal favor to me? And maybe someday I could pay you back. You're certainly not going to lose anything. I'm here by myself. I can't possibly harm you."

Max Breskin was unconsciously shaking his head in a positive direc-

340

tion. He was aware what a favor from a presidential aide could mean. Maybe a little help if they had trouble with the FCC? Or the D.C. building code inspectors?

"John," Breskin said, "let's look at it this way. You said before that God was beyond human logic. I think that's the way to look at this thing. It is beyond logic or common sense. It's out of sight. Don't logic it. Do it as a personal favor to me."

Burns was obviously very fond of Max Breskin. That was the kind of request that he couldn't turn down. He smiled at Breskin, nodding his head up and down.

"Okay," John Burns said. "I'll make a deal with him." He turned to Keyes. "I believe that's the word you politicians use, isn't it? Deal?"

The video recorders were spinning and the oscilloscopes were displaying waveforms and the air conditioner and dehumidifier were humming; it was a high-tech world. But John Burns and Max Breskin and Malcolm Keyes were all on their knees in the praying position.

"Jesus," John Burns was saying, "this is a prayer for politicians. We're about to pray for all the politicians in Washington, D.C. and we hope that you will lead our politicians into the path of righteousness."

Burns paused while Keyes and Breskin repeated his words.

"First, we pray that you help our politicians to be unselfish," Burns continued. "Help them to put the needs of the people above their own immediate political imperatives."

Keyes wasn't having any problem with it.

"We ask, Jesus, that you make our politicians courageous, so that they may take risks with their careers rather than with the planet."

Keyes liked that. He repeated the words with a smile in his voice.

"And, finally, Jesus, we ask for nothing less than a miracle, for divine intervention. We ask you, Jesus, to help our politicians to be truthful, even though we all know how difficult it is for a politician to be truthful. Even so, try to help them, Jesus."

". . . try to help them, Jesus," Breskin and Keyes repeated.

"Amen."

"Amen."

Keyes stood up, brushed off his knees, and took out a tape measure and a protractor and a red grease pencil.

*   *   *

John Burns was the very definition of the word "aplomb." As he took his clothes off, he was busily dealing with his videotape editor, involved in the editing of his latest sermon. Keyes—who was making red grease pencil marks on Burns's body in preparation for the measurements— might have been measuring Burns for a new suit. The man was totally unselfconscious, absorbed as he was with his own image on videotape, as the editor shuttled it back and forth looking for edit points.

"I have never understood why so many fundamentalist Christians are opposed to the theory of evolution," the taped Burns was saying.

"There," Burns said. "Cut it there. Then go to the wide shot."

The hubs spun.

Keyes measured.

The editor edited.

Breskin glowered.

"The fact of the matter is," the taped Burns was saying, "that there is no mention in Genesis of the skin color of Adam and Eve. We've always tended to assume that they were white and that, therefore, we have a white God, since man was made in His image; but then how do you account for the passage in Exodus where the races are mentioned? Browns, blacks, yellows. Those conservative scribes left out the reds," he added in a fast aside. "But where did these colors come from? White doesn't contain black, brown, yellow, red. White is the *absence* of all those colors. So where did color come from except by evolution? After all, there was only one creation, was there not?"

"Cut," John Burns said. "Run through the audience reaction shots."

The editor edited.

"Please don't move your right leg," Keyes said.

Breskin stood with his fists on his hips watching the ridiculous process, eyes narrow, mouth grim, outrage in his face.

"But there are problems with this," the taped image was saying. "*Big* problems. Oh, the implications."

Burns was strutting, moving funny, a look on his face that said he was moving in on a bit of truth. Someone had once told him that he loved standing reality on its head, and his reply was that reality was already on its head; he was merely standing it right side up.

"If the whiteness of Adam and Eve evolved into the yellow and brown, the red and the black, that *could* mean that people of color are at a higher state of development than the pales, the bleached, the whites. Could *that* be why so many fundamentalist Christians can't bear the thought of evolution?"

"Cut," the live Burns said, scratching his chin, not sure of which of the three camera angles to go to.

Keyes was delicately trying to check the color of his pubic hair.

"John," Max Breskin said, "I'm really sorry about this."

Burns shrugged. He had an almost demonic ability to get to the heart of a matter, even when he didn't know anything about it.

"It's an imperative of imperialism," he said to Breskin. "Let's go to the profile where I'm holding out the Bible toward the audience."

"Now, how can the Good Book save our white superiority? I'm here to tell you we've got problems. I'm here to tell you our options are limited."

"Stop," Burns said. "There's a nice pause after 'options.' Cut on the pause to the close-up. I like the smile on my face." Saying it, Burns had the same smile on his face.

Keyes, meanwhile, was measuring and looking worried. Keyes was beginning to look like a doctor who has turned up a bad biopsy and doesn't look forward to breaking the news to the patient.

Breskin fumed.

The editor spun the reels and made the tape transfers and built a program.

"The problem, of course, is to produce all those colors without calling for additional creations and without surrendering to evolution and its subversive implications for the superiority of the white race."

Burns was doing his humble act now. Shrugging. Extending his hands out to the audience, head tilted. A mere human trying to deal with the difficulties of the infinite.

"The only answer I can come up with is that it was something like a rainbow coalition. If Adam was white, Eve had to be somewhere in the vicinity of a shade of lavender. I'm not sure, but I think you can pull yellow and red out of lavender. And if you put lavender against lavender often enough, you can get brown and black. The only worse possibility, of course, is that Eve was white and *Adam* was lavender."

At bottom, John Burns was a kind of intellectual Milton Berle of Christendom. He was a crowd pleaser. His taped audience loved him. They were stamping their feet and clapping their hands. Their faces were happy. They were transported. Burns was a slayer of hypocrites. He was David sailing out paper airplanes of truth and fantasy and slaying the Goliaths of self-righteousness and hypocrisy and racism, and they loved him.

Keyes finished. He looked at Breskin. He nodded toward the control-room door. When they were outside, Keyes gave him the bad news.

"I can't tell you why. All right? Don't ask. But your guy is in trouble. Watch him. Stay with him. *Never* leave him alone."

Breskin looked at him.

"I suppose I should thank you for warning me."

"You don't have to thank me. I happen to think he's a valuable piece of humanity. For that very reason, he's in big trouble."

"You've gone this far," Breskin said. "Can't you go a little farther?"

"No. Forget about it."

"But it's big."

"Yeah."

Breskin stood in the hall outside the control room shaking his head up and down. They could hear the applause and the fervency coming from inside the control room, the hallelujahs and the cheers, the amens and the shouts and the sobs. Breskin was talking to Keyes, but he was looking inward, his mind was elsewhere: He was already doing planning.

"Okay, then that's it. That's the situation. I owe you one. Thanks a lot, fella. We shall see what we shall see," he said absently.

44

SONG OF SOLOMON

ALEXANDER ALBRITTEN was manic; he was finally in a position to take *action* and the prospect was exhilarating. He was going to go into *action,* and then the goddam GOD Project would come to an end for him and he'd be able to forget about the Book of Mark. One more time and he was never going to measure a male body again, or follow Karmarkar's algorithm anymore, restlessly traveling the country like a dying salesman.

Albritten was standing in the rear of a van parked on Massachusetts Avenue, watching dirty pictures.

There were three cameras concealed in John Burns's hotel room, and Albritten wasn't missing a trick; the technician sitting at the console had control of focus and could also pan and tilt each of the cameras. Albritten was wearing headphones and had a microphone suspended in front of his mouth so he could keep Elmer Jessup informed.

"He's getting some genuine, old-fashioned religious fervor into it, I'll tell you. We are getting usable footage. Yes, indeed. He's stripping her now. My, my. Those baggy clothes she wears have been concealing something. The preacher has good taste."

Albritten's voice was beginning to tremble with excitement.

"Elmer, it's happening. This has to be the high-tech event of the *century.* Monk is a genius; you have to give him credit. Will you look at that? Look what those madmen at the Consortium have achieved. The most powerful driving force in the universe, and they've replicated it, the geniuses, with plastic and chips and ones and zeros; they've done it; Christ is risen!"

Albritten paused, pressing his earphones against his ears, listening to Jessup.

"I'd say about six inches," he replied, then turned back to the three screens, not wanting to miss a thing. He also felt compulsive about narrating the event, like some fiendish, depraved football announcer.

"*Aha,* they're not sticking to the missionary position. That lovely girl is now in the praying position. She's on her knees performing the act of communion, taking into her mouth the body of Christ, and if she keeps going like that, she's going to be getting the blessed wine before long. But no! That's not the plan. They're feverishly turning down the bed-clothes, and now they are rolling around on the bed doing some rather serious kissing."

Albritten was ecstatic. The best-laid plans, as it were, were *not* going agley. The entire operation was proceeding flawlessly. John Burns was a tiger in bed, and the epiphany was approaching.

"There's rapture and ecstasy happening, Elmer. Awake, O north wind; and come, thou south; blow upon my garden, that the spices thereof may flow out. Let my beloved come into his garden and eat his pleasant fruits, bingo, bango, bongo!"

Albritten sat down, exhausted. He closed his eyes. He felt like having a postcoital cigarette, although he hadn't smoked in a month. Albritten was at the end of his rope.

"We'll give them an hour for the deep, deep sleep of the double bed," he said flatly into his microphone.

Albritten was feeling uncannily calm. He was sitting alone in the darkness on a bench in Dupont Circle. Sooner or later it always happened when he was commencing an operation. The calm came over him and his eyes felt cold. He had done maniacal planning, factoring in the known universe, but there was always the possibility of bad luck, accident, coincidence; that was what made his eyes cold. His cold eyes were able to disintegrate everything, looking for hidden flaws, looking for accidents before they could happen.

346

The accident promptly happened. The handset lying on the bench beside him started squawking, and he picked it up. It was the worst possible news. The two Christians they had infiltrated into the Twenty-fifth of December Movement had been taken off the job of guarding the hotel room. It was no longer a walkover.

But Albritten had layered the operation: He had alternatives to alternatives. He had resources. He didn't even have to think about it. The important point about operations was that you had to be psychologically sound. You didn't necessarily have to be realistic; realism was over-rated. You had to be emotionally relevant; you had to keep in mind whom you were dealing with. He didn't hesitate.

"Cue the Whore," he said.

Blau and Mulcahy had the duty standing guard outside Room 602 of the Madison Hotel—the midnight-to-8:00-A.M. shift. They expected to be bored, but it was in a good cause; it was in the service of John Burns. There was no higher calling. They both felt like apostles. They were the usual bearded, blue-jeaned, safety-shoed Christians who also happened to be gorillas. At 2:00 A.M., a drunk got off the elevator. He staggered into the corridor, out of control. There was a woman with him trying to hold him up. The woman was gamely trying to help him, but he was too far gone; he was bouncing off both walls of the corridor. As they drew closer, the man began to have dry heaves. The whole scene was disgusting.

Blau and Mulcahy shook their heads at each other.

It got even worse. The woman had a hooker's face. It was unmistakable. She had sold herself too many times, and her self-contempt and cynicism were etched into her features. It showed in her painted face— the weariness, the cynicism, the degradation. Evil went straight for the face, and hookers were vulnerable to it. It was what you saw in a hotel corridor at two in the morning. The only sound you could hear was the jangling of her earrings, which were so long and edgy that they looked positively lethal.

The man almost knocked Mulcahy over, first with his dead weight, second with his breath. But Mulcahy was a beefy apostle; he righted the man.

"Brother," he said, "do you see what you're doing with your life?"

"Nothing wrong with me," the man said. He was having a little trouble with his tongue. "A little balance problem, that's all."

"Amen," Mulcahy said to him. "A little balance problem. You

347

just said more than you know. Don't you know that balance is everything?"

"Listen to him, brother," Blau put in. "He knows what he's talking
about."

The man was drooling.

"Balance," he said, holding on to Mulcahy's shoulders. The man's
eyes were dead. His trousers were wet. He was a disgrace. He was
looking nauseous, and there were funny sounds coming from his in-
sides.

"Sooner or later, you're going to have to stand on your own two feet,
brother," Mulcahy told him. "And you can't do that without Jesus
Christ, now can you? You've walked away from Jesus. A *long* way from
Jesus, and you have a long way to go to get back to Him. Are you
listening to what I'm saying?"

"Jesus? Jesus who?" the man said, and Mulcahy suddenly went
down, poleaxed. Blau was right behind him. The woman had taken him
out with a cosh. Then she took a handset out of her purse and extended
the antenna.

"This is the Whore," she said into it. "Proceed with the mission."

Albritten stood there with his arms folded, looking fondly at the clinging lovers. Riordan had picked the lock so skillfully they had gotten into
the room without waking them. The bedclothes had been pushed back,
and the naked, young bodies made a pretty picture; a Raphael, perhaps.
Adam and Eve about to be tossed out of Eden. Adam, anyway. Eve
could go back to the Salvation Army, where she had come from. Or
maybe a Rodin. It was an area Rodin had entirely neglected—*after* the
encounter.

Albritten was looking at the closest he had ever come to the solution
to the politics of counterrevolutionary warfare. The only one to have
passed nineteen of the twenty checkpoints. The omens were good.

"Do the chloroform," he said to Riordan and Slocum.

45

SAVING THE SOUL
OF ELMER JESSUP

THERE WAS A quart of bourbon in one of the kitchen cabinets. He got it out and put it on a black-and-red plastic tray. Then he found three glasses; they were clean; someone was actually keeping the place up. He emptied both ice-cube trays into a bowl and carried the tray into the living room. He put it on the glass-and-wrought-iron coffee table.

"Swizzle sticks," he mumbled, and went back to the kitchen.

Albritten's long nightmare was over. They had him; they had the little son of a bitch: John Burns had come through with a perfect score of twenty. Albritten had come through a task that could justifiably be called Sisyphean. And it was over. Sisyphus was contentedly looking at himself in the mirror over the fake mantelpiece, buttoning his top shirt button, tightening up his tie knot, putting on his jacket.

The irony was that Albritten had resisted it. He'd never believed in John Burns. Malcolm Keyes was his man. He'd been so high on Keyes that—once he was given free rein to pick up John Burns—he'd promptly broken all the rules and abducted Malcolm Keyes, risking all manner of catastrophes. He'd had to satisfy his curiosity. And Keyes had failed the last two checkpoints. Albritten accepted the data and moved on to John Burns, even though Nye would get all the credit. Albritten didn't care about credit anymore. He was exultant. He was finished with the infernal GOD Project. He smiled at himself when the side-door bell rang. He waited. Riordan was on the doors. When Monk and Jessup entered the living room, Jessup came up to him and gave him a satisfying thwack on the back. Albritten ostentatiously picked up the attaché case he had hidden behind the couch.

"I officially return the Book of Mark to you, sir," he said to Jessup. Jessup nodded.

"Well done, Alex."

Monk had a tic around his left eye.

Jessup made himself a rare bourbon on the rocks, drinking before five, before the sun had set below the yardarm, before the proper time to splice the mainbrace; but this was an occasion: The GOD Project had welded seams again.

"Did you salt the room?" Jessup asked, settling onto the couch with his drink and his cigar.

"A videocassette of the action, along with a few Polaroid stills. Some pretty steamy stuff. The kid's an athlete. I think they'll get the message: One peep out of them and every major newspaper and magazine in the country will get copies."

Monk's eye was still twitching.

"I know you did a careful job of measuring," he said in that emaciated voice.

"You betcha."

"Could we see him?" Monk asked.

"Of course."

Albritten left the room.

Monk and Jessup didn't look at each other. Monk was staring out the window, avoiding any eye contact. He didn't have to worry. Jessup was communing with his cigar smoke. The two had absolutely nothing in common; only the imperatives of international power politics could have brought them into the same room together.

Then John Burns was in the room with his hands manacled in the praying position.

"Sit in that chair," Albritten said. The categories were clearly drawn; there were warders and there was a prisoner.

"Have you been treated well?" Monk asked in a soft dying voice.

"Do you mean apart from the fact that I was kidnapped? Apart from the fact that I'm being held against my will? Apart from the peculiar things this man did to me? Apart from—"

350

"Stop preaching," Jessup said. "We've had about all the preaching we want out of you. Goddam guardhouse lawyer."

"I want you to know this wasn't my doing, John," Monk said.

"His name isn't John. His name is Henry. His name is Henry Patrick and he's a goddam traitor."

Albritten's eyes swiveled toward Monk, but Monk made no response; dead, thud silence in the room as the two men studied the captive.

Jessup spoke through his cigar.

"The plague bacillus," he said. "That's what Churchill called Lenin. But genetically altered in this case. Absolutely unpredictable results. Dangerous to the environment. There was no environmental impact study."

"I can feel the coldness radiating from you," Burns said to Jessup. "You're a troubled spirit."

"You think so?"

"I've heard that you're born again. Is that true?"

"So what?"

"How can you believe in Jesus and do the things you do? And to the poor, for the most part. Don't you know what Jesus said about the poor? And what He said about the rich? Is it really necessary for me to give you Bible instruction?"

Albritten had never really listened to Burns before. He found himself surprised by the young man's self-possession. His poise. He was almost dominating the room, which wasn't easy in the presence of the Director of Central Intelligence.

"It isn't too late to change, you know. Jesus forgives. But you don't have forever. Your soul is soaked in blood, the blood of innocents."

Jessup was like a slow-burning fuse; you could almost smell the acrid odor of black powder sputtering along the living-room floor.

"I personally am willing to pray for you," Burns went on. "You're going to need all the help you can get."

"You do that, kid."

"But I want you to help me."

"That's what we're here for."

"I want you to help me understand how greed and Jesus can coexist in the same soul. I'm leery of that. It's possible you only think you were born again. You ought to give it some thought. You've got to realize that what's at stake is nothing less than the fate of your immortal soul."

Burns suddenly stood up, and they all recoiled, but Burns wasn't physically threatening. They relaxed again as he began to pace around the room. He was in the preaching mode and was, therefore, tapping

351

something deep inside himself. He looked exactly the way he did on the stage of the Pentagonal Church of Christ, except that he had handcuffs instead of a Bible.

"Are you at least worried about your soul?" Burns asked.

"No, I'm not worried about my soul. My soul is safe. My soul is in a safe house," Jessup said, winking at Albritten. "You don't have to worry about my soul. All I'm doing is what *you* should have been doing. Defending the United States of America from its enemies."

"But they're not *my* enemies," Burns said. "These poor countries around the world aren't the enemies of ordinary Americans. I realize they may be the enemies of the rich. You aren't confusing the enemies of the rich with the enemies of the people, are you?"

Burns was pointing both hands, perforce, at Jessup.

Jessup was shaking his head in disgust. He sipped bourbon, puffed on his cigar, frowned, shook his head, sucked on a tooth.

"You got the best. You were given everything. And look what you turned into. A bearded commie Jesus freak who runs at the mouth. We've been looking for you for a long time, baby, and now that we've got you, we're never letting go."

Burns was calm. He was gazing roughly in the direction of Jessup's shoes.

"Stop calling me names," he said quietly, "and show me where I'm wrong. Show me that it *isn't* a war of the rich against the poor."

Jessup sighed. Albritten almost passed out; he had never seen Jessup sigh. It almost seemed as though Jessup had been touched, disarmed. Jessup! Burns the preacher had connected up with Jessup the born-again Christian, and Jessup seemed willing to drop his authoritarian stance and do an approximation of being human.

"It's the system, Henry," he said patiently. Patiently! "It's our system against their system. It's a competition. A confrontation. In the course of which we have to do some things that Jesus wouldn't like. It's an imperative. The two systems cannot coexist."

"Why can't they coexist?"

"Because they can't. They don't belong on the same *planet*."

"But what about your free play of the market? What about free competition? Why can't we defeat them in the marketplace? Why do we need all those nuclear warheads?"

John Burns was about six inches away from Jessup's face when he said this. Jessup remained calm.

"You don't know the facts," he said.

352

"Oh, I see. The facts are secret?"

"That's it. You don't have all the facts. If you did, you'd think differently about these things."

"I don't get to see the secret cables."

"That's it."

"So what do I know?"

"You've got it."

Burns made two circuits of the living room before replying. The handcuffs were cramping his style; you could see that he wanted to put both hands in his back pockets.

"Why is it that we are always on the side of the rich oligarchs and we always accuse the Russians of being on the side of the poor peasants?"

Albritten was astonished. Jessup was continuing to be civil.

"Now look, Henry. You have to understand something about the status quo."

"What don't I understand about the status quo?"

"It has to be maintained."

"But Jesus wasn't satisfied with the status quo. Jesus tried to change the status quo. Jesus *changed* the status quo as it's never been changed before. The world hasn't been the same since."

Jessup's head nodded slowly up and down.

"That's true," he said.

"So the status quo is not ipso facto sacred," Burns said.

"You'd better believe it is."

"I *hate* the status quo. The status quo is sinful. We're all over the world. Bribing politicians, infiltrating labor movements, infiltrating churches, buying off the media. Here helping armies to fight guerrillas, there helping guerrillas to fight armies. All for the benefit of the status quo, which means keeping the rich rich and the poor poor. The people you work for want to live in a world of peasantry; they want to keep it *all*. They want to bring back the Middle Ages, when the aristocracy owned it *all*."

"It's no sin to be rich," Jessup said.

Burns was circling around the coffee table past the couch, past the cheap cabinet standing catercorner with all of its cheap china.

"You're rich, aren't you?" Burns said across the room to Jessup. "Do you remember what Christ said about your chances of getting into heaven?"

"Yeah, I know that. But I'm a nice guy. I'm not worried. I believe in

Jesus as much as you do. I know that a few bucks one way or another won't make that much difference to Him."

"Jesus knew what He was talking about. He knew what you have to do, and be, to get rich. Big rich."

"Is that right?"

"You know what you've had to do."

"Fuck you."

Burns stopped pacing. He looked as if he had been struck in the face. He stood there a moment, his eyes far away. He clasped his hands together, interlacing his fingers.

"Fuck," he said.

"That's it. You got it."

Long pause, now looking up at the ceiling.

"You."

"Now you've got it."

Another long pause.

Then he said it as though hearing the phrase for the first time in his life.

"Fuck you," he said, not aiming it at Jessup, simply trying it out. Then he was back in motion around the room, on the prowl.

"The vulgar expression for carnal love, used as an epithet. The tired brain using a cliché, falling back on the tried and the trite. And yet, somehow, I'm feeling vibrations about that phrase. You've said something important. Because, you know, God made us carnal creatures. Satan didn't do that. That was God's work. We are made in the image of God. Genesis five, one: 'In the day that God created man, in the likeness of God made he him.' The penis was not created by Satan, you see; I personally believe that Satan doesn't even *have* a penis, *that's* one of his problems. He is incapable of the ultimate expression of love. No, Satan didn't create the penis, God did. *God* has a penis! So sex is godly. The penis is an instrument of love. Of course, sometimes it's used as an instrument of hate, but *that* is the true perversion, the true violence.

"Now, Mr. Jessup," he said, sounding something like a grade-school teacher trying to help out a slow pupil, "God gave us the bodily organs and the emotions with which to make love. He made it possible for us to fuck each other. You could argue that fucking is a religious act; we are following God's design, doing as He bade us, doing as He made us, carrying out His will. So we see that fuck really means God, since it is the essence of God's design; it is nothing less than the ability to express love, which is the highest possible form of human activity."

354

Burns was starting to shake. His taut limbs were making exaggerated motions as he strutted around the living room.

"So I'll say the same thing to you, Mr. Jessup, but I'll say it in better language, in clearer language. Are you listening? Pray you, joy you, serenity you, heaven you, *Jesus* you, *God* you."

Burns ended with his manacled hands pointing at Jessup's face.

"I'll make a deal with you," he said.

Jessup took the cigar out of his mouth. He was looking at John Burns, but he was talking to Dr. Theodore Monk.

"This is your fault," he said. "You did this to us."

"*His* fault?" Burns said. "Him? You're not confusing him with God, are you?"

"Maybe I am."

"What deal do you want to make, John?" Monk asked.

"His name isn't John; his name is Henry," Jessup said.

"Will you shut up at long last, you obnoxious old bastard?" Monk replied. Jessup almost swallowed his cigar. "You have no tact. No sense of the play of human relationships. You're an unregenerate boor, you fascist prick."

Monk had unloaded a lot of rage, but he was paying a price. He had to breathe deeply for thirty seconds before he could resume.

"Tell us what your deal is, John," he said.

"I don't know why I'm here," Burns said. "I don't know what's going to happen. I don't know what you want with me. But whatever it is, I'll promise to cooperate. I won't resist."

It was uncanny. Burns didn't have the faintest idea what it was about, but he had put his finger on the one issue that mattered: They were going to try to find out what had gone wrong with him. They didn't want to disturb him in any way. It was why they hadn't used X-rays or tomography; they didn't want to disturb the Problem, perhaps undo the Problem. They wanted to understand the Problem so they could prevent it from ever happening again, ever ever ever.

"What's it going to cost me, preacher?" Jessup asked.

"We all get down on our knees and pray my prayer to Jesus."

The three of them looked at each other. Jessup winked.

"I'm always ready to pray to Jesus," he said. "Gentlemen?"

Six knees cracked as they got into position. Only Burns had performed the exercise of late. A few tears were sliding down Monk's face. Albritten was looking sheepish, embarrassed, a teenager.

The four men placed their palms together in the praying position, accompanied by the jingling of handcuffs. Jessup still had the cigar in his mouth.

"Repeat after me," Burns said. "Jesus, we ask you to strengthen our powers of love." Burns waited.

"Jesus, we ask you to strengthen our powers of love," the three said.

"All forms of love, Jesus."

"All forms of love, Jesus."

"Tender, platonic, parental, filial, carnal."

"Tender . . . filial . . . what?" Jessup said.

"Platonic."

"Platonic."

"Parental."

"Parental."

"Carnal."

"Carnal."

"In particular, Jesus, we ask you to help us to see that the way to survival, and revival, is to understand that the Godly path, the straight and narrow path . . ."

Burns waited as they repeated it. They got it mostly right.

". . . is for us to fuck each other instead of killing each other."

"I'm not going to say that," Jessup said through his cigar. "That's the most ridiculous prayer I've ever heard of. It's obscene. An obscene prayer. An X-rated prayer, for God's sake."

"Then you've missed the point of everything I've said."

"Then I've missed it. Because I'm not going to say it."

Jessup was still holding his hands in the praying position, palms opposed.

"Then the deal is off," Burns replied. "The deal was that you would pray my prayer to Jesus. I will not cooperate. I will resist in every way I know."

Jessup sighed for an unprecedented second time. Albritten didn't have the faintest idea what Jessup was going to do. Jessup looked at Albritten and at Monk and at Burns. He closed his eyes.

"Jesus," he said, Albritten and Monk quickly joining in, catching up. ". . . the straight and narrow path is for us to fuck each other instead of killing each other."

Jessup looked as though he had swallowed a grasshopper.

"Amen," John Burns said.

"Amen," his flock replied.

356

46

LIBERATION THEOLOGY

MAX BRESKIN WANTED to get out of his skin and escape to never-never land. He was sitting in his regular bar, trying to pour gin on his agony, and it wasn't working. They had stolen his Federal Express, his Volkswagen. The best account he had ever had in his life. Or would have. How many times did a phenomenon like John Burns come along? He had always known that life was unfair, crazy, stupid, but this was the limit. The kid was getting the truth out; that was some kind of sin. Thou shalt not tell political truth. Thou shalt keep the suckers in the dark. He didn't have the faintest idea what to do about it. He had had all he could do to keep the girl from going to the police. Breskin needed thinking time.

They had caught Christ in the saddle. *Jesus,* that stuff was raunchy. The kid was a real stud. Be the biggest fundamentalist scandal of all. It could ruin left-wing fundamentalism for all eternity. Those photographs locked Breskin in. The public didn't take to the idea that a preacher was also a sexual being. John had been caught fucking. What could he do about that? If Breskin went public, he *might* save John Burns, but he would wreck the Twenty-fifth of December Movement. Was that the right thing to do?

357

He wondered where they had him, why they wanted him, what they were doing to him. They always got the people with leadership ability, the people with the ability to create change. Had things actually reached the point where the U.S. had its own *disappeareds?* He ordered another double; he couldn't stand himself. While making the drink, the bartender switched the program on. Breskin had clout in the bar; he was a neurotic tipper. It was a rerun. A year old. Breskin couldn't bear the thought of putting on a substitute preacher. There was no substitute for John Burns; he was one in a billion.

Burns was pulling at his chin, seemingly working the idea through on camera. "There's something I absolutely don't understand about the situation we find ourselves in. The communists are our enemy. And everybody hates them. 'Communist' is a curse word in this country. And the people who hate the communists the most are the military, who happen to be the only people in this country who live the communist life: Give up your freedom and take orders and you are cared for from enlistment to the grave. Now, how do you figure that? What do *they* have against communism?"

Max Breskin smiled paternally. *Better* than Federal Express. No competition; the kid was in a league by himself.

"Free medical care," Burns was saying. "Free dental care. Low prices at the post exchanges. No layoffs. No give-backs. No *competition*. Oh, maybe a little from the Marine Corps, but not serious, cutthroat, free-market competition."

Breskin had been alone at the bar. But now a second man sat down two stools away from him and ordered a vodka freezing, with a twist.

"Now, if the Pentagon were on Wall Street," Burns continued, "the Securities and Exchange Commission would have to raise a question here. As long as they can convince us of this big communist threat, they can go on enjoying their nice communist existence, without worrying about being laid off. Or giving away give-backs. Doesn't that sound as though commie-baiting might be something like advertising, something like salesmanship, something like a conflict of interest, or maybe insider trading?"

"This is an amazing country," the stranger said to Max Breskin. "Where else would the ruling circles allow something like this to take place? In Russia the government would transport him to Siberia, where he could preach to the bears."

"Yeah," Breskin said, feeling maudlin, almost weeping in his gin.

"But this is America; that kind of thing can't happen here, right?"

Breskin drank, emptied it, ordered another double, all the time seeing images of John Burns lovingly fucking his girlfriend, twisting sweaty bodies on the white sheets, catastrophic orgasms, taking the Lord's name in vain. Breskin belched. What could he do about *that?*

"Why, if they ever did anything to John Burns," the man was saying, "his manager would make such a stink there would be hell to pay. Be another Watergate. Heads would roll. After all, this is a government of laws. They can't pull crap like that *here.*"

Breskin's nose wrinkled in disgust as he stared into his gin.

"Unless the guy's manager is stuck for a particular reason and he *can't* do that."

"Why couldn't he?"

"He can't. He just can't. He doesn't know what to do."

The man nodded and ordered another drink. He thought about it for a while.

"Of course, there's another approach the manager could take," the stranger said. "It's a hallowed practice in this country. The manager could take nonviolent, civil-disobedient action."

"What do you mean?" Max Breskin asked.

"Snatch him back. Nonviolently, of course. The judge sentences you to a hundred hours of community service. You help old ladies across the street for a while."

"Yeah. Ha ha. We really take care of old ladies in this country. Trouble is, you'd have to know *where* to be civil, *where* to be disobedient. Where have they got him? The guy's manager would have to know that before he could orchestrate anything."

What happened then was nothing less than cognitive dissidence. Breskin had pulled that trick a thousand times on the public: something that comes out of nowhere, off the wall, forcing your attention. Your eyes blink. What the hell is this? The man was pushing a slip of paper across the bar to him. Breskin had a little problem opening the one fold; knowing you were drunk was the pits. And then his eyes popped. He almost fell off the barstool. It was a message made out of a chaos of upper- and lowercase letters and numbers that had been cut out of a magazine. It looked illicit. Dangerous. Subversive. It was an address in Maryland. Dawn was starting to come up.

"Oh, Jesus," Max Breskin said, looking around for the man, who was gone, having left a twenty-dollar bill on the bar. Breskin looked at the address again. The magazine type made it look authentic; somebody somewhere wasn't kidding around.

"Oh, my God," he said.

He started to get up off the stool. It wasn't easy. His nervous system was disconnected from his body; it was going on its own, randomly, struggling to find its own center of gravity.

"To arms!" he said to the bartender. "Sound assembly! Call out the militia! Pilots, man your planes! Onward Christian soldiers!"

He was reeling now. He looked at the bartender.

"When in the course of human events, don't shoot till you see the whites of their eyes!" he said, falling flat on his face.

Breskin found that sitting was uncomfortable. He had to stand. He had never gotten drunk before and had never experienced what it was like to have a hangover. He was holding the ice pack to his head while sipping black coffee, but slowly, giving it time to be accepted by his sour stomach, which was close to rejecting everything. But he had an interest in life, which was what really kept him going. He was watching Joe Poole at work.

Until now, Max Breskin hadn't particularly cared for Joe Poole, because Poole was a film director by profession, and film directors had a tendency to be obnoxious: Nobody knew anything about anything except Joe Poole. And yet Poole had volunteered immediately, pitching in enthusiastically, giving it everything he had, and taking complete charge as though shooting a feature. But then everybody had; everybody in the Twenty-fifth of December Movement esteemed John Burns, loved him, was ready to defend him, would apparently do anything for him. Breskin was watching Poole commence the operation now, sitting in front of the radio transmitter, the big map of Maryland mounted on corkboard and standing up on the top of the transmitter cabinet.

"Car Two," he was saying. "Where is Car Two?"

The speaker came promptly to life.

"Car Two. At Minnesota Avenue and Bennings Road."

Joe Poole stuck a red pin in the map.

"Stay there. Motor running. Stay tuned. Car Three."

"Car Three. Nebraska Avenue at Roosevelt Place."

Poole threw a glance over at Breskin. This was no longer a mere rehearsal. They were going on and they were ready.

"Keep your motor running, Car Three. Come in, Car Four."

360

Onward Christian soldiers, Breskin thought.

"*Where* is Car Four?"

Nothing but static and beeps and electronic sighings, electrons flying to the positive pole.

"Do I have a Car Five?"

"Five."

"Where?"

"Decatur. Just off Minnesota. Motor's running."

"Good show, Five. Six?"

"Here."

"*Where?*"

"Baker Street at the intersection of North Carolina."

"Okay, Six, keep your motor running. Four, where the hell are you?"

"Hello, Poole? Is Poole there?"

"Yeah, Poole is here. Is this Four?"

"This is Four, Poole. Can you hear me?"

"*I can hear you.*"

"Three checking in. They're leaving. They've turned left on Harrison Lane."

Poole moved the one blue pin an eighth of an inch on the map.

"All cars on final alert," he said.

"Is this Poole?"

"*This is Poole.*"

"We're at Montcalm and Fontaine."

Poole started to say something, caught himself, inhaled.

"Keep your motor running, Four," he said calmly.

"They're going along Lefcourt," Three said. "Easterly."

Max Breskin moved the ice pack to a new place on his head. He hiccoughed a dozen times and then got back in control. Sober now, he was wondering if the Central Intelligence Agency could be thwarted by a bunch of screwball Christians from the Twenty-fifth of December Movement.

Poole stuck his head into the cab and told the driver to start heading east. Poole was bearing down on the map. It was too early to say where they were headed. There was National Airport, close in, and there was Dulles, far out in Virginia. There were also a number of small airfields in the area which the CIA could conceivably use. The problem was to somehow get in front of the CIA limo without knowing the direction it would be going in at any given moment.

"Three, what's their speed?"

"A God-fearing forty."

"Two, Five, and Six, step on it. Get ahead of them. Four, get behind Three on Harrison."

Breskin was praying for subtlety. He didn't want a Cecil B. De Mille epic; the CIA would *notice* that. What they needed was closet drama. Finesse. They had to keep the CIA from knowing that they were being followed (as well as *advanced*) by five cars and a van. If they knew, they could radio for help. Breskin figured they might be able to handle a carload of CIA types, but the marines arriving would be too much. Breskin was beginning to get excited, in spite of his awful head and marginal stomach. It was Joe Poole's intensity and confidence. He was like a film director serenely going twenty million dollars over budget.

"Now they're going north on Fishkill," someone said.

Poole nodded. It was looking like Dulles.

"I want this to happen before they get to Route 95," he said into his microphone. He was busy moving pins with one hand, pressing the button on his microphone with the other.

"Car Two, report."

"I'm parallel on Hawkins. I'm ahead about a quarter of a mile."

"Car Three, report."

"Parallel on Ellsworth, half a mile ahead."

"Four, report."

Static.

"*Four!*"

"We're right behind Three, like you said."

"All right, folks. Now we're going to do this thing. Drivers stay on your toes. Troops get ready to move. If they stay on Fishkill for another thirty seconds, we're going in. Car Two will cut across at Fifth Street moving west. Car Three will cut across on Seventh Street moving east. Cars Four and Five will overtake. Car Six, you're going to have to go against the one-way on Fishkill to take them head-on. Everything to be done on my signal. Car Three, are they still on Fishkill?"

"They're still on Fishkill and they are not decelerating."

Poole was manipulating a pattern in his head that must have felt something like differential calculus. He repositioned the pins a final time and then breathed.

"And . . . *action.*"

Max Breskin almost tossed his cookies as the van accelerated, squealing east onto Brentwood, getting up to sixty in half a block. Up ahead on Fishkill, but out of sight to the right, they could hear the

362

pained squealing of brakes, the animal sounds cars made when dumping momentum. He cocked an ear, but there were no crashes. Then the van slewed around onto Fishkill and he saw Joe Poole's piece of perfection up ahead at the next intersection: the CIA limo surrounded by five cars, all with their hoods pointed into the long, black sedan, a lovely pentagon of shiny metal. The van screeched to a halt, and Breskin got out carrying a baseball bat, Poole right behind him.

All the Christians were carrying baseball bats. There was people power on Fishkill Street. Breskin went up to the rear door and yanked it open. Burns was sitting in the back, handcuffed, a CIA agent on either side. Dr. Theodore Monk was on a jump seat. Joe Poole shot some stills.

"Now *we've* got incriminating photographs," Breskin said. "Unlock those damn things. *You,*" he said to the driver, "*out.*"

"Now we'll all do what they say," Alexander Albritten said. "No violence, no scene, we obey. Carmichael, take the cuffs off."

Max Breskin wreaked havoc on the communications equipment in the dashboard. When he got back out of the car, John Burns was standing there smiling at him.

"Hallelujah, Max."

"Hallelujah, John. Get in the van, John. I have one more thing to do here."

Breskin moved around to the front of the car and broke the windshield with one soul-satisfying bash. Then he popped open the hood and broke the bat with one gigantic smash at the ignition cables. He remembered to pick up the two pieces and take them with him.

"You try this again," he said to them.

His hangover seemed to have disappeared.

363

47

THE FLIGHT OF THE DOVE

Keyes was rotating the bottle in the cooler. He was going back and forth between excitement and detachment. He kept trying to hold on to the excitement, but it wasn't easy. He checked his watch on the night table. She was fifteen minutes late. He went back to the wine. All he had on was a silk bathrobe and slippers. He knew her schedule. If she was more than about twenty minutes late, the whole thing would be a scrub.

The door suddenly flew open and she was there, striding across the room with her attaché case, smiling at him, kissing his cheek. She was wearing a conservative gray suit, the skirt a good two inches below the knee.

"Sorry I'm late," she said. "Round up the usual excuses."

She had been attending a banquet in honor of the ancient Democratic senator from the great state of Alabama in the ballroom of the hotel, which was why Keyes had gotten the room for that day; there would be an easy and inconspicuous transition from politics to love. Only Madeleine's chief of staff knew. She trusted him because, among other things, he was a lousy writer.

Madeleine took her skirt off and was hanging it carefully in the closet. Keyes was working the corkscrew.

"I've been trying to pick up some conservative support for a test ban proposal," she said. "You wouldn't believe what I'm running into. There are some very intelligent people in the Senate who don't want to get rid of the bomb."

She was taking off her jacket and blouse. The basic power problem seemed to be going away rapidly. Keyes was feeling the centripetal force assembling, gathering. She was down to her bra and panties when the phone rang.

"Nobody knows I'm here," Keyes said. "It must be for you."

She sat on the edge of the bed, prettily crossing her legs, and picked up the phone. Keyes was pouring the wine; he could tell she was talking to George, her chief of staff, who was obviously warning her about being late for the next meeting. She hung up. He went to the bed and handed her a wine. They clinked and sipped, looking at each other over the tops of the glasses. He sat down next to her.

"Trying to save the world again today, huh?"

"The world doesn't want to be saved. Not the world of big-league Washington politics. *One* phone call, Malcolm."

She punched in the number like a touch typist driving hard toward lunch.

"Senator Ripley is a bit thick," she said. "Do you know what I mean by thick? I mean thick. He hasn't had a new thought in about fifty-seven years." And then she was talking to one of the biggest curmudgeons in the U.S. Senate.

"Is this the charming senior senator from South Carolina?" she said in her best girlish voice. Pause. "Oh, I'll bet you say that to all the Vice-Presidents." She winked at Keyes and rolled her eyes up into her head. Keyes slowly slid his hand over her back to the far shoulder and commenced a slow caress.

"Do you know," Keyes whispered, prompting her to quickly cover the mouthpiece, "that you have remarkably soft shoulders."

"Is that a fact."

"Soft shoulders are dangerous on highways and women."

"Heh. I've never been compared to the New Jersey Turnpike before. Why yes, Senator Ripley, that would be the general idea. *Nobody* would test. *They* wouldn't test and *we* wouldn't test. With one hundred percent guaranteed verification, of course. That's how we'd end the arms race."

Keyes slid his right hand down her arm and then made a quick little darting movement—the old hand-is-quicker-than-the-eye—alighting on her waist.

"Why, Senator Ripley," she was saying, "now who on earth ever told you that the arms race was over? That reminds me of a famous line by Mark Twain, who was almost a Southerner himself, you know."

Keyes had slyly insinuated his right hand inside her panties. "No, sir," she said, "not the one about being happy as a Christian with four aces up his sleeve, you devil. The one about rumors of my death being exaggerated."

Keyes's left hand was now in its favorite place: cruising aimlessly along one of Madeleine's thighs.

"But, Senator, have you taken a good look at the military budget lately?" Sudden hand over the mouthpiece. "Quick, what's the military budget?"

"Four hundred and thirty-two point seven billion."

"Why, it's four hundred and thirty-two point seven billion, sir. Now, does that sound like the arms race is over?" Short pause. "Well, it certainly is. Now you have one of your people take a look at that thing and you'll see I'm not exaggerating." Very short pause. "*Yes.* Billions."

"You've really had a tough day at the office," he said after she'd hung up.

"That old chauvinist son of a bitch knows damn well what the military budget is. To the nickel."

"Is he doing King Midas?" Keyes said, keeping his hands on her.

"I'm afraid so. Right now King Midas is wringing his hands. You see, there's this fiendish commie plot. They keep making concessions. It gets harder and harder to justify the military budget. Washington sits terrified awaiting the next commie concession. Poor Midas. When he thinks of all that cold hard cash out there he rubs his hands. Then he thinks about the possibility of nuclear suicide and he wrings his hands. Do you know, I actually believe it's a close call."

"The concession gap certainly seems to be growing bigger and bigger," Keyes said, starting to have a little trouble breathing.

"I'll say it is," she said, caressing him. "You're making a major concession right now. Oh dear, the liberal's heart's desire, big government."

She quivered as they kissed, and his right hand went straight to the clasp at the back of her bra, releasing it with an expert practiced movement. Reaching from behind, he cupped both breasts in his hands.

"Having said all this," she said, "there *is* something to be said for atomic explosions."

"My sentiments exactly."

"Who takes them off?" she said.

"The Vice-President never takes off her own panties while I'm around," Keyes said. "I'm your special assistant for panties."

She lifted up and he slipped them off.

He was on top of her before she could even get her head on the pillow.

As he entered her, he said, "But you have to get it right. This isn't atomic. It isn't fission; fission is where the little atom breaks up. It's hydrogen. It's fusion. That's where the two little atoms come together."

She wrapped her legs around him.

"Tell me about it, lover."

It was vacation time, the Nuclear Princess on vacation from the Button, no decisions to make, no angles to work, no lines to be walked, no responsibilities, the world not at stake, her arms flung wide across the bed while she was having her own button pushed. The dove was out of the cage and on the wing, flying high, up where there was nothing but the winds of buoyancy and *space,* space to be herself in a hawk-free zone, briefly, space to cavort and romp and frolic, the dove writhing through death-defying aerobatics, before going critical and experiencing the explosion that heals, the kilo-tonnage of love, followed by the fluttering detumescent descent to earth.

He came to slowly, hearing sounds coming from the bathroom. When he got his eyes open, she had emerged, naked, showered, ready to go. She had reserve underthings in the lid of her attaché case; she could even open it in public and no one would see them. Then she did a very sexy reverse strip for him, getting back to her conservative professional look in minutes.

"This is a little too close to wham bam, thank you sir, but we'll have to live with it for the time being," she said, speeding across the room. "Bye-bye," she said, going out the door.

"Bye-bye," he said.

48

HUMANKIND DOES
NOT COMPUTE

D R. THEODORE MONK'S hands were shaking. They were shaking more and more of the time these days, and he was afraid it was incipient Parkinsonism. His only hope was that it was psychosomatic: repressed fury at Elmer Jessup of the Marginal Intelligence Agency.

Monk had driven himself to the limit. He had given the project everything he had. There wouldn't have been a project if it hadn't been for him. And now he was Covert Enemy Number One, having to spend more and more time with spooks, which was a total waste—there was no communication in either direction; they existed on nonintersecting planes. He looked across his desk at the two of them, Jessup and Albritten, who were impenetrable security hardheads.

"We lost John Burns because someone compromised that safe house in Maryland. That's how those crazy Christians were able to follow the car. I happen to believe that compromiser was you."

"I'm sick and tired of your accusations," Monk said.

"When I get back to Washington, the first thing I'm going to do is have your security clearance revoked. We don't need you on this project anymore, anyway."

"You people have a bad habit of blaming your security failures on scientists," Monk replied. "It saves you from confronting your own incompetence. Have you figured out yet how the Vice-President got *out* of here?"

Jessup bristled. The damn woman had apparently gone up in smoke. "Why don't *you* tell *me* how?" he said. "You arranged it, didn't you?"

"*You* are responsible for the security here. This is the first time you've ever admitted that I'm smarter than you are. That's a good mental set. Hang on to it."

"I want a complete status report on this project right now," Jessup said.

"Mark Eight won't do. That's all you need to know."

"Why won't he do? He cost two billion dollars. Why won't he do?"

"He's too dumb."

"I'll be the judge of that," Jessup said.

"You can't even do your own job. Stop trying to do mine."

"I want to talk to Mark Eight. I insist."

Monk let out a long, slow, sulfurous sigh.

"You're interfering in matters you don't understand."

"Yeah, sure. Only you scientists understand these things. Where is he?"

To see Mark Eight, they had to suit up and go through the inner security portal, which promptly rejected Jessup; he had gained too much weight since his characteristics were entered into the portal computer. But the computer memory was controlled from an input device in CIA headquarters in Langley, Virginia—to which Jessup himself was carrying the only key. They had to shut down the entire apparatus, which was a major job since it wasn't supposed to be easy to shut down. Numerous alarm systems had first to be turned off, all of them having two-key locks, the keys having been distributed among different scientists so that it would have taken a treacherous cabal of at least fourteen high-ranking scientists to disable the thing. The mere task of finding the fourteen was arduous. It took two hours to get Jessup through to the heart of the GOD Project.

On their way to Mark Eight, they passed through the museum, and Jessup paused, contemplating Marks One through Six.

"Morons," Jessup was mumbling. He shook his head in disgust at Mark One. "Eighteen billion dollars," he said. "You ought to hang a price tag around his neck. Eighteen billion dollars for the Bubblehead."

Monk had used a bubble memory for Mark One, which was ideal for bad environments, but memory access time turned out to be way too slow. As Monk walked along the cases, he remembered all the major decisions he had made over the years. Mark One had used LISP, which was the standard artificial intelligence language in the United States. It hadn't been good enough. For Mark Two, he had used the Japanese AI language, PROLOG. For Mark Three, he had invented his own AI language: SAPIENS. *That* was the one that worked. For Mark Four, Monk had put a team to work on gathering together the 200,000 most commonly known facts for the knowledge base. It was a major step forward. For Mark Five, Monk had incorporated highly sophisticated heuristic procedures—rules of thumb which humans use to narrow the possibilities in any given situation. Common sense, in other words. Monk had programmed it. Monk had made major advances in cognitive science, which was something like a cross between psychology and computer engineering. All Jessup could talk about was the cost of diamonds.

"I've started going over your books," Jessup was saying, standing in front of Mark Six. "Why did you have to use diamond-coated chips? Are you aware of how much money you've spent on diamonds?"

Monk closed his eyes.

"They're faster," he said.

"So why can't we get along with slower? Slower and cheaper."

"See, this is one of the ways your ignorance is invincible," Monk replied. "Let's just take vision. Do you realize that human vision requires the ability to process several billion bits of data every *second?*"

Monk didn't even bother making the point that because diamond-coated chips ran cooler, they brought down the temperature of the SIR from 106.8° F to a barely feverish 98.9° F.

As usual, Jessup changed the subject.

"They look threatening as all hell. But any halfway motivated guerrilla could take on all six at once."

Monk kept his peace and led them in to Mark Eight, not even bothering to tell Jessup that even Mark One would have been worth a Nobel, if it hadn't been for the secrecy.

"Good afternoon, Dr. Monk," Mark Eight said brightly.

"Good afternoon, Gordon," Monk said affectionately.

On the surface, Mark Eight was user-friendly.

"This is Mr. Jessup and Mr. Albritten."

"Very nice to meet you, gentlemen," Mark Eight said.

Jessup wasn't quite sure what to talk *at;* Mark Eight was a pile of electronics, jury-rigged on a workbench.

"You ready to kill commies, Gordon?" he said.

"We're gung ho here, sir. This is the best battalion in the army. Just point us where you want us to go."

You could almost hear a salute in his voice; if he had had heels, they would have clicked.

"That's the spirit," Jessup replied. "You're the kind of man this country needs."

"What we've got in this country is worth defending, and we'll go anywhere on the planet to do the job."

"What's your rating?"

"Private soldier, infantry, the backbone of the armed forces."

"I don't know what you're talking about," Jessup said to Monk. "He seems perfect to me. Ideal. Design center. *Why* do you want to kill commies?" he said to Mark Eight.

It was obvious. If Mark Eight had had shoulders, he would have shrugged them.

"I'm a freedom fighter."

"But what's wrong with the commies?" Jessup persisted.

"They're evil."

"Why?"

"Why?"

"What is it they do that makes them evil?"

"They're always getting people to revolt against law and order. *And* they're godless atheists. Isn't that right, Dr. Monk?"

"That's right, Gordon."

Jessup looked at Monk.

"Offhand, he seems perfect for the job."

Monk was trying to be discreet in front of Mark Eight.

"He wouldn't be able to cut the mustard," he said quietly.

"Why not?"

"Too dim," Monk whispered.

"He certainly has the right attitude."

Monk had his back to the pile of electronics on the bench. He spoke as softly as he could.

"It's a question of basic abilities, perceptions, learning skills."

"*Another* moron, in other words."

"Would you kindly watch your language?" Monk replied.

"I'm not a pointy-headed intellectual, if that's what you mean," Mark Eight said. "And, I wouldn't be too quick about calling other people dumb if I were you."

Jessup took a step back from the workbench.

"Hostile son of a bitch, isn't he?"

"That's the *idea,*" Monk said softly. "Right?"

"Yeah, right. What went wrong?"

Monk was doing his best to be patient.

"Henry Patrick was made with the heptode, a device with seven discreet states of being, as compared with the go/no-go diode. All right, he didn't work out. So we backed off." Monk's voice was barely audible. "We made Mark Eight with the pentode, five states. Not enough. What you might call immature technology. There's only one more possibility."

"I'm listening."

"We could try the hexode with Mark Nine. Six states of being."

"Will it work?"

"I don't know. There'll be gains and there'll be losses. We're going to have to give up color, for example."

"You mean we won't have black ones?"

"I'm talking about *vision*. Mark Nine won't be able to see in color. We're going to use a modified Vartec algorithm. They'll see everything in shades of gray. It saves brain. For other things. The AIQ will definitely be higher than Mark Eight, but whether it will work or not, I can't tell you."

"Hell, I hope it turns out better than the last one. The last product of your labors is currently a religious maniac sowing subversion all over the country. That's what *you* did for us."

"You don't understand the problem," Monk replied.

"Is that a fact?" Jessup said, somehow working a Churchill out of an inner pocket. It was pure spinal cord; he was wearing a mask.

"There's no smoking here," Mark Eight said.

Jessup's eyes flicked over the pile of electronics on the workbench.

"*You're* going to get turned off," he said. "One thing we don't need is another moron."

"You're looking for it, aren't you?"

"You think so, huh?" Jessup walked up to the workbench and scanned it. "A two-billion-dollar pile of shit."

"Don't get me started," Gordon warned.

Jessup raised his arm and was about to sweep Gordon onto the floor.

"Jessup," Monk said sharply.

The Director of Central Intelligence looked at him, his right arm poised in the air.

"You're a fool," Monk said. "You're in over your head. You don't understand the issues. You *never* did. You don't have the most elementary understanding of what's going on here."

Jessup dropped his arm. He was obviously shocked at his own actions. He had actually communicated with himself.

"Well, I'd appreciate it if you'd explain it to me. That is, if you think I'm capable of understanding it."

Monk's hands were shaking so hard he put them in the pockets of his white jacket, but the vibrating pockets looked ridiculous. He took them out again and clasped his hands behind his back.

"We have a million genes," Monk said. "Each one can be expressed by an equation, an extremely complicated equation. Do you see the level of complexity I'm talking about? One million very long, very complex simultaneous equations?" Monk searched for an image that would get across to Jessup. "It's like the matter of going by rocket ship to another habitable planet. The nearest likely possibility is so far away that we don't live long enough to be able to get there, even if we could travel at the speed of light. That's the way it is with understanding humankind. Even computing those million simultaneous equations at the speed of light, we don't live long enough to understand even the first thing about the human being."

Jessup looked stunned. In a moment, something had cut through and dreams had come crashing down.

"Do you see what I'm saying?" Monk continued. "It's a basic limitation. It's fundamental. You make a man, you get a man. You're back at politics. Any third-rate poet could have told us that sixteen years ago."

"A third-rate brain like Mr. Jessup's wouldn't have believed it," Mark Eight said.

"Relax," Monk said.

Jessup began pacing around the room.

"We don't live long enough," he said, talking to himself. "Okay, you're right. I haven't understood. I admit it. We're out at the frontier somewhere, out at the limits. There are some things you just can't solve with money. I see that now."

He came to a stop. And a conclusion.

"Then there's only one thing we can do," he said to Albritten. "That goddam kid is a menace."

49

JAMAIS VU

KEYES WAS SITTING at the bar in the Willard Hotel dressed in his most conservative, boring suit and his drabbest, dullest tie, ready for a hot evening with Madeleine. Halliday was touring Iowa, South Dakota, and Nebraska on a profoundly forgettable fence-mending trip, so Keyes had the evening off.

He had three jam-packed briefcases with him, a Manhattan telephone book in each one. He was going to have one white wine while fantasizing about what was going to happen when he got to Madeleine's place in Georgetown, the briefcases being camouflage for the benefit of the Secret Service. Her chief of staff would be there too, plus several of her aides. The others would be dismissed one at a time until only Keyes was left.

He had managed three sips of the wine and was just about to pull Madeleine's dress up over her head when his beeper went off. It was the last thing he had expected. He hated the beeper; it was pretentious. He went to the nearest phone and called the White House; they switched him to the Vice-President's office.

"Get here," she said, "ASAP."

"Where?"

"My office."

"Your office?"

"Change in plans."

He hung up and went back and paid his bill. He much preferred a bed. Now he was going to have to do it on a desk with the phones ringing. Of course, a desk had its undeniable charms. Spontaneity. Kinkiness. Sex in unexpected places. It reminded him of politics, where the unexpected was the norm.

When he got there, he found Dr. Theodore Monk sitting distraught in a chair situated at one end of the Vice-President's desk. The unexpected. Disgustedly, he dropped the prop briefcases onto one of the couches and sat down in the chair at the other end of the Vice-President's desk in her rectangular office in the EOB.

Monk's long, anorexic body seemed to culminate in two large hands that were clinging to each other and pressing down against his thigh to keep from shaking.

"They're going to kill him," he said. "They've given up trying to finesse the situation. They've lost interest in trying to solve the Problem. So they want to kill him to get him out of the way."

"I don't understand that," Keyes said. "Albritten has been working so hard to find him, and doing it the hard way; why would they give up on solving the problem now?"

"Because they've given up on the Mark Seven series. They realize that Mark Seven is hopeless. Mark Nine is the only remaining possibility."

"What made them decide that now?" Keyes asked.

Monk gestured helplessly with his clenched hands, eyes closed, a look of desperation on his face.

"I talked them into it. I explained the situation to them."

"How will it be done?" the Vice-President asked.

"They absolutely cannot get close to him. He's already been kidnapped twice, and so there are people guarding him constantly. They're going to do it while he's performing at the church."

"How do you know this?" she asked.

"They thought I was asleep on the flight back from the Consortium."

"And then what would they do?" the Vice-President asked. "Steal the evidence? The—uh—*body?*"

"Something like that," Monk replied. "You can be sure they'll have an elaborate scenario prepared. Even if it's implausible, the public will buy it. The media will buy it and so the public will buy it. So *The Nation* raises a few questions. Who will care?"

Madeleine was sitting primly behind the desk, her honey-blond hair done up in a bun, her glasses on straight, her dove invisible, grounded.

"I have a question," she said.

Monk blinked in slow motion, waiting.

"Why do you care?"

Monk uncrossed his long legs and then crossed them the other way. He spoke looking down at the blasted fingernails of his clenched hands.

"I can't explain this too well. We're in a funny area. It's artificial, but it's intelligence. Every bit as real as yours and mine. They're going to kill this intelligent, feeling entity. In a way, it's almost as though they were going to kill my son. How can I let them do that?"

Keyes and the Vice-President avoided looking at each other.

"What did you say the name of the operation is?" the Vice-President asked.

"Operation Calla Lily."

"Operation Calla Lily," she repeated, admiration in her voice at the way the CIA and the Pentagon had of gilding the ghastly. "I'll tell you frankly, Dr. Monk, my own interest is somewhat selfish. I think the assassination of any public figure is bad for all of us. It gives the crazies ideas. For that reason, I don't want to see this happen any more than you do. The question is, when does it get laid on?"

It was the ultimate security absurdity. Monk seemed to be having trouble getting it out. In the act of blowing the whistle, he was having second thoughts; the inner establishmentarian conscience was asserting itself. It was the ultimate act of bureaucratic betrayal, but paternal instinct was stronger.

"Tonight, at the Pentagonal Church of Christ," he said.

Madeleine looked at her watch and then went to a white telephone situated on a large red base placed on an end table. It was a secure phone that had cost seventy-five thousand dollars, far more than Keyes's net worth. About a second passed between picking up the receiver and the commencement of communication. "I want to talk to Richard." Pause. "All right. Leave word. It's urgent." She hung up. "He's in the middle of a speech in Ames, Iowa." The second time she actually dialed a number. "This is the Vice-President. I wish to speak with the Director." Pause. "All right. Leave word. It's urgent." She slammed the receiver back down. "He's having dinner in Washington, but they don't know where. Can you believe that?"

Total silence as the three of them sat thinking.

"What about the deputy director?" Keyes said.

Madeleine went back to the funny phone. The deputy director had never heard of Operation Calla Lily but he promised to look into it immediately.

"What do you do now?" Keyes asked. "Call the FBI?"

"No. I've got my own troops. They're better than the FBI. Certainly when it comes to assassinations. And I can assemble them faster."

She went back to the enormous phone and called the Secret Service.

Keyes was leaning against the rear wall of the church, taking in the scene, experiencing a strong feeling of jamais vu, which was when the familiar looked foreign. He had already gone backward down the three major aisles, feeling paranoid once removed, looking at faces. It was hard to read faces. What was he looking for? He didn't know. A slavering, twitching, madman's face? A cool professional cucumber? As usual, he was in over his head.

The Secret Service was all over the place. The idea was to find Alexander Albritten or his equivalent in the Pentagonal Church of Christ and then haul him before the second top executive in government, waiting outside in her limousine. She would then order him to call off Operation Calla Lily. In the meantime, ten Secret Service men were drifting through the church doing their specialty: looking for the murderous impulse before it manifested itself. By staying in her well-guarded car, the Vice-President was also plugged in to the White House switchboard, in case the President or the DCI called.

To Keyes it was a normal Twenty-fifth of December Movement audience. They were with Burns, tuned in, raring to go, ready to be turned on. Everything was as usual. Three TV cameramen in different locations in the audience, a fourth discreetly placed behind the stage and off to one side for audience reaction shots, and a fifth all the way to the right of the stage to get the Burns profile. Tough-looking Christians were everywhere. They were even throwing Keyes dirty looks until Max Breskin came along.

Breskin was wearing earphones and a chest mike, and a pair of field glasses were dangling from his neck. There was a heavy Christian at each elbow.

"Balcony, come in," Breskin was saying. "What's happening?"

Breskin seemed satisfied by the answer.

"After you search the balcony, stay there. One man at the top of each aisle."

Breskin looked at Keyes.

"You're sure about this, are you? We're finding nothing so far."

"Only about ninety-eight percent," Keyes said.

Breskin nodded slowly.

"I tried to talk him out of going on tonight. Like talking to the wall."

"It's barely possible," Keyes said, "that all these preparations of yours—which are a bit obvious—will scare them off. Get them to abort the operation."

"Let's hope so," Breskin said, going off. "Does everyone have baseball bats?" he said into the chest mike.

John Burns was in good form; the spirit was upon him. The intoxication. He could feel it surging through his veins. He looked out at the capacity crowd and felt the vibes coming back at him, the love, the eagerness. They were going to have a wonderful time together this evening; they were all going to communicate; they were going to strip away the fakery and falsity in their lives and get down to a bit of truth, face truth, let truth sweep over them and make them free.

Burns knew himself. He knew that he liked to perform for people. If he hadn't become a preacher, he believed that he would have become a jazz bassist. Performing brought him to life. Performing was a trip. It was so exciting that he sometimes thought the bright television lights artificially stimulated his pineal gland into producing endorphins, which produced the body's natural elevated highs. Whatever it was, when he confronted a live audience, he was transformed, energized, elevated.

Burns had his right hand in his back pocket; his left hand was holding the Bible tucked under his arm. He was wandering around the stage more or less at random.

"You know, hate is an odd emotion," he said. "It's an emotion that's bad for us. It's bad for the heart and the liver and the digestion and the blood pressure." Pregnant pause. "Not to mention the planet. As long as there are thousands and thousands of nuclear warheads lying around, hate menaces us all. So we want to be careful about this hate. It's not good for us. It's nuclear. And yet they keep telling us to hate the communists. Now what are the reasons for this? Why do they ask us to

378

engage in such an unchristian and unhealthy act as hating the communists?"

Dr. Theodore Monk had found a seat in the audience fairly close to John Burns. Unfortunately, it was in the middle of a long row, so he was surrounded by ardor, fervor, fever. He tried to tune it all out so that he could watch and listen to John. John was a marvel. In some way that Monk would never understand, John had unified himself, body and soul. By what process? How could it have happened? Monk was consumed by curiosity and sadness. He was never going to be able to find out. He was never going to get the final data; one way or another it would be denied him. Now all he could hope for was that his son would be allowed to go on living.

"Now what do the communists do that is evil?" Burns was saying. "Well, that's an easy question to answer. Our leaders tell us all the time. Any place on earth where peasants decide to rebel to get a bigger piece of the action, you can be sure there's a commie in on it somewhere, usually down a cellar with a candle stuck in a wine bottle. But isn't there something wrong here? *They* are evil because *they* are always on the side of the poor? The godless, atheistic communists! On the side of the poor? With Jesus? And we are righteous because *we* are always on the side of the rich, the landowners, the big corporations? I'm confused. Does that sound Christian to anyone here?"

Madeleine Smith was sitting in her car watching John Burns on the built-in television set adjacent to the built-in bar. The program wasn't broadcast live, but someone had set up a feed from the control room inside the church so she could watch it in real time. She was having a martini to calm a rare attack of nerves. All the reports coming back from Anderson inside the church were negative. They could find nothing wrong. It would be heaven-sent if it turned out that there wasn't going to be a firefight between the Secret Service and the CIA. She was sitting there drinking and listening and praying that *someone* would get back to her—Richard, or that son of a bitch Elmer Jessup.

* * *

379

Keyes went to the control room, where Joe Poole was directing the program, shouting at his cameramen as usual. Even Poole had a Christian with him for protection: armament, one baseball bat.

Keyes wandered up to the big console and looked at all the monitors, one for each camera.

"Now where does Jesus stand on these issues?" Burns was saying on four monitors, the fifth showing a long wide shot of the audience. "But then you know the quotes as well as I do. 'Blessed be ye poor, for yours is the kingdom of God. . . . But woe unto you that are rich! for ye have *received* your consolation.' Luke six, twenty and twenty-four."

"Camera Two, move in on John," Poole said. "Slow move. Camera Four, tighten up that shot. I'm not interested in anything but John Burns. Camera Two, start your move. Camera Five, tilt up slightly. We're not seeing enough of the balcony. Camera Two, *move* it."

"And then, of course, 'It is easier for a camel to go through the eye of a needle, than for a rich man to enter into the kingdom of God.' For the yuppies among us, think of a Mercedes-Benz roaring through the eye of a needle."

Laughter, clapping of hands, hallelujahs. A mass giggle came back at Burns, and his endorphins flowed.

"How much clearer can it be?" John Burns said, shrugging his shoulders. "Jesus is saying to us that it is evil to be rich. It is sinful to be rich. 'Ye have received your consolation.' That means you're not going to receive any consolation in heaven; heaven is not your destination. If you're rich."

John Burns thought for a moment as he prowled the boards. He knew that he was in dangerous waters. He was going against the American dream, rags to riches, hit the jackpot, make a killing.

"Make a killing," he said to them. "That's what we say when somebody makes a lot of money, isn't it? When somebody gets *rich*. A *killing*. Oh, Jesus knew what people have to do to get rich. Conniving, scheming, stepping over bodies as you make your *killing*. To become *rich*."

"Camera Two, what are you *doing?* Don't you know how to do a slow zoom, for Christ's sake?"

Keyes tore his eyes away from the monitors and looked at Joe Poole.

"Two! What the hell are you waiting for? Straighten the shot; you're off vertical. What is this, galloping arthritis?"

"Oh my God," Keyes said.

Poole looked at him.

"The gunman is Camera Two," Keyes said. He was starting to run as he said it. He was shouting it. "The gunman is Camera Two," he said again, running out of the control room into the auditorium.

"And even if you didn't make your killing, even if you inherited your killing, you're *still* going to hell if you don't give it all away to the poor." Burns held the book out toward them and quoted from memory.

"Acts of the Apostles four, thirty-four and thirty-five. 'Neither was there any among them that *lacked:* for as many as were possessors of lands or houses sold them, and brought the prices of the things that were sold and laid them at the apostles' feet: *and distribution was made unto every man according as he had need.*' "

Burns was holding the book out, slowly moving it through 270 degrees of arc.

"Now what are we to make of this? What does that sound like? How can Jesus be denied any longer? How can we deny that Christ and His apostles believed in the redistribution of wealth downward *and who does that sound like?*"

John Burns didn't know how they were going to take it. He would undoubtedly be called a witting agent of the KGB. Are you now, or have you ever been, witting? It was his biggest gamble yet as a preacher, but his endorphins were flowing, surging, cresting; he was confident. He'd brought them a long way in the past and they'd followed him, but *this* was a step. Inerrantists all, they were looking at him open-mouthed. He sympathized with them. It had to come as a shock. At the same time, it was so obvious; how could they all have missed it for so long?

"Brothers and sisters, there is no way to escape it, there is no way it can be denied. Jesus Christ was the first communist and His apostles spread the word of communism to others, and *Judas* was a degenerate capitalist spy in the camp who used the very life of Jesus Christ to make a profit, the everlasting profit, to make a killing! Judas was the first anticommunist. This is the word of God!"

The audience finally began to react. There were moanings and groanings and Christ the Kings. Jesus save us. They were holding their heads and moving from side to side. There was speaking in tongues, there were writhings in the aisles. John Burns had brought them to the edge of something, and they didn't know if they wanted to step over that edge and enter a new country.

"I understand," he told them. "I do understand. I know the problems this makes for all of us. Oh, the problems. Karl Marx and Jesus Christ were talking about the same things? These godless atheistic communists are the ones aiding the poor and this is why we should hate them? This is what the bomb is for? This is what all the fighting is about? This is what all the hating is about? Putting our livers at risk, putting our planet at risk?"

John Burns stretched out his arms as though trying to embrace everyone in the Pentagonal Church of Christ.

"Brothers and sisters. Hate is unchristian. Hate is unhealthy. Hate is un-Jesus. John thirteen, thirty-four: 'A new commandment I give unto you.' A new *commandment*. That means this is big stuff. Jesus isn't kidding around with this. This is the *eleventh* commandment. That ye love one another. And He said, 'Love thy enemy,' and I do. I love this enemy of ours. I love the communists. Oh how I love the communists. Come. Let us all love the communists together. Think it, speak it! *I love the communists.*"

Blam.

The carbonation in John Burns's eyes fizzed out as the bullet crashed into his brain. He was like a baby going to sleep in a flash, falling to the stage floor without theatrics, dead on arrival as he hit the boards, his secondhand soul flying straight up to heaven, which was a warm place.

Malcolm Keyes, up on the stage now and commencing a tackle of John Burns, took the second bullet to the head.

50

THE RAPTURE BEGINS

OLD BRAHMS WAS on the podium, preparing to conduct his Fourth Symphony. Which was the Word of the Lord, the Book of Job, Modern Man in Search of a Soul. It was all there. Despair, death, resurrection, joy. No, wait a minute. There was no chorus in the Fourth. Why have a thousand singers if there was no chorus? It *wasn't* the Fourth. It was the *Fifth*. Brahms's Fifth. Brahms's Fifth? Ah, a posthumous work: the Brahms Choral Symphony! That had to be the explanation. That old devil was making a final attempt to truly top Beethoven. Who else would attempt—could attempt—such an enterprise? And the choral was in the *first* movement.

Brahms had forces at his command now, one thousand singers standing ready to deliver "Joy to the World," a host that could have been assembled only in heaven since union scale would have been ruinous. That explained everything. He was dead and he was in heaven. And Old Brahms was on the podium, tapping his baton, raising it high over his head: The suspense was excruciating. *Of course.* It was the Twenty-fifth of December Movement! When old Brahms descended with the downbeat, the opening, joy, would reverberate from the near end of heaven's mansions to the far.

Except that nothing happened. Only one instrument responded to the maestro, a friendly flute that sounded familiar. He heard it as music before he got the sense of it.

"Hel-lo, how is my little boy today?" his Aunt Helen was saying.

Then he heard something that was intrusive, harsh. It was a vibration, but it wasn't music; it was a driving pumping relentless noise that was profoundly boring but that he realized was also very familiar. He opened his eyes.

Pope was sitting next to his bed checking his own blood pressure.

"One-fifty over ninety. I seem to be taking this whole thing rather well," Pope said.

Keyes looked around, but slowly. His head was swathed in bandages; there was a respirator stuck up his nose, and an IV bottle was dripping something into a vein in his left arm. It was colorless, so at least he wasn't getting a blood transfusion.

It was a peculiar room. The furniture near the bed was all hospital white. But beyond that, the place looked like an enormous hotel room—oak furniture, oriental area rugs, a professional-looking bar.

"Where am I?"

"The Presidential Suite of the Bethesda Naval Medical Center," Pope said. "The entire floor is yours."

"They say you're going to be all right," someone said sourly. It was Doolittle. "If I'd known that, I wouldn't have bothered coming down here."

"How are you feeling?" Pope asked, shutting the lid on the plastic carrying case of his automatic sphygmomanometer.

"Horrible."

Keyes closed his eyes. It was starting to come back to him. He remembered being in the Pentagonal Church and there was something wrong, a serious problem had come up and he was going to do something about it. He opened his eyes.

"How is John Burns?"

Pope looked awkward. He started to feel for beard growth, which he always did when he was at a loss.

"He's dead?" Keyes said.

"Yes."

"Ah, gee, ah, goddammit. Ah, if I could have gotten there a second sooner."

"You did yeoman work. Don't start blaming yourself."

"Goddammit to hell."

384

"And take it easy. You spent the last twenty-four hours on the critical list."

"Did they get the guy who did it?"

"Yep. You alerted them. They were coming at him from all sides. His camera was right near a side door, and he tried to shoot his way out. I have a feeling he didn't realize he was up against the Secret Service. They killed him. Those Secret Service guys are good; they managed to miss everyone else. I'll take the Secret Service over CIA any day."

"They shouldn't have killed him," Keyes said. "Dammit, they're forever killing the evidence."

"Yeah, I know. But then it was a crowded auditorium and the guy was shooting. You could make a case that it was legit."

Keyes could vaguely hear the sound of a small commotion in another room, and then Halliday walked in.

"How is he?" Halliday asked.

"Having second thoughts about politics," Keyes said weakly.

"Malcolm, I apologize for this. It wasn't part of the deal."

"How's your memory?" Doolittle put in.

"I don't know. Ask me something."

"What did Second Philly do in 1948?" Doolittle said.

Keyes looked up into his forehead.

"Truman 234,897, Dewey 178,902."

Pope wrote it down and then went to the phone to call his computer.

Halliday was circling around the room, and Keyes was following him with his eyes.

"There's something I'd like to ask you," Keyes said.

"I'll bet."

Keyes flicked his eyes toward Doolittle and then ricocheted away.

"I don't know but I wouldn't be surprised if it's classified."

"You bet your ass it's classified," Halliday replied. "Gentlemen, I'm going to need five minutes with Malcolm."

Doolittle looked mortally wounded at being excluded, but Pope hung up the phone triumphantly.

"He's right! He got it to the vote! Keyes beats Dewey!"

When they were gone, Keyes said, "He was real, wasn't he?"

"Yeah, he was real. I looked at the body in the morgue. John Burns was a mere mortal."

"How did they expect to get away with it?"

Halliday drifted over to the bed and sat on it.

"They had an 'ambulance' waiting outside. They had 'doctors' in the house. They were going to rush 'the body' to the 'hospital.' You were probably shot because you were too close to 'the body.' Of course, 'it' turned out to be 'him.' The assholes."

"What are you going to do about it?"

Halliday left the bed and went over to the best-stocked bar in Washington, D.C. He came back with a shot glass and a bottle of scotch. He opened the bottle and poured out an ounce of scotch and took a long look at it before demolishing it.

"Nothing," he said.

"You going to let that bastard get away with killing John Burns?"

"I can get more mileage out of it this way."

"I wouldn't be surprised if you're going to let him stay in office, too."

"Stop looking for justice, Malcolm. That isn't the name of the game. The name of the game is politics. Yes, I'm going to let him stay there. I'm even going to let him threaten the Twenty-fifth of December Movement with those sex tapes he's got. They'll have to buy the cover story so as not to ruin the reputation of their martyr. As a martyr, John Burns will be very profitable for them."

Keyes was looking up at the ceiling and concentrating on not moving, for fear of scrambling his brains.

"I wouldn't have expected you to do that," Keyes said.

"Malcolm, you've got to get over these juvenile attitudes. There are three and a half testicles in the entire Democratic Party and I've got one of them."

Keyes shook his head, chuckling.

"Doc Halliday has one ball."

"Now, Malcolm, you're not going to tell me that you believed your own television spots, are you? I am not now, nor have I ever been, Doc Halliday. That is pure public relations. I'm like all the others. We're all angle merchants and odds players. We lie, we manipulate, we cheat, we con. Every politician in this country is bought and paid for, and that includes me."

Keyes lifted his head up off the pillow about half an inch to get a better look at his President. Halliday poured another ounce into the shot glass and disappeared it. Then he was on the prowl again.

"I've got the depth of a suntan to work with, and I'm doing rather well with it, thank you. I'm going to get us a test ban treaty. In *this* term. It will be the beginning of the end of the nuclear age. No new weapons can be developed if they can't be tested. We won't be able to maintain any kind of superiority over the Russians. They'll just crank out a few more of the old ones until we're even. At that point, even the American establishment will see the wisdom of getting rid of the damn things, because even from *their* point of view, the warheads will be worthless. Free at last, Malcolm! By then the biggest nuclear problem will be to get the French to stop testing. *French* lunacy is a special brand. But we'll come up with something to squeeze them."

Halliday paused by the bed and looked down at Keyes. He was afraid of losing his cassette recorder. But he had a special problem with him; he wasn't dealing with a politician. How could you deal with someone who was basically unwilling to deal, who wanted the whole loaf? He put his drink down on the night table next to the rectal thermometer and resumed wandering. His face was ashen; he hadn't been to sleep in thirty-six hours.

"You're an oddball. God, are you an oddball. You're a freak, as a matter of fact. Which is what we have in common. I'm a freak too. Neither one of us fits the mold."

"I'm not so sure of that," Keyes replied, head back on the pillow, eyes closed. "I may be a freak, but I'm having my doubts about you."

Halliday stopped in the middle of the room and clapped his hands.

"Malcolm," he said, "you're not seeing it. You don't see that we're winning. We're on our way! Getting a test ban will begin to reduce the channeling of the federal budget to the rich via the military-industrial complex. There'll be money set free for social programs and reducing the deficit. I figure we could get the deficit down to *zero* in five years. Getting a test ban will be the beginning of the end of the military takeover of the United States."

Halliday was getting excited, elated. Keyes had never seen him this emotional. He was giving away his game plan. He had it all worked out. He understood all the balances of forces and where reality could give and where it couldn't. Politics was a game of billiards and you had to know the angles, but you also had to know how to put a spin on the ball and sort of beat physics at its own game. Halliday believed that he could.

"Now what follows from our losing nuclear superiority? Why, our generals won't be too hot to interfere around the world. Without our nuclear shield, the Russians might not be too shy about interfering back. They could openly resist us in Central America, the Philippines, anywhere. So our conventional forces begin to get less useful and we begin to allow the world to go its own goddam way. And I'm doing this on a suntan's difference!"

Halliday was starting to move funny. He was moving around the big room at a faster pace, and Keyes was almost certain that he could see spasms rippling through his arms and legs. He was like a lay preacher of politics selling a vision of heaven to the persuadable voter.

"But it can't happen fast, and there's a price. John Burns was part of that price. If it makes you feel any better, I think he was on to something in that last sermon. I would love to see the word 'communist' fumigated so it could be used again, not as a curse, but as a description of the opposite of conservatism. Until we can have a respectable left wing in this country—authentic opposition to the right wing—we'll never have a rational politics. But people's minds have been poisoned for generations. It's going to take a long time to turn this thing around. Remember? It takes a thousand hours of truth to cancel out one minute of lies, and all I can do is try to get the process started and hope that it works before the bombs go off. That's all you can expect from me."

Halliday poured another ounce of scotch into his shot glass. He held the glass in his right hand, looking at it, then looking at Keyes. When he spoke, it was a little like talking to a child, or anyway an adolescent.

"Now what are you going to do, Malcolm? Go back to New York and Doolittle and spend the rest of your life reelecting Hackenlauter? Come on, stay at the center with me for the eight years and then, by God, we'll write a book that'll knock their socks off. We're going to break the news to the public, remember? Adlai Stevenson hinted at it in the fifties. Let's tell the American people the truth, he said. He never got around to it. You and I are going to do it. But I can't do it without you. I need my tribal historian, my shaman, the magical man who remembers everything. You want to get the truth out so goddam much, then stick with me. What do you say?"

"I say goddammit to hell," Keyes replied.

"That's a good answer. That's a *good* political answer. You're trapped dead center between telling me to go fuck myself and saying yes. That 'goddammit to hell' signifies there's a compromise coming. Welcome to politics, my boy. I'm moving your office into the West Wing. You'll be next door to Akers. How about it?"

Keyes was mortally exhausted, strung out, ready for a long sleep. He kept his eyes open just long enough to get it out very quietly.

"I just want you to know, sir," he said, "that I *hate* scotch."

51

GAZOUTA

H<small>E WAS BUNDLED</small> up against the still-crisp air of May, and the male nurse was slowly pushing the wheelchair along the quiet path, slowly, as though being supercareful about not scrambling Keyes's brains. Keyes had already found out that his doctors were right; merely riding to the cemetery had exhausted him. Keyes had insisted on going. Not because he'd been that close to Burns, but because he'd been a leader, and there were very few natural leaders per generation. The fact was, John Burns was irreplaceable. John Burns did things that wouldn't have been done without John Burns, and when you were irreplaceable you were in trouble.

There were about fifty people standing around the grave; a public service had already been held at the Pentagonal Church of Christ, and they'd managed to jam in fifteen hundred people. This one was for relatives and friends only.

The nurse stopped at the edge of the crowd, and Keyes sat there listening. It was a short simple service. The minister sounded inhibited. He was attempting no oratorical flights. He knew whom he was burying. Every mourner would inevitably compare any rhetoric with that of Burns himself, so he wasn't even trying.

Keyes started to drift. He was thinking that the only one who could have done justice to the moment was John Burns himself. Burns would have had fun with it.

He'd work the crowd, making new connections, cutting across boundaries, going in harm's way, taking them by surprise, pushing them further than they'd ever been pushed, going too far, shocking them, then looking down at his shoes for inspiration, finding the thought, sharing it with them, winning them back, reveling in the rapport, waving his Bible. Be one hell of a funeral; be the best goddam funeral anyone ever had. And it would end with John Burns sitting lotus fashion on the descending coffin delivering what Max Breskin referred to as "the gazouta."

"Peace on the earth, goodwill to men. And women. And the children. And the land. And the air. The water. The seas. The lakes. The rivers. The living planet given to us by the Lord. Goodwill to it; may God and man preserve it. Amen and so long."

Keyes nodded to the nurse, who pushed the wheelchair toward the grave. Max Breskin was standing there in his shirt sleeves, watching as each mourner paraded by to throw a spadeful of earth onto the coffin.

Breskin looked at him.

"What are you doing here? You're a mess."

Keyes nodded. He was having the headache of a lifetime. His head was pounding and drumming; it was like a minimalist atonal concerto for percussion instruments. It wasn't helped any by the *thud* sounds the spadefuls of earth made as they hit the coffin; mankind went out with neither a bang nor a whimper, but with a dull *thud*.

"Can you tell me why this had to happen?" Breskin said.

"No, I can't."

"It's because he was getting a following, that's why. He was getting popular."

"I can't say," Keyes said.

Thud.

"Peace Is Our Profession. Only the Strategic Air Command is allowed to be for peace. Otherwise you've got the FBI on your tail."

"I can't argue with you there."

Breskin was still looking at the hole gouged out of the earth, shaking his head, not wanting to believe that it had really happened.

"Because he was for peace he was a public enemy. Public Enemy

390

Number One. No, not a public enemy. The public is for peace too. Corporate Enemy Number One. Banker's Enemy Number One. That's why he's in that box. He was *Oligarchic* Enemy Number One."

Thud.

Keyes said nothing.

"All we've got now are his tapes. I want you to tell your big-shot friends we're going to *play* those tapes."

Thud.

"You may find this hard to believe," Keyes said, "but they'll be glad to hear it."

Breskin took a long, slow look at him.

"You know, I don't understand you. I don't understand you at all."

"Yeah. I can understand that."

"Am I ever going to understand this?"

"Use the Freedom of Information Act in about forty years."

Thud.

When Keyes was wheeled away, Breskin was still standing there in his shirt sleeves looking down into that hole in the ground, still not believing it.

52

PHOTO OPPORTUNITY

RICHARD HALLIDAY WAS doing his best to look mean, which was difficult, because what he was feeling was elation; he had the old bastard cornered at long last, as all DCIs eventually were cornered, because they were America's official outlaws. Jessup was sitting in Halliday's favorite easy chair, looking a bit like a schoolboy in the principal's office. Halliday was wandering around; this was not a coffee-and-danish session.

Halliday was going to use Elmer Jessup—relentless right-wing hawk who had been suckled on nitroglycerine—to help start the millennium.

"Your agent almost killed a valued aide of mine. As far as I'm concerned, that's treason."

"It wasn't treason. It was a blunder."

"When you make blunders of that magnitude, it isn't far from treason. How could you possibly believe that you could get away with murder? At least in Washington, D.C. anyway."

Jessup was talking through his cigar.

"It wasn't murder. That is, it wouldn't have been murder had those

392

goddam scientists known what the hell they were talking about. The odds were supposed to be out around where the sun comes up every morning. Fuckheads."

"You can't lay this on Monk."

"Yes I can."

"I suppose Mark Seven will turn up in an automobile junkyard one of these years."

"Maybe."

"What a monumental screwup."

"It can be contained."

"How?"

"Stick to the cover story."

"Religious crazies killing each other."

"That's it."

"And if I don't stick to the cover story, you, Elmer, are finished. There'll be a special prosecutor, congressional committees, the standard disaster."

"And your CIA will be finished too. The public will crucify us. You won't want to govern without intelligence. Without the covert tool, you'll have a mess on your hands."

"But if I don't want to intervene in other countries, I won't need the covert tool."

Jessup was shocked. He was looking at the President of the United States as though he were a left-wing demonstrator out in Lafayette Park. *That* possibility had never occurred to him. To Elmer Jessup, not intervening overseas would mean, ultimately, the end of capitalism in America.

"Take this for what it's worth. If you try that, you'll be impeached, and I don't mean by Congress."

"What do you mean?"

"By a bullet."

"Elmer, are you threatening me?"

"No, I'm not threatening you. As your DCI, I'm informing you about the realities. This system is not going to let itself be destroyed by you. You've got to know that."

"You think the CIA is that important, huh?"

"*We* are keeping this system *going*. Your CIA saves your ass three hundred and sixty-five days a year and you don't even know it."

Halliday paced, prowling the room of all curves, preparing to throw a few of his own, holding back his response for more than three minutes just to make the bastard sweat. Then he sat down on a couch at right angles to Jessup and put his hand on Jessup's knee.

"All right, I'd just as soon avoid a circus. That doesn't help anybody. Smears us all. People start thinking about their government. That's the last thing anybody in politics wants, right? To have people thinking about their government? By the way, Elmer, can I quote you on verification?"

It was too sharp a turn even for the Director of Central Intelligence. "Can you quote me on what?"

"Verification. That the CIA is one hundred percent convinced that the Soviet Union could not possibly cheat on verification of a comprehensive test ban treaty."

"That's been true for twenty-five years. Everyone knows that."

"But you never said it out loud," Halliday replied.

"What's that supposed to mean?"

"Like before the Senate committee that's going to consider the comprehensive test ban treaty that I intend to get with the Russians."

Jessup was nodding his head up and down. It wasn't agreement; it was merely that he had gotten the message and he was weighing it all in the balance. Avoiding scandal, disgrace, hearings. Plus keeping his job. As compared with the loss of nuclear weapons. Without testing, the nuclear arms race would be over, along with the Strategic Defense Initiative. And it would be the end of nuclear superiority and nuclear intimidation.

"What about the GOD Project?" Jessup asked.

"I am willing to continue it under certain circumstances."

Jessup's head was still going up and down. Only God knew what his glands were pumping at the moment. He sat there thinking for ten minutes. Halliday got up and made a couple of phone calls while waiting. It was like a climactic moment in a chess game, a grandmaster at bay, caught by intersecting forces, no way out. And anyway, if he didn't do it, someone else would. At the end of the ten minutes, he knocked over his king.

"Deal," he said.

Halliday went wordlessly to his desk and mashed down a button on the intercom.

"Send in Moody," he said. Then he went back to his seat next to Jessup.

A herd of photographers came in, shepherded by Moody, who had the usual strained look on his face.

"This okay for you guys?" Halliday asked, posing, smiling, gesturing toward Jessup, stretching his neck as far as it would go, because he photographed better that way.

There had been rumors of bad blood between Halliday and the DCI. This would at least cool off the story for a while. Halliday had no smile problem; he actually felt like smiling. Jessup had to work at it. He really needed two tiny hydraulic jacks at each end of his mouth to get his lips up. He had to settle for a modified snarl.

Click!

53

CONFESSIONS OF A MONK

> "Oh, fifteen arms went round her waist
> And then they ask can a barmaid be chaste."

Scrape, scrape, scrape.

Keyes was sitting at his empty desk in his empty office waiting for Pope to get presentable. It was 11:00 P.M. and they had an appointment in the Oval Office. Keyes had two windows, but soon he was going to be "moved" to the West Wing, where he would have four windows, which was mortifying to the rest of the White House staff.

> "I must go down to the seas again, for the call of the running tide
> Is a *wild* call and a *clear* call that may not be denied."

Scrape, scrape, scrape.

Keyes yawned from his toes on up. He had not gotten his energy back yet, although the bandage now was only on the left side of his skull. His elbows were resting on the desktop and his hands were holding his chin up. He was one of the walking wounded.

"And pile them high at Gettysburg
And pile them high at Ypres and Verdun.
Shovel them under and let me work.
Two years, ten years, and passengers ask the conductor:
What place is this?
Where are we now?"

Scrape, scrape, scrape.

Pope stepped back and took a good look at his face. The Nixon shading was gone; he was ready to be seen by his President. Keyes waited while the ritual continued. Pope took his pulse and frowned. Pope was still frowning at his pulse, no matter what it was. Then there came the rolling up of the sleeve, the slapping on of the cuff, and the pushing of a button.

"We're late," Keyes said, knowing that Pope wouldn't talk or move while taking his pressure. The machine slowly chirped down to Pope's pressure, and when he saw the digital readout on the LED display, he shook his head in disgust.

"Son of a bitch, back at the old homestead. One-eighty over one-twenty."

"Could you belly breathe while we're walking over there?"

"Okay," Pope said reluctantly, snapping the case shut, carrying it like a briefcase.

Halliday was making it an informal, friendly occasion. He was the bartender. He made a special little business out of pouring a Canadian on the rocks for Keyes; Keyes had won his spurs. Monk looked totally out of place with a glass in his hand. He didn't seem to know what to do with it or what it was for. Monk was still looking affectionately at Keyes, paternally, as though still not 100 percent sure about him. Madeleine was looking her best librarian self with her horn-rimmed glasses and long gray skirt that went well below the knee and shut off everything. Akers, sitting next to her on the couch, had on his usual sphinx look, the great immutable poker face. Having finished playing host, Halliday plopped down in his green chair and smiled at Monk.

"So," he said.

Monk sipped his drink and made a face. It was hard to tell whether he was feeling cornered or liberated; the bureaucrat who was still trying to defend his budget or the bureaucrat who knew that it was all over.

397

Halliday got right to it.

"We now know that John Burns was not Henry Patrick. We now know—that is to say, *you* now know—that Malcolm here isn't Henry Patrick."

Monk looked at Keyes, then focused on the bandage. He looked away.

"The question is," Halliday continued, "where the hell is Henry Patrick?"

Monk's little mouth produced its little smile.

"I don't think we'll find out for a very long time, if ever," Monk told them. "He has a strong survival instinct. He knows how to take care of himself." Monk couldn't help glancing at Keyes. "Who knows how high he may rise in life?"

"So we'll never know what went wrong," Halliday said flatly.

"Oh, I know what went wrong," Monk replied.

Halliday almost dropped his scotch, which he never did.

"You do?"

"Certainly. We were too successful. We managed to get too close to the original model, and *that's* the problem. We didn't make a slave. We made an autonomous individual. Henry has too much discretionary ability."

"Heh," Halliday said.

"The goal was too ambitious. We were unwise."

"Unwise?"

The reply came as a low-frequency lugubrious rumble of a confession.

"Yes."

"To me, 'unwise' is a euphemism for 'damn fool.' "

"I'd say that about describes it, yes."

"I'll tell you frankly, Dr. Monk," Halliday said, "I have a theory about how Henry's records disappeared from the army base he was assigned to."

"Oh?"

"I think you had something to do with it."

Monk sipped his drink and cleared his throat and tried to hide his eyes, looking everywhere but at people.

"How did you manage that?" Halliday asked, maintaining a friendly quality in his voice, even getting a touch of admiration into it.

Monk shrugged. He was a scientist, accustomed to accepting the data, whatever they were, and the jig was up.

"I sent them the wrong records to begin with."

"Why?"

"Jessup."

"Why Jessup?"

"I felt that if anything went wrong with the experiment, Jessup would take the easy way out. He's a fascist, after all, and he has this belief in explosions as problem solvers. I was afraid he would have Henry killed. How could I cooperate in that?"

Everybody drank.

"I *might* be able to keep that peccadillo from getting back to Elmer," Halliday said. "But tell me, is there any possible justification for further funding of the GOD Project?"

"Of course."

"Why?"

Monk thought. He was obviously struggling to make complex thoughts clear to morons.

"You see, man is a seventh-generation computer. That's what Henry is. And, of course, the seventh generation is no longer a computer. The eighth generation we made deliberately simpler. I believe the Vice-President is acquainted with Mark Eight."

"Yes, indeed," she said.

"You made quite an impression on Gordon, I might add. Unfortunately, he isn't very bright. But he's got feistiness and hostility. All he needs is more intelligence and he might be a good soldier. What we're proposing is the production of Mark Nine, whose intelligence would lie somewhere in between Seven and Eight. He'd be less than human, but perhaps close enough to be effective in combat."

"An army of dummies," Halliday said slowly. "Hostile dummies."

"It's the only possibility left."

"What's a Mark Nine going to cost me?"

"Eighteen billion."

"Ouch."

"If we ever got to the point of mass production, the economies of scale would be huge. I can assure you it would be cost-effective."

Akers was looking at the Vice-President, but he wasn't actually looking at her. Keyes was amazed; there was an expression on his face, a real expression. Akers was not only feeling an emotion, he was letting it show. There was a sort of enchanted glow on his face.

"You've got the formula for man out there in Colorado, huh?"

"You could put it that way."

Akers had finally found something that had bowled him over. He had dropped his guardedness, his eternal detachment. Akers was being himself.

"But then, I mean, can't you, like, explain everything? Solve everything? Tell us how to solve all the problems? That man sitting across from you has the power. You've got his ear. Tell him how to solve the problem of greed. That's the big one. Tell him how to solve the problem of power hunger. Tell him how to solve the problem of people who want to run other people's lives. Tell him how to solve the problem of aggressiveness. Right now. Here's your chance to change the world."

Monk smiled, sipped a little alcohol, made a face, and then gave Akers an affectionate look.

"I'm afraid it doesn't quite work that way. The brain is a bit of infinity in all of us. The formula is simply too ponderous, too complicated, to work with in that way. Every scientist on the project has been forced to accept it, and I suppose it's a terrible admission for a scientist to have to make: Intuition is faster than mathematics. Shakespeare was right: We're a piece of work."

Akers's face had fallen. He had been lifted out of himself momentarily and then it had crashed; everything was back to normal. He was nodding his head up and down, back in the old mode. The enchanted look had vanished. It felt right. It certainly did. Intuition was faster. Yup. Back to shrinks.

"Be a can of worms anyway," he said to Monk. "Now that I think about it, there are some things I don't want to know."

"The whole idea sounds like a plague," the Vice-President said. "Armies of robots. It sounds like the last book of the Old Testament written by a lunatic automobile mechanic. Dr. Monk, do you think Mark Nine stands a chance of being successful?"

Monk was thinking again. For all of his ivory-tower qualities, he was an astute bureaucrat and he knew how to go about protecting his budget.

"I can't give guarantees," he said. "It might turn out that your eighteen billion gets wasted. A fundamental problem, as I see it, is ego. Ego is made of nitroglycerine and has to be handled with extreme care or it detonates. However, the metaphor only works for small quantities. This nitroglycerine of ours has the odd characteristic of losing its explosiveness as it gets bigger. Make it big enough and it gradually turns into the milk of human kindness. The problem being that if you make them with a big ego, there is a much less felt need for combat."

"Could that be what's wrong with the right wing?" the Vice-President put in. "They all have small egos. That's why they're always hot to trot overseas?"

400

Monk smiled obediently; gaiety was missing from it.

"There are other problems," he went on. "We're dealing with a funny area, after all. For example, uniqueness is an inevitable aspect of AI. Each one is different. We are not making clones. We *can't* make clones. We wouldn't even want clones. We need a variety of abilities. In any case, the fact of the matter is that they're all different. So we don't really know what we're getting. You know, there's something called the 'risk equation' in transitioning from development to production. With Henry, the transition risk was very, very high. There was an unpredictable factor involved. I hesitate to say this. I *blush* to say this. I'm talking about the risk factor of *humanity.*"

The Monk looked around. No one was laughing at him.

"Plus the fact," he continued, "that you're taking a fairly sizable intelligence and trying to make a fanatic out of it. That is, an intelligence that believes killing is the answer to its problems even though— over an estimated service life of twelve years—it never works. They have to go on killing. A fanatic, in other words. The fanatic is voluntarily stupid. He has to be intelligent to function. But he also has to be operationally stupid, as it were, and manage to deny the evidence of his senses that his course of action is not rewarding. It's yet another line that has to be walked, and we haven't been successful yet, and yet I still think it's worth a try. It's an imperative."

"Which particular imperative are you talking about?" Halliday said.

"All the key players are going to get around to trying it sooner or later. The Common Market already has an AI program called ESPRIT. In Britain, the Alvery Directorate is working on AI. If *they* ever get it they'll go back to being Great. In Japan, it's ICOT, the Institute for New Generation Computer Technology. I don't see how you cannot do it. *Someone's* going to do it."

Monk's voice was shaky; his hands were shaky. He had had a nervous breakdown while trying to solve the mysteries of the brain; it was as though the brain had turned on itself, rebelling at the thought of being understood. Monk had never entirely gotten over it. He had paid his dues. And his straight-arrow approach gave him credibility. He was a terrific salesman for his mad idea.

There was a long silence in the room, and then the tape recorder spoke up.

"If aggressiveness is genetic, why hasn't the human race purified itself long since?"

Monk looked at him fondly, as though a bright child had just asked a good question.

401

"Of course," Monk replied. "Why haven't the aggressive genes been killed off over the millennia? Why hasn't the human race gotten progressively more peaceful? It's because only the potential for aggressiveness is genetic. The warriors are basically created anew in each generation, in the caldron of childhood. Because mommies don't know how to be mommies, and daddies don't know how to be daddies."

"Tell me something," Halliday said, projecting friendliness, beginning to refill drinks, playing the helpful bartender. "Where do you stand on verification?"

"Where do I stand on what?"

"Verification."

Theodore Monk looked into his drink and then chugalugged it.

"You mean in reference to the test ban treaty?" Monk said.

"Precisely."

"May I have another one of these?"

"Of course."

While Halliday mixed the drink, Monk tied both shoelaces. He was working it through, solving a problem, finding a cube root, saving his life. By the time Halliday had made the drink, Monk had made up his mind.

"I'm convinced beyond any shadow of a doubt that verification procedures are more than adequate. There is no way the Soviets could possibly cheat. I know any number of top-flight geologists who would support that."

"Are you willing to say that publicly?"

"Anytime, anywhere."

"Thank you very much, Dr. Monk. It's been a great pleasure talking to you, and very enlightening. I'll be in touch. Can I help you out with transportation?"

"I have a car," Monk said, rising. He shook everyone's hand, taking a last, long, quizzical look at Keyes, and then padded out of the Oval Office, walking on eggshells, arms not moving, a classic case of someone whose mommy didn't know how to be a mommy, whose daddy didn't know how to be a daddy.

Total thud silence in the Oval Office.

"You know," Halliday said after a while, "for all his apparent weakness, that guy is made out of steel. He's all balls. That's the American character. We're the ballsiest people to have ever walked the face of the earth; we should use them on the flag instead of stars. We come up to the abyss and then adrenaline starts pumping and we spend a few bucks

402

and then we start cantilevering our way across it, never looking back."

"Are you leaving the GOD Project in place?" the Vice-President asked.

"Sure. It's part of the price. It's quid pro quo. There's no way I can get a test ban otherwise. But there's a built-in self-destruct mechanism. If we can't test nuclear weapons, the Strategic Defense Initiative goes down the drain. In that case, the Strategic Computing Initiative *also* goes down the drain, because it is supposed to be in support of the Strategic Defense Initiative. Remember? That's the truth they're hiding behind. That's the truth that's protecting the GOD Project. It's a funny thing. Lenin was right. All these capitalists I deal with are selling me the rope. They're getting a good price for it, but they're selling."

54

PRESS CONFERENCE

MOODY WENT INTO the room striding confidently. He stepped up onto the small stage and settled himself before the podium. There was the usual moronic buzz in the press room. He waited a moment and then said, "I have an announcement and then I'll take questions."

That was the signal to roll tape and shut up, although the still cameras kept going off; *those* guys never seemed to get enough pictures of *anything*.

"The battalion that had previously been dispatched to the Philippines to defend Clark Air Force Base is about to be expanded to brigade size. This signals no deepening commitment and heralds no further deployments. It is merely an acceptance of the fact that a battalion is not sufficient to defend Clark Air Force Base, given the recent successes of the New People's Army. I'll take questions."

Q: This is reminiscent of something.

Q: Doesn't the administration know that seventy percent of Americans are opposed to military intervention in Third World countries?

A: This is *not* a military intervention. This is a beefing up of the guard force for Clark Air Force Base. We have been in the Philippines since 1898.

Q: But isn't this Vietnam all over again? Starting off small and then escalating?

A: This is *not* an escalation. It is a purely defensive action designed to protect American airplanes and installations and personnel. That is all it is; do not read anything else into it.

Q: Are you still calling this Low Intensity Conflict?

A: Most certainly.

Q: How about Not So Low Intensity Conflict?

Moody's armpits weren't giving him away anymore. He had come to see that Washington was a cinch after Albany. These big-shot reporters never asked the *really* tough questions. They were tough about nuts and bolts, but they never got around to the basics. It was journalistic three-card monte. In this case, they were staying away from land reform, which would have defused the entire insurrection. That brigade would be defending more than Clark Field. They'd be defending the status quo in the Philippines. And if they had a *clue* that the brigade was part of the price of a test ban treaty, they were behaving themselves, they weren't giving it away. Moody knew that his job description had been written a couple of hundred years ago by Benjamin Franklin, who said that diplomats were people who went overseas to lie *for* their country. Moody's corollary: Press spokespeople were people who stayed at home in order to lie *to* their country. He'd have to stay on his toes, but basically these guys were pushovers. He looked around for the next question.

55

POLITICAL BEDFELLOWS

THE VICE-PRESIDENT had no clothes on.

"Just remember that if I ever die of an orgasm, you're to dress my naked body and throw me on the floor."

"Which dress do you want?"

"The gray one. It's the longest."

"Okay."

"And make the bed before you sneak out."

"All the political niceties will be observed, Madam Vice-President."

"Your hair is starting to grow back. God, what a nightmare."

"Oh, just another day in politics."

"You'll have to go soon. I've got to make a speech to the Daughters of the American Revolution about that brigade going to the Philippines."

"I hate that whole idea."

"Richard can't do everything at once. He'll get the test ban this term. We worry about the Philippines in the second term. A Republican could lose *Alaska*. Maybe Richard will be able to lose the Philippines in the second term. In fact, I hope he does, so I won't have to do it in my first term."

"And to think that only six months ago I was a virgin," he said.

"I hope I didn't hurt you, honey," she said suavely.

"It was very disillusioning."
"But innocence kills," she told him.
"Uh-oh."
"Bye-bye."
"Bye-bye."

1-800-759-5961

$134.10

407